Antc

MW01674792

Treatise on Grand Military Operations

Vol. 2

SALZWASSER
VERLAG

Antoine Henri Jomini

Treatise on Grand Military Operations

Vol. 2

Reprint of the original, first published in 1865.

1st Edition 2022 | ISBN: 978-3-75259-082-1

Verlag (Publisher): Salzwasser Verlag GmbH, Zeilweg 44, 60439 Frankfurt, Deutschland
Vertretungsberechtigt (Authorized to represent): E. Roepke, Zeilweg 44, 60439 Frankfurt, Deutschland
Druck (Print): Books on Demand GmbH, In de Tarpen 42, 22848 Norderstedt, Deutschland

TREATISE

ON

GRAND MILITARY OPERATIONS:

OR A

CRITICAL AND MILITARY HISTORY

OF THE WARS OF

FREDERICK THE GREAT,

AS CONTRASTED WITH THE MODERN SYSTEM.

TOGETHER WITH A FEW OF THE MOST IMPORTANT PRINCIPLES
OF THE ART OF WAR.

BY BARON JOMINI,

TRANSLATED FROM THE FRENCH

BY COL. S. B. HOLABIRD, U.S.A.

ILLUSTRATED WITH MAPS AND PLANS.

IN TWO VOLUMES, WITH AN ATLAS.

VOL. II.

NEW YORK

1865.

CONTENTS.

CHAPTER XIV.

CHAPTER XV.

CAMPAIGN OF 1759.

CHAPTER XVI.

CHAPTER XVII.

CHAPTER XVIII.

35

CHAPTER XIX.

CHAPTER XX.

CHAPTER XXI.

CAMAIGN OF 1760.

CHAPTER XXII.

CHAPTER XXIII.

CHAPTER XXIV.

CHAPTER XXV.

CHAPTER XXVI.

CHAPTER XXVII.

CAMPAIGN OF 1761.

CHAPTER XXVIII.

CHAPTER XXIX.

CHAPTER XXX.

CHAPTER XXXI.

CAMPAIGN OF 1762.

CHAPTER XXXII.

CHAPTER XXXIII.

CHAPTER XXXIV.

CHAPTER XXXV.

LIST OF MAPS

TO ILLUSTRATE

JOMINI'S GRAND MILITARY OPERATIONS.

VOLUME II.

A TREATISE

UPON GRAND MILITARY OPERATIONS.

THE SEVEN YEARS' WAR.

CHAPTER XIV.

GENERAL OBSERVATIONS UPON LINES OF OPERATIONS; MAXIMS OF THIS IMPORTANT BRANCH OF THE ART OF WAR.*

In giving an account of the campaigns of 1756 and 1757, we have enunciated a few maxims which were deduced directly from the events. However, it appears necessary to collect, in a chapter, all the combinations which are connected with lines of operations.

This task should undoubtedly be undertaken by one more experienced than myself. It requires one of those rare men, who unite profound acquirements with a talent for composition, which would disguise the dryness of the subject under the charms of style. Conscious of our incapacity, we have

* We have hesitated long as to the place and the limits which should be given to this chapter. If we had placed it at the beginning, it would not have pointed so accurately to the events with which it is connected; since the maxims would have preceded their relation. If placed at the end of the work, it might have been conceived on a more extended plan, but then the account of the twenty campaigns would have been without any knowledge of the principles upon which the criticisms and judgments were founded. Hence, at last, it was concluded to place it immediately after the invasion of Moravia.

indicated that our sole ambition was to furnish some points of comparison, and to show the consistency between the principles of the art, as illustrated by facts drawn from these two most celebrated and important periods. Under these restrictions we hope to attain the end in view. Before passing to the discussion of the combination of lines of operations, let us define what is to be understood and comprehended under this denomination.

Lines of operations should be considered under two points of view. The first are *territorial lines.* The second are *lines of manœuvre.* This distinction may be reluctantly admitted, because it is new, but we will endeavor to justify its use.

We understand by territorial lines of operation, those which nature or art have traced for the invasion or defense of states. Frontiers covered with fortresses, those which are defended by nature, mountain chains, great rivers, the sea, and other insurmountable obstacles, form, in my opinion, the first combination of lines of operation; the dispositions of the general-in-chief necessary to embrace them in their development, to traverse them offensively, or to cover them defensively, require a second combination still more important, and almost always decisive. They are undoubtedly connected with the preceding, but as they present a very different point of view, it has appeared necessary, in order to designate them more exactly, to term them *lines of manœuvre* or *manœuvre-lines;* for they are really the basis of strategy. Some examples may be useful to make my ideas more intelligible.

The three great lines of operations of France against Austria are, on the right, Italy; in the centre, Switzerland and the Tyrol; and Germany on the left. The most natural lines for entering Germany are those of the Mein and the Danube. Such is the material of lines which can only be subjected to a few rules, dictated, so to speak, by nature.

Frederick entered Bohemia by his line of the centre, upon four points. The French armies invaded Germany in 1796 and 1799 upon two lines subdivided. Napoleon has never operated, save upon one principal line. Such are the combination of lines of manœuvre. This latter part of the military art has never yet been reduced to rules. Its relations with the others have not been established, and it is this which it is proposed to do as well as may be possible.

DEFINITION OF LINES OF OPERATIONS CONSIDERED AS THOSE OF MANŒUVRE.

The relations of these lines traced by nature, the positions of the enemy, and the views of the general-in-chief, form so many different classes, which are named from the character of these relations. It is important to establish this classification before going any farther.

We will call *single lines of operations* all those lines of an army operating in the same direction upon the same frontier, without the formation of a large detached corps.

Double or multiple lines of operations are those of an army which operates upon the same frontier by forming two or three separate corps, which act toward the same or different ends, for one or more objects.

Interior lines of operations are those formed by an army to oppose several lines of the enemy, and to which is given such a direction that the different corps may be concentrated and their movements combined, without the enemy being able to oppose to them a greater mass.

Exterior lines are the opposite of interior; they are those which an army might form, at the same time upon the two extremities of one or several lines of the enemy.

We will call *lines of operations upon an extended front* such as are undertaken on a large contiguous development by isolated divisions, belonging to the same force, and operating to the same end. Under this denomination we will comprehend the lines formed by two separate corps on a single given front.

Deep lines are those which, starting from their base, cross a great extent of country to gain their extremity.

Concentric lines of operations are several lines, or a single one divided, which parts from two or more distant points, to attain the same point in advance, or in rear of their base.

By *eccentric lines* are understood those which start from the same point, and diverge so as to send corps upon distant separate points.

Lastly, the final combinations presented by general operations of armies are *secondary lines* and *accidental lines.* The first term is intended to designate the connection between two armies, which are acting on the same development of frontier; thus the army of the Sambre and Meuse was the *secondary line* of the army of the Rhine in 1796. *Accidental lines* are those arising from events which have changed the original plan of campaign, and thus give a new direction to the operations. These last are rare and of the highest importance; they are not generally resorted to except by commanders of a vast and active genius.

Glancing over these different combinations, a wide difference will be observed between our views and those of the authors who have written upon this subject up to our day. The fact is, that these lines have been considered merely in their material relations. Lloyd and Bulow have only attached to them the importance which pertains to the magazines and depôts of an army. The latter has even advanced the idea, *that there are no lines of operations when an army is encamped near its magazines.* The following example will explode this paradox. Let us suppose two armies to be encamped, the first upon the Upper Rhine, in advance of Brisach, the second upon the Lower Rhine, in front of Dusseldorf, or any other point of this frontier. Admit that their large depôts are immediately across the river, which would be the safest and most advantageous position. These armies would have an offensive or defensive object in view, hence they would have *territorial lines* or *manœuvre-lines.* First, their defensive territorial lines would join the points which they occupied to the second line which they were to cover. Now they would both be cut off, should the enemy establish himself upon the latter line. The army of Melas would have had ten years' supplies in the fortress of Alexandria, but was nevertheless cut off from its line as soon as a victorious enemy occupied that of the Po. Secondly, their line of manœuvre would be a double one against a single one, if the enemy should concentrate for the purpose of overwhelming one of these armies. There would be a double exterior against a double interior, provided the enemy separated into two corps, but gave them such direction as to enable them to reunite promptly.

It will thus be seen that Bulow has set out from a principle entirely false; his work is therefore necessarily based upon and enforced by erroneous and dangerous maxims.

We shall now pass to the examination of the most important lines of operations which have been employed from the Seven Years' War in 1756, up to 1800. We shall classify them on the principles laid down, and after comparing results with their causes, we shall confirm by this mass of proof the maxims given in Chapter VII.

OBSERVATIONS UPON THE THREE LINES OF OPERATIONS OF FREDERICK IN 1756, 1757, 1758, AND THE DEFENSIVE LINES WHICH HE ADOPTED IN THE SUCCEEDING CAMPAIGNS.

The plan of campaign rests upon six essential combinations: 1st, The political condition of the two parties; 2d, Their position at the moment; 3d, Their relative force and means of making war; 4th, The dissemination and posting of the armies; 5th, The natural line of operations; 6th, The most advantageous line.

It is not contended, that a plan of campaign can be arranged solely on an exact equilibrium of warlike means; it will be conceded, however, that they enter largely into the calculation. These plans, which are nothing more than lines of manœuvre, are subject to many secondary considerations; still they should be subordinated to the rules of the art; to the invariable principles recognized as its foundation. Hardihood, audacity even, qualities which are necessary and often decisive, are compatible with their application. The greatest proofs of it which history can furnish are exhibited in the operations of the army of reserve in 1800. Never was there a bolder enterprise, nor one more rich in great combinations; none were more prudently or wisely conducted, since the enemy was threatened with total destruction, without other risk than the sacrifice of the rear-guard.

In applying these maxims to Frederick's different lines of operations, we are forced to acknowledge that the accidental plans, which were originated by him in the course of the campaign, owing to the unexpected turn of events, were vastly superior to his primitive ones.

It has been seen from a description of the theatre of war, that the Prussians had three lines of operations against the Austrians; that of the left against Moravia; that of the centre upon Bohemia; that of the right through Saxony. The first was most favorable to the operations in a military point of view; for in this direction the communications were less difficult. Had Frederick fixed his eyes upon Vienna, which was the centre of the power of his enemies, this line led him there more directly and with fewer obstructions. But were he to limit his views to the provinces adjacent to his states, it would then be found to be the longest of the three, since it was most distant from Brandenburg, which was the centre of his own power.

The king well knew that a coalition was formed against him, and though perhaps he might not be certain of all the members of it, still he knew that it was formidable. The preparations of Austria had given rise to some diplomatic communications, and Frederick, feeling persuaded that they were trifling with him, resolved to anticipate his enemies, and to attack the most formidable of all.

But the choice of his line did not correspond to his intention. He desired to inflict a terrible blow upon Austria, and thus sufficiently frighten the others to prevent their simultaneous action. However, he did nothing to attain this result. It is more probable that he might have accomplished it, had he pushed on to Vienna with his one hundred and five battalions and one hundred and sixty squadrons, during the stupor of his other enemies, than that he would be able to defend himself in his own states with eighty thousand men, as he afterwards did, when the Russians were masters of Prussia, the Swedes of Pomerania, the French of Saxony, and the Austrians of half of Silesia. Ought he to have feared twenty thousand Saxons, left at a distance from his right flank, and which were not at war with him? Had he pushed forward to the banks of the Danube, as no doubt he might have done, the Elector of Saxony, intimidated as he would have been, would scarcely have hesitated to break the forced obligations which bound him to Austria. He would have restrained himself from a rupture with a prince who shook the first power of Europe to its centre.

When Frederick contemplated invading Saxony, it is certain that there were less than thirty thousand Austrians in Bohemia and twenty thousand in Moravia. If, at this time, he had carried out the march related in Chapter X., that is to say, had he assembled his army at Neisse for the purpose of menacing the two provinces at the same time; of keeping up a separation of the imperial forces, and operating vigorously by the left, it can hardly be denied that he might have destroyed the army of Moravia before it could have been reënforced or sustained. In fifteen days, eighty battalions and one hundred and twenty Prussian squadrons would easily have moved to the gates of Vienna, covered by the rest of the army, which should have been masked at Olmutz. The troops guarding Bohemia would have been embarrassed to find an outlet through which they could concentrate their forces to succor the capital. What would Frederick risk by such an enterprise? Nothing; he might either have dictated terms to Austria, or have retreated with the loss of a few thousand men; this difference of the chances should have furnished the most powerful motive for the attempt.

It may be objected that the thirty thousand Austrians stationed in Bohemia, might have compromised the safety of the army; but can we believe that they would have remained tranquilly at their posts when the capital was in danger, though, by so doing, the retreat of the Prussians might be cut off? However, admitting this improbable supposition, would not the twenty-five battalions and forty squadrons, which the king had left in Moravia, have been sufficient to keep open his line of operations? Would it not have been necessary, in order to cut off his retreat, to have guarded the lines of Saxony, of Bohemia, and of Moravia, upon a front of one hundred and fifty leagues? It is not easy to cut off an army of one hundred thousand men from a frontier of such extent, when they are led by a Frederick. If the thirty thousand Austrians had been withdrawn upon the Danube, the king could have drawn to him the corps in Moravia, and have delivered battle, with the mass of his forces, under the walls of Vienna; a battle which would have decided the fate of Austria, and, if lost to Frederick, it would only have resulted in the evacuation of the conquered provinces.

At the beginning of the campaign of 1757, the king might still have undertaken this enterprise with success. The Austrians were divided; the French were not acting against him; the Russians still kept their frontiers, and the army of the Circles did not exist. The Prussian army amounted to upwards of one hundred thousand men, which number included thirty thousand of the best cavalry in the world. Frederick, by leaving some of his garrison battalions in Saxony, had nothing to fear. He could have moved *en masse* upon the centre of the Austrian lines, the front of which, starting from the frontiers of Saxony, and extending along those of Bohemia, Silesia, and Moravia, nowhere presented an insurmountable obstacle.

The great man saw at last, in 1758, that his natural and advantageous line was that of Moravia; that by invading that province, the Austrians would be compelled to uncover Bohemia, for the purpose of moving to the succor of their capital. He undertook that invasion with an army much inferior to that of Daun, encamped at Konigsgrätz, and which was more capable of sustaining and defending this line than in the preceding campaign. Besides that, the presence of the Russians upon the Oder, and of the army of the Circles in Saxony, had compelled him to divide his forces, and should have prevented him from moving too far from his centre of operations and supports. Notwithstanding this enormous difference in the circumstances, had the king been less slow in conducting the siege of Olmütz; had he concentrated his forces to attack Daun when he took position at Predlitz; and finally, had he not so imprudently exposed all his resources in a single convoy, he would, in all probability, have thrown back the Austrians upon the Danube. But to carry out this, it was necessary to combat Daun incessantly, without giving him the least chance of rest. This sort of vigorous war was not then well understood. The idea of the destruction of men to which it led was exaggerated, and the king, at that period, had not sufficient means of reënforcing his army in proportion to the depth of his line, and to its consequent enfeeblement. Such were, probably, the motives which restrained Frederick from acting at the most promising period of this campaign.

Be that as it may, the choice of the line of Moravia was controlled, in 1756 and 1757, firstly, by the political situation of the two parties; secondly, by the relative force and means of war, since, in place of four armies, there was but one to fight; thirdly, by the distribution and the stations of the enemy's forces, for they were scattered and did not cover this province; fourthly, by the natural line of operations; fifthly, it offered to the king, at that time, the greatest chances of success.

When Frederick, in 1758, transferred thither the theatre of war, this choice, on the contrary, was more governed by the consideration of natural lines; for the other chances had all turned in the enemy's favor. Had he carried out in 1756 that which he planned in 1758, there is no doubt Austria would have been invaded with half the loss; its provinces would have been laid under contribution, and Prussia would have acquired a superiority over her rival. We shall see directly some very striking instances of the importance of the choice of lines of operation, and of their influence upon the fate of armies and of empires.

After having examined what Frederick could and ought to have done in these three campaigns, let us glance for a moment at what he actually did do. The invasion of Moravia not having been attempted in 1756, that of Saxony was undeniably the best operation to undertake, not so much in a military and topographical, as in a political sense. Had Saxony even been a province of Austria, it would have been much better to invade Bohemia, because the disposition of the frontiers is such, that Saxony is necessarily in the power of the Prussians as soon as Bohemia is conquered. But it was not a question of driving an Austrian army out of Saxony. The project of the conquest of this province appeared under a very different aspect. Frederick, in considering it, had in view the fact, that, by seizing it, he covered the most feeble part of his frontiers, sheltered his hereditary states from invasion, reënforcing his army with the Saxon troops, recruiting from the population of this electorate, administering it, and, in fact, forming therefrom a Prussian province. Viewed from this point, it can not be denied that a *temporary* invasion of Bohemia could not be placed in the balance against the advantages resulting from the conquest of this country.

But when the king had become master of it, in 1756, there was nothing to prevent him from entering Moravia the following year, as he afterwards did when there was no longer an opportunity. He delivered the sanguinary battles of Prague and Kollin without reaping any benefits therefrom; whereas by moving from the Neisse upon Olmütz, Daun would have been beaten before Prince Charles had arrived to his succor; and had the latter prince hurried to the protection of Vienna and the Danube, Prague and all of Bohemia would have been at the mercy of the Prussians, as has been proved by the operations narrated in Chapter X.

It follows from all this, that in the second campaign the king chose a bad territorial line, and the manœuvres whereby it was developed, and which we term *lines of manœuvre*, were equally dangerous, for they were *double* and widely separated, as will be exemplified in the following figure:

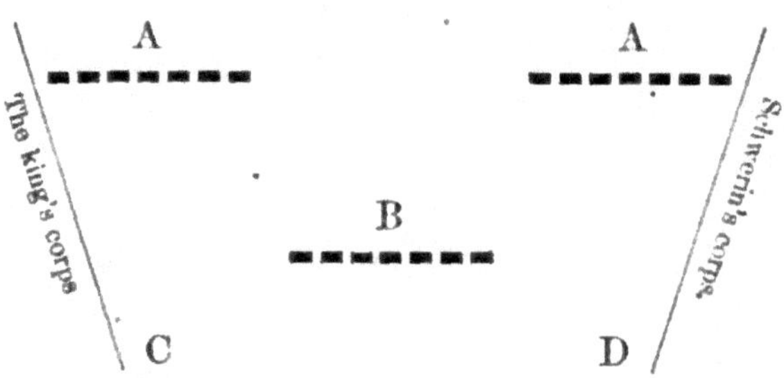

A large river (the Elbe) ran between the two *corps-d'armée*, which separated them by at least fifteen marches. Had the Austrians occupied either of the positions A, or B, which would have thrown their mass upon one of the banks of the Elbe in C, or D, by destroying the bridges and clearing the course of this river, one of these corps would certainly have been destroyed. What would then have become of the other? would it not have been forced to retreat like the army of the Rhine, in absolutely the same position in 1796?

The sole view under which the dispositions of Frederick would appear defective, was that of the possible concentration of the Austrians; but they pursued a system directly the reverse of this; their army, in the attempt to cover everything, was divided into four great divisions; the two extreme ones being much farther off than were the two lines of the Prussians between them. These four divisions thus formed an exterior line, and their junction could only be effectuated on a concentric point well in rear of their frontiers. Thus Frederick knew how to profit by the faults of Marshal Browne. A proof that this great man, in every other case, regarded a double line as vicious, may be adduced from the fact that he always condemned the practice of making large detachments, and that he tried his best to force the Austrians to adopt that system.

The territorial lines taken by the king in the campaigns from 1759 to 1762 were constantly the same; because they were defensive lines. The Russians, acting always in concert, prevented Frederick from continuing, without being exposed to great dangers, a war of invasion which should separate him from his centre of power and from his resources, since it would enable one of three armies to inflict irreparable blows. Besides, he always operated upon three interior lines, moving his mass in succession against each one of them, whilst the two others maintained a well-combined defensive.

Figure 1st, Plate XX., demonstrates the advantages of these dispositions. The three interior lines, A, represent the three Prussian *corps-d'armée;* the four exterior lines, B, represent those of the enemy. The king moved rapidly with his masses upon that one of the three points A, where the danger was most pressing. He there restored his failing affairs and flew to another. After the battle of Hohenkirch, he knew how to concentrate his separate corps in Saxony, and, by a master-stroke, stripped Daun of the fruits of his victories. Thus, after 1758, the king operated successfully in Saxony, in Silesia, and in Brandenburg. In 1756, he had allowed the favorable moment for a war of invasion to escape; he was aware of it, and it is perhaps due to the change which he introduced into his system, that he was able to successfully maintain himself, for such a length of time, against forces so greatly disproportioned to his strength.

Upon referring back to the different epochs of the Seven

Years' War, we shall become convinced of one thing; that though the king may have failed in his first selection of lines of operations, his choice of accidental lines was always skilful. Witness his marches against the combined army, and his return into Silesia, in 1757; the invasion of Bohemia after the siege of Olmutz; the movements subsequent to the battle of Hohenkirch; finally, his march into Silesia, in 1760; all are master-pieces of the art.

There is undoubtedly merit in a well-combined plan of campaign; but it is rare that such a plan can be fully carried out. An unforeseen event, as a battle lost, often changes completely the direction of the war. In such moments as these, at the crises of campaigns, genius displays itself with the greatest splendor. An ordinary general is then embarrassed; Frederick never was, and his unpremeditated operations are, so much the more, lessons to military men. It has already been remarked in the preceding chapter, that the king, by his march into Bohemia, pointed out and confirmed an important maxim, *that of directing a retreat in a direction parallel to the line of our frontiers.* By its application the Prussian army, instead of drawing the theatre of war into Silesia, carried it into the enemy's provinces. Had the Austrians made use of this lesson, in the wars of the French revolution, they would not have abandoned so much territory as they did, and the field of operations would not have been transferred, in two campaigns, from the banks of the Oise, upon the borders of the Danube, to the heart of Germany. This is sufficient to enforce the importance of accidental lines. There is no use of citing a greater number of instances to support it. Let us now proceed to the analysis of the lines of operations of the Austrians upon their own frontiers, and of the French in Westphalia.

OBSERVATIONS UPON THE LINES OF OPERATIONS OF THE FRENCH AND AUSTRIANS IN THE SEVEN YEARS' WAR.

A description of the territorial lines of the Austrians has already been given; it only remains to examine the manœuvres, by means of which the Austrian generals embraced their development, whether defensively or in the invasion of the enemy's provinces.

A glance at the general map will show that Bohemia is, as it were, a central zone, upon which the Austrians might direct the bulk of their forces with the greatest advantage.

The frontiers of the three lines form almost a salient angle. (See Plate XX., figure 2). We shall have occasion hereafter to demonstrate how very advantageous this configuration is to Bohemia, although Lloyd has argued to the contrary; it is necessary to observe, that, by this position, the Prussians were forced to act upon two exterior lines of operations; whilst their enemies could occupy interior, or perhaps a single one; in fact, if the Prussians had left Saxony or Silesia open, nothing would have prevented the grand Austrian army from seizing it, by manœuvring with vigor against the one so abandoned. This *central* position of the mass of the Austrian forces became of much greater advantage, as a large river divided the salient angle, and ran diagonally toward Saxony and the centre of the Prussian states. Their operations against some of these provinces were favored by the line of the Elbe, by means of which a division might hold in check one of the enemy's corps, whilst the army overwhelmed the other. The king owed his salvation to the vicious manner in which the enemy's generals operated.

In 1756, the Austrian army was incapable of other efforts, nor did they undertake any but the delivery of Saxony. In

1757, the dispositions of Marshal Browne were equally defective in their offensive and defensive relations. Instead of making use of his central position, in order to maintain his troops concentrated, he broke up into four grand divisions upon an extent of sixty leagues. Such a system is neither good for the defensive nor the offensive. After the battle of Kollin, in place of operating *en masse* upon the Elbe or in Saxony, whither the French army had marched, Prince Charles exhausted his efforts far from the principal object in view, and wasted precious time before the fortresses of Silesia.

In 1758, Daun was wiser. After the raising of the siege of Olmütz, and the march of the king against the Russians, he marched himself upon Dresden; but then the French army was no longer in Saxony, and the marshal wasted his time in positions which could not be approached. He detached twenty thousand men upon Neisse, though that expedition offered but little attraction, when Prince Henry might have been overwhelmed, and the theatre of war quickly transferred to Brandenburg. The formation of that double line, and the intolerable slowness of his movements, were the causes of the loss of all the fruits resulting from his plan. The king was thus allowed to repair the disasters of Hohenkirch, by the skillful manœuvres related in Chapter XIII.

In 1759, Daun took Dresden, and manœuvred in Lusatia; the Russians gained the battle of Kunersdorf, and marched towards the same province. This concentric combination of the operations, the only one which was adopted in this war, brought Frederick to the brink of ruin; the slowness of the Austrian general spoiled everything, and experience proves that: *two armies which manœuvre upon the same frontier under different commanders, are of no more value than two exterior lines of operations.* The Russians returned into Poland without having agreed upon a plan of operations.

In 1760, the first plans of the members of the coalition were not better combined. The king, in marching into Silesia too late, drew all the enemy's forces into that province; but he preserved a central position, and beat Laudon at Lignitz. The Austrian and Russian armies, separated by merely a few days' march, were not able to come to an understanding nor to combine their movements. The Russians began an eccentric march in their departure from their allies, in order to descend the Oder, and make a diversion upon Berlin. Daun, repulsed and isolated, remained in the mountains of Upper Silesia. When the Russians returned into Poland, the operations became more active; the armies on the two sides marched into Saxony, where the king gained the battle of Torgau over a part of the Austrian forces.

In 1761, the leading efforts were made in Silesia, although the possession of Dresden admitted of their being developed and directed with much more success in Saxony, and even in Brandenburg. The king by his dispositions, and by the camp at Buntzelwitz, arrested Laudon and the Russians, who, in spite of their enormous superiority, confined themselves to parades, and a few demonstrations which amounted to nothing. Daun remained all the campaign at Dresden without making any use of his situation.

In 1762, no longer embarrassed by the Russians, the king retook Schweidnitz, and rejected Daun into the mountains. Prince Henry beat the double line of operations in Saxony, and Austria made peace after seven campaigns, in which her generals gained a number of battles without any important result.

The French generals were neither more skillful nor more fortunate.

After the campaign of 1758, they formed two lines of

operations in Hesse, and upon the Weser, on a development of one hundred leagues. Ferdinand, by manœuvering upon the extremity of this line, had merely to contend with isolated corps, which he drove back behind the Rhine.

Contades, who, after the battle of Creveldt took the chief command, seized the advantages of the line of the Rhine, all the fortresses along which he held, and which his adversary had the temerity to avoid by his right, placing himself between the North Sea, a superior army, and the frontiers of France. It has been seen to what extent the marshal ought to have availed himself of these advantages, had he operated by his right with celerity and vigor. He held a position similar to that of Napoleon upon the Saale, in 1806, only more advantageous; since Wesel, which was to the line of the Rhine what Magdeburg was to that of the Elbe, was in his power, whilst Bonaparte did not hold Magdeburg.

At the end of the campaign, the two French armies lost all the fruits of their partial success; for the reason that the duke, by taking a central position, broke up the concert of their operations; their time was thus sacrificed to movements which were disconnected; to a correspondence without an object, and to plans without results.

On the opening of the campaign of 1759, Ferdinand, desirous of profiting by the advantages which his interior line of operations presented, determined to overwhelm the corps which was then in the country of Hesse, whilst the grand army should be lying quietly in winter-quarters; the success of this plan would involve the entire ruin of Broglio's army. The battle of Bergen decided that it should be otherwise, for the simple reason that the duke was not strong enough to replace his losses, and renew an attack the next day after a check. At length the French comprehended that it would be advantageous to operate unitedly, and the armies were concentrated in Hesse. The conquest of this country, and of a great part of Westphalia resulted from this combination. The loss of the too famous battle of Minden, which would have led to great disasters had the armies been isolated, gave rise to no greater inconveniences than the retreat of Contades, who repassed the Weser, although he might easily have held his position on the right bank; but for this occurrence, the beaten army would have preserved its conquests, and possibly might have gone on to others from the mere effect of concentration.

In 1760, Broglio concentrated all his forces in the electorate of Hesse. This system assured an honorable and successful campaign to the French armies; although the marshal did not know how to profit by his advantages of superiority, and did not undertake a single important enterprise, nevertheless his army made conquests, and held its position therein.

But in 1761, the scene was changed; it has been said that the Versailles cabinet allowed the commander-in-chief to combine his own plans. The armies were reënforced, and raised to one hundred and ninety-nine battalions and one hundred and ninety-seven squadrons. France had never had a more formidable army on a single frontier; *but it was divided into two corps at a great distance apart;* one of which was commanded by Broglio, and the other by the prince of Soubise. They made war by a flourish of the pen; one of the generals formed plans not suitable to his colleague. Memorials took the place of combats, for whilst they were coming to an agreement on a plan, the enemy had time to anticipate them, and by changing his dispositions, he obliged them to have recourse to a new series of memorials. At length they were obliged to unite, but the command remained divided. The two armies attacked Ferdinand; that of Broglio commenced its operations too early, and the prince of

Soubise too late for the day named for their combined effort. One was beaten; might not the other have been? Similar causes produce similar effects.

Comparing the *manœuvre-lines* of the Austrians, the Russians, and the French, with those of Frederick, it will be seen that the manner of their combination set at naught all principle, and therefore the difference in their results is easily explained. Had the king of Prussia, in his first campaign, known how to make use of his victories to the same extent as has been done in our day, the consequences of these differences in lines would have become more evident and more decisive.

OBSERVATIONS UPON THE MANŒUVRE-LINES OF THE LAST WAR. (1792 to 1800.)

At the commencement of this terrible contest, which presented such varied fortune in its changes of the prospects of the contending mass, Prussia and Austria were the only enemies known to France, and the field of operations was merely extended to Italy for the purposes of observation reciprocally; inasmuch as this latter country was too far removed from the scene of action. The development of the lines of operations, which extended from Huningue to Dunkirk, presented three leading divisions; that of the right, which shut in the line of the Rhine, from Huningue to Landau, and thence to the Moselle; that of the centre, which was composed of the interval between the Moselle and the Meuse; that of the left comprised the extent of frontier country from Givet to Dunkirk.

When France declared war against the emperor, her object was to prevent a re-union of her enemies. She had then one hundred thousand men upon the extent of the three lines of which we have spoken, and the Austrians not over thirty-five thousand in Belgium. It is impossible then to discover the motive which prevented the French from seizing that province, when there was nothing which could have resisted them. Four months elapsed between the declaration of war and the concentration of the allies. Is it not probable that the invasion of Belgium would have prevented that of Champagne, by affording the king of Prussia a measure of the strength of the French forces, and leading him to hesitate to sacrifice his armies for a secondary interest, such as that of a form of government? and although that invasion did not have the consequences expected from it, how does it happen that it changed the face of all Europe? This question is not difficult to solve, but as it does not enter into our plan, we shall not stop to furnish a solution, but merely cite it as an instance, proving the importance of the choice of the line of operations.

At the end of July, when the Prussians reached Coblenz, it is certain that the French were not able after that to make a war of invasion, and that this rôle was cast for the united armies. We shall see in what way they carried it out.

The forces of the French, upon the development of frontier already stated, were then about one hundred and fifteen thousand men. They were distributed on a front of one hundred and forty leagues, divided into five army corps, and it was impossible for these troops to oppose an effective resistance; for, to prevent their action, it was only necessary to operate upon their centre, and thus prevent their junction. To this military motive were joined all the reasons of state. The end which it was proposed to attain was merely a political one. It could only be reached by rapid and vigorous operations. The territorial line, situated between the Moselle and the Meuse, which formed the central part of the frontier, was less fortified than the rest, and presented the excellent fortress of Luxemburg as a base of operations to the allies. It was therefore chosen with discernment; but it will be seen that the execution did not correspond with the plan.

The court of Vienna took the greatest interest in the war, owing to its family relations, and also to the dangers to which its provinces were exposed in case of reverse. But on account of some political whim, for which it would be difficult to assign a reason, the principal rôle was abandoned to the Prussians; the house of Austria only coöperated in the invasion to the extent of thirty battalions; fifty thousand men remained in observation in the Brisgau, on the Rhine, and in Flanders. Where were concealed at this time the formidable forces, which this power afterward deployed in the war? what more useful occupation was there than guarding the flanks of the invading army? This strange system, for which Austria has paid dearly, may explain the resolution of the Prussians, to abandon, after the first campaign, a war in which they ought never to have appeared.

If too much carried away by this subject, which is foreign to the art of which we treat, it is on account of its close connection with the existence of a corps which ought not only to have covered Brisgau, but the flank of the Prussians, by fronting the Moselle, and restraining Luckner in the camp of Metz. It must be conceded, however, that the Prussian army did not exhibit in its operations the amount of activity necessary to ensure success. It remained uselessly eight days in the camp at Kons. Had it only anticipated Dumouriez at Islettes, or set to work more seriously to expel him therefrom, it would still have maintained all the advantages of a mass concentrated against isolated divisions, with the power of overwhelming them successively, and rendering their junction impossible. It is probable that Frederick, in a like position, would have confirmed the language of Dumouriez, who said at Grandpré, that if he had been campaigning with the great king, he would have found himself before this beyond Chalons.

The Austrians proved, in this campaign, that they had overcome the mania which formerly possessed them, of covering all to guard all. The plan of leaving twenty thousand men in the Brisgau, whilst the Moselle and the Sarre were stripped of troops, still showed, however, their mortal fear of losing a village, which brought them back to their old system of forming large detachments, which was so pleasing to many of their generals. They have never relied exclusively upon strong battalions; but have always deemed it necessary to occupy the entire development of a frontier to prevent them from being subject to invasion, when, in fact, it is the very course which renders them everywhere assailable.

We will not here enlarge further on this campaign; solely observing that Dumouriez abandoned, without a proper object, the pursuit of the allied army, in order to transfer the scene of operations from the centre to one extremity of this line; besides, he did not understand how to act to attain a great end, and went to attack the army of the duke of Saxe-Teschen in front, when, by descending the Meuse upon Namur, with the mass of his forces, he would have been able to throw it upon the North Sea, towards Nieuport or Ostend, and to annihilate it entirely by a battle more fortunate than that of Jemmapes.

The campaign of 1793 offers a novel example of the tendency of a bad choice of lines. The Austrians gained victories and retook Belgium, because Dumouriez understood but slightly the scene of his operations. Thus far they are open to no criticism. The desire of reconquering those rich countries warranted the enterprise, which was most judiciously directed against the extreme right of Dumouriez' immense front of operations. But when the French army was driven back under the cannon of Valenciennes, when it was disorganized, torn by dissension, as was also the interior of the country, and incapable of resistance, why did the Austrians pause eleven months before a few fortresses, and give the republicans time to recover and form new armies? When the wretched condition of France, and the desperate situation of the army of Dampierre are brought to mind, can anything be conceived more absurd than to parade the allies before the forts of Flanders?

A war of invasion is particularly advantageous when the power of the state is concentrated in the capital. Under the government of a truly great prince, in ordinary wars, the chief place of importance in the empire is at the general headquarters; but under a feeble prince, or in a democratic state, and still more, in a war of opinion, the capital is usually the centre of national power.*

If this truth were doubted, it ought to have been confirmed on this occasion. France was to such an extent in Paris, that two-thirds of the nation were in arms against the government which oppressed it.

After the French army was beaten at Famars, if the Dutch and Hanoverians had been left in observation before its remains, and the English and grand Austrian army had directed their operations upon the Meuse, the Sarre, and the Moselle, acting in concert with the Prussians, a war of invasion might have been carried on by a mass of one hundred and twenty thousand men, flanked by two strong corps. The Dutch and Hanoverian armies, without even changing the direction of the war, or running great risks, might have been left to mask Maubeuge and Valenciennes, whilst the bulk of the army pursued the remains of that of Dampierre. As

* The capture of Paris by the allies decided the fate of Napoleon; but this fact does not destroy the force of my assertion. Napoleon had all Europe on his hands, and the French nation had abandoned his cause. Had he possessed fifty thousand more men, it might have been seen that his capital was truly at head-quarters.

it was, *after several victories, two hundred thousand men were occupied six months in sieges, without gaining an inch of ground.* At the moment when they threatened to invade France, they posted fifteen or sixteen corps in defensive attitudes, to cover their own frontiers! This appears something like the course pursued by Prince Charles of Lorraine in 1757, who decided, in a council of war, not to attack Breslau with ninety thousand men, for fear that the garrison of Schweidnitz, about six thousand strong, would cut off his retreat!

It is no less astonishing, that, from the commencement having made all their efforts against the right of the general front of operations, they should suddenly have shifted them to the extreme left; so when the right of the allies was acting in Flanders, it was not seconded by the imposing forces which stood upon the Rhine. When the latter, in turn, commenced their operations, the allies remained inactive. Do not these faulty combinations resemble those of Soubise and Broglio in 1761, and all the double lines of the Seven Years' War?

In 1794 everything was completely changed. The French, from a painful defensive, assumed a brilliant offensive. The combinations of this campaign were undoubtedly well established, but they have been exaggerated into a new system of war.

In order to corroborate the justness of my assertion, let us take a glance at the armies in that campaign and in 1757. It will be observed that they were nearly the same, and that the direction of the operations was absolutely similar. The French had four corps, which were united into two grand armies, corresponding to the four divisions of the king of Prussia, from which were formed two armies at the outlet from the mountains. The two grand corps also took a direction centred on Brussels, similar to that of Frederick and

Schwerin, in 1757, upon Prague. The only difference in these plans consists in the Austrians having occupied a less extended position in Flanders than that of Browne in Bohemia; but this difference is assuredly not in favor of the plan of 1794. Besides, the proximity of the North Sea was against the latter position. To turn the Austrian flank, General Pichegru had to defile between the shores of that sea and the mass of the enemy's forces—the most dangerous and mischievous direction possible to be given to grand operations. This movement is precisely the same as that of Beningsen upon the Lower Vistula, which ought to have compromised the Russian army in 1807.

The fate of the Prussian army, thrown upon the Baltic, after being cut off from its communications, is another proof of this truth.

Had Coburg operated as a general would in our day, he might have made Pichegru bitterly repent of having undertaken this bold manœuvre, which he executed a full month before Jourdan was in a condition to second him.

The grand Austrian army, destined for the offensive, was in the centre, before Landrecies. It was composed of one hundred and six battalions and one hundred and fifty squadrons. On its right flank was the corps of Clerfayt, for the purpose of covering Flanders, and on its left the corps of Kaunitz. A battle gained under the walls of that place would have caused it to open its gates. A plan of the diversion in Flanders was found on the person of General Chapuis, and a reënforcement of *twelve battalions* was sent to Clerfayt! Long after the knowledge of the success of the French had become general, the corps of the duke of York marched to his succor. But what could then be done by the army before Landrecies, since the departure of these troops compelled it to defer its invasion? Did not the prince of Coburg thus lose all the advantages of his central position, by allowing his large detachments to fight in detail, and permitting the French to consolidate in Belgium? At last, the army was put in motion, after a part of it had been sent off to the prince of Kaunitz, and a division left at Cateau. If, in place of parcelling out this grand army, it had been at once directed upon Turcoing, one hundred battalions and one hundred and forty squadrons might have been concentrated there. What would then have become of the famous diversion of Pichegru, cut off from his frontiers, and inclosed between the North Sea and two of the enemy's fortresses? The French plan of invasion had not only the fault due to exterior lines, but was also defective in the execution. The diversion upon Courtray was effected upon the 26th of April, and Jourdan did not arrive at Charleroi until the 3d of June, more than a month after. What an opportunity the Austrians had to profit by their central position!

Without doubt, had the Prussians manœuvred by their right, and the Austrian army by its left, that is to say, both upon the Meuse, the result would have been very different; they would, in reality, have been upon the centre of a scattered line, and their mass might have prevented the concentration of its several parts.

In a pitched battle, it may be dangerous to attack the centre of a continuous line, which possesses the power of simultaneous succor from both wings; but this is a very different thing from a line of one hundred and thirty leagues.

In 1795, both Spain and Prussia withdrew from the coalition; the theatre of the war was diminished, and Italy became a new field of glory for the French armies. The lines of operations in that campaign were still double. They wished to operate by Dusseldorf and Manheim; Clerfayt, wiser than Coburg, transferred his mass alternately from one of these points to the other, and gained such decisive victories at Manheim, and in the lines of Mayence, that the army of the Sambre-and-Meuse was compelled to repass the Rhine, in order to cover the Moselle, and threw back Pichegru under Landau.

In 1796, the lines of operations on the Rhine were based upon those of 1757, and those of Flanders in 1794, but resulting, as in the previous year, in a very different manner. The armies of the Rhine and of the Sambre-and-Meuse started from the two extremities of the base, for the purpose of taking a concentric direction upon the Danube. They formed, as in 1794, two exterior lines. The Archduke Charles, more skillful than Coburg, took advantage of the interior direction of his own, to give them a less distant point of concentration than that fixed upon by the enemy. He seized the moment when the Danube covered the corps of Latour to conceal several marches from Moreau, and to throw all his forces upon the right of Jourdan, whom he overthrew. The battle of Wurzburg decided the fate of Germany, and forced Moreau's army, extended as it was upon an immense line, to retreat.

Bonaparte commenced his extraordinary career in Italy. His system was to isolate the Piedmontese and Austrian armies. He succeeded by the battle of Millesimo in forcing them upon two exterior lines, and afterwards beat them in succession at Mondovi and at Lodi. A formidable army was collected in the Tyrol, to succor Mantua, which he had besieged. This army committed the error of marching upon two lines *separated by a lake.* Quick as thought, the French general raised the siege by abandoning everything, and moved with the greater part of his army against the first column, which debouched by Brescia, beat it, and thrust it into the mountains. The second column arrived upon the same ground, was beaten in its turn, and forced to retire into the Tyrol to communicate with its right. Wurmser, on whom these lessons were thrown away, desired to cover the two lines of Roveredo and Vicenza; Bonaparte, after having overthrown and repulsed the first upon Lavis, changed direction to the right, debouched by the gorges of the Brenta, against the line of the left, and forced the remnant of that fine army to seek safety in Mantua, where it was ultimately obliged to capitulate.

In 1799, hostilities were recommenced. The French, though punished for having two exterior lines of operations in 1796, had three, in 1799, upon the Rhine and the Danube. An army of the left watched the Lower Rhine; that of the centre marched to the Danube; Switzerland, which flanked Italy and Suabia, was occupied by a third army as strong as the other two. *The three corps could only be united in the valley of the Inn at eighty leagues from the base of their operations!* The archduke had equal forces, but he united them against the centre, which he crushed at Stockach, and the army of Helvetia was obliged to evacuate the Grisons and Eastern Switzerland. The combined armies then committed the same errors, and instead of following up the conquest of this central bulwark, which afterwards cost them so dearly, they formed a double line in Switzerland and upon the Lower Rhine. Their army in Switzerland was overwhelmed at Zurich, whilst that of the Rhine was amused about Manheim. In Italy, the French formed the double line of Naples, in which place thirty-two thousand men were uselessly stationed, whilst upon the Adige, where the heaviest blows should have fallen, their army was too weak, and experienced overwhelming reverses. When the army of Naples returned to the north, it again committed the fault of taking a direction away from that of Moreau; Suwarof skillfully availed himself of the advantages of the central position in which he was left, marched against the first of these armies, and beat it at a distance of several leagues from the other.

In 1800, everything was changed. Bonaparte had returned from Egypt, and that campaign presented a new combination of the lines of operations.*

One hundred and fifty thousand men filed across the flanks of Switzerland, and debouched on one side upon the Danube, and on the other upon the Po. This superb march secured the conquest of an immense extent of country. Up to that time, modern history had offered no similar operation. The French armies formed two interior lines of operation, which reciprocally sustained each other. The Austrians, on the contrary, were compelled to adopt an exterior direction, which deprived them of the power of communicating. By this manœuvre, the army of reserve cut the enemy off from his lines of operations, and preserved all its own relations with the frontiers and with the army of the Rhine, which formed its secondary line. Figure 3, Plate XX., confirms this statement, and exhibits the positions of the two parties respectively. A A, represents the armies of the reserve and of the Rhine; B B, those of Melas and Kray; C C C C, the passes of the Saint Bernard, the Simplon, the Saint Gothard, and of the Splugen. It is seen by this figure, that Melas was cut off from his base of operations, and that, on the other hand, the French general ran no risk, since he preserved all his communications with the frontiers and with his secondary line.

An analysis of the memorable events, of which we have barely sketched the outlines, will be sufficient to convince any one of the importance of the choice of manœuvre-lines in all military operations. In fact, the salvation or destruction of empires depends upon this. By it the disasters of a lost battle may be repaired; an invasion rendered a nullity,

* This chapter was composed in 1803. Since then, we have witnessed events equally brilliant, but they did not result from wiser combinations. The manœuvres of the French before Ulm and Jena, the march of the Russians upon Kaluga and the Berezina, and that of the allies upon Leipsic, offer new applications of the same combinations with still greater results.

the advantages of a victory extended, and the conquest of a country secured.

By comparing the combinations and the results of the most celebrated campaigns, it will be observed, that all the lines of operations which have led to success may be brought under the general principles as grouped and presented in Chapter VII.; *for single and interior lines have for their object, to place in action, at the most important point, and by means of strategic movements, a greater number of divisions, and consequently a greater mass than the enemy.* Likewise it may be remarked of such as lead to failures and are unsuccessful, that they also may be referred to errors opposed in their nature to these principles, since double exterior and all multiplied lines have a tendency to expose feebler or isolated parts to a mass which shall overthrow them.

It now remains to point out the influence which the configuration of the frontiers has upon the direction of grand operations, and to make a few observations upon eccentric lines.

Lloyd and Bulow have applied them to retreats; the latter especially has argued, that a retreat, in order to be a good one, ought to be eccentric, as in the following figure;

that is to say, an army commencing this operation from a given point, ought to follow several diverging lines, for the purpose of covering a greater extent of frontier, and *menacing the flanks of an adversary by the two extremities.*

With these high-sounding words, flanks, a partial air of importance is given to the most erroneous principles; such as are totally opposed to the rules of the art. A retreating army is always both physically and morally weaker than its adversary, because its numerical inferiority, or a series of reverses have compelled it to retire. Ought it therefore to be still further enfeebled by spreading and diverging? We would not oppose a retreat made by several columns to facilitate and expedite the movement, so long as these columns were capable of mutually sustaining each other. But it is those which are conducted on diverging lines, which are referred to, and which the above figure defines. Let us suppose that an army of forty thousand men is in retreat, before one of sixty thousand. Should the first now form four isolated divisions of about ten thousand men, the enemy, by manœuvring upon two lines of operations of thirty thousand men each, would easily be able to turn, envelope, and disperse in succession all these divisions. In what way can they escape such a fate? *merely by concentrating.* But this mode is opposed to the system proposed by the author we are discussing; hence the absurd and impossible nature of his theory is evident.

Let us test this mode of reasoning by the great lessons which experience has given us. When the first divisions of the army of Italy were repulsed by Wurmser, Bonaparte collected them all at Roverbella, and although he had but forty thousand men, he beat sixty thousand, for the simple reason that he had merely to combat with isolated columns. Had he made an eccentric retreat, what would have become of his army and his conquests? Wurmser, after his first check, made an eccentric retreat by diverging his two wings from the extremities of his line of defense. What was the consequence? the right, although sheltered by the mountains of the Tyrol, was defeated at Trent; Bonaparte then directed his march behind the left detachment, and destroyed it at Bassano and Mantua.

When the Archduke Charles yielded to the first efforts of the two French armies, in 1796, would he have saved Germany had he manœuvred eccentrically? On the contrary, was it not the concentric direction which he gave his retreat, which preserved it? Finally, Moreau, who had marched upon an immense development, by isolated divisions, discovered that this incredible system would lead to his own destruction, as soon as it became a question of fighting, and above all of retreating; he concentrated his scattered divisions, and all the efforts of the enemy failed before a mass which it had to observe on a line of eighty leagues. After such examples it seems to me there is nothing more to be said.

Bulow has, moreover, committed the grave error of calling those retreats parallel, which start from a given point, and are directed on the frontier. On the contrary, they are called direct or perpendicular retreats. Lines of retreat are parallel when conducted parallel to the line of the frontiers, over a considerable extent of country, such as was made by Frederick the Great, of Prussia, in marching from Moravia into Bohemia; the line of battle of the army will then be perpendicular to the frontiers, as is shown in the following figure:

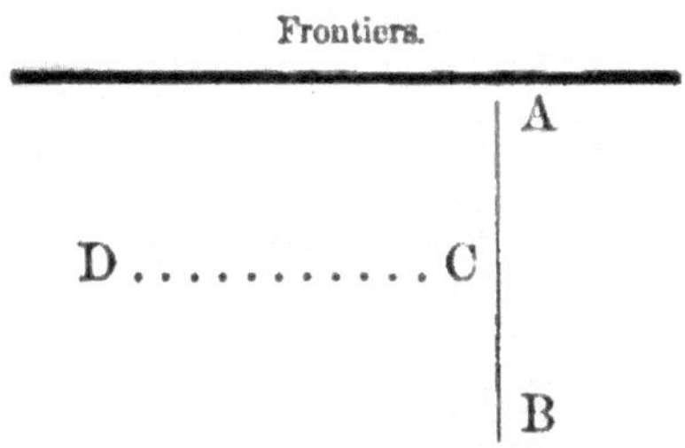

A B represents the line of battle of the army, C D indicates the one which would be passed over in retreat. But when the army's line of battle and the frontiers are parallel, the line of retreat is then necessarily perpendicular. The figure given by Bulow himself will serve to show it.

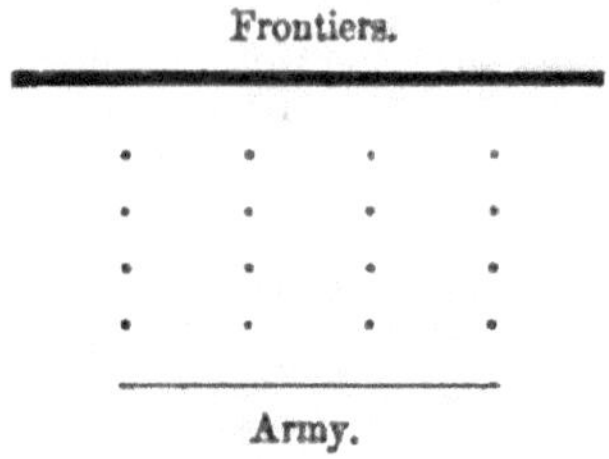

Recapitulating the different ideas presented in this chapter, it appears that:

1st. *In order to manœuvre properly, two armies should never be formed upon the same frontier.*

2d. *Double lines against a single one will always fail, the chances being equal, for the reasons pointed out in Chapter VII.*

3d. *Interior lines will resist most advantageously exterior lines, whether on the same frontier or on two different frontiers.*

The success of all the great strategic movements of Frederick, especially the one which followed the battle of Hohenkirch; the reverses of the Austrians in the Seven Years' war; those of the French in the war of Hanover; upon the Rhine and the Danube in 1796 and 1799; and, finally, the immortal campaign of 1800, all prove the truth of the third maxim. The invasion of Belgium in 1794, which succeeded in opposition to these principles, can hardly be cited as an exception, since the Austrians made no use of their central position, to fall, as they should have done, *en masse* upon the left of the French, which for more than fifteen days was beyond the reach of succor.

4th. *The most advantageous direction to be given to a line of manœuvre is upon the centre of the enemy's line, when his* *forces are scattered over an extensive front; but in any other case it should be directed against the extremities, and thence against the rear of the enemy's line of defense. The combinations of the campaign of* 1800 *have clearly demonstrated the truth of this maxim.**

The advantage of that direction not only arises from the fact, that in attacking one of the extremities of the line there is but a part of the enemy's forces to contend against, but there is a still greater one derived from the fact that his line of defense is threatened in reverse. The army of the Rhine, after having made demonstrations against the left of Kray, marched rapidly along the border of Switzerland, and thus, placing itself upon the right extremity of his line of defense, conquered, without fighting, the greater part of Suabia. The results of that part of the combination which placed the army of reserve upon the rear of Melas, cutting him off from his line of operation, was not less brilliant.

5th. *The configuration of the frontiers may be of great importance in determining the direction of these lines. Central positions, which form a salient angle towards the enemy, as Switzerland and Bohemia* (see Figure 3, Plate XX.), *are the most advantageous, because they are naturally interior, and because they lead to the rear, or to one of the extremities of the enemy's line of defense. The sides of this salient angle become of so much importance, that all the*

* We have considered it best to give this article as written at the camp of Boulogne, before the campaigns of 1805, 1806, and 1809. It is a great satisfaction to have been able to discover, in the first operations of Napoleon, the basis of the system which he henceforth followed.

The march of the grand French army upon Donaüworth, where it was established upon the extreme right of Mack, and whence it afterwards cut him off from his base and secondary line of operations, and the movement executed in 1806, by the sources of the Mein and Saale against the extreme left of the Prussian army, embody the same principles, and exhibit like results. Lastly, the memorable victories of Abensberg and Eckmuhl furnish us with incontestable proof of the superiority of central masses, or of interior lines skillfully put in action against divided corps, provided all the chances are equal.

resources of art should be joined to those of nature to render them unassailable.

6th. *In the absence of these central positions, their places may be supplied by the relative direction given to manœuvre-lines, as is shown in the following figure:*

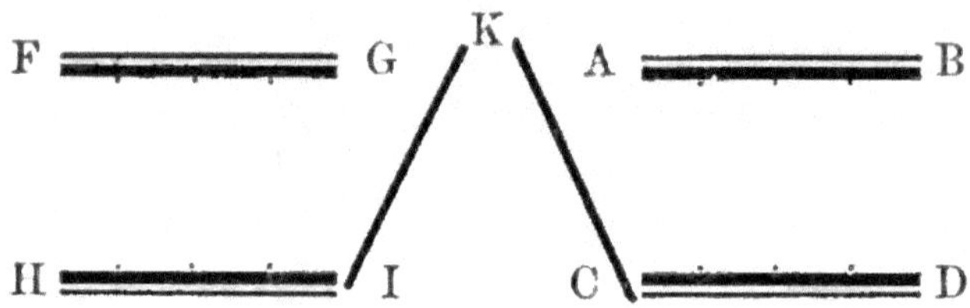

C D, manœuvring against the right flank of the army A B, and H I, being moved upon the left flank of F G, they will form the two interior lines, C K, and I K, upon one extremity of the exterior lines, A B, and F G, which they will be able to overthrow in succession, by moving against them alternately the mass of their forces. This combination exhibits the results of the lines of operations in 1800, and 1809.

7th. *The configuration of the theatre of war may possess as great importance as that of the frontiers.**

In fact, the entire theatre of war forms a four-sided figure. To place this idea in a clearer light, let us point to the theatre of the war of the French armies in Westphalia, from 1757 to 1762, and that of Napoleon in 1806.

In the first of these theatres of war, the side A B, was closed by the North Sea; the side B D, by the line of the Weser, which was the base of Duke Ferdinand's army. The line of the Mein formed the line C D, the base of the French army, and the face A C, formed by the line of the Rhine, was equally guarded by the armies of Louis XV.

* The above article 7, is the only one of the chapter which has been added since the first edition; all the others were written in 1804.

It will therefore be seen that the French armies, operating offensively upon two faces, had in their favor the North Sea

forming the third side, and, consequently, had only to gain by their manœuvres the side B D, in order to be masters of the four faces; that is to say, of the base and of all the communications of the enemy, as the following figure will show.

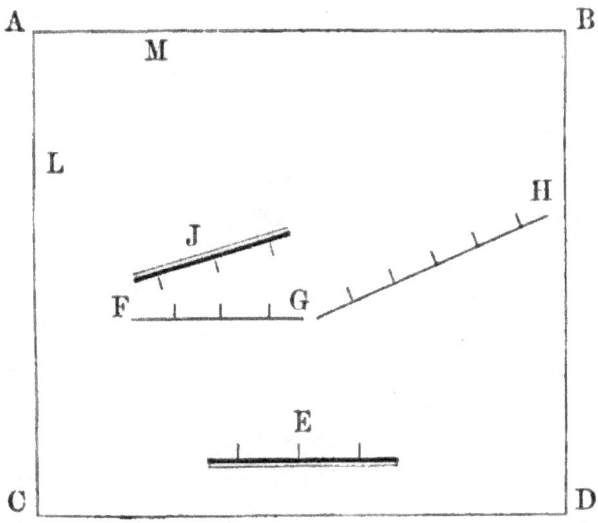

The French army E, starting from the base C D, for the

purpose of gaining the position F G H, cuts off the allied army J from the side B D, which forms its only communication, and only base. The latter would then be thrust into the angle L A M, which was formed toward Emden by the line of the Rhine, the Ems, and by the North Sea, whilst the French army E, can always communicate with the Mein.

The manœuvre of Napoleon upon the Saale, in 1806, was combined in precisely the same way. He went to occupy Jena and Naumburg, the line F G H, and afterward marched by Halle and Dessau to expel the Prussian army J, to the side A B, formed by the sea. The fate with which that army met at Erfurt, Magdeburg, Lubeck, and Prenzlau, is sufficiently well known. The great art, then, may be reduced to this: to seize upon the enemy's communications without the loss of our own. It is easily seen that the line F G H, by its prolonged position, and the crochet left upon the extremity of the enemy, keeps up its communications with the base C D; this is the exact application of the manœuvres of Marengo and Jena.

When the theatre of operations does not rest upon the sea, it will always be bounded by a great neutral power which will guard its frontiers, and will form in that manner one side of the square. This, it is true, never can become a barrier equal to the sea; but in general, it may be regarded as a dangerous obstacle, and one upon which it is not safe to retire after being beaten, and therefore it will be advantageous to push an enemy against it. The territory of a neutral power, which has at its command two hundred thousand men, is not violated with impunity, and should a beaten army be forced to run this risk, it is not the less cut off from its base. If the adjacent power should be a feeble one, then the frontier is thrown back until the territory of a formidable one is reached to limit the theatre of war.

To confirm the principles here laid down, it will be merely

necessary to glance at the theatre of war in the campaign of Poland in 1806 and 1807. The Baltic Sea and the frontiers of Austrian Galicia formed the two faces A B, and C D, of the square before given. It was undoubtedly important to both armies that neither of them should be thrown upon either of these obstacles.

The configuration of the frontiers will sometimes modify the shape and position of the quadrilateral. It may have the general form of a parallelogram or of a trapezoid; as in the figure given below.

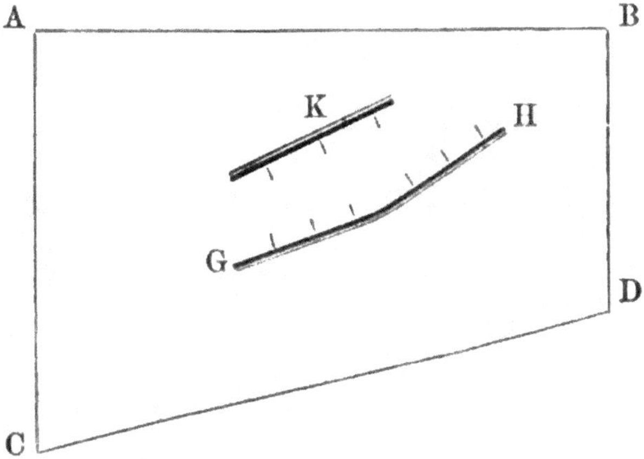

In the latter case, the army G H, which will be in command of the faces A C, and C D, will still have the advantage; since the base of its adversary is narrowed toward B D, which renders it more difficult to regain its communications; the front of this base, offering less development, will also possess fewer resources of manœuvre. On the contrary, it will enable the army G H, to operate with more success, since the direction of its line CD, will naturally lead it upon the communications of the enemy, and as the space which it would have to hold to cut him off from it is less in extent, that operation, of course, becomes more easy and practicable to concentrated forces.

The theatre of the war in Prussia and in Poland, spoken of above, was precisely similar to that figure. The frontiers of Galicia, extending as far as the Narew, formed, by the line of the Vistula, the short side B D. The manœuvre by which Napoleon embraced that side at Pultusk and Eylau, was absolutely the same as that sketched above.

However, that operation presented an unfavorable phase; founded, firstly upon the limited amount of confidence which could be reposed in the neutrality of Austria; and secondly, on account of the great distance from the base of the armies, leaving their communications with the Oder at the mercy of the Vienna cabinet; nothing else could be done at that time to put an end to these incessant invasions. The manœuvre of the French general was good; the operation of the statesman was merely audacious.

It is believed that sufficient examples have been given to illustrate the manœuvre of embracing the theatre of war, so as to reduce all cases to a few combinations which fall under the same principles, which are:

1st. *To direct our masses toward the decisive points of the lines of operations; that is to say, upon the centre, if the enemy have committed the fault of parceling out his troops; or upon one of his extremities, if he remain upon a contiguous line.*

2d. *To endeavor, in the latter case, to attain that one of the extremities opposite to an impassable obstacle, which bears upon the enemy's communications without exposing our own.*

CHAPTER XV.

CAMPAIGN OF 1759.

PREPARATIONS FOR OPENING THE CAMPAIGN; OPERATIONS OF THE FRENCH AND ALLIED ARMIES; COMBAT OF BERGEN; BATTLE OF MINDEN.

The armies passed the winter tranquilly in the cantonments given in Chapters IX. and XIII. A few movements took place in Saxony and upon the Rhine, without much of an object, among the principal of which, was the occupation of Frankfort, by the prince of Soubise, and that of Erfurt, by General Knobloch of Prince Henry's army.

The belligerent powers profited by this interval of repose, to prepare themselves for still more sanguinary combats. They renewed their efforts to fill up their armies, established their depôts, and introduced into their plans more unity than had marked them heretofore.

The turn of the maritime war between England and France attached the cabinet of Versailles still more strongly to an alliance which seemed to open a brighter future, seeing no other compensation for the loss of its colonies than the destruction of the king of Prussia, and the conquest of Hanover. It was not understood, nor even perceived by this cabinet, that in endeavoring to remedy a slight evil, it was sapping the very foundation of national interest, and giving a direction to the policy of Europe entirely opposed to its own preservation. It has already been remarked that the alliance of France and Austria presented some advantages;

but this should have been confined to a reciprocally defensive treaty, such as might have enabled France to concentrate all her resources upon the maritime war; very different from that alliance of invasion which employed the large armies of Louis XV. to break up the German equilibrium in favor of the House of Austria.

The victorious efforts of Frederick in this great struggle had unveiled to the allies the defects of their plans; but agreeing upon this, they differed widely as to the mode of improving them. The French government hoped to arrive at it, by centralizing in some measure the operations of the allied armies; by sending men whose merit was recognized to the camps of their confederates. M. de Montalembert was attached to the Russian army, count of Montazet to the Austrian army, and the marquis of Caulaincourt to the general headquarters. Would these ministry-generals have attained the objects of their missions, if they had secured the unlimited powers of all the several sovereigns? Reduced as they were to the part of observers and counselors, they contributed solely to introduce more unity into the operations.

Austria, an impassible witness of the efforts which the allies made to sustain a struggle which concerned herself more than it did them, and deceived by the miscalculations of a crooked policy, lost the advantages which she might have derived from her European supremacy.

England wished the war prolonged, and was in a condition to carry it on; her victorious fleets secured her incalculable resources. Her armies, and those of her allies, had at their head men of great reputation, and whose successes gave each day more weight to her pretensions. The cabinet of Saint James had just renewed its treaties, by which subsidies were granted to the king of Prussia and the Hessians, and the army of Duke Ferdinand was soon seen to expand to seventy thousand men.

At the opening of the campaign, the position of the French army differed little from the one occupied by it the preceding year. It was a double line of operations exposed to superior forces. The marquis of Contades commanded the army of the Lower Rhine, toward Wesel. The duke of Broglio commanded that of the Mein, and was connected with the army of the Circles, which, since the evacuation of Erfurt by the Prussians, had occupied, with a strong division, the archbishopric of Fulde, and several important posts upon the Werra.

Duke Ferdinand, possessing the advantage of a central position, undertook to show a front to the two armies. His task was a difficult one; whilst moving his mass against one of them, he exposed himself to a dangerous invasion from the other. The duke adopted the sound plan of forming a double interior line of operations, reënforced at the decisive point. The absence of the marquis of Contades induced the belief that his army was not in readiness for action, and saved the necessity of choice, as it was natural to seize this moment for the purpose of thrusting the army of the duke of Broglio beyond the Mein, or even the Rhine. The allies made the necessary arrangements for carrying this out.

The duke first communicated his plan to Prince Henry, in order to have him make a slight diversion on the side of Saxony, to prevent the troops of the empire from annoying the expedition. He left the command of the corps of observation of the Lower Rhine to Generals Sackville and Sporken, and on the 21st of March, directed himself, with the divisions of the prince of Holstein and the hereditary prince, upon Cassel, where the corps of the prince of Isenburg joined him on the 24th. The army arrived at Fulde on the 30th; and the advance-guard at Gersfeld.

In the meantime Prince Henry detached the Generals Knobloch and Lindstedt into Franconia, for the purpose of attracting the attention of the troops of the empire, whilst the hereditary prince attacked them on the side of Hesse. The latter, in his movement, seized upon Meiningen and Wasungen, made two thousand prisoners, and determined the Austrians to retreat upon Bamberg.

The duke rested at Fulde until the 10th of April, as much to secure his communications by Cassel, as to establish the necessary depôts for his operations. The loss of that precious time illustrates the defects of that system of war; it afforded the duke of Broglio time to make his preparations. The French troops were encamped in such a manner that they might be united at Bergen in two days' march; a chain of light troops was placed at such a distance that timely information would be given, so that the troops could be assembled without being disturbed.

Whilst these events were passing, the Marquis d'Armentières, who commanded upon the Lower Rhine, set about extricating the duke of Broglio from his embarrassment. Under command of the Count Saint Germain, he formed a *corps d'élite* of upwards of ten thousand men, which was transported to the Lahn, but which arrived too late to take part in the action. The allied army at last took its departure from Fulde, on the 10th of April, and on the 12th, went into camp at Windeken. The duke of Broglio, having learned, since evening, of that movement, took his measures to meet the attack at Bergen.* (Plate XXI., No. 2). That position was excellent; the hamlet, which covered the right, is situated upon the reverse of a chain of ridges, which extended along the right of the Frankfort causeway to Bischofheim, and which in the vicinity of Bergen are very steep. A beautiful plain in advance, and to the left of the hamlet, descends to the forest of Wilbel, but it is cut transversely by a hollow way, which leads to that village. Bergen was surrounded by a wall, and by gardens embellished with evergreen hedges.

It was occupied by eight battalions. The regiments Piedmont, Royal-Roussillon, and Alsace, were placed more in rear; and behind the latter, four Swiss battalions, with the regiments Rohan and Beauvoisis, disposed in column by battalion, for the purpose of sustaining the troops which occupied Bergen, or filing to the left to turn the enemy. The left, which was formed of the Saxon corps, was unattackable. Between that wing and the right, eleven battalions in columns were also placed. An intermediate reserve of thirty-two squadrons was established in three lines in rear of the tower of Berg-Wartha. The artillery swept with a cross-fire all the approaches.

On the 13th of April, at daylight, the allied army advanced in five columns directly upon Bergen, and between eight and nine o'clock was formed on the reverse of the hills which extend from Birschofsheim to Wilbel. During this time the duke of Broglio had assembled his generals at the town of Berg-Wartha, and given them his orders, wherein he insisted particularly upon the defense of Bergen.

On the other hand, Ferdinand concluded that the only attackable point admitted of a vigorous defense, and not wishing to risk the fate of a campaign in an action which presented so few chances in his favor, determined to engage at first only the brigades of his left, under the prince of Isenburg, and afterwards to cause them to be sustained by the hereditary prince, who had possessed Bischofsheim, in order to turn the enemy. The right, under General Granby, was refused.

This movement was commenced at ten o'clock. The moment the duke of Broglio perceived the design of the prince, he threw in front of Bergen the six French and four Swiss battalions, where they were formed at the moment when the Hessian grenadiers vigorously began their attack.

This infantry combat was murderous, and raged upon the same ground until all their ammunition was exhausted.

Whilst this took place, the division of the hereditary prince, skirting the right of the hamlet, sought to turn the left flank of the French corps which defended it, at the instant it was attacked by the prince of Isenburg. The moment was decisive. The duke of Broglio reënforced the troops in front of Bergen by the regiment of Beauvoisis, and, at the same time, led the regiment Rohan against the right of the hereditary prince, whilst the two regiments of the centre turned the left of the Hessians. This simultaneous effort, executed at the moment that the prince of Isenburg was killed, obliged the allies to fall back. The regiments Rohan and Beauvoisis, yielding themselves too ardently to the pursuit, were charged and broken by the cavalry, which, up to this time, could not act, owing to the nature of the ground.

The duke had merely been repulsed, and nothing was lost provided the French could be drawn from their position. For this purpose he retired at first to the valley, in which the army was formed in the morning, but immediately after took post upon the height, making demonstrations against Wilbel and the Saxon corps, whilst the left opened a fierce cannonade. But the imperturbable duke of Broglio confined his movements to merely posting his reserve so as to sustain his wings, if necessary, in such a way that his adversary was obliged to regain, in the night, his position of Windeken.

The consequences of this combat offer nothing important. The count of Saint Germain joined the army the next day; but this reënforcement did not induce the duke of Broglio to change his mode of operating and follow up his success. The Duke Ferdinand seemed to court it, by making a feint of besieging the chateau of Marburg with the corps of General Hardenberg. Broglio, faithful to his system, only disturbed the rear-guard, and, after sundry skirmishes, discovering that the duke had cantoned his army in the neighborhood of Fritzlar, established his own behind the Lahn.

The marquis of Contades was still at Paris when he heard the news of the combat of Bergen. He set out therefrom as soon as he had received his last instructions, and arrived at Creveldt on the 4th of May. His first care was to throw a bridge over the Rhine between Wesel and Rhées, to deceive the enemy, whilst the army was assembling near Cologne and Dusseldorf. This movement attracted the attention of Ferdinand upon Westphalia, for he left with General Imhof only twelve thousand men in order to cover Hesse, and moved himself with all dispatch upon Lipstadt.

The marquis of Contades had now learned by experience, that the establishment of a double line of operations upon the Lippe and the Mein was not a suitable way of arriving at great results. It would become evident that Ferdinand, master of the fortified places of Munster, Lipstadt, and Hameln, could regard without fear the temporary progress of the French army in Westphalia, and profiting by his central positions of Fritzlar and Cassel, could operate in succession against the one which at the time presented the greater chances of success. He therefore resolved to operate *en masse* by Hesse, descending the Weser, in order to force the allies to repass that river, and thus evacuate Westphalia, of which the duke d'Armentières had possession, and was besieging Munster with twenty-five thousand men. The French army left its quarters on the 20th of May, for the purpose of assembling at Giessen. On the 3d of June it occupied the following positions:

82 battalions, 54 squadrons, Marburg.
18 " 31 " reserve under the duke of Broglio, on the Ohm towards Homberg.
15 " 20 " upon the Lower Rhine, under the duke d'Armentières.

7 battalions,		at Frankfort and Hanau.
	20 squadrons,	carbineers and gendarmes, under General Pcyanne, at Cologne, before joining the army.
126 "	125 "	not including some volunteer corps or legions.

Ferdinand, since the projects of his adversary were so pronounced, sought to gain time for concentrating his forces, and with this object in view, he sent the hereditary prince with three thousand men, as partisans, to Dusseldorf, in order to render the French uneasy in regard to their communications and their magazines. But this insignificant effort resulted as should have been expected; for whilst the duke concentrated his army at the camp of Werla, the marquis of Contades took advantage of his absence to invade Hesse, which he carried out with all the activity which, in those days, could be infused into an operation.

The advance-guard of fourteen battalions, of which ten were grenadiers, left Marburg on the 5th, and moved on the 9th towards Corbach. The reserve started at the same time from its position of Jantershausen, and arrived on the 9th at Niederurf. The grand army encamped on the 8th at Sachsenberg. The object of this movement appeared to be to isolate the corps of Imhof, but the execution was not rapid enough, for that general, having learned of the march of the French, moved on the 9th to Warburg, and on the 11th formed a junction with the corps of General Wutgenau. The duke of Broglio also entered Cassel without opposition, on the 11th, and finding no enemy thereabouts, he afterwards pushed forward his advance-guard to Munden.

Whilst these events were passing, the marquis of Contades had marched his army on the 10th to Corbach, with the intention of seizing the defiles of Stadtbergen, or, if required, to sustain the expedition conducted by his lieutenant. These defiles, so important and so easy to defend, were abandoned by Wutgenau, and the marquis of Contades, knowing of the occupation of Munden, led his army through them on the morning of the 13th. It was encamped in rear of the Dimel, and the marquis of Auvet covered the camp by taking post at Essen, upon the left bank, with four battalions supported by two brigades. The duke of Broglio was ordered to move upon Paderborn. Ferdinand, on his side, was joined, on the 11th, by the corps of Generals Sackville and Sporken, at Soest, where he halted until the 12th, and on the 14th encamped at Buren, where the corps of Imhof and Wutgenau joined him. It would seem that the duke wished to anticipate the French at the passage of the Dimel, but Contades, not wishing to subject the corps of Auvet to the risk of fighting alone, had passed that river in six columns on the morning of the 14th.

Ferdinand saw clearly that the object of the French was to cut him off from Minden and the Weser. However, as he could not direct his march towards that stream without losing his communication with Munster, Lipstadt, and especially with the corps of Wangenheim, left in the camp of Dulmen, upon the Lower Rhine, he therefore continued to retire parallel to the Weser.

Let us abridge, in a tabular form, the marches which resulted from these combinations.

	June 18, The *duke of Broglio*, at Etteln and Paderborn. *Fischer's corps* towards Ruden, the *army* at Meerhof.
June 19, The *duke* retired between Lipstadt and Ervitte. *General Wangenheim* at Dulmen.	June 19, *D'Armentières* at the camp of Schembeck; awaits the arrival of the convoys of provisions coming from Hesse.
June 20, The *duke* at Rittberg. Rested in position.	
	June 23, The *duke of Broglio* at Neuhaus.
	June 24, The *army* at Paderborn. The *corps of Chevreuse* at Buren; the *legion of Fischer* at Dettmold.

June 29, *Wangenheim* at Wolbeck. Evening, the *duke* started his advance-guard.	June 29, *Duke of Broglio* at Osterhold The *army* at Ostschlagen. The *corps of Chevreuse* at Neuhaus, in order to cover Paderborn and the magazines.
June 30, The *army* followed, and encamped at Marienfeld.	
	July 2, The *duke of Broglio* at Orlinghausen. The *army* at Struckenbruck, near Bielefeld.
July 3, The *duke* at Dissum, near Ravensberg. *Wangenheim* at Ladberg, afterwards joined the army.	July 3, The *duke of Broglio* at Heppen and Hervorden.
	July 4, The *army* at Bielefeld.
	July 6, *D'Armentières* invested Munster.
July 7, The *duke* at Osnabruck.	July 7, The *duke of Broglio* at Engern. 3 brigades of infantry at Hervorden. 1 of cavalry at Hervorden.
	July 8, The *army* at Hervorden.

It will be seen by this table with what a degree of slowness the operations were conducted on both sides; and that the French, after the 24th of June, were so situated that they might have seized all the communications of the allies. Finally, when the duke was decidedly retreating, Broglio resolved upon an enterprise against the fortress of Minden, whose bad condition and weak garrison held out strong hopes of success. He advanced, July 9th, at midday, to within double cannon-shot of the place, and summoned it. General Zastrow, who commanded the fortress, disregarded the summons, and prepared for its defense. He had already destroyed all the boats to be found on the Weser. Fortunately for the French, a peasant pointed out the only one overlooked, which was found some leagues from there. The duke of Broglio made use of it to send across the river, during the night, the Lanoue volunteers and Fischer's corps. These troops assaulted the horn-work which covered the bridge of the Weser, whilst a battery, which had been established on the opposite side during the night, took the troops which defended it in flank, and enfiladed the bridge. The attack, which was at first repulsed, was renewed with success. The legion Fischer, after having captured the horn-work, pursued the garrison upon the bridge, forced it to enter and open the gates to the grenadiers, who entered the city without firing a shot.

This operation, which was carried out with vigor, gave a fortress and one thousand two hundred prisoners to the French.

Thus terminated the first part of the campaign in Westphalia. Before proceeding farther, we desire to offer some observations.

Nothing more strikingly proves the advantages of a happy choice of lines of operations, than the progress made by the French armies during this period. The combination which carried the army of Contades to the Lahn, perpendicular to the Rhine, and afterwards pushed it by its right towards the Weser, would have given rise to results of the greatest importance, if this general, in place of merely threatening the communications of the allies, had seized upon and held them.

*The greatest secret of war consists in becoming master of the communications of the enemy.** Had Contades appreciated this truth, it is probable that the allied army would have been destroyed. It is difficult to conceive how the general who combined so well, should have executed so badly. As soon as he became master of Munden, and the defiles of Stadt-Bergen, he was sure of gaining the communications of

* Napoleon expressed himself thus in an audience at which the writer was present, at the opening of the campaign in 1806. This truth was confirmed a few days after in a most brilliant manner, by the march upon Gera and the Saale, which brought about all the results of the battle of Jena.

Ferdinand. In order to turn the chances in his favor, it would have been sufficient to change his direction to the left, and to march swiftly upon Buren and Geisecke, in order to cover his own line of operations, and shut up the duke so closely that it would be impossible for him to gain a march either to the right or to the left. Marshal Contades would thus have turned and held the duke between the Rhine, the North Sea, and the French army. He could then have deliberately attacked the allies, overwhelming them at a single blow. Such was the position in which Napoleon knew how to entangle Brunswick at Jena, Mack at Ulm, Melas at Marengo, Wurmser at Bassano, and in which he allowed himself to be caught by the Russians at the end of the campaign of 1812.

Although the first combination made by Contades exhibited some skill, yet its execution did not correspond to the plan which he had formed. After the duke of Broglio had seized upon Minden, on the 9th, which was the most favorable moment to march to the attack of Duke Ferdinand, the French general remained five days in his camp of Hervorden, and allowed the duke to reëstablish his communications by taking position, on the 14th, at Stolzenau on the Weser.

Some men, who deny the influence of the art of war, as an excuse for not studying, have objected that it is not founded upon principles, since this plan of Contades, which had been so skillfully combined, led to nothing but reverses. A pitiful argument, to which it is not necessary to reply.

There can be no doubt, but that the basis of a plan of campaign should be founded upon principles; since from it proceed the great results; thus the concentric march of Napoleon upon Gera, in 1806, was by itself a victory; for it secured all the advantages of one. But of what use is a good plan, when all principles are abandoned in its execution, and what would have been produced by this great march, if the French army, after having gained the communications of the Prussians, had halted at Salfeld and Schleitz, until they had again recovered them, by moving to Gera, between the Elster and the Mulde? A plan, formed on great principles, and of which the execution is throughout conformable thereto, will lead to extraordinary victories, and the most decisive results; such were Napoleon's wars, until he became intoxicated with ten years' success; such were likewise those of his enemies, after they had become enlightened by experience, so as to be enabled to apply the principles which lead to it.

A new confirmation of the advantages of the application of principles is furnished by the battle of Waterloo. Napoleon having skillfully concentrated, without the knowledge of the English and Prussian generals, would have overwhelmed Blücher at Ligny, if the orders which he had given to the *corps-d'armée* of his left had been executed, and if the Count d'Erlon had debouched by Bry, as he should have done. Although these orders were not executed, he gained on the 16th a great victory; but two days after he was beaten for having despised his enemy, and directed Grouchy to make a movement contrary to the principles of the art; whilst the allies, letting the marshal manœuvre unnoticed, debouched on the rear of Napoleon, by a hardy and well-combined march. If, on the 17th, he gave Grouchy the order to fall back upon him, as has been affirmed, it repaired the fault he had committed, and his defeat was the result of the fortuitous events which prevented the execution of this movement. It was a decree of destiny, which so often forms a part of victory.

As to duke Ferdinand, Tempelhof has greatly extolled his perseverance in remaining in the vicinity of Lipstadt; nevertheless, it was a fault similar to that committed by the Prussians in their march upon Gotha and Eisenach, in 1806.

The German author justifies it on the ground that he did it to save the corps of Wangenheim, encamped at Dulmen; but ought he to have risked his communications and possibly the loss of his army, to save a detachment which ran no danger? It appears to have been an easy matter to send an order to this detachment to move by forced marches upon Munster, Osnabruck, or Minden, and thus have given it a secure concentric direction toward the points whither the army was to move.

Ferdinand succeeded merely by a hazard upon which he could not have relied, since the primitive plan of the French generals announced the broadest views, and more resolution than had been exhibited in the preceding campaigns. If the duke had been opposed to an active and enterprising general, his manœuvres, which have been so highly lauded by Tempelhof, would have led to his destruction.

BATTLE OF MINDEN.

The unexpected capture of Minden, by securing to the French a place of arms on the Weser, rendered the arrival of subsistence from Paderborn safe, and placed them in a position for acting vigorously against the Electorate of Hanover, the conquest of which appeared inevitable.

The marshal of Belle-Isle, who was minister, being forcibly impressed by this idea, filled his correspondence with Contades with this subject alone; discussing the best means of preserving the electorate, and avoiding the necessity of again evacuating it. But matters had arrived at such a pass, that a battle alone could decide the fate of the campaign.

Wishing to ward off the fatal consequences which would follow from the loss of Minden, Ferdinand quitted the camp of Osnabruck, in the night of the 10th and 11th of July, and reached Stolzenau in three marches.

The allied army not having a single fortress upon the Weser where it could establish its depôts in security, the duke turned his eyes upon Bremen, and felt himself authorized to seize it, from the example furnished him by the enemy in 1758. With this view he detached thither General Drewes, with four regiments of infantry, by Vechte. This detachment arrived in the night of the 14th and 15th, at daylight secured all the outlets, surprised the guard of the advanced works without giving any alarm; and penetrated into the city by stratagem.

Neither did Contades on his side lose any time. The reserve under the duke of Broglio was transferred to Minden on the 12th of July, and was replaced in the camp at Engern by two brigades of infantry, the French grenadiers, the royal grenadiers, and the brigade of cavalry Dumenil. Another division of infantry, and one of cavalry, was sent to Goofeld on the 13th, and passed the Weser near Minden on the 14th. They replaced the reserve of the duke of Broglio in the camp which it had just vacated, in order to move to Buckeburg two leagues from that point.

The grand army set out from Hervorden on the 14th, and encamped the next day near Minden, with its right wing at that village, and its left at Hartenhausen. The right flank was covered by the Weser, the front by the stream from Barte, and the left by the morass which extended even beyond Lubbecke, having behind it the chain of mountains which border the Werra. (Plate XXII.). The count of Rougrave was placed in advance in the plain between Minden and Kuttenhausen, with a strong division, to observe the allies. The count of Saint-Germain, who was posted at Bielefeld with the brigade of Auvergne, and a regiment of cavalry, marched against Hameln to restrain its garrison and cover the convoy, which came to the army from Cassel by Paderborn and Hervorden. Lubbecke, at the extremity of the morass, was occupied by the hussars of Berchini and Turpin; Hille, by the volunteers of Hainaut and Haller. Fronting this village, and across the morass, at Eichorst, the little corps of General Andlau was posted, supported by the division of Brissac, encamped at Kofeld, whose object it was to cover the road of Hervorden. The corps of the duke of Broglio was on the other side of the Weser, at Bukeburg. The partisans of Fischer scoured the country and spread terror to the very gates of Hanover; whilst the volunteers of Dauphiny extended their incursions on the right bank as far as Nienburg. Several bridges had been laid across the river, in order to facilitate the communication between the corps of the duke of Broglio and the grand army. The duke of Chevreuse blockaded Lipstadt, and d'Armentières besieged Munster.

The position occupied by the duke of Broglio rendered the communication with Hanover very difficult, and enabled the French to take possession of that capital. Their generals concluded that Ferdinand would pass the Weser, or at least that he would send across a strong corps to ward off this misfortune, and his construction of several bridges near Stolzenau confirmed them in this opinion. But this prince was too skillful to adopt such a system. He preferred allowing his adversary a slight temporary success upon the right bank of the river, to the exposure of his army to defeat by enfeebling it by detachments, which after all never have a decisive influence on the operations. On the other hand, he concentrated his forces, and was meditating recalling even the isolated corps in order to strike a decisive blow at the first opportunity; and in the night of the 15th and 16th, he put his army in motion in three columns against Minden, and encamped in the rear of Petershagen, with his right at

Brunikostige, and his left at the Weser. Thirteen battalions and eighteen squadrons of Hessian and Hanoverian dragoons constituted the advance-guard, commanded by the hereditary prince of Brunswick, who went into camp in two lines before Petershagen.

The duke, who wished to bring on an action in a situation unfavorable to the French, closed up their position, feeling persuaded that they would come out to attack him. On the 17th, the prince of Brunswick encamped in advance of Tonhausen and Hammern. The army was divided into nine columns, and was posted with its right at the village of Sudfeld, and its left at the woods in rear of Tonhausen, near the Weser.

This movement made a strong impression upon the French. Rougrave's corps, which lay in the plain in advance of Minden, was withdrawn under the cannon of the fortress, and all the troops were put under arms. Marshal Contades, not considering himself strong enough, ordered the duke of Broglio to rejoin the army with his corps.

The position of the enemy was, however, too strong to allow the duke of Brunswick to attack it with success; hence all his efforts to draw them out. Finding that it would be difficult for him to succeed in this, he returned, at four o'clock in the evening, to his camp at Petershagen; the duke of Broglio followed his example and withdrew.

Ferdinand, seeing the failure of his first attempt, caused the villages of Kuttenhausen, Hammern, and Friedwald to be occupied by strong detachments of infantry, and cut large openings in the dyke of Tonhausen, to enable the army to advance into the plain of Minden by division and squadron fronts, and moved his advance-guard to Tonhausen.

Munster having surrendered on the 23d, Ferdinand resolved to take the offensive without delay. He sent General Drewes to Osnabruck, to bring off the magazines which might be found there. The hereditary prince marched on the 27th upon Lubbecke with six battalions; on the 29th upon Hervorden, and encamped facing that village at Rissel, where General Drewes arrived, after having retaken the magazines of Osnabruck. The same day the duke Ferdinand, informed of this success, marched his army by line, and by the right in three columns. The first was composed of the first line, the second of the artillery and the baggage, and the third of the second line. They encamped with the right at Hille and the left at Friedwald. The general headquarters were in the first-named village, guarded by two English regiments. General Gilse occupied Lubbecke with three battalions.

On the 30th the duke assembled his generals, and recommended them to study carefully all the roads and the peculiarities of the ground, for the purpose of being able to conduct their several columns respectively in such a way that they might be quickly formed into a contiguous line. On the 31st he again called their attention to the same thing, and directed them to examine minutely the vicinity of the windmill of Hammern, in order to employ all arms with the greatest success. In considering the wisdom of these measures, and their propriety and connection with the very hour, even the instant in which the French generals were observed in movement for the purpose of forming in the plain of Minden, one is tempted to think that the duke was present at their council of war.

The detachments which the allies had made from their army, finally induced Marshal Contades to attack them, and the day was fixed on the 1st of August. To carry it out the following order was given:*

* This order, translated from the German, undoubtedly differs slightly from the original. It will be seen from the perusal of this long document (many passages of which have been suppressed), that it embodies but few instructions con-

"The reserve, commanded by the duke of Broglio, forming the right wing of the army, will march forward fronting on the village of Tonhausen, and will attack at the same time the camp of the prince of Bevern, upon the road of Petershagen. This attack will be sudden and vigorous, in order to overthrow his troops, cut off his retreat upon the army, and thence spread dismay and confusion.

"To insure the success of this operation, the reserve will be reënforced by the royal grenadiers and the grenadiers of France. Six guns and four howitzers will be added to its ordinary artillery. The duke of Broglio will attend to the assembling of the artillery, and transmit the necessary orders to the grenadiers. Every means will be employed to contribute to the success of this attack, which will render us masters of the enemy's left flank, and therefore upon this operation will depend the success of the day.

"The *retreat* will sound in place of the *generale*. As soon as it shall be beaten the reserve will break up its camp, pass the bridge, traverse the village, and leave it at the gate leading to the camp of the grenadiers. Its heavy baggage will be sent to Rehmen, where that of the army will be collected. There it will pass the Weser by the last bridge of boats, in order not to interfere with the march of the troops.

"The ground on which the army will have to deploy being cut up and furrowed, it will not be able to form in its accustomed order of battle. There will therefore be placed in the centre of the first line the brigades of cavalry Colonel-

cerning the attack, and that it is almost altogether devoted to the manner of extricating the army from its position, forming it into columns, and deploying it before the enemy. It would be well for the reader to take a glance at Chapter V., Volume I., where we have discussed Frederick's orders of march. A single instant will suffice to comprehend the difference which exists between the combination and execution of his manœuvres and those of the French general. We desire, also, to refer to the remarks which have been made at the end of this chapter.

General, Cravates, and Mestre-de-Camp, under the command of the duke of Fitz-James, Lieutenant-Generals Vogué and Castries, and the Major-Generals Lutzelbourg, Saint-Chamand, Vilbonne, and Courmainville. The four brigades of infantry, Picardy, Belsunce, Touraine, and Rouergue, under the Lieutenant-Generals Nicolai, Beaupreau, and the Major-Generals Planta and Monty, will form the right of the first line. Thirty-four pieces of heavy artillery will be attached to it. The left of this line will be composed of the four brigades of infantry, Condé, Aquitaine, the King, and Champaign, under Lieutenant-General Guerchy, and the Major-Generals duke of Laval and Maugiron. It will be provided with thirty pieces of artillery of position, which the Chevalier Pelletier will place upon the front of the two wings, so as to cover the front of the cavalry by a cross fire in the centre.

The first battalion of each brigade will be formed in column; the others will march in their customary manner (line of battle). The brigade Auvergne, placed at the left of the infantry of the right wing, will be formed in inverse order, that its first battalion may be formed in column, resting on the brigade of cavalry Colonel-General. The infantry brigade Condé, posted at the right of the left wing, will be formed the same as the others, that is to say, its first battalion in column, *appuied* upon the Mestre-de-Camp cavalry.

" The second line will march in the same order as the first. The brigades of infantry Auvergne and Anhalt, under Lieutenant-General Saint-Germain, and Major-Generals Leyden and Glaubitz, will constitute the right. The brigades of cavalry King, Bourgogne, and Royal-Etranger, under Lieutenant-Generals Dumesnil and Andlau, and the Major-Generals Orlick and Galfeld, will occupy the centre. The left will be composed of the Saxon brigades under the command of the Marquis of Lusatia.

"This second line being much less strong than the first, and yet having to occupy the same front, the battalions of which it is composed will be extended a good deal more than common.* The reserve, formed of the gendarmerie and the carbineers, under Lieutenant-General Poyanne, and the Major-Generals Bellefond and Bissy, will be placed in a third line behind the centre of the cavalry.

"The brigades Navarre and Lowendahl will receive a particular destination.

"The army, thus formed, will take up its first position. The left will be in rear of the village of Hahlen, resting on the morass; the right will be prolonged in rear of the red houses in the plain of Minden, as far as the woods. The lines will march at four hundred paces apart. The duke of Broglio will rest his right upon the steep banks of the Weser, presenting his front towards Tonhausen, and connecting his left with the right of the army, with his infantry in the first line and his cavalry in the second. This division, as well as the royal grenadiers and the grenadiers of France, will receive orders from the duke of Broglio.

"Whilst these troops are attacking Tonhausen and the camp of Petershagen, the army will deploy and march in line of battle against the enemy. If that march can not be immediately effected, the brigades of infantry and of cavalry will continue their movements in column upon battalion and squadron front, keeping their distances so as to be ready to form.

"The first battalion of each brigade which is to remain in column, will preserve this formation throughout the march and during the battle. The brigades of infantry will be

* This is a strange disposition; extending the second line intended as a reserve, was to deprive it of all its force by attenuating it. Had the second line remained in columns of attack, the battle would not have been lost. This line should only be deployed when a defensive post is occupied, and it is desirable to impose upon the enemy by an appearance of numbers.

preceded by one hundred workmen with wagons and the necessary tools.

"Since the enemy's right is at Hille, and his left behind Holzausen, the march will be directed upon his left flank, in order to inclose him. If the attack of the duke of Broglio succeed, he will endeavor to gain that flank in order to envelop it. The manœuvres executed by the army will depend upon those made by the enemy. Marshal Contades will, in any event, give suitable orders.

"The brigade of Navarre, the volunteers of Hainaut, Dauphiny, and Muret, under the command of Lieutenant-General the duke of Havre, will make a false attack upon the dyke which leads from Hille across the marsh.

"To carry this out, the artillery park will furnish four eight-pounders. The duke of Havre will direct a sharp fire upon the enemy's redoubt which commands the dyke; but the morass will only be crossed in case the army should penetrate to the vicinity of Hille, and where a junction could be effected with it. Up to that time it will confine itself to simply annoying the enemy, and preventing him from resting his right upon the morass. This corps ought, in case of necessity, to cover the retreat of the army, by holding the dyke and defending its passage. It should be careful also to crown the heights in rear with infantry and light troops, to hold in check any parties which the enemy may detach from Lubbecke. This precaution is important.

"The duke of Havre is informed that the duke of Brissac occupies Goofeld, for the purpose of observing the hereditary prince. He will communicate with him through the valley of the Bergkirchen, employing for this service the volunteer cavalry of Dauphiny, which is acquainted with the country and the roads. The posts of Kolhof and Hartenhausen will be maintained, because they overlook the surroundings of the morass.

"The brigade Lowendahl, under the command of Major-General Bisson, will enter Minden as soon as the retreat shall be sounded. It will occupy the ramparts and the three bridge-heads. The greater part of the heavy artillery will be placed upon the cavaliers; that, in case of necessity, it may cover the retreat of the army. Some pieces will also be placed in the work which covers the stone bridge, in order to defend the approaches to the têtes-de-pont against the attack of the light troops which infest the left bank of the Weser.

"The *retreat*, which will replace the *generale*, will be beaten at the usual time.

"The army immediately after will fall in, under arms, in front of the camp, and will march out in eight columns. The first, under the command of count de Guerchy, will be composed of the brigades King and Champagne. It will leave the woods situated near Amelbeck, at its left, will pass the Bartha upon the last bridge near the morass, and will march to the farthest hedges in front of Hallen, where it will remain in column until daylight. Then the army will be formed; the left will rest upon the above-mentioned hedges, and the right in the direction of the red houses which are situated in the plain. Eight pieces of heavy artillery will join these two brigades in the evening, and will remain before their front during the battle. M. de Saint-Ville, assistant quartermaster-general, will direct this division.

"The second column, which will be composed of the brigades Aquitaine and Condé, commanded by M. de Maugiron, will be conducted by Assistant-Quartermaster Baudonin, who will show them the bridge where the Bartha is to be passed, the place where the brigades will remain until daylight, and the ground upon which they will afterwards be formed. This column will have six pieces of heavy artillery.

"The third column, composed of two Saxon brigades, under the command of the count of Lusatia, will be conducted by the Assistant-Quartermaster Montaut, who will designate the place where they will remain in column behind the height, awaiting daylight, when it will form in a second line four hundred paces behind the first.

"The fourth column, comprising the brigades of cavalry Mestre-de-Camp, Cravates, and Royal Etranger, under the command of the duke of Fitz-James, will be directed by the Assistant Quartermaster Angers, who will indicate the place where the column will rest until daylight, when it will form; the brigade Mestre-de-Camp will rest its left on the infantry brigade Condé; that of Cravates will give its right a direction upon the red houses; and that of the Royal Etranger will be placed in a second line to the brigade Mestre-de-Camp, and at four hundred paces distant.

"The fifth column will be composed of the brigades of cavalry Colonel-General, King, and Bourgogne, under the command of Lieutenant General Dumesnil, and conducted by the Assistant Quartermaster Dumay, who will indicate the point where it will await the arrival of daylight. When daylight begins to appear, the brigade Colonel-General will be formed in the first line, resting upon that of Cravates, and conforming its direction to the red houses. The brigades of King and Bourgogne will be formed in a second line behind that of Cravates and Colonel-General.

"The sixth column, under Lieutenant-General Beaupreau, will be formed of the brigades Touraine and Rouergue of the infantry, which will pass the Bartha on the bridge pointed out to them by the Assistant-Quartermaster Germain, will march to the redoubt which is in front of Picardy, and there halt until daylight, when they will be formed on the right ot the brigade Colonel-General. This division will take eight pieces of artillery of position, which will remain in advance of its front during the battle.

"The seventh column, commanded by Lieutenant-General Saint-Germain, will comprise the brigades Auvergne and Anhalt. The first will cross the bridge pointed out by M. d'Ouné, an officer of the general staff, and will go as far as the camp of the second in the gardens in front of the village. The brigade Anhalt will be formed in a second line to those of Picardy and Belsunce.

"The eighth column, under the Chevalier Nicolai, will be composed of the brigades Picardy and Belsunce, will direct its march upon the red houses, and halt there until daylight. It will then be formed with its right extended to the woods, taking its direction upon the left of the reserve, commanded by the duke of Broglio. The Assistant-Quartermaster Grandpré will conduct this column. Towards evening, the park will send eight pieces of cannon, which will remain with these brigades during the action.

"The corps of the duke of Broglio will form the ninth column. The gendarmes and grenadiers will be mounted, and remain in advance of the front of the camp until they shall receive the order to place themselves in a third line behind the centre.

"There have been nineteen bridges thrown across the stream, which runs from the morass to the Weser in front of the camp, in order to facilitate the retreat of the army in case it should be forced to fall back. The centre and the left will retire across these bridges into their camps. The right and the reserve will retire upon the city, line the hedges, occupy the gardens which surround it, and will place the artillery in their front, to check the enemy in concert with the cannon of the place."

In conformity with these dispositions, the army was put in motion immediately after sundown, and the several columns reached their destination a little after midnight. Ferdinand, prepared for this event by the turn which affairs had taken, gave orders to his army on the 31st, at five o'clock in the afternoon, to hold itself in readiness to march at one in the morning. It was then put in motion in eight columns, and at six o'clock in the morning was formed in line of battle, with its right resting on the morass in rear of Hahlen, and the left connected with the corps of Wangenheim, which took post behind the batteries in advance of Tonhausen. The cavalry was to be distributed upon the two wings, but that of the English, forming the right, was kept back by the obstinacy of Lord Sackville, and did not arrive at its post in time.

The French army had a hill before it which concealed its march. The generals, who were engaged after daylight in deploying their troops, had not taken any notice of the movements of the allies. *Their columns were not able to disentangle themselves quick enough; some were too near, others too distant, and confusion reigned in them all.* The army was scarcely arranged in battle at eight o'clock, except the division of Broglio, which began its attack, about five in the morning, by a fierce cannonade upon the corps of Wangenheim.

Instead of falling furiously upon the enemy, the duke of Broglio lost two hours in the employment of his artillery, to which the enemy replied. Perhaps he flattered himself that this tremendous noise would be sufficient to drive the corps of Wangenheim from its position; but the latter maintained its post firmly. The duke, finding the village guarded by stronger forces than he had supposed, went in person to Marshal Contades to ask for reënforcements.

At that instant the allied army began its movement, and Ferdinand, who expected to be anticipated, arrived upon the enemy's line before any of his troops were formed, except the cavalry, and that was in the centre. The position of this arm, contrary to all tactical rules, broke the continuity of the infantry line, and deprived it of all force by admitting of a separation of the two parts from a cannonade alone.

No sooner had the duke discovered this fault, than he ordered the Hanover and English infantry, and the regiment Hardenberg to attack immediately, that they might throw themselves against the flanks of the lines of the French infantry, at the moment when the remainder of his own should attack the French right, and the prince of Anhalt should assail their left, with all the pickets of the army, which were under his command as *general of the day*. This infantry of the allies, advanced swiftly, although exposed, for the distance of fifteen hundred paces, to the fire of all the batteries which covered the front of the French squadrons.

That cavalry, the strength and pride of the French army, advanced to meet the German infantry, and charged it with spirit; but the fire of the latter was so well directed, and so well sustained, that, after fruitless efforts, the first line retired in disorder, followed closely by the allied infantry, which overthrew successfully whatever attempted to bar its progress.

Contades, coming up to the centre whilst these things were being enacted, directed the marquis of Beaupreau, with the brigade of Touraine, and eight pieces of artillery, to occupy some houses and gardens surrounded by hedges, in advance of the front of the cavalry; this movement tended to take in reverse the infantry of the allies, which advanced with such audacity. In the mean time some brigades of cavalry charged anew with the greatest impetuosity, but were equally repulsed.

At length the carbineers and gendarmes arrived. These brave corps at first broke the front line of the allied infantry, but were received by the second line with a quick and continuous fire, and were obliged to retreat. Lieutenant-General Poyanne, who commanded these troops, received two musket balls in his body and several sabre cuts on his head.

The right brigade under General Vogue made a fourth attack, which also failed; for at the moment it was about to wheel, General Urf, with some squadrons from the left wing, took it in flank, and routed it.

The French cavalry of the centre were thus totally beaten, and the duke needed but a few squadrons to render his victory complete. He sent Lieutenant-Colonel Ligonnier to Lord Sackville, with the order to send forward the cavalry of the right wing to the left, through the wood, and to charge the enemy vigorously. This order, though reiterated by Captain Winzingerode and Colonel Fitzroy, was without avail; on this account the English infantry suffered a good deal. The duke, not being able to do anything with Lord Sackville, directed Lord Granby, commanding the second line, to make this movement, but at the moment it was about to be commenced, Sackville went and arrested it.*

However, the allied infantry continued to advance. The count of Lusatia arrived with his Saxons, and doubled it up for an instant, but it was re-formed and resumed its offensive march.

At this moment the prince of Anhalt attacked Hahlen, and repulsed the French as far as Dutzen, passing along the morass.

The brigades of Aquitaine and Condé, which endeavored to sustain the Saxons, were repulsed, and Lieutenant-General Maugiron, who led them, was wounded with two musket balls.

* Lord Sackville, tried by court-martial, was declared incapacitated from serving in the armies of his majesty. Nevertheless, he was employed some time after, and contributed not a little to the failures in the war against the United States.

Whilst the right wing of the allies was obtaining this success, the left was not idle. The Prussians, Hanoverians, and Hessians, made a fine charge upon the grenadiers of France and the Royals. Some squadrons gained the right flank of the brigades Touraine and Rouergue, overthrew them, and captured a great part of the latter. Lieutenant-General Beaupreau was here wounded.

The allies seized some houses and the ground which the enemy desired to occupy, and repulsed the brigades of Auvergne and Anhalt, which were interposed by Marshal Contades to cover the retreat.

In spite of all this confusion, the duke of Broglio still continued to cannonade the corps of Wangenheim; his infantry advanced, it is true, but out of the reach of musketry. The cavalry which was posted to sustain the right flank of the army, already roughly dealt with by the regiment Hammerstein, was overthrown by the dragoons of Holstein. Then the regiment Marine, in order to make a way for its escape, opened its fire upon the Prussian dragoons, when the latter, wheeling to the left, charged the Marine regiment, and captured it with two flags and ten pieces of cannon.

At eleven o'clock the French army was in disorder, excepting the corps of the duke of Broglio, which had not been engaged. It covered the retreat of the right upon Minden, and the Saxons that of the left.

This battle, in which the French lost seven thousand men, would have been less decisive, had not the duke brought against their rear the corps of Drewes and that of the hereditary prince. This latter commanded the expedition of which we have already spoken. He arrived on the 31st at Quernhein, and, the next day, beat the corps of Brissac, posted at Kofeld with eight thousand men, to cover the communications by Hervorden. This success placed Contades in a critical situation; for immediately after the combat, the prince occupied the position of Behmen, and the defiles of Bergkirchen. The retreat becoming impracticable by the left bank of the Weser, it was necessary to pass that river at Minden, and to retire upon Cassel with all diligence. The baggage of the army was nearly all seized near Detmold, by the chasseurs of Freytag; the marshal here lost his own and that of the prince of Conti.

Minden capitulated the next day.

Tempelhof regards this battle as one of the most interesting, and most remarkable, in its connection with the rules of the art. The dispositions which preceded the affair, and those which were made during the action, according to his views, deserve the study and attention of posterity. Ferdinand here showed himself a general conversant with the most astonishing resources of the art. His manœuvres to draw the enemy to the desired point are master-pieces; nothing shows better the soundness of its maxims, than the hardy idea which he conceived of *weakening himself in order to become stronger*. The division of his army, which was already weak, into several corps, had in effect, all the appearance of a fault, and offered the French generals so many advantages, that they could hardly fail to undertake to profit by it.

According to our view, however, Contades ought to be blamed less for fighting than for not having better understood his adversary, and therefore have divined the exact motives for his making a faulty disposition. It can hardly be repeated too often, that the first quality of a general is to be able to judge of the talents and character of his adversary, to penetrate his most secret views and comprehend the aim and drift of his operations.

The order of battle in which the French army was formed, was exceedingly defective. It is an old mode of proceeding to place the cavalry in a plain and the infantry in a broken country. Still this custom should be subordinated to the great principle of never parcelling out a line of infantry, by cutting it by an arm which has not sufficient consistency by itself.

The plan of quickly overwhelming the corps of Wangenheim was a good one, but it is not by a cannonade that a general can be driven from a position, when he knows its effects. Cannonades are compliments to which a reply may be made without trouble. They are almost always as insignificant as was the one at Minden. Infantry must always be brought into action when there is a decisive blow to be struck.*

Hence it follows that the infantry should have charged the enemy with all possible promptitude as soon as they were formed, without wasting time by a musketry fire; for, after all, it would serve merely as a line of sight for the enemy's artillery to fire by.

Besides, a long experience has shown that the fire of artillery is much less destructive in a battle than is commonly supposed. However, it is well to make a distinction between the physical and moral effect. Ordinarily the prelude to a battle is a fierce cannonade. It is intended to dismount the enemy's guns, and thus enable the infantry to advance with less danger; but in this there is great deception. Tempelhof has cited many examples in which batteries of twenty and thirty pieces have cannonaded his own for hours without hitting men or horses, and much less a line of infantry. If his experience does not fully bear out his assertion, it may be strengthened by arguments drawn from the construction

* Cannonades have become more serious since the above was written. Armies have had as high as one thousand pieces which have vomited destruction into columns which are oftentimes too deep. Thus, artillery has played a more important part in battles, but yet remains merely an accessory.

of the pieces and of their different fire. It is very certain that if one hundredth part of the round shot had attained their mark in the last war, neither party would have had a piece of artillery left.

The result of the battle depended upon the success of the attack upon the corps of Wangenheim. Contades, who had enforced this, ought to have traced his line of direction in such a manner that he might have sustained vigorously the attack of Broglio, refusing his left, and thus engaging his army according to the turn which his principal attack might have taken. (See Chapter VII., *Reflections upon the oblique Order of Battle.*) That disposition would have afforded him more facility for his advance, as he only had to march by lines and by the right.

The most essential faults were, then, 1st, The slowness of the duke of Broglio, which enabled Wangenheim's corps to recover from its surprise and form in front of the village. 2d, The length of time consumed in the deployment of the columns, which lasted four entire hours, and at the expiration of that time the infantry were not even in order.

Ferdinand's conduct, the wisdom of his manœuvres, the readiness with which he decided to attack the French cavalry with his infantry, deserve, on the other hand, the highest encomiums.

When treating, in Chapter V., (vol. i., page 191) upon the orders of march and their influence upon the success of Frederick, and the wide difference between his deployments and those of Guibert, the affair of Minden was quoted to sustain the ideas advanced, because it demonstrates, in an especial manner, the absurdity of the system of the French tactician; but since then, the battles of Prague, Kollin, Zorndorf, Rosbach, and Leuthen, have added a new force to my opinion.

We have seen the long instructions of Contades to his generals, to explain the mechanism and composition of the march, and the formation of the columns. Although they were nine in number, and of two or three brigades at most, it took them four hours to form imperfectly, though it was much easier to preserve the distances, as the columns were not of great extent. How could Guibert get out of this difficulty with his four columns of five or six brigades, having to preserve distances out of sight?*

It appears that this author took his system from Ferdinand, who, in fact, succeeded in forming eight columns. But, probably military annals do not furnish another instance in which such a prodigy has been performed. Of what use would have been these eight marches had the marshal made his attack in column, or had he advanced, like Frederick, by lines and by the right, upon an extremity of the position of the allies? Dispositions like these, in face of the enemy, are only suitable when his point of attack is known; for, to be useful, it will be necessary to assume that we are constantly masters of the ground which serves for a field of battle, and that the enemy will take the same place upon the front which we may assign to him; for if he extend his position to the right or the left, it is certain that the opening of the march will be wrong, or that the line will be turned.

A field of battle precisely like that of Minden, enclosed between the morass and the Weser, was absolutely necessary to allow the duke to arrange, in advance, his deployments and make use of such a system.

There is a vast difference between these dispositions, arranged long beforehand, and which the enemy might have caused to miscarry by a single unexpected movement, and

* The reader is reminded that if these observations related to a system of deployed lines exclusively, then these conditions are not indispensable. As has been mentioned, we prefer an order in columns by battalions, or a modification of the two orders united.

the dispositions hastily made on the spot, even on the day of battle, and executed rapidly by Frederick's order of march.

For the execution of his plan, Contades had to give to each of the brigades of his army an exposition of these dispositions, the precision of which is admirable, but the length useless. Frederick, saving himself all these writings, would have said the same morning, *The army will march by lines, by platoons, by the right; will take its direction from the right, and will form at the signal of . . . . The advance-guard, composed of ten battalions and fifteen squadrons will make such an attack . . . . . The left will be so disposed as to sustain the engaged wing.* It is certain that the columns taking the same direction, which it is desired to give the two lines, upon an extremity of the enemy's army, or upon some point of his position, will be able, after arriving opposite to the point of attack, to form, in a few moments, at a given signal, by platoon to the left into line of battle.

We will close this chapter by some observations upon the position of cavalry in the centre of the first line. In an order of battle in deployed lines, this mode of stationing cavalry ought to lead to a defeat; since a victory depends upon the maintenance of a permanent line. Now all generals know at this day, whether a sufficient force and stability is found in cavalry for the defense of a decisive position in the first line.

The inconvenience of such a line will be increased as the line is lengthened and the cavalry extended. The reason of it is, that the interval left by the broken cavalry being greater, one of the wings of the infantry may be overwhelmed before the other can be brought to its support. The position, the nature of the ground, and circumstances, will determine which of the wings it will be most convenient to attack.

It will be seen that the same inconveniences arise in this case, that appear when an army is attacked upon an extremity of its line in the open oblique order, like that of Frederick at Leuthen. (See Chapter VII.) The attacked extremity, composed of infantry alone, which can not be sustained by its cavalry, nor by the other wing of the infantry, will most undoubtedly be overthrown if the enemy employ against it the three arms in superior force. And what will become of this infantry wing, if the enemy, availing himself of the natural advantages of the open oblique order, turn its flank with a mass of cavalry, which may be placed in column to the right or left of the infantry? Hence, we believe, that if circumstances require the presence of several squadrons of cavalry in the first line, it would be better to dispose them in columns in the intervals of the centre and of the wings, which will leave them free to charge without affecting the solidity of the line.

OPERATIONS AFTER THE BATTLE OF MINDEN.

The retreat of the marquis of Contades across the Weser gained the allies greater advantages than even the victory. This retreat was altogether premature. The French might have held their position in the camp at Minden, which they had succeeded in reaching in sufficiently good order; nor ought they to have been alarmed at the presence of the hereditary prince at Goofeld, since, after the capture of Munster, the duke d'Armentières was stationed between Lipstadt and Paderborn, and the division Chevreuse occupied Bielfeld. But the marquis feared that Ferdinand might reënforce the corps of the hereditary prince, and by attacking d'Armentières, succeed in anticipating him at Cassel, which contained his depôts and covered his communications. As it was, the duke d'Armentières started on the 3d of August for Hesse, and on the 10th took position at Warburg, after having thrown reënforcements into Munster and Wesel. On the 4th, the French army marched to Hastenbeck. The duke of Broglio was detached the next day with twenty-six battalions and thirty-six squadrons, along the Weser, to cover its march upon Eimbeck and Gottingen, and to take possession of the defiles of Munden and Witzenhausen. The hereditary prince passed the Weser at Rinteln and followed the enemy's rear-guard towards Eimbeck.

Ferdinand, on his side, started, on the 5th, with the army from Goofeld, and in six marches went into camp, on the 12th, at Stadtbergen. Meanwhile, the marquis of Contades, having continued his retrograde movement, arrived, on the 10th, at the defiles of Munden. He established the count of Saint-Germain at Dransfeld, in order to protect the passage of the army. The hereditary prince attacked this corps vigorously on the 10th, but without success. Saint-Germain happily effected his junction with the army at Cassel, on the 12th, and the division of d'Armentières moved from Warburg to Wolfshagen.

Tempelhof has written a long dissertation to prove *that he ought not to have left a fortress in his rear*, and that Contades experienced this reverse only for having passed Lipstadt without having made himself master of it. We will not undertake to refute this assertion, for the experience of ten campaigns and the most important events of the later wars answer it better than any reply we can make to these labored calculations, which merely serve as a historical monument of the combinations of that period.

We have stated that the Marquis d'Armentières had marched to Wolfshagen in order to cover the left flank of the army, and the roads of Fritzlar and Marburg. Ferdinand, wishing to dislodge him in order to oblige Contades to abandon the vicinity of Cassel, put all his detached corps in motion, to overwhelm that division, but want of unity in these multiplied attacks gave d'Armentières time to retire. However, the object at which the duke aimed was accomplished. Contades fell back behind the Eder, and even behind the Ohm to Gros-Seelheim; d'Armentières to Goofeld.

Ferdinand, not contented with these partial successes, again resolved to dislodge the French army, and continued to manœuvre against its left. He attacked or summoned the different posts of the enemy, even in presence of their army. Cassel and Ziegenhain surrendered at the first cannon shots. Meanwhile the duke moved, on the 19th of August, to Corbach, and afterwards to Munchhausen, where he assumed a position, on the 25th, facing the enemy, from whom he was separated by the Lahn. The Marshal d'Estrées joined the French army the same day. He had been sent by the court to reconcile Contades and Broglio, who mutually accused each other of the loss of the battle of Minden, and their rivalry was becoming fatal to the interests of the army.

Ferdinand, wishing to make use of the defensive attitude of his enemies to recover Munster, detached General Imhof with six thousand men into Westphalia. No sooner had Marshal Contades heard of this, than he sent d'Armentières to Wesel, to take command at that place of some regiments just arrived from France, and which, with the garrison, formed a corps sufficiently strong to succor that fortress. This expedient succeeded. Imhof was delayed by rains, and only began the siege on the 3d of September, and was obliged to raise it before d'Armentières, and to retire, on the 6th, to Telligt.

Ferdinand, hearing that Fischer's corps was at Obervetter, separated from the French army by the Lahn, ordered the hereditary prince and Wangenheim, on the 27th of August, to capture it. The post of Obervetter, situated as it was in a kind of peninsula and surrounded by rocks, appeared so strong to that partisan, that he considered it unattackable, and guarded it carelessly. Wangenheim, having gained the steep and rocky heights which supported his left flank, fell unexpectedly upon the enemy. Fischer cut his way through with a few brave men; a part of his corps was saved, but four hundred men were killed or taken prisoners. This surprise enabled the allies to gain the extreme left of the enemy, and force him to abandon his intrenched camp. The hereditary prince took post at Wetter, in front of Broglio, and the army encamped between Melnau and Amenau. Broglio remained alone upon the right of the Lahn, and fearing he might be cut off, recrossed that river and retired, on the 29th, by Marburg.

September 2d, the hereditary prince and Wangenheim crossed the Lahn at Gosfeld. Luckner's legion surprised an advance-post near Ober-Waimer, and caused a loss of five hundred men to the enemy. General Wangenheim established himself there, and the hereditary prince marched to Alma, pushing scouts upon Hohensolms. Ferdinand then recalled the prince of Bevern from Marburg, and stationed the duke of Holstein at Schwarzenborn.

These movements finally decided Marshal Contades to quit, on the 4th, the fine position of Gros-Seelheim, and to retire upon Munzlar. No sooner had he gone, than the allies summoned the château of Marburg; but Colonel Duplessis, who was in command, compelled the duke to besiege it. The French army, far from attempting to save this post, continued its retrograde movement, and encamped toward Giessen. Broglio was behind the Lahn near Dudenhofen, covering Wetzlar. Ferdinand successively moved and encamped, the 10th of September at Ober-Waimer, the 18th at Salzboden, and the 19th at Krofdorf; the corps of Wangenheim occupied the heights in front of Wetzlar.

The two armies remained some time in these positions, for the reason that the allies were distant from their magazines, and desired to await the fall of Munster. On the other hand, Marshal Contades could not retire any farther without abandoning the right bank of the Mein, and perhaps even that of the Rhine.

The Duke d'Armentières, after having revictualed Munster, withdrew on the 12th to the Rhine, and General Imhot again resumed the blockade, receiving some reënforcements. The siege artillery did not arrive until the beginning of November, and the trenches were opened on the night of the 8th and 9th. The commandant made frequent and happy sorties; d'Armentières tried in vain to return to its succor; he found Imhof so well posted at Roxel, that he was obliged to turn back. The place finally capitulated on the 21st of November. The garrison was allowed to march out, a just recompense for the bravery displayed in its defense.

During this period, nothing of any importance occurred between the armies stationed in the neighborhood of Giessen. The duke of Broglio, it is true, gained a victory, but his battle-field was the French court, and his adversary Marshal Contades, who was recalled, and Broglio was left in command of the army.

The course of affairs was no more favorable than before; the new general *manœuvred by detachments, to harass and cut off the enemy's communications.* The division sent against Marburg failed. The duke of Wurtemberg, who was to occupy Fulde with ten thousand men, for the purpose of cutting the allies off from Cassel, having taken up a bad position, with the city and the river at his back, the hereditary prince of Brunswick was directed to attack him. This corps, being in a measure surprised, was obliged to retire through the village with precipitation, and was so hotly pressed, that it could not reform. A part of the infantry and cavalry escaped; three battalions of Wurtemberg grenadiers were compelled to lay down their arms. The duke of Broglio, seeing his army thus menaced upon its right flank, abandoned the camp of Klein-Linnes, and withdrew between Friedberg and Butzbach, leaving a garrison at Giessen, which was invested. The armies went into barracks, the weather being too cold to allow of living in camp.

Ferdinand was obliged to send a reënforcement of thirteen battalions and twenty squadrons to the king of Prussia, whose affairs had taken a bad turn in Saxony since the combats of Maxen and Meissen. This fact induced the duke of Broglio to profit by his superiority, and endeavor to save Giessen. For this purpose, he resolved to send the Duke d'Armentières with the corps of the Lower Rhine upon the right, and that of the duke of Wurtemberg upon the left flank of the allies, whilst he should attack them himself in front, upon Giessen; the Marquis du Voyer was also moved to Limburg, in order to join his troops to those of d'Armentières. After some insignificant movements, the allies raised effectually the blockade of Giessen, and Ferdinand, determining to canton his army, struck his camp at Krofdorf on the 5th, to approach Marburg.

The march of the troops under the Duke d'Armentières was retarded. owing to the floating ice in the Rhine; it did not therefore arrive upon the banks of the Dille until the 3d of January. Du Voyer then marched to Dillenburg, placed the Swiss regiment Waldner in that village, and put his division in cantonments. Duke Ferdinand, judging it imprudent to leave a corps upon the right flank of his winter-quarters, repaired on the 7th to Gladebach, to see General Wangenheim, and on the same day directed his corps in three columns upon Dillenburg. An advance-post of dragoons was surprised by the right column at Wiselbach, whilst that of the centre moved directly upon Dillenburg. The regiment Waldner, believing itself guarded, had scarcely time to seize its arms; its colonel, Paravicini, was killed, and a great many brave men met the same fate, and near seven hundred were taken. The campaign was terminated by this event, which decided the duke of Broglio to take up his winter-quarters from Giessen to within the Hundsruck. The allies did the same; the corps of General Imhof remained in Hesse, and covered its cantonments with intrenched positions. The army was dispersed in the province of Munster and in the bishoprics of Osnabruck, Paderborn, etc.

The maritime affairs of France suffered vastly more during this time than those of their armies in the field. Guadeloupe had been lost since the month of May. The provinces of Canada, against which the English had sent superior forces, had been ably defended for three years by Montcalm, but were utterly lost by the death of that brave man, killed at Quebec, in a combat which his death immediately changed into a defeat. In India, the defeat of the squadron of Count d'Ache changed into a rash and dangerous enterprise the project of Lally to besiege Madras; soon afterwards repulsed himself he was obliged to capitulate.

Nevertheless the old and irascible marshal of Belle-Isle, contemplated repaying the English for the audacious visits they had dared to make to the coast of Normandy in the preceding year. Preparations were made at Toulon and Brest to unite all the squadrons; the troops were assembled under Chevert, near Dunkirk.

But Admiral Laclue, who commanded the twelve vessels which sailed from Toulon, did not know how to rally his squadron properly. Separated from five of his vessels, he was defeated off Lagos, by the English Admiral Boscawen, who had double the number of vessels. Four French ships were taken or burned, and three sought refuge at Lisbon.

Laclue lost his legs, but still was not able to justify himself for the dispersion of his squadron.

This was but a prelude to more bloody disasters; as obstinate in the choice of her admirals as in that of her ministers, the marchioness of Pompadour, whose fatal influence might have been traced for a long time, had induced Louis XV. to intrust the fate of his navy to the stupid and pusillanimous Marshal de Conflans, and persisted in having him leave Brest, in spite of the check which had been experienced by the Mediterranean fleet.

The fleet of the enemy, which was in observation, was dispersed by a storm, without his knowing enough to take advantage of it, and pursue them. Conflans sailed, finally, on the 14th of November; but scarcely had he signalled the English squadron of twenty-three vessels, than he threw his fleet upon the coast, imagining that the enemy would not dare to follow among the unknown rocks and shoals. His rear-guard thus became engaged in this false movement, and quickly separated from the rest of the fleet, it had to sustain an unequal conflict.

The cowardly marshal, without attempting to disengage them, ran ashore with the admiral's ship; one of his divisions sought refuge in the Vilaine, which was not thought capable of sheltering even frigates. The result of the most unfortunate battle could not have exceeded this shameful retreat, which cost six ships sunk, stranded, or burned. Had the vast resources wasted upon the Hanover army been applied to the navy, France would not have been called to lament over these reverses, which subsequent alliances could never repair.

CHAPTER XVI.

GENERAL POSITION OF THE ARMIES; FIRST OPERATIONS TO THE RIGHT AND LEFT.

We have already seen at the end of the preceding campaign, how Frederick repaired the defeat of Hohenkirch by concentrating his forces in Saxony, where, after a series of glorious operations, they went into winter-quarters.

At the opening of the campaign, the armies of the different powers were found stationed as follows:

The king had in Silesia..................	54	battalions,	88	squadrons.
The corps of Fouquet, in Upper Silesia, opposed to Deville, consisted of.........	18	"	20	"
Prince Henry commanded in Saxony......	43	"	60	"
The count of Dohna, in Pomerania........	26	"	35	"
Total............	141	"	203	"

The Austrians had,

The corps of General Deville in Moravia...............	26	battalions,	32	squadrons,	3,500	Croats.
That of Laudon, in Bohemia, between the Elbe and Silesia..................	10	"	20	"	6,400	"
That of Beck toward Politz...	10	"	15	"	3,000	"
That of Harsch about Nachod.	16	"	25	"	3,300	"
The army under Marshal Daun, at Gitschin.............	47	"	60			
The corps of Gemingen, on the frontiers of Saxony on the Eger..................	9	"	39	"	3,000	"
Total *........	118	"	191	"	19,200	"

* The Austrian battalions were two or three hundred stronger than the Prussians. The latter can only be estimated at from six hundred to six hundred and fifty men.

The army of the Empire, of upwards of fifteen thousand men, is not included in this estimate.

The army of the Circles was cantoned in Franconia, near the frontiers of Saxony, with one division on the Werra, in the confines of Hesse. That army, including its Austrian corps, contained upwards of forty-five thousand men. The Russian army was stationed in Poland. It might be estimated, including its light troops, at sixty thousand men. The Swedes had fifteen thousand combatants in Pomerania. Finally, the French armies recruited anew, and placed upon a formidable footing, disquieted Saxony and the hereditary States of the king.

Frederick, having a formidable enemy behind him, was constrained to present a front in every direction and divide his forces. He could not undertake a single offensive operation without subjecting his impoverished and weak states to an invasion from the enemy, although he drew from these same states all his resources for continuing the war. This condition of things will account for his gaining great battles, without, nevertheless, being able to undertake any very brilliant operations. Since the late invasion of Moravia, his plan contemplated nothing more than to gain time and disembarrass himself, by a victory, of the one of his enemy's armies which should press him too closely. Such were those of the campaign of 1758, and following.

The Austrians had, at the commencement of that campaign, a line of operations from which they could derive no advantages. Daun resolved to act upon the defensive until the Russians should have drawn off a part of the forces of the king. It appears that no plan of concentration was originally arranged between the allies; for the first events were only surprises of outposts, or small expeditions against magazines; the most important operation being the capture of a battalion of grenadiers at Greifenberg.

Frederick, certain that the enemy could not operate against the provinces without provisions, saw no better means, at present, of warding off invasion, than that of destroying their magazines and depots. For this purpose, in February, he directed some troops upon the Wartha and Posen, and there destroyed those of the Russians.

In the middle of April, he planned two enterprises which were more serious. General Fouquet was to enter Moravia, in order to seize the magazines which the Austrians had there, whilst Prince Henry should penetrate into Bohemia, and destroy the great depots which had been formed by the army of the Circles and those of the troops destined to operate against Saxony.

Fouquet marched through Troppau to the Mora; but he could not prevent the evacuation of the magazine of Hof, and retired without having succeeded. Prince Henry was more fortunate. He entered Western Bohemia, the 15th of April, in two columns, by Leutmeritz and Saatz. That part of Bohemia was only protected by the corps of Gemmingen, whose cantonments were widely extended. His expedition succeeded; he led back eighteen hundred prisoners, and destroyed the magazine of Saatz, which contained thirty-two thousand tons of flour and an abundance of forage.

As soon as Daun heard of this expedition, he dispatched the corps of General Beck to cover Prague and protect the great depot of his army; but Prince Henry was satisfied, and had withdrawn into Saxony.

However, as the great operations of the campaign would be dependent upon the movement of the Russian army, it was probable that Frederick would soon be obliged to transfer the greater part of his forces to the Oder, to oppose their march. He detailed the army in Saxony for this expedition; but, whilst waiting, he disposed it so as to attack the army of the Circles, in order for a time to disable it from further action, and allow of his stripping Saxony of troops with greater safety. The fact was, its preservation depended upon that of Dresden, then capable of sustaining a siege of more than nine months—a period of time long enough to enable Frederick to terminate decisive operations against the Russians. Prince Henry was then ordered to proceed into Franconia.

The combined army of the empire and of Austria, commanded by the duke of Deux-Ponts, was divided into several corps. At the end of April General Haddick occupied the excellent camp of Monchberg, which he had begun to intrench. General Maquire had occupied one at Asch, near Eger. The Margrave of Baden was posted at Stadtsteinach. The bulk of the army, conducted by the duke of Deux-Ponts, moved, on the 4th of May, to Culmbach. Some detachments of light troops scouted as far as Hof and Nordhalben, on the roads accessible to the enemy.

Prince Henry resolved to attack the camp of Monchberg, before it was brought to a state of defense. In consequence of this determination, all the troops were concentrated at Zwickau in the early part of May. His plan was to send General Fink with a division, by Asch, upon the right flank, and General Knobloch, by Nordhalben, upon the left flank of the enemy, whilst he should himself attack in front by the great road to Plauen. But it was difficult to conceal his march in a country where roads were so rare, and the army of the Circles, getting information of the movement in time, abandoned the camp of Monchberg, not wishing to risk the chance of a battle. It appears certain that, according to the general plan of operations, that army was to remain absolutely on the defensive, and under no pretext to become engaged in a decisive affair. Such at least seems to be the only explanation for the promptitude with which it retired.

Below is a table of the daily positions:

PRUSSIANS.	IMPERIALISTS.
May 4, *Knobloch* at Auma. *Fink* at Waldkirch near Reichenbach. The *army* at Zwickau.	Position already indicated. *Haddick* at Monchberg. *Maquire* at Asch. *Margrave of Baden* at Stadt-Steinach. *Duke of Deux-Ponts* at Culmbach.
May 5, *Knobloch* at Schleitz.	
May 6, *Knobloch* at Lobenstein. *Fink* at Bergen. The *army* at Polh.	
May 7, *Knobloch* at Nordhalben. *Fink* at Adorf. The *army* at Œlnitz.	
May 8, *Knobloch* halted.	May 8, *Maquire* retired from Asch after a slight cannonade with Fink's corps.
May 9, *Knobloch* at Zeyern. *Fink* halted. The *army* at Hof. The *advance-guard* at Birck.	May 9, *Haddick* retired from Monchberg to Culmbach.
May 10, *Knobloch* before Cronach. *Fink* goes by Sparneck and Monchberg to Weissenstadt. The *army* at Monchberg.	May 10, The *army* at Culmbach. *Maquire* at Wunsiedel, before moving upon Bareith.
May 11, *Knobloch* before Cronach. *Fink* at Dobern. The *army* at Penck, near Bareith.	May 11, The *army* marches on Bamberg. *Maquire* at Kemnath directing his retreat upon Nuremberg by a new order.
May 12, *Knobloch* before Cronach. *Fink* at Bareith. The *army* at Penck.	
May 13, *Knobloch* at Zeulen. *Itzenplitz* at Melkersdorf. *Finck* joins the army at Alstædt.	
May 14, *Knobloch* at Lichtenfels. *Itzenplitz* at Alzendorf. The *army* at Hollfeld. The *advance-guard* at Heiligenstadt is moving upon Bamberg.	May 14, The *army* evacuates Bamberg and encamps at Hochstadt. *General Kolb* at Bamberg.
May 15, *Knobloch* at Zapfendorf. *Itzenplitz* at Scherlitz. The *advance-guard* at Nistendorff.	

May 16, The *three corps* united at Bamberg under General Itzenplitz. The *army* still at Hollfeld.	May 16, *General Kolb* at Sommerfeld. The *army* at Herzog-Aurach.
May 17, The *army* encamps at Sachsendorf.	May 17, The *army* encamps in rear of Nuremberg, where it is joined by Maquire and Kolb.
May 25, The *army* with Itzenplitz begins its movement to return into Saxony.	

The remainder of the movements were made with reference to small expeditions from the corps of Itzenplitz against the magazines of Schweinfurt, etc.

It will be seen by this table, that Prince Henry did not succeed in bringing on a battle. The only event worthy of notice in this expedition was the operations against the corps of Maquire. Driven from Asch, on the 8th, by Fink, that division was ordered by General Haddick to retire upon Bareith. Fink, having been informed of this, halted in the neighborhood of Nagel, to allow him to become entangled in the gorges of the Fichtelberg, and sent word of what had passed to Prince Henry. The latter immediately detached four thousand men to Saint-Johann, to close against Maquire the only outlets which were not as yet occupied by the Prussians on the right. That division, in consequence, ran the risk of being inclosed, since Fink was in its rear. Fortunately, Haddick had ordered him to gain the Nuremberg road, which he succeeded with difficulty in doing, by the aid of the peasants, who led him into it by cross roads. Thus, after escaping almost by a miracle as it were, this corps was directed through Kemnath upon Neustadt and Nuremberg, as has been given in the table.

This expedition also gave rise to some slight combats; the most important of which occurred at Himmelskron. The Prussian cavalry charged a rear-guard, which covered the retreat of the camp equipage upon Culmbach, and made a thousand prisoners. Fink's advance-guard had a similar success near Nagel.

Prince Henry, seeing the impossibility of striking an important blow, concluded that a distant invasion would be opposed to the system adopted by the king, and might compromise his affairs at the decisive point. On this account he led back his army into Saxony. The Prussians were cantoned on the 3d of June, in the vicinity of Zwickau; the prince reënforced Dohna's army with ten battalions and twenty squadrons, under the command of General Hulsen. Fink was transferred, with four battalions and five squadrons, to the neighborhood of Dresden, to observe the Austrians in Lusatia.

The army of the Circles was encamped at Forcheim; its advance-guard was at Wustenstein. Haddick was separated from it with the Austrian troops, and by order of Marshal Daun attached to those constituting the corps of Bohemia.

POSITION OF THE GRAND ARMIES

Whilst these events were in progress in Franconia, in the course of the month of May, the Russians began their movements to approach the Vistula.

The armies under Frederick and Daun were in observation of each other. The king had occupied a very formidable position between Landshut and Liebau, in which he was calmly waiting to have his adversary develop his projects. On his side, Marshal Daun, whose plan was wrapped up in the march of his auxiliaries, carefully avoided everything which would have placed the Austrian army on the scene of action before the arrival of the allies.

Frederick, observing the timidity of the Austrian marshal, resolved to destroy the magazines, which the Russians had established anew at Posen, for the purpose of delaying their entrance upon the field of action, and with the hope of breaking up the unity in the operations of his enemies.

General Wopersnow was selected to carry out this enterprise, with six battalions and fifteen squadrons drawn from Silesia, which arrived at Guhrau on the 18th of May; but the news of the invasion of the Marche by an Austrian corps caused the destination of this division to be changed to Naumburg, on the Bober, where it joined the divisions of General Seidlitz and Czetteritz.

Daun, seeing Saxony unprotected on account of the withdrawal of the corps of Prince Henry, desired to take advantage of it to throw Wehla's corps, upwards of four thousand strong, between the two armies, whilst General Gemmingen should support this feeble division by marching, as has been stated, upon Chemnitz and Zwickau. Such an enterprise deserved the fate of all partial and miserable operations, which passed in those days for brilliant conceptions. Wehla marched as far as Spremberg, but was prudent enough to retire into Bohemia, through Hoyerswerda, and thereby avoided being cut off altogether.

In the course of these events the rumor spread abroad that Daun had been ordered, by his court, to penetrate into Silesia. This report, confirmed as it was by the reconnoissance of the king's position, made by Laudon on the 21st of May, led to the recall of the Prussian corps, detached to Naumburg. That of Fouquet was cantoned between Kamens and Frankenstein, and the king encamped between Johnsdorf and Grissau. Nevertheless, all the movements of the marshal were limited to threatening the county of Glatz and the communications of his adversary. Frederick, understanding too well the character of the Austrian generals to be duped by those demonstrations, held on to his camp until the early part of July, merely having some of his important posts reënforced.

All this time the position of the armies in Saxony and Franconia remained about the same. Prince Henry had cantoned his troops between Dresden and Zwickau. The army of the Circles having quitted its camp at Forcheim, the 2d of June, occupied, on the 23d, that of Hocheim, upon the road from Asfurth to Konigshofen. Its light troops scoured the country in the direction of the Werra, towards Meiningen from one side, and towards Salfeld, Schleitz, and Hof on the other.

The grand Austrian army under Daun was encamped at Schurtz. Deville, Laudon, Beck, and Harsch, still occupied their old positions. This quiet state of affairs was caused by the determination to await the Russians; as soon as the court of Vienna was finally able to estimate with certainty their arrival at Posen, and the period at which they would begin their operations in Silesia, orders were sent to Daun to advance to the Queiss. The grand Austrian army started from Schurtz on the 28th, and moved in two columns to Horzitz and Neudorf.

On that day, Laudon and Beck continued in their positions with the light troops, and afterward marched to Hohen-Elbe and Eipel to cover this movement. A corps under the command of General Harsch was left at Pless in order to cover the frontiers of Bohemia. Generals Haddick and Gemmingen were directed to pass the Elbe and move towards Upper-Lusatia, in order to protect the left flank of the army from Prince Henry.

The king, having been informed the same day that a movement had been observed in the camp of the enemy, made a reconnoissance of Schatzlar, but could not actually deter mine the direction which they had taken. He inferred natur ally enough, that Daun's first operations would be directed against Upper Lusatia, in order to second those of the Russians; but this movement seemed to him premature, since the Russians had not yet united their columns at Posen; and besides, it appeared possible that General Dohna might attack one of their columns, should he have an opportunity, and overthrow it, and thus the plans of the court of Vienna would become deranged, and Daun himself exposed to embarrassment. As it was, the first column, commanded by General Frolof Bagrew, only arrived on the 22d of June at Uscia, on the Netze. Supposing even that Dohna was not in a condition to embarrass the operations, it was probable that this corps would not be able to arrive in Upper Silesia, or even on its frontiers, before seven weeks had elapsed, on account of the difficulty of the transport of provisions from Poland. Now, during this interval, Bohemia would remain open on the side of Konigsgrätz, for Generals Harsch and Deville were far too feeble to guard it. On this supposition a fine opportunity would be presented to Frederick to take the offensive. He might easily penetrate into the circle of Konigsgrätz, cut off these two corps from the grand army, and reach even into the circle of Buntzlau. The marshal, thus losing his communications and principal magazines, which were established at Jung-Buntzlau and upon the Elbe, would be obliged to retrograde, and perhaps even accept a battle under most unfavorable circumstances.

These considerations left Frederick in suspense; the venturesome movement of the Austrian general was inconsistent with his ordinary prudence. As it was very necessary to know the direction which the enemy had taken, General Wedel was ordered with twelve battalions and fourteen squadrons through Schatzlar upon Trautenau, and Seidlitz was detached with eight battalions and fifteen squadrons upon Hirschberg and Lahn, with the view of there attacking the Austrian corps which had proceeded along the mountains of Riesengebirge, for the purpose of gaining the Queiss, and the right flank of the Prussians. Bulow's corps, being of no further use at Tonhausen, was to rejoin the army.

During the progress of these movements, the Austrian army continued its own behind the chain of the Reisengebirge mountains. On the 29th, it encamped in three divisions at Gitschin, Lomnitz, and Horzitz. It sojourned the next day, and was transferred, July 1st, to Turnau, Bredl, and Gitschin. Laudon took up a position, on the 30th, at Hohenstadt, and on the 1st of July, at Bohmisch-Gablenz. General Beck was at Hennersdorf. On the 2d, two columns of the army united at Reichenberg; the third marched to Turnau, Laudon to Busch-Ullersdorf, and General Beck to Hochstadt. They remained, on the 3d, in these positions, to await the arrival of the artillery train, which marched with great difficulty through a mountainous country, where the roads were naturally bad and injured by the recent rains. On this day the third column also joined the army.

The king finally ascertained Daun's movement, and doubted not that his sole object was to facilitate the operations of the Russians and reënforce them with his army; consequently, the Prussians made preparations to follow General Seidlitz through Hirschberg, as soon as it should be positively known that Harsch's corps left at Jaromirs was not strong enough in conjunction with that of Deville to attempt any dangerous enterprise against Glatz and the camp of Landshut. Seidlitz crossed the Bober on the 3d, encamped at Husdorf near the Lahn, and pushed patrols along the Queiss. One of these detachments engaged the advance-guard of Laudon, who had reconnoitred Greifenberg and Lowenberg. As soon as the Austrian general became aware of the position of Seidlitz, he fell back to Gebardsdorf near Friedberg, where he reunited his division.

Daun followed his movement, on the 5th, in four columns to Friedland. He encamped, on the 6th, in the order of battle here given, at Gerlachsheim, where he awaited information from the Russians. On the 8th, Gemmingen was

ORDER OF BATTLE OF DAUN'S

FIRST

GENERALS.............ODONELL. SINCERE.

LIEUT.-GEN'S...........................WIED. GU-

MAJOR-GEN'S.

Lichtenstein.
- 4 squads. Grenadiers.

Martigny.
- 5 squads. Darmstadt.

Saint Ignon.
- 5 squads. Portugal.

Stainville.
- 5 squads. Odonell.

Unruhe.
- 3 bat. Wolfenbutel.
- 2 — Gelruck.
- 2 — Charles Lorraine.
- 1 — Grenadiers.

SECOND

LIEUT.-GEN'S.. ....ANGER.

MAJOR-GEN'S.

Odonell.
- 5 squads. Stambach.
- 5 —— Kollowrath.

Kalnocky.
- 5 squads. Anspach.

Los Rios.
- 2 bat. Durlach.
- 2 — Louis Daun.
- 2 — Neuperg.
- 1 — Grenadiers.

Brinken.
- 2 bat. Tillier.
- 2 — N. Esterhazy.

RE-

LIEUT.-GEN'S...OREILLY.

MAJOR-GEN'S.

Wiese.
- 5 squads. Archduke Leopold.

J. St. Ignon.
- 5 squads. B. Daun.

Hartenegg.
- 2 bat. Anger.
- 1 — Cleriel.
- 2 — Baaden.
- 3 — Pallavicini.
- 2 — Waldeck.

Elrischshausen.
- 1 bat. Staremberg.
- 2 — Palfy.
- 2 — Bethlem.

ARMY AT MARCLISSA IN 1759.

LINE.

D'Ahremberg. Buccow.

Arco. D'Arberg.

Bibow.
- 2 bat. Lascy.
- 2 — Puebla.

Migazzy.
- 2 bat. Old Colloredo.
- 2 — Sincere.
- 2 — Joseph Esterhazy.

Buttler.
- 1 bat. Grenadiers.
- 2 — Emperor.
- 2 — Wallis.
- 2 — Kollowrath.

Zolern.
- 5 squads. Deville.

Pellegrini.
- 5 squads. Archduke Joseph.
- 5 — Archduke Ferdinand.

Ayassasse.
- 4 squads. Grenadiers-à-cheval.

LINE.

Esterhazy.

Weix.
- 2 bat. Haller.
- 2 — Old Wolfenbutel.
- 2 — Teutschmeister.

Herbersthein.
- 1 bat. Grenadiers.
- 2 — Henry Daun.
- 2 — Molke.
- 2 — Merci.

Thurn.
- 5 squads. Zerbst.

Berlichingen.
- 5 squads. Palfy.
- 5 — Bathyani.

-SERVE.

Deynse.

Bulow.
- 2 bat. Los Rios.
- 2 — Ligne.
- 2 — Luzani.

Pellegrini.
- 8 bat. Grenadiers.

Ziskowitz.
- 5 bat. Grenadiers.

Rebach.
- 5 squads. Wurtenburg.
- 5 — Buccow.

Total.—77 battalions, 88 squadrons of heavy cavalry, not including the hussars and light infantry, Croats, etc., 282 pieces of cannon, and 12 howitzers.

detached to Ullersdorf, and General Wehla to Ostritz, to guard the rear against the enterprises of Prince Henry. Laudon marched, on the 10th, to Lichtenau, near Lauban, in order to cover the left flank, and was replaced at Gebardsdorf by Beck.

In the course of these events, Frederick directed Fouquet, on the 7th, to relieve the army at Landshut, and ordered Wedel to abandon Trautenau and rejoin him. At the same time he sent off the artillery train and heavy guns to Vogelsdorf, and on the 5th, put himself in march at the head of the advance-guard for Hirschberg. The army followed him, on the 6th, in two columns. The king moved to Waltersdorf, and General Krokow remained at Landshut awaiting Fouquet's corps, the advance-guard of which arrived the same day.

All the army was concentrated, on the 10th, at the camp of Schmotseifen or of Durings-Vorwerk. This position was very strong, and commanded all the surrounding country. The army remained here until the end of August.

MOVEMENTS OF THE AUSTRIANS TO EFFECT A JUNCTION WITH THE RUSSIANS; GENERAL DISPOSITIONS OF THE KING.

It has already been stated that the march of the Russians was to regulate the enterprises of the allies, and that Frederick was disposed to send against them Prince Henry with his army, whilst he should oppose Daun in person.

The moment he saw that Daun was making arrangements to send a corps to sustain the Russians, it was natural that he should attempt to devise measures to prevent their junction; the position of Prince Henry favored this object, since he could gain Sagan and the line of the Bober before the enemy. Daun also had received information, on the 12th of July, that Soltikof was awaiting reënforcements on the

Wartha, to enable him to operate with success against the count of Dohna, whereupon he assembled a council of war, in which it was resolved to unite the divisions of Haddick, Gemmingen, and Laudon, and to send this corps, thirty-five thousand strong, along the Spree and the Neisse upon the Electoral Marche. Tempelhof argues that this movement might have had important consequences.* According to him, it was to draw off the attention of Prince Henry, and induce him to denude Saxony of troops, thus favoring the operations of the army of the Circles against that province, in order to oblige the king to make a considerable detachment from his army in Silesia, and thereby secure an opportunity of attacking him with a decisive superiority.

All these fine results are hypothetical, and at this time, in the eighteenth century, ordinary generals have often mistaken the accessories for the principal part. Be that as it may, this project prevailed, and was to be seconded by the march of the army of the Circles upon Erfurt and Leipsic, as well as by an expedition to be made by the corps of Deville and Harsch united against Fouquet at Landshut, or against the fortresses of Upper Silesia. As it would be impossible to detail the movements of these numerous small corps, and would, above all, swell this work much beyond the limits prescribed, they will be presented in a tabular form in which the relations between them during the different operations will be seen at a glance. We will confine ourselves simply to a sketch of the facts essential to a thorough understanding of the plans of the generals

* Of course it was better to annex these separate corps to the Russian army than to have them isolated upon an extended line and taken up with insignificant details; still, Daun's plan was not in conformity to the true principles, for he might have made a better use of these divisions.

TABLE OF THE PRINCIPAL MOVEMENTS UNTIL THE BATTLE OF KUNERSDORF.

Prussians.	Combined Armies.
July 3d, The *king's* army encamped since the opening of the campaign near Landshut. *Seidlitz* moves to Lahn. *Wedel* at Trautenau. *Fouquet* at Ullersdorf opposed to Deville and Harsch. *Prince Henry* in Saxony, about Dresden. The *Count of Dohna* on the Wartha about Posen. *Kleist* observed the Swedes with six battalions.	July 4th, *Daun* at Reichenberg with the army. *Laudon* at Gebardsdorf. *Gemmingen* marches from Aussig to Gabel. *Wehla* from Gabel to Zittau. *Haddick* was at Toplitz. *Beck* for a long time at Hochstadt. *Harsch* and *Deville* about Konigshof. The *army of the Circles* at Romild, in Franconia. The *Russians* at Posen. The *Swedes* behind the Peene.
July 5th, The *king* with the advance-guard at Hirschberg.	July 5th, *Daun's* army at Friedland. The *reserve* halts at Reichenbach.
July 6th, The *king* at Waltersdorf. The *army* in two columns at Hirchberg and Seifersdorf.	July 6th, *Carbineers* at Marclissa. The *army* at Gerlachsheim. The *reserve* at Friedland.
July 7th, *Fouquet* replaces the army at Landshut. The *king* halts.	July 7th, The *reserve* joins the army.
	July 8th, *Gemmingen* at Ullersdorf. *Wehla* at Ostritz. *Beck* at Neustadt.
July 9th, The *army* passes the Bober and cantons between Spiller and Johnsdorf.	
July 10th, The *army* encamps at Schmotseifen near Liebenthal.	July 10th, *Laudon* at Lichtenau covers the left flank. *Beck* replaces him at Gebardsdorf.
July 11th, *Mosel* halts at Neudorf.	
July 12th, The *Duke of Wurtemberg* detached to Goriseifen by the king.	
July 13th, *Fouquet* still at Landshut.	July 13th, *Deville* and *Harsch* unite at Trautenau.

IN LUSATIA AND LOWER SILESIA.

July 13th, *Prince Henry* about Dresden in Saxony. *Fink* at Bischofswerda.	

PRUSSIANS.	COMBINED ARMIES.
	July 15th, *Laudon* at Lauban. *Haddick* at Leutmeritz.
July 17th, *Fink* at Marienstern. *Wurtemberg* at Buntzlau.	July 17th, *Harsch* and *Deville* at Schönberg. The *reserve* leave to replace Laudon at Lauban.
July 18th, *Knobloch* at Stolpe.	
July 20th, *Prince Henry* learns of Haddick's movements and marches to Camens. The *Duke of Wurtemberg* from Buntzlau to Sagan.	July 20th, *Deville* at Conradswalde to turn Fouquet.
July 21st, *Duke of Wurtemberg* retires to Buntzlau. The *king* still at Schmotseifen. *Fouquet* still at Landshut.	July 21st, *Laudon* at Radmeritz on the Neisse. *Daun* still at Marclissa. The *reserve* at Lauban. Other *corps* in the same positions. The *army of the Circles* in march for Saxony through Gotha.
July 22d, *Fink* at Bautzen.	July 22d, *Haddick* and *Gemmingen* united at Ullersdorf.* *Maquire* from Kamnitz to Krewitz. *Reserve* not posted. *Carbineers* at Gebardsdorf.
July 23d, *Prince Henry* at Bautzen. *Duke of Wurtemberg* at Freiwalde by order of the king. *Lentulus* replaces him at Goriseifen.	July 23d, The *Russian army* finally arrives near the Oder, beats Wedel at Kay near Zullichau.
July 24th, The *Prussian army* on the Oder is beaten by the Russians at Kay.	July 24th, *Laudon* at Rothenburg. *Maquire* at Krewitz. *Haddick* at Lauban. *Deville* fails in his operations against Fouquet. *Daun* still at Marclissa.
July 25th, The *Duke of Wurtemberg* retires to Burau. The *king* still at Schmotseifen. *Fouquet* sustains himself against Deville in Upper Silesia.	July 25th, The *Russians* are at Crossen.

* There are in Saxony and Silesia twenty villages of this name; care must be taken not to confound them.

Prussians.	Combined Armies.
Prince Henry at Königswartha. *Fink* remains at Bautzen. *Wedel* is retired to Sawada.	
July 26th, *Prince Henry* hears of the defeat at Kay, and marches to Weisswasser.	July 26th, *Haddick* at Lehnau in the evening. *Maquire* at Bischofswerda. *Laudon* still at Rothenburg.
July 27th, The *prince* at Muska. July 28th, The *prince* at Sorau; in the evening at Sagan. July 29th, *Duke of Wurtemberg* joins him.	July 27th, *Haddick* sets out and marches steadily to arrive at Pribus the 29th. *Laudon* joins him. The *Russian army* at Crossen since the 28th.
July 30th, The *king* arrives in the night at Sagan.	July 30th, *Haddick* is at Tribel. *Laudon* still nearer to Sommerfeld. *Daun* at Lauban. *Buccow* remains at Marclissa.
July 31st, The *army* marched at first to Naumburg, and afterward returned to Sommerfeld. *Prince Henry* goes to take command in Silesia.	July 31st, *Haddick* at Pforten. *Laudon* at Sommerfeld. *Beck* at Naumburg.
Aug. 1st, The *king* orders Wedel to join him at Mulrose, also Fink.	Aug. 1st, *Laudon* and *Haddick* at Guben: the former goes to join the Russians by forced marches; the latter seeing the approach of the king retires to Weissac.
Aug. 2d, The *army* at Markersdorf. The *advance-guard* passes the Neisse and falls upon the baggage of Haddick.	Aug. 2d, The *Russian army* at Aurith.
Aug. 3d, The *army* at Gros-Briesen. *Cavalry* at Beskoow. *Fink* near Torgau. *Wedel* about Crossen.	Aug. 3d. *Laudon* joins the Russians at Frankfort.
Aug. 4th, The *army* at Mulrose. *Cavalry* at Hohenwalde. *Fink* leaves Sagan to join the king. *Wedel* the same from Logau.	Aug. 4th, *Haddick* retires to Spremberg.
Aug. 6th, *Wedel* joins the king at Mulrose.	Aug. 6th, *Daun* at Lauban since the 30th.

PRUSSIANS.	COMBINED ARMIES.
	Buccow at Marclissa.
	Beck at Pribus.
	Maquire at Hoyerswerda.
	Wehla about Sagan.
	Ayassasse replaces Beck at Naumburg.
Aug. 7th, The *army* at Boosen. *Seidlitz* at Leubus.	
Aug. 8th and 9th, *Fink* joins the army.	Aug. 9th. The *Russian army* still encamped about Frankfort.
Aug. 10th and 11th, *Passage of the Oder* at Reitwen.	Aug. 10th, *Deville* in march to join Daun. *Haddick* at Guben and sends forward his cavalry to join the Russians. *Maquire* is ordered to move to Gorlitz.
Aug. 12, The *army* about Leissow and Bischofsee.	Aug. 11th and 12th, *Daun* marches from Lauban to Gorlitz. *Marquis of Aynse* replaces him at Lichtenau near Lauban.
	Aug. 12th, *Daun* at Rotemburg.
Aug. 13th, *Battle of Kunersdorf.*	Aug. 13th, *Daun* at Phibus. *Beck* is moved toward Soran and Christianstadt.

IN UPPER SILESIA.

July 17th, *Fouquet* at Reichennersdorf.	
July 18th, *Ramin* is moved to Lindenau; fights Janus and returns to camp.	
	July 20th, *Deville* at Conradswalde to turn Fouquet. *Wolfersdorf* at Guldenoelse.
	July 22d, *Deville* near Schweidnitz. *Combat of Freiburg.*
July 23d, *Goltz* at Friedland. *Krokow* is replaced at Hirschberg and comes to join Fouquet.	
July 24th, *Fouquet* marches to Gottesberg to occupy the defiles behind the enemy.	
July 25th, At *Conradswalde.*	
July 27th, *Fouquet* occupies the position of Todtenhubels to stop the retreat of the enemy.	July 27th, *Deville*, having decided to retreat, seeks to force a passage but is repulsed and obliged to march by detours.

Prussians.	Combined Armies.
	July 28th and 29th, Upon *Johannesberg* and *Braunau*. *Deville* sets out the 10th of August to join Daun with twelve battalions and twenty-five squadrons.

OPERATIONS AGAINST THE RUSSIANS.

Prussians.	Russians and Allies.
April 10th, *Dohna* carried the intrenchments of Pennamunde.	April 10th, *Swedes* behind the Peene. The *Russians* behind the Vistula.
May 1st, *Dohna* encamped at Greifswalde. *Kleist* remains opposed to the Swedes with six battalions and seven squadrons at Schwerinsburg.	
	May 18th, The *advance-guard* leaves Thorn.
	May 22d, *Frolof Bagrew* at Mewe.
May 26th, The *army* at Stargard.	
	June 3d, *Prince Galitzin* at Posen.
June 7th, The *army* at Soldin.	
	June 11th, *Frolof Bagrew* at Uscia on the Netze.
June 12th, The *army* at Landsberg, twenty battalions and thirty squadrons.	
June 19th, *Hulsen* comes from Saxony with a reënforcement of ten battalions and twenty-two squadrons.	
June 23d, The *army* at last breaks up and marches to Schwerin.	
June 26th, To *Birnbaum*, the advance-guard to Kamiona.	
June 27th, To *Sirakow*. A *movement* to cut off a division of the enemy at Filehne.	
	June 29th, *Army* unites at Posen.
July 1st, The *army* at Obernicky threatens the communications of the enemy, fails in an enterprise against Posen, and retires the 6th behind the Wartha.	

PRUSSIANS.	RUSSIANS AND ALLIES.
July 9th, *Dohna* anticipates the enemy at Casimirs.	July 9th, *Soltikof* marches to Tornowa to cut off the Prussians.
July 11th, *Dohna* still anticipates the Russians at Wilzina.	July 11th, The *army* marches upon the heights of Wilzina to gain the left flank of the enemy.
July 12th, and 14th, *Dohna* marches from Senkowa to Polnisch-Neustadt.	July 12th, *Soltikof* moves his advance-guard to Pynno and seeks to cut off the enemy from Silesia.
	July 14th, The *army* about Polnisch-Neustadt in presence of the Prussians.
July 15th, The *army* at Brecz.	July 15th, *Army* stationary.
July 16th, At *Meseritz*.	July 16th, The *army* at Pobrouka.
	July 17th, At *Bentschen*.
July 18th, *Wopersnow* is detached to the convent of Paradise, to prevent the enemy from turning the army.	
July 19th, The *army* follows.	July 19th, At *Bomst*. *Stoffel* at Zulichau.
July 20th, *Wopersnow* pursues Stoffel to Zulichau. The *army* follows.	
July 21st, The *army* encamps the right at Zulichau, the left toward Kalzig.	July 21st, The *army* encamps between Langmeil and Schmollen.
July 22d, *Wedel* replaces Dohna.	
July 23d, The *Russians* wish to turn the left.	July 23d, *Soltikof* wished to turn the left and gain Crossen; he beat the Prussians at Kay.
July 24th, *Wedel* retires behind the Oder and encamps at Sawada. *Wedel* approaches Logau.	
	July 25th, *Advance-guard* at Crossen.
	July 28th, *Army* at Crossen.
	July 31st, *Advance-guard* at Frankfort.
	Aug. 1st, *Army* at Kurtsch.
Aug. 2d, *Army* near Crossen.	Aug. 2d, *Army* at Aurith.
Aug. 3d and 6th, It *marches* to Mulrose and is united to that of the king.	Aug. 3d, *Laudon* joins the Russians at Frankfort.
Aug. 7th, The *Prussian* army, formed of the débris of Wedel, of the corps of Prince Henry,	

Prussians.	Russians and Allies.
and that of Fink, encamps at Boosen.	
Aug. 10th and 11th, It *passes* the Oder at Reitwen.	
Aug. 12th, *Encamps* near Leissow and Bischofsee.	
Aug. 13th, *Battle of Kunersdorf.*	Aug. 13th, *Battle of Kunersdorf.*

It will be seen by an inspection of this table, that Daun, manœuvring as he did by the right of the king and then occupying the position of Marclissa, indicated great designs. His line of operations was perfect; but he extracted from all this no other advantage than to cover Haddick during his movement against the king, whilst the army of the Circles operated in Saxony and retained Prince Henry. Notwithstanding these good dispositions, the enterprise was on the very point of miscarrying, because the prince, instead of remaining in Saxony, anticipated the Austrians upon his arrival between the Bober and the Neisse. As it was, Haddick, after having left the little corps of Brentano at Aussig in Bohemia, had gone from Leutmeritz the 15th, and was united with Gemmingen the 22d, at Ullersdorf, whence he was directed through Loebau and Lehnau upon Pribus. Laudon, on his side, had quitted Lauban, and was posted, on the 21st, at Radmeritz on the Neisse. These two corps effected their junction at Pribus, on the 29th, and marched by Sommerfeld to Guben. Then Laudon left all his heavy baggage and trains with General Hadick, and went himself with all haste to Frankfort, where he joined the Russian army the 3d, with fifteen thousand men, of whom the greater part were cavalry. It would appear that Haddick's corps was also to join the Russians, but when that general heard of the approach of the king, he changed his plan and quitted Guben, the 1st of October, to approach the Neisse.

We will now resume the narrative of the movements of

the Prussian troops before relating what passed in Upper Silesia.

On the 22d of July, the king was encamped at Schmotseifen with the army of Silesia. Fouquet's corps was still about Landshut; Prince Henry had assembled his forces at Dresden the 10th, and detached General Fink to Bischofswerda, and afterward to Bautzen. When, on the 19th, the movement of Haddick was known, Prince Henry moved to Bautzen, and left only a detachment in Saxony, under the command of General Knobloch at Bischofswerda.

The king sent the duke of Wurtemberg in the direction of Pribus; but that general, hearing of the arrival of Laudon at Rotenberg, and believing that he ought not to expose himself to the attack of a superior force, quitted Freiwalde the 25th, and retired to Burau. Prince Henry, leaving General Fink at Bautzen with twelve battalions and ten squadrons, moved himself, on the 25th of July, with twenty battalions and thirty-five squadrons to Königswartha, where he learned for the first time of the battle of Kay. The prince marched in three days by Muska to Sagan, and was there joined, on the 29th, by the Duke of Wurtemberg. The king arrived in the night, and then resolved to join the corps of Prince Henry, the Duke of Wurtemberg, and Fink to the army of Wedel, for the purpose of delivering a new battle to the Russians. Prince Henry repaired to the camp of Schmotseifen, to take the place of the king in the command of the army of Silesia.

The army remained at Sagan until the 31st. The king, informed of the arrival of Haddick at Tribel, and knowing that his enemies ought to effect their union at Crossen according to their agreement, was deceived, and moved on Naumburg on the 31st. However, when he learned that the enemy had marched by Sommerfeld, he went in pursuit of him with all his cavalry the same evening; he overtook a detachment of the rear-guard at Altwasser, and pushed it as far as Sommerfeld. Frederick encamped, August 2d, at Malkersdorf; his advance-guard crossed the Neisse and fell upon Haddick's baggage, capturing a battalion of the escort, two pieces of cannon, and three hundred wagons. The next day the army was moved to Gros-Briesen, and all the cavalry to Beskow; the king encamped at Mulrose on the 4th.

Whilst these changes were taking place, the army of the Circles concurred in favoring the union, and at the same time menaced Saxony, holding in check General Fink, who had retired from Bautzen to Kamentz on the 27th, and was reported, on the 30th, at Hoyerswerda. That army, which we left at the Hocheim camp, left there July 5th, and advanced to Auerstedt, where it encamped on the 31st. General Fink, hearing of these movements, instead of continuing his march through Spremberg upon Pforten and Guben, returned, on the 3d of August, to Torgau, which contributed very materially to the success of the Austrian enterprise. He received the king's order to join him, started the 4th, and arrived the 9th of August, by Lubben, at Hohenzesar.

After the battle of Kay, Wedel retired by Sawada to Logau, where he encamped the 2d of August, and on the 6th, received the order to join the army at Mulrose.

Frederick marched, on the 7th, with the army in two columns, and encamped between Boosen and Wulkau; the advance-guard, under the command of Seidlitz, at Lebus.

We have seen that Daun wished to attack Fouquet at Landshut. In consequence of this, Generals Harsch and Deville were united, on the 13th of July, at Trautenau; their forces amounted to thirty-three battalions and fifty-one squadrons, without including the light division of General Janus. Fouquet had but twenty-three battalions and twenty squadrons to oppose them.

General Harsch falling sick, Deville took the command at the camp of Schomberg, and marched, on the 20th, to Conradswalde. He intended to turn Fouquet's position, and cut him off from his communications with Schweidnitz; but the latter place being provisioned, was no longer dependent upon his position. The Austrians left six thousand men, under General Wolfersdorf, at Goldenoelse, to protect the depots at Trautenau, and marched, on the 22d, by Gottesberg in the direction of Schweidnitz. He encamped near Kunzendorf; the light troops of Janus were about Mount Zisken. This movement gave rise to a slight combat between the Austrian advance-guard and the two hundred men of the garrison of Schweidnitz, who occupied the village of Freiburg.

On the 23d, Fouquet remained in position, and contented himself with detaching General Goltz with seven battalions and eight squadrons to Friedland, to seize the equipage the Austrians had in that place. Frederick, before quitting the camp of Schmotseifen, heard of the enemy's attempt on Upper Silesia; but he regarded it as of so little consequence, that he merely sent three battalions to Landshut to take the place of General Fouquet, who was ordered to encamp between Conradswalde and Friedland, to cut off the Austrian army from Bohemia, by seizing the defiles through which it was to come.

As soon as General Deville heard of this, he concluded he had no time to lose before retiring, and resolved to open a passage on the road from Alt-Lassig to Friedland, and imposed the duties of advance-guard upon General Janus.

Fouquet, when reënforced by three battalions under General Goltz, took up an advantageous position on the heights of Vogelgesang and Todtenhubels, where he was attacked in vain at two different times. Deville, discouraged by so many obstacles, turned about against the position of Goltz, at

Friedland. Janus was detached thither on the 28th, and was to be sustained by General Wolfersdorf; but there was but little unity in the attacks, so that this Austrian corps was at last obliged to retreat into Bohemia, there being no other mode of escape but by the road to Wustengiersdorf and Johannesberg, which makes a long detour. However, his measures were so well taken that this movement was executed without loss in the night of the 28th and 29th.

Fouquet wished to envelop their rear-guard near Waldenburg, with a corps under General Ramin, consisting of eight battalions and four squadrons, whilst he himself marched by Conradswalde upon Gottesberg; but the retreat was conducted with so much order that it was impossible to break the rear-guard, and the Prussians were obliged to retire to their camp at Conradswalde on the 30th.

The Austrian army encamped at Brauna, Janus returned to Friedland, and Wolfersdorf, with nine battalions and five squadrons, moved to Konigsheim. Fouquet, finding the position of the latter hazardous, thought he might be able to seize it, and made his dispositions for the enterprise; but when his columns arrived in front of it, it had already been abandoned. The Austrians, who had been ployed in good time behind Bersdorf, quietly continued their retreat upon Trautenau, losing their equipage and two hundred dragoons. The Prussians, after thus terminating this expedition, returned to their camp at Landshut.

Deville was soon after recalled to Daun's army, with five regiments of cavalry, and turned over the command to General Harsch.

Before detailing the series of operations conducted by the king, we will resume those of the Russians since the opening of the campaign.

CHAPTER XVII.

FIRST OPERATIONS OF DOHNA AGAINST THE SWEDES AND RUSSIANS; BATTLE OF KAY; THE KING ARRIVES TO THE ASSISTANCE OF HIS LIEUTENANT; BATTLE OF KUNERSDORF.

It will be remembered from the preceding chapter, that the Russian army, in May, was still encamped beyond the Vistula.

General Dohna had taken advantage of its absence to repel the Swedes into Stralsund, and to deprive them of the means of undertaking anything further during the campaign. He had assaulted and carried the entrenchments of Penamunde on the 10th of April. Having terminated this expedition, he left General Kleist in observation, with six battalions and seven squadrons. at Schwerinsburg, and, after several marches, moved himself to Landsberg, on the Wartha, June 12th, intending to capture the Russian corps of Galitzin, which guarded Posen at a great distance from the army. But not being strong enough to accomplish this, he awaited the arrival of Hulsen, who led him a reënforcement from Saxony of ten battalions and twenty squadrons of cuirassiers, so that the enemy had time to join the main body at Posen. Soltikof there took the command.

The count of Dohna, after being obliged to abandon this enterprise, wished at least to cut off a corps of ten thousand men, which was to remain behind at Filehne. He crossed the Wartha for that purpose, and advanced as far as Obernicky on the 1st of July. This corps having been already withdrawn, the Prussians made demonstrations against the depôts of Posen, which were too well guarded to be disturbed. The count, afraid of suffering from hunger in a country abounding in everything, recrossed the Wartha, to approach the bakeries, and encamped at Obierzerze on the 6th of July.

On the 9th, Soltikof pushed forward a detachment of Cossacks to Samter, on the right of the enemy, to conceal the movement of the army, which went into camp between Tornova and Wiekowitz, for the purpose of cutting off its adversary from the frontiers of Silesia and the army of the king. The latter, hearing of their dispositions a little too late, resolved then to move himself to Casimirs, where, on account of the defiles, he did not arrive until the 10th at noon.

At length the two armies were in each other's presence. The Russian army having its right badly posted, it was proposed to Dohna to attack it at daylight in echelon by the left. He approved of the plan, but deferred the attack until the next day, under the pretence that his troops were fatigued. Soltikof did not think it advisable to await the attack, and gained the heights of Wilzina by Pytin, bordering the lake on which rested the right of the Prussians. This well-combined movement established him upon their extreme right, and cut them off from their secondary line of operations and from Silesia. Happily Dohna arrived on these heights by a flank movement at the very instant when the Russian advance guard was about to seize it. The armies again encamped in each other's presence.

The next morning, July 12, the Russians resumed their march. The views of Soltikof had changed. He left a considerable corps to draw off the attention of the enemy, or restrain him if necessary, and turned his left with the remainder of his army between Casimirs and the lakes of

Czerkowitze. This movement was executed so near the Prussian line, that Dohna perceived it and extended to his left along the swamps. If the historians can be believed, it was proposed to Dohna to imitate Frederick at Rosbach, and attack the Russians during their march; but he undertook nothing of the kind.

The king was dissatisfied with a general who allowed such fine opportunities to escape him, and superseded him by General Wedel. Meanwhile Dohna sought to approach the Oder, and moved on the 14th to Neustadt, on the 15th to Brecz, and on the 16th to Meseritz. It is said *that this movement was caused by the want of ovens!* The army was to remain some days in this position, in order to recover from its fatigues and privations. Its repose was not long. Soltikof, renewing his system, sought to cut it off from Glogau and the Oder, and on the 17th established himself at Bentschen.

Dohna, wishing to thwart the designs of the enemy, moved on the 19th to the convent of Paradise; on the 20th to Zullichau, where he took position the next day, with his right at the village, and his left forming a crochet in rear toward Kaltzig. (See Plate XXIII., No. 1.)

General Wedel arrived at the army on the 22d. The next day at sunrise, he reconnoitred the camp of the Russians, who had taken position, the 21st of May, between Langmeil and Schmollen on the Faule-Obra. Not being able to discover anything from the right, he concluded from the tranquillity which pervaded the left, that there had been no change, and returned to the camp at ten o'clock. But he had mistaken for the left, the rear-guard with which Soltikof intended to hide the movement which he had commenced at daylight, for the purpose of transferring his army upon Heinersdorf, Niekern, Palzig, and Crossen, in order to gain the Oder, and effect a junction with the troops which Generals Laudon and Haddick were bringing to him.

At noon, the left wing of the Prussians discovered the heads of the enemy's columns. An account of it was immediately carried to the general, who, at first, was not disposed to believe it, and lost no time in making sure of it by seeing with his own eyes the imminence of the danger. His instructions were precise; he was ordered to prevent the junction of his enemies even at the risk of a battle; his part was quickly taken. The occasion for attacking an army in its march was a fine one, and he had good grounds for believing that, seconded as he was by troops skilled in manœuvres, he might quickly overtake the heads of the enemy's columns. He then immediately gave the order of march by lines and by the left; the first in the direction of Kay, and the second upon Mohsau.

The armies were separated by a marshy stream which runs from Kay to the Oder, and which could only be passed near the mill of that village; the road leading to that point was very narrow, and bordered by a swamp. The heads of the Prussian columns arrived near Kay at three o'clock in the morning. The cavalry of the left hurried to seize this crossing, which was already in the possession of the Cossacks; they were followed closely by six battalions of the advance-guard, under the command of General Manteufel. The Cossacks were repulsed, and the Prussian cavalry crossed, debouched from the bridge, formed by squadron, and immediately charged the Russian cavalry, which showed itself between Palzig and Kay, and threw it back against its own infantry. During this interval, the advance-guard having also passed the defile, and being formed in the little plain as it came up, the cavalry took post in its rear in two lines. The attack was made with spirit, and the heads of the enemy's columns were thrown back.

However, these six battalions were soon contending with the bulk of the Russian army. The fire then increased with great fury. General Manteufel was wounded, and his troops were forced to retire with loss, to make room for the left wing, which came to its relief, being left in front under the command of General Hulsen. This infantry marched against the enemy with boldness, whilst twenty squadrons marched by their left, along the woods situated between Palzig and Glocksen, in order to turn Soltikof's right and take him in reverse.

The movement of the infantry was hurried; the battalions moved forward as they were formed, and the Russians, whose flank was already menaced, managed these isolated attacks so well, that they were able to form line during the time gained, and to fill the cemetery with formidable batteries, as well as the issues from Palzig, which covered their centre. The Prussian infantry arrived, in fact, around this village, in spite of all the efforts of the enemy; but it was there overwhelmed by a fire of grape and canister, which forced it to retire with a heavy loss. Nevertheless, the broken battalions were replaced by fresh ones as they passed through the defile, and the charge was renewed in concert with the right wing, which succeeded in pushing its way forward, notwithstanding the multiplied obstacles of ground. But these few battalions, always parceled along the line, were taken in flank by the Russians, and the infantry thus beaten was forced to retire upon Kay; its retreat carried with it that of the cavalry, which had charged with success the enemy's infantry from the right.

The Prussians acknowledged six thousand men *hors-du-combat;* they especially regretted General Wopersnow. The loss of the Russians was about equal to theirs. The battle lasted from four o'clock until seven. General Wedel availed himself of the night to repass the defile of the Kay, and reunited his columns at Mohsau; he passed the Oder the following day near Ticherzig, and went into camp at Savada, from which he afterwards moved to Logau; here it was, that he received the order to join the king, as has been stated in the preceding chapter.

The Russians made no use of their victory; all their advantages consisted in occupying Crossen, the 25th, and afterwards uniting themselves with the Austrian corps, which had been sent to reënforce them.

By a circumstance which seemed curious, Wedel, who endeavored to imitate Frederick at Rosbach, lost the battle of Kay through the operation of the same causes which were fatal to Soubise; this was due to his having engaged by individual battalions, or by heads of columns at a distance, troops already formed; for aside from this, his plan was conformable to principles ;. it was to its vicious and imperfect execution the Russians owed their good fortune. No great blame could be attached to the Prussian general, who had only joined the army the evening before; however, encamped as near the Russians as he was, one can hardly understand how a movement of such length as that from Langmeil to Palzig was not discovered and opposed. It is astonishing that he did not take time to reconnoitre the ground, and make the discovery that a defile separated him from the enemy. In this case, persistence in his object required him to make his attack in columns, in order to bring simultaneously into action, a sufficient number of troops, and to form close column on the centre, for the passage of the defile. In place of which, the army marched at full distance, by the left, and consumed a great deal of time in clearing the defile and forming forward into line; which allowed the Russians time to oppose a strong and well supported line to the attack of single and isolated bodies.

It appears besides, that Wedel was too precipitate in conducting this enterprise. From the account given, it would seem that he did not know of the movement of the enemy through Palzig, upon Crossen, until it was too late to prevent it; except, to cut them off from the Oder by Netkau, which would have been a climax of rashness. It then became necessary to decide to repass the Oder immediately, in order to try and anticipate the Russians at Crossen, by the left bank; or to wait until the next morning to attack them, making in the night all the preparatory movements. The Prussians, who had done no marching during the day, could have accomplished all this without inconvenience, and have opened an engagement at daylight. This error of a general as skillful as he was brave, was probably caused by the embarrassment into which he was thrown by the movement of the Russians upon his left; he saw no other way of working out a satisfactory explanation to give the king, than the one which would be furnished by a victory. In Frederick's eyes it would have appeared doubly absurd to have allowed the enemy to manœuvre, and not have fought him.

As to the conduct of Soltikof, it will be admitted that he manœuvred well enough against Dohna's army to accomplish the end he had in view; and not only that, but he also gave evidence of talent in his conduct of the battle.

BATTLE OF KUNERSDORF OR FRANKFORT.

In Chapter XVI., Frederick was left encamped at Boosen before the Russians; Daun at Marclissa; Prince Henry at Schmotseifen in Silesia; Fouquet and Harsch in their old positions. After the departure of General Fink to join the king, Saxony was left open to the army of the empire, which had moved to Naumburg on the Saale, thrown forward some detachments into the duchy of Magdeburg, and taken possession of Leipsic.

Marshal Daun, without possessing exact information concerning the operations of the Russians, and desirous of favoring their junction with the corps of Haddick and Laudon, set out, on the 30th of July, from the camp of Marclissa with the left wing of the army, and marched upon the heights of Lichtenau, near Lauban, leaving the right wing at Marclissa, under the command of General Buccow and the duke of Ahremberg. Beck, who had remained such a long time at Lichtenau, was moved toward Naumburg on the Queiss, for the purpose of interrupting the communications between the Prussian corps at Schmotseifen and the one then marching upon Sagan.

The 4th of August, Daun heard of the victory of Kay, and received information that Haddick had retired upon Spremberg, but that Laudon had effected his junction with the Russians. The distance between the two Prussian armies led Daun to hope that he might be able to isolate the army of Prince Henry, and cut him off from the Marche and from the king. Nothing in truth would have been easier, with celerity and vigor of action; but unfortunately qualities leading to such a course did not distinguish Daun. He dared not begin his march before calling in General Deville with twelve battalions and twenty-five squadrons, and it was not until eight days after, in the night of the 12th, that he started from the camp of Lauban to move by Gorlitz to Pribus, where he arrived on the 13th. Beck was moved to Sorau to observe Silesia; Haddick detached his cavalry from Spremburg to carry out that junction which he did not think he could effect with his infantry.

At Boosen, the king received the news of Ferdinand's victory at Minden. He had already ordered the pontoons and necessary boats from Custrin to permit him to lay two bridges across the Oder near Reitwen, which were put down during the night of the 10th, without the enemy obtaining the least knowledge of it; the advance-guard covered this operation. The army marched in the night, in three lines by the left, and arrived at the bridges at daylight, when the advance-guard immediately crossed to occupy the heights of Oetscher; the bulk of the army quickly followed. The cavalry crossed the Oder at Oetscher. All the baggage and equipage remained at the bridges under the guard of nine battalions and seven squadrons, commanded by General Wunsch.

The rest of the army, comprising fifty-three battalions and ninety-five squadrons, forming in all forty thousand combatants, took a position, with its right at Leissow, and its left in rear of Bischofsee; the advance-guard was in echelon in advance of the left wing and the village. Fink's corps was established upon the heights in rear of Trettin, in echelon, adjoining the right, and between the advance-guard and the right wing of the army. (Plate XXII.) The king went in person upon the heights of Trettin to reconnoitre the position of the Russians, and on his return gave the following orders:

"If the enemy remain in position, the army will march at daylight by lines and by the left. General Fink will make demonstrations on the heights with a head of column, to convey the impression to the Russians that the king intends to attack them from that point. But before engaging he will wait until the army under the king opens fire; then he will crown the heights in advance of Bischofsee and Trettin with infantry and considerable artillery. The cavalry of this corps will take up an intermediate position in the plain, for the purpose of sustaining the infantry at need, and taking advantage of favorable moments to charge the enemy. While this is being executed, the army will continue its march in two lines by the left. Seidlitz, with the cavalry of the left wing, will precede the first line of infantry, and the prince of Wurtemburg, with the cavalry of the right wing, will follow it. These two generals will form their troops in a third line; when the infantry comes into action, the hussars of Kleist will turn the right flank. In general, care will be taken to refuse the left, for the purpose of directing all the efforts towards the right."

A little later the king added the following: "Should the enemy march in the night to Reppen, the army will follow him at three o'clock in the morning, in three columns by lines." It was thought that he would take position with his right at Reppen, his left at Neuendorf, and his front covered by a creek.

Before beginning an account of this battle, it will be well to glance at the position of the Russians. On the right bank of the Oder is situated a valley, or more properly a bottom-land, caused by the overflow of the river, about three thousand yards wide, near Frankfort, and which, lower down, opens to about three leagues. This portion of the country has been gradually conquered from the river, reclaimed and converted into farms and sites for villages. It is bounded by a chain of heights which extend along the road to Kunersdorf. The Judenberg, which first presents itself, as we go out of Frankfort, is a group of several steep heights, which command the plain as far as Kunersdorf. From this point, the ground is almost smooth as far as the hill of Spitzberg, which rises up at a distance of eight hundred yards from that village. At the right of Kunersdorf, in returning towards Frankfort, is found the Kuhgrund, a kind of ravine which cuts the plain transversely, and thus forms two plateaus. Three dams of considerable size divide the village, and extend to the left as far as the forest; finally, a quarter of a league in rear of Kunersdorf, is situated the Muhlberg, as high as the Judenberg, and which commands the interval between these two elevations. The field of battle is bounded by the forest of Reppen

The Russians were upon the heights, at first facing the Oder, with their right upon the Muhlberg, which was intrenched, and their left on the Judenberg; but when it was seen that the king wished to turn their position, the Russian general made a change of front so that their right was at the Judenberg and their left at the Muhlberg. Each wing was covered by intrenchments and formidable batteries. This was also true of the Spitzberg, which protected the centre. Laudon formed the reserve; his infantry was at the red farm, and his cavalry more in rear towards the suburbs of Frankfort. The Russian cavalry was also in the plain to the left of the Austrian. Laudon, anticipating the attack, took post in the bottom formed by the last inequality of the ground of the Judenberg.

On the 12th of August, at three o'clock in the morning, the king's army was in motion by the left. At first, he wished to adopt the order of battle which he had used at Leuthen, and turn the left wing of the enemy with his right, whilst General Fink should attack it in reverse; but, it appears that, however much he had reconnoitred the ground, he had not obtained sufficient information, for the columns, after marching a long time by the left, encountered the dams of which we have spoken, and were forced to return again to look for openings through which they might pass. This circumstance was most unfortunate, for the heat was excessive, and the troops were, in consequence of this, greatly harassed and lost precious time. Finally, at ten o'clock, the army was in line of battle in the forest; its right was upon the heights near the stream called Hunerflies, and the left at the woods. A strong battery was placed on the Kleistberg, at the right, without the enemy observing it.

The Russians, occupied by the demonstrations made by Fink upon the heights of Trettin, did not disturb this movement; and when the Prussians arrived at the edge of the forest, they confined their action to sending some Cossacks to their front, thinking that this was only a detachment sent to make a diversion in favor of the other attack.

Frederick now caused eight battalions, formed in two lines in echelon before the right wing, to advance, for the purpose of storming the intrenchments and seizing the batteries of the Muhlberg. All the cavalry was collected behind the left wing, with the exception of some squadrons of dragoons. The army was brought into line of battle facing the left flank of the enemy, at about half-past eleven, when the cannonade commenced. In the interval, a battery was established upon the Seidlitz mountain. All this noise was merely to shake the Russian infantry, because the batteries were too distant; the one on the Kleistberg, which enfiladed the enemy's line, and fired in ricochet as far as Kunersdorf, alone caused ravages in the enemy's ranks.

The Russians themselves were not in want of artillery. They had upon their left near one hundred pieces of heavy calibre and a great number of howitzers. They answered the Prussian fire with an immense superiority, and forced themselves to set fire to the abatis. Nothing can give an idea of such a terrible scene. At this instant the king ordered the grenadiers to seize the intrenchments and batteries of the Muhlberg. General Schenkendorf, with the brigade of the first line, and General Linstedt, with that of the second, moved out and penetrated into the valley between the wood and the intrenchments, with a coolness and bearing difficult to describe. Thus far, it is true, the grenadiers had suffered little, because the enemy's batteries were badly arranged, and did not bear upon them until they were ascending the heights and about one hundred and fifty paces from the intrenchments, when they received salvos of cannon and volleys of musketry which spread death through their ranks. This reception did not discourage them, for after one discharge they crossed bayonets. The Russian reputation for obstinacy, so justly accorded them, caused a most desperate resistance to be expected, when, to the great astonishment of all, disorder seized their battalions. The Prussian grenadiers then leaped into the ditch, climbed over the parapet, and, in less than ten minutes, seized seventy pieces of cannon.

The left wing of the Russian army was thus thrown back. All the ground between the Muhlberg and Kunersdorf was soon covered with small parties of troops, as frequently occurs in armies of that nation. Nothing but a strong division of cavalry was now wanted for a charge home to render the victory complete; but unfortunately that arm was with the left wing, as has been previously stated, and the artillery was yet in rear, so that it was not possible to gather all the fruit of this glorious attack. If thirty pieces of light artillery had been quickly placed upon the Muhlberg, and opened upon the disordered masses of the enemy, the results would have been incalculable, for it would be difficult to imagine a more suitable place for artillery. The slope of the Muhlberg towards Kunersdorf was so gentle, that the balls would have ricocheted two thousand paces without rising above a man's head, and the enemy, not being able to deploy more than two regiments, would have been crushed throughout all his depth. But the Prussian artillery was so slow that it was not able to keep up with its infantry.

However, the king, keeping back his left, sustained these two brigades with the right wing, which soon crowned the elevated heights. The grenadiers, whose ranks had become somewhat disordered, were immediately reformed. The Russians made use of these moments to advance some battalions, and to reëstablish order among those who had been expelled from their position. The grenadiers, at the sight of the king, who came among them, and of the first line which was advancing, again fell upon the enemy and overthrew him.

Notwithstanding this advantage, the march of four lines of infantry from the right was not to be accomplished without some confusion. The Russians had leisure to withdraw the guns from the right, and to turn the batteries of the Spitzberg towards their left. Although cut up into platoons, these masses of brave men were determined not to yield up the field of battle. Their generals covered the plain which extended from the little mill to Kunersdorf with infantry and artillery, thus forming a crochet with their first order of battle, and offering a formidable front, instead of the flank which had been surprised. Laudon bestirred himself to second their efforts.

On the other hand, the Prussians had put their left in motion; Fink had passed the creek at the big mill and at Beckers. The cannonade was then re-opened with greater fury, and Frederick led his first line against the enemy. The latter held on better than before at the first attack; the musketry was close and destructive, cartridges were burned on both sides without yielding. Finally Fink was about to turn the Russians, when they fell back behind Kunersdorf. Their ranks became a second time disordered, and Laudon was obliged to hurry up and occupy the edge of the Kuhgrund.

From this moment fortune deserted the Prussian colors. Those battalions which had so often covered themselves with glory gave way, and neither the presence of the king, nor the danger to which he subjected himself, was able to arrest them, although the second line, the entire left wing, and Fink's corps had scarcely been seriously engaged.

We have said that Frederick was not aware that the dams would arrest the march of his left wing, for it is probable that his intention was to bring that wing into action when the proper time for it to engage should arrive. This not being practicable, except by breaking into subdivisions or platoons, or again re-forming in front of the obstacles under the fire of the batteries on the Spitzberg, nevertheless he had ordered the cavalry, which was formed behind it, to charge. General Seidlitz and the prince of Wurtemberg defiled slowly by sections between the dams at the left of Kunersdorf. After forming under the fire of the enemy, they advanced against him with boldness, but the canister spread death and terror in their ranks. Seidlitz was wounded, disorder was introduced, and the appearance of Austrian and Russian squadrons upon the flanks completed the rout of this cavalry, which fled to re-form behind the left wing. The latter, notwithstanding this occurrence, moved forward and carried Kunersdorf, the cemetery of which remained in the hands of the Russians. It afterwards attacked the Spitzberg with great bravery, under the eyes of the king, who hurried there, harangued his troops, and then returned to the right wing, which had been stopped by the Kuhgrund.*

Here the combat was recommenced with new fury. Frederick himself led the battalions to the charge, whilst Fink extended to the right, and endeavored to dislodge the adversary from the heights of Elsbuch.

The enemy, on his side, had massed all his forces towards the Spitzberg, where the infantry was posted in four and five lines on account of the slight extent of ground. Everything depended upon the capture of the Kuhgrund; this hollow way might have been four hundred paces long and sixty wide, and varied from fifteen to twenty feet in depth,

* Frederick has given in his works an exact account of this battle; there is no question about this ravine which had so much influence; he says, also, that the enemy was pushed as far as the Jewish cemetery and to the Judenberg, because he has mistaken the Spitzberg for the cemetery; finally, he has greatly censured the charge of cavalry which took place on the left, whilst Tempelhof assures us that he gave the order himself.

with a sharp, rough slope. The Prussian infantry threw themselves into it and sought to ascend the opposite side, which Landon had lined with all his infantry. The heat was excessive; the Prussian troops, who had marched and fought for nearly ten hours, were already exhausted; all their efforts to surmount this slope were vain; a few brave men reached the top and died among their enemies. The carnage was terrible, for musketry and canister were delivered at only fifty steps. Still the king did not lose the hope of success, and sent back to the charge the bravest of his repulsed battalions, until at length the greater portion had fallen. Fink's corps was not more happy in its assault of the height of Elsbuch; it was constantly overthrown, and the left wing, which endeavored to seize the Spitzberg, experienced the same fate.

In this critical position of affairs, Frederick sent an order to his cavalry to fly to the right, and try to break the enemy's infantry. The duke of Wurtemberg set out immediately at the head of several regiments, and formed near the great mill as many squadrons as the ground would permit, and made ready to charge the opening of the Kuhgrund, when, severely wounded, he turned his eyes to the rear, and beheld his squadrons flying, frightened by the terrible fire of the enemy. In vain General Putkamer advanced with his hussars; he lost his life, and the attack was unsuccessful. In less than six hours, the Prussians had sixteen thousand men disabled. Everywhere they performed prodigies, to maintain their position; but some Austrian squadrons, having charged the right flank of Fink's troops at the foot of the Elsbuch, overthrew them and decided the retreat. The disorder was so great while passing the bridges over the creek of Hunerflies, that the greater part of the king's artillery, amounting to one hundred and sixty-five pieces, was abandoned. Frederick, covering the retreat with the regiment of Lestewitz, received a contusion, and saw two batalions captured behind him. He did not pass the defile until towards the last, closely followed by the enemy.

The adverse army was so badly off, that Soltikof only sent in pursuit some Austrian squadrons belonging to Laudon; the rest of the army passed the night hap-hazard, and in confusion, upon the heights of Oetscher. The king rallied the debris of his own forces at the bridge of the Oder, and passed the night reorganizing it, which operation was terminated the next day at noon.

In order to render the victory decisive, Frederick had ordered General Wunsch, left with the guard of the bridges and the bateaux, to move against Frankfort with some battalions, to capture that city, and cut off Soltikof's retreat by seizing the bridge. Wunsch had made such capital arrangements that he took the garrison prisoners and guarded the bridges; the loss of the battle alone forcing him to retrace his steps.

On this memorable and bloody day of Kunersdorf, the Prussians lost twenty thousand men, of whom eighteen thousand were killed and wounded; it was half of the force present. The loss of the enemy was upwards of sixteen thousand Russians and three thousand Austrians killed and wounded. Soltikof wrote to the empress *that if he should gain one more victory like this, he would have to go and carry the news himself, with his baton in his hand.*

The king here exhibited amazing courage; it became necessary to drag him out of the *melée*, and had it not been for the devotion of Major Prittwitz, he would there have lost his liberty or his life. The army passed the Oder the evening of the 13th, and immediately broke up the bridges. On the 16th, it moved to Malvitz; the 18th, to Furstenwalde, where it guarded the passage of the Spree and covered Berlin. The king, at his order, was joined by General Kleist, who, up to this time, had been watching the Swedes on the Peene, with six battalions and seven squadrons. He replenished and refitted his parks, and thus reorganized a small army of from twenty-eight to thirty thousand combatants.

On the other side, Soltikof, after having passed the Oder on the 16th, encamped with his right at Tzetschnow and his left at Lossow, with Laudon's corps near the right, and Haddick, with from twelve to fifteen thousand men, at Hohenwalde. The allies remained in their positions until the end of the month—a strange result of a victory without example in the history of that war, and a most faulty employment of a numerical superiority which ought to have guaranteed to them the conquest of Prussia.

Frederick has been blamed for not having been satisfied with the capture of the Muhlberg, and for persisting in continuing his attacks. To exculpate him, Tempelhof enters into a long dissertation, which it is not worth while to cite; for it is essentially absurd to reproach a general, after the event, for having followed up his success. Undoubtedly, the king would have done better to have contented himself with a partial victory, than to have lost a battle so terrible as this, could he have foreseen the result of his second attack. *Recollect that only eight battalions had thus far been engaged. Did he not possess the fairest possible chance of giving the final blow to an army which, so to speak, was surrounded?* Nevertheless it can not be concealed that, after the capture of Kunersdorf, the king had strong inducements to content himself with holding it and remaining there; for then he would have had possession of the two roads resting on the enemy's line of operations, those of Reppen and Zielenzig. By allowing his troops to rest, and posting ten squadrons of hussars in the plain of Reipsig, to observe the enemy during the night on the road to Crossen, Frederick would have subjected Soltikof to the alternative of surrendering the next day, or of cutting his way through, which would have been most difficult, since the advantages of the ground, and of the victory of the previous evening, would have insured the success of the Prussians in a defensive battle.

But how shall we blame a great captain, who has captured half of his enemy's camp, for endeavoring to get hold of the other half? It is not in such a case that these observations are admissible. Fault may be found with the king for a different error: *that of having badly sustained his first attack*, and it will be shown that this was a fault independent of all the circumstances.

The original combinations of the king were good; he had gained the line of operations of the Russians and had insured the chances in his favor; however, it might perhaps have been better to have passed the Oder above Frankfort, and to have reached them by the Crossen road, the point of communication with their secondary line, the Austrian army; and in the end, it was of more consequence to cut them off from this, than from their base; for by leaving them the Crossen road, they preserved the power of effecting a junction with Daun, which would have been fatal to the interest of the king. But without discussing these general points of view, let us indicate more especially the errors committed on the field of battle.

The king having gained the rear, and the extreme right of the enemy, he arrested his attack upon that right, (because the left wing of the Russians had faced to the rear.) This operation, founded upon great principles, should have produced the same results as the battle of Leuthen (Chapter VII.); but the execution was too slow; *for if the attack is not rapidly sustained, the extremity is not the most feeble part, seeing that the enemy may have time to move thither all his means of defense.*" It was this that happened on the occasion in question. As everything depended on the first attack, it was necessary to hurry it, and not allow the enemy sufficient time to organize effective resistance. The echelon of eight battalions in front of the right was well ordered; but it would have been better to have held the infantry of this wing in columns of attack, to enable them to follow rapidly the attack and outflank whatever opposed them, or endeavored to reform; finally, there should have been a division of cavalry at this point, to sustain the infantry, and to charge as opportunity offered.

This march of the right in columns of attack would have accomplished the double end, of *mobility and force which it would have been necessary to oppose to the platoon masses of the Russians.* The four lines of infantry had all the inconveniences of columns, without any of their numerous advantages.

As to the cavalry, it is indisputably certain, that Frederick placed his own badly. It is true, that occasionally there must be assembled masses or reserves of this arm, but it is nevertheless certain, as a general rule, that a division of cavalry is wanted at each wing, to take advantage of the occasions which may be presented for finishing the victory, or reëstablishing the combat should this become necessary.

Frederick must have regretted that he neglected this maxim at Kunersdorf.

It appears likewise, that the king engaged his front at an unfavorable time, in the second attack, and was uselessly obstinate in his endeavor to capture the Kuhgrund. We have been over the field of battle, and are convinced that all would have been gained, if the ravine had been turned, and the Spitzberg carried; that was truly the key of the second position. The king was able to see easily this intrenched height, and ought to have felt its importance. After occupying Kunersdorf, he should have supported the movement by allying it with his left. Fink should have replaced his right wing before the Kuhgrund; this wing, returning by Kunersdorf, should have turned the Spitzberg, whilst the left attacked it in front; after that, the hollow way would have been no longer tenable. Moreover, the enemy would not have had time to take post there and organize his defense, had the right, formed in columns of attack, as has been said, executed its movements with rapidity, to complete what the grenadiers had so well begun.

CHAPTER XVIII.

OPERATIONS IN SAXONY AND SILESIA AT THE PERIOD OF THE BATTLE OF KUNERSDORF, AND IN CONSEQUENCE OF THAT AFFAIR.

It will be remembered that Fink left in Saxony only the garrison of Dresden, and some troops at Leipsic, Wittenberg, and Torgau. Frederick had just fought the Russians, and Daun was marching to Pribus, to connect himself more closely with Soltikof, and to protect the operations of the army of the Circles; the latter, master of the battle-field, sent a detachment to summon Leipsic, which opened its gates on the 6th of August.

The army marched to that place, and encamped on the 8th; the duke of Deux-Ponts soon after detached the prince of Stolberg, with his corps of from fifteen to eighteen thousand troops, against Torgau. This expedition possessed no other interest, than that connected with the name of Colonel Wolfersdorf, the heroic commander of the place.

The fortress of Torgau was then defended only by a wall and ditch, to which had been added some earthen parapets. Notwithstanding its bad state of defense, and the weakness of the garrison, Wolfersdorf sustained three assaults; a fourth was commenced; the garrison was in want of provisions; it was about to succeed, when the brave commander sallied out at the head of four hundred men, took the column of attack in reverse, and routed it with considerable loss.

At length, after such an honorable resistance, he agreed to deliver up a city without defense, on condition that he should be allowed to retire freely with all his baggage. He marched out on the 8th, with the honors of war, and was ordered by the king to Potsdam.

On the 20th, Wittenberg was summoned; General Horn, who occupied it with three Saxon battalions, not wishing to attempt the defense of the place with troops whose fidelity he suspected, delivered up the city, and also marched to Potsdam.

Whilst these events were passing, Daun moved the divisions of Wehla and Brentano before Dresden, to observe that place, and to concert measures with the army of the Circles; he afterward reënforced them with the division of Maquire, which formed altogether a corps of some fifteen thousand men. The duke of Deux-Ponts, leaving General Saint André in the vicinity of Leipsic, with twelve thousand men, in order to cover his conquests, went in person to Meissen, where he arrived the 27th of August. On the 26th, Maquire was already before the new city of Dresden, and had unsuccessfully attacked the faubourg.

The count of Schmettau, who had so ably defended that place the preceding year, was still in command, and made all the preparations for a vigorous defense; he answered the threats and the first attacks of the Austrians by burning the splendid suburb, and evacuated the new city, that he might concentrate all his means of defense in the old town, upon the left bank of the Elbe. But all misfortunes seemed to burst at this time over Frederick's head. He had written to the count of Schmettau immediately after the battle of Kunersdorf, to try and arrange a capitulation to save the garrison and the twenty millions in the military chest, since he could expect no assistance from him. The court of Saxony, dreading a bombardment, influenced Maquire by solicitations, to propose advantageous terms to Schmettau. The count profited by this step of Maquire, and demanded, until the 3d of September, not only the liberty of the garrison to march out, but permission to remove all the Prussian property, which was at first refused, but was granted soon after, at the approach of the corps of Wunsch.

This latter general had started with his regiment the 21st of August, and collected a corps of seven thousand men; retaken Wittenberg and Torgau, by allowing the garrisons to march out freely. Obliged, unfortunately, to halt in this latter village, to await the arrival of his artillery from Magdeburg, he did not set out until the 3d of September, and arrived on the 4th at Grossenhain, where for the first time he heard from Colonel Wolfersdorf the state of the discussion; he then hastened his march in order to deliver Schmettau. The latter, however, far from supposing he was about to be relieved so soon, had signed the capitulation the same evening, and had delivered the place to the allies.

The next day, Wunsch, still thinking that the Prussians were in Dresden, overthrew the corps of Brentano and Wehla, on the heights of Boxdorf, from the woods of Moritzburg, and advanced as far as Weissenhirsch, where he heard of the surrender.

That officer had not, previous to this time, commanded any but small detachments of light troops; but nevertheless, on this occasion he displayed the audacity of a soldier, and the skill of a general; not contented with having beaten and driven upon Dresden two corps double the strength of his own, he at first resolved to storm the city guarded by Maquire, and gave orders to have the bridges over the Elbe destroyed, to prevent the allies from issuing upon his rear.

Night, and the fatigue of the troops, who had marched and fought constantly for twenty-four hours, obliged him to defer his attack until the next day. But the next day, calm reflection upon the hazardous nature of this enterprise induced him in the evening to take the road to Torgau, whither General Saint-André was also directed.

Wunsch arrived before the city on the 7th; the next day he received a summons from General Saint-André to surrender, to which he replied by an immediate attack on the Imperialists in the advantageous position which they occupied near the village of Zinna. He directed his effort against their left, which was separated from the line by a small stream, and thus overthrew it by a skillful manœuvre, routed the enemy, capturing seven hundred prisoners and twelve pieces of cannon.

This combat, though apparently of slight importance, had all the consequences of a victory; it raised the *morale* of the Prussian army, and enabled it to recover a part of Saxony, when everything would have been lost as far as Magdeburg, had Wunsch been defeated.

OPERATIONS OF THE GRAND ARMIES AFTER THE BATTLE OF KUNERSDORF.

In Chapter XVII. we have left Frederick's army encamped at Furstenwalde, on the 18th of August. Prince Henry still remained at Schmotseifen, and Fouquet shielded the position of Landshut against General Harsch. These two latter Prussian corps numbered upwards of fifty thousand men. The king had not more than twenty-eight thousand.

The Russo-Austrian army was encamped about Lossow, between Frankfort and Mulrose. Daun moved, on the same day, to Tribel, to connect his operations with the Russians, and to cover, at the same time, the enterprises of the army of the Circles against Saxony. Buccow was at Lauban, with twenty battalions and thirty squadrons; the marquis of

Ainse was with the reserve at Rothenburg; Deville at Marclissa, with twelve battalions and twenty-five squadrons, covering the communications from Lusatia with Bohemia; Beck, with his light troops, was about Naumburg; Harsch in Upper Silesia; finally, Maquire and Wehla had joined the army of the Circles, as we have before mentioned.

After the catastrophe of Kunersdorf, whilst the remnant of the king's army was covering Berlin, separated from the greater part of the troops which guarded Silesia, the fall of the Prussian monarchy appeared inevitable. But astonished Europe saw Frederick rise again from its ruins, and his enemies, thanks to the apathy of their generals, were found, at the conclusion of the campaign, very near the point at which they started. Were any one to look for the causes of this inactivity, it would soon be discovered to arise from the pusillanimity of their generals-in-chief, men of honor on the field of battle, and not lacking energy in council. This may be the difficulty with all coalitions, when they do not receive the impulses which govern them *from a single man of genius.*

The Austrian army was a fine one, and superior in numbers to the one opposed to it; yet it had not fired a shot, although the Russian army, victorious in two bloody battles, had lost half its numbers. Although Soltikof owed, in part, the winning of the last battle to Laudon; nevertheless, there were indications of an after-thought by the Austrian cabinet, and from that time there was a coldness between the generals which continued to increase. Daun at first sent to Soltikof Lascy, the chief of his staff, for the purpose of combining a plan of operations; but he returned without having accomplished anything. The Russian marshal declared *that his troops had done enough, and if it was not the intention of the Austrians to sacrifice them altogether, the Austrian army ought to pursue the king, and finish what he had commenced.*

That until that time he should let his army rest at Guben, and approached the Oder and his depots at Posen.

Daun, to prevent this injurious and dangerous separation, sought an interview with Soltikof; and it was then agreed *that the Russian army should halt upon the left bank of the Oder until after the capture of Dresden, on condition that the Austrians should furnish it with provisions; that the two armies would afterwards march into Silesia and there pass the winter; provided the Austrians captured Neisse, which they were intending to besiege.*

Whilst the enterprises of the coalition were subordinated and made dependent upon a paltry accessory, and whilst Daun, instead of dealing vigorous and decisive blows, contented himself with covering the communications, dreading the king as much when he was beaten as when victorious, Frederick set about making use of the precious moments which he had not expected.

This great man had received, on the evening of the battle, an aid-de-camp from Ferdinand, bringing the news of the battle of Minden. He hurried him back, after his defeat, with this remarkable reply, "*I am sorry not to be able to give a better reply to so agreeable a message; but if you find the roads open and are able to reach the duke, and that Daun is not at Berlin, and Contades at Magdeburg, assure the duke for me that we have lost nothing of importance.*"

The communications with Prince Henry having been interrupted, he was not informed of the result of the battle until the 18th. His position was embarrassing, and he extricated himself from it with consummate skill, concluding that the only salvation, under the present condition of affairs, depended upon opening communication with the king anew; and with the design of establishing himself upon Daun's rear, he traversed Upper Lusatia, to seize the magazines of his enemy, and to protect the most valuable provinces.

In consequence of this determination, he caused a division to rejoin him, and on the 27th of August directed himself, with thirty battalions and fifty-eight squadrons, upon Lusatia. General Ziethen, with an advance-guard, had followed, on the 15th, the movements of Daun upon Pribus, and on the 28th he was at Sagan. The prince marched there on the 29th, and Ziethen marched to Sorau.

Daun heard of this movement, and feared that the enemy, by gaining several marches upon him, might prevent him from communicating with the Russians. Concluding that his force was too feeble to prevent this, he ordered General Buccow to quit Lauban and join him at Tribel, and directed the marquis of Ainse to march to Pribus. Soon after the sudden appearance of Ziethen at Sorau inspired the marshal with such fears that, without waiting for his reënforcements, he fell back behind the Neisse, at Muska, where he joined General Buccow.

This false movement might have had fatal consequences; for the Austrian general, by the loss of a march, uncovered the magazine of Guben, to which Ziethen was thus placed as near as himself. Fortunately, the Prussians remained in their position, and Daun, hearing of the smallness of Ziethen's corps, returned to Tribel on the 1st of September.

Whilst these events were passing, the Russians, who had halted at Lossow, were driven out by the want of forage, and expecting to find every variety of resources in abundance, in Saxony, were at length in march to approach that province, and encamped, on the 30th, at Lieberose, with Haddick at Lambsfeld. Daun, advised of this movement, feared that Prince Henry might intercept their communications with the Oder and Poland, and resolved to capture Ziethen's corps, in order to make a diversion, or to deprive the prince of the means of undertaking anything serious. General Beck was to leave Wiesen for the purpose of seizing the defile of Buschmuhle, on the Sagan road, upon the rear of the Prussians. Prince Esterhazy was to direct himself, by Sommerfeld, upon their right flank, whilst the marshal, with the main body, should attack them in front. Obstacles having delayed Beck's arrival, the expedition failed. Ziethen had time to fall back upon Prince Henry, whom he joined at Sagan. Daun went into camp at Sorau, Beck about Wolsdorf, covering and watching the army.

On the other hand, Frederick, hearing of the departure of the Russians, immediately left his camp of Furstenwalde, and moved, on the 30th, to Woldau, on the road from Lieberose to Lubben. By this wise march he covered, at the same time, Lubben and Luckau, the central points of his communications with Berlin, Saxony, and Lusatia. A detachment was pushed upon Lubben and Vetschau, the environs of which were invested with the enemy's light troops. This position of the king led Haddick to fear that his intention was to cut off his communications with the Austrian army, and to prevent it, he quitted Lambsfeld, marched between Peitz and Cottbus, and afterwards as far as Kahren, where he arrived on the 5th.

Daun, the same day, received news of the surrender of Dresden. He then ordered Haddick's corps to march into Saxony to effect its junction with the army of the Circles, for the purpose of consolidating his conquests and enabling him to operate securely against Silesia.

The capture of Dresden was announced to the Russian army on the 6th of September. Frederick, who had merely heard of the first operations of Wunsch, did not despair of yet saving the place, and dispatched General Fink, with nine battalions and twenty-seven squadrons, to unite with that corps, and take command of the whole. The instructions to the first-named directed him to follow Haddick, upon his flank, to prevent his junction with the army of the

Circles, and to attack him on the first occasion. He marched on the 7th, and arrived at Grossenhain on the 9th. Learning there the surrender of Dresden, and of the junction of Haddick, which he was to prevent, nothing remained for him to do but to march towards Torgau, and there rally Wunsch's corps, and suspend the rapid progress of the allies in Saxony.

During the progress of these events upon the great theatre of operations, nothing of importance took place in Upper Silesia between the corps of Fouquet and Harsch. After various movements they took post—the Austrians at Trautenau, the Prussians under Goltz at Landshut, and those under Stutterheim at Schmotseifen, to observe Deville, stationed at Marclissa.

The general situation of affairs, and the concentration of the allies in Lower Lusatia, seemed to portend decisive events. Never was Frederick in a situation so desperate; but Daun was not the man to profit by it. A hardy operation made him lose confidence; his best founded hopes would suddenly sink into absurd fears. Such, for instance, was the effect produced upon his mind by Prince Henry's march upon Sagan.

When the prince received information, in that village, of the march of the Russians towards Saxony and the position which the king had taken, he felt there was not a moment to be lost, and that he must reach that province. Consequently, he resolved to turn the enemy by Buntzlau and Gorlitz, and fall upon Upper Lusatia, as the Austrians had denuded it of troops. The army started, on the 4th, from Sagan, and arrived, on the 7th, near Lowenberg, where it joined the corps of Stutterheim. Ziethen was detached against Marclissa with eleven battalions and twenty-five squadrons, to drive Deville from Lauban, and destroy the magazines which that general guarded. On the 9th, Stutterheim was sent against the depot of Friedland, which he seized. Prince Henry marched the same day to Lauban, and Deville retired at his approach upon Gorlitz, where he was joined by Beck's corps, which had retired from Rothwasser. On the 12th, the Prussian army went to encamp at Gorlitz; Ziethen occupied the Landskrone; Stutterheim took position between Radmeritz and Seidenberg, to cover the left of the army, and the Austrians retreated upon Bautzen.

No sooner was Daun apprised of these movements of Prince Henry, than he brought to a climax the errors he had committed during this campaign; he left the camp at Sorau and marched at first to Spremberg, hoping thus to cover his conquests in Saxony and preserve the unity of his operations with the Russians; but when he heard that Prince Henry had begun an offensive enterprise, menacing at the same time his detached corps and his magazines, he considerably lowered his plans, and thought of nothing but his depot at Bautzen; without reflecting upon the embarrassment into which he would be thrown, he marched on the 12th of September, and encamped, on the 13th, at Teichnitz. In order not to lose his communications with the Russians and to observe the king, he ordered Haddick to detach Wehla towards Hoyerswerda, and General Palfy towards Spremberg. Beck had to move to Friedland to prevent the incursions of the Prussians.

As soon as the allies began to take a divergent direction, Frederick might hope everything, and this last blunder of Daun, in reality, completely reëstablished his affairs. When Soltikof ascertained the fact of a retrograde movement of the Austrian army, he broke forth in loud reproaches, and wished immediately to retire upon Crossen. The marquis of Montalembert, sent from France to the headquarters of the Russian army, succeeded, by his entreaties and representations, in calming Soltikof, and even in deciding him to lay siege to Glogau; but the errors of Daun were nevertheless real and in their effects irreparable. The Russian general demanded a new reënforcement; on the 15th, Daun regretfully sent to him a corps of ten thousand men under the command of Campitelli, who left the camp of Bautzen with his command, and joined the Russian army by way of Muska.

Nearly all the generals were in favor of recrossing the Oder at Crossen, and operating by the right bank of that river, for the purpose of drawing nearer their depots; however, the efforts of the marquis of Montalembert, and the arrival of the new Austrian reënforcement, decided Soltikof to march to Christianstadt. He moved, on the 18th of September, from his camp at Guben, and reached Christianstadt on the right bank of the Bober, on the 21st, where he was joined by Campitelli. Laudon covered the army in this movement, and took post at Freystadt.

Frederick, who had not observed the march of the Russians from Lieberose to Guben, started the 16th for Wetschau, and encamped the 17th at Cottbus. It appears to have been his design to move against Daun, with the belief that the Russians had repassed the Oder; but finding that they still remained upon the left bank, and intended to besiege Glogau, he resolved to attack them. On the 19th, the army moved to Forste, and on the 20th to Schönwalde; from this place the king sent to Prince Henry and Fouquet, to send him all their disposable troops. Frederick having pushed a reconnoissance upon Sagan, which drove in the feeble detachments found there, established himself and his army, on the morning of the 21st, with his left on the Galgenberg toward the city, and his right at Elkendorf.

This skillful march was the finishing stroke in the reëstablishment of his affairs; it placed him in a condition to link his operations with Prince Henry, in order to save Glogau, and ruptured forever all unity in the operations of his enemies. *The Russians at Christianstadt, and the Austrians at Bautzen, had between them the mass of the Prussian armies, which occupied the interior positions of Sagan and Gorlitz.*

Daun, informed on the 21st, that Frederick was marching in the direction of Glogau, resolved to act with all his forces against Prince Henry, to expel him from Upper Lusatia into Silesia, and thus to secure the possession of Saxony. To effect this, he moved General Odonell to Reichenbach with the grenadiers-à-cheval; the army followed on the morning of the 23d, and encamped near that city. Daun pushed a reconnoissance upon the Landskrone near Gorlitz, and resolved to capture Zeithen's corps, after the latter had ceased to be in his power.

The interest which the Austrians attached to the preservation of Dresden, and the conquest of Saxony, manifested in all their operations, did not escape the notice of Prince Henry, who, wishing to draw off the army of Daun from Silesia, and give the king means of operating safely, judged that by gaining the left of the enemy, and menacing Dresden, he would oblige him to direct his march upon the Elbe.

On the 23d of September, the prince commenced his movement, and, after a forced march, arrived at daylight on the 25th near Hoyerswerda. Finding that General Wehla was still in observation behind the Elster, he endeavored to surprise him; made his advance-guard halt in the woods, and sent detachments of cavalry against his flanks to reach and cut off the enemy when the advance-guard should march against the town.

The operation was executed perfectly. As soon as the cavalry had passed the river, it was formed by squadrons, and charged the Austrians, whom it dispersed. A part of the corps succeeded in gaining the woods. Wehla was taken, with one thousand eight hundred men.

This rapid march of Prince Henry, which was made with the equipments of the magazines, twenty leagues in two days, in the midst of the enemy's armies, was the most splendid operation of that war. When Daun received information of the departure of the Prussians, he went to Gorlitz on the 25th to reconnoitre, and ascertain the object of their movement; informed that they were marching by Hoyerswerda, he returned the same day to Bautzen to protect Dresden if necessary.

Two days after his arrival at Hoyerswerda, Prince Henry learned of the junction of Haddick's corps with the army of the Circles, and that these troops united were to attack and repulse General Fink from Meissen; we will now proceed to give an account of that operation, beginning for that purpose further back.

We have seen that Fink was joined, September 11th, by Wunsch's corps. The next day these two generals moved in advance; after occupying Eulenberg and Leipsic, in which they captured three of the enemy's battalions, they directed themselves upon Dobeln and Meissen. As soon as the duke of Deux-Ponts heard of this, he resolved to attack them there immediately; but he uselessly placed sixteen battalions in Dresden, which might equally well have been left in charge of a smaller corps. The corps of Fink was encamped near Korbitz, and was there attacked, on the 21st of September, by the Austrians under General Haddick. Wunsch occupied the heights of Siebeneichen, where the army of the Circles wasted the entire day cannonading his position. After a trifling combat, General Fink repulsed the enemy with the loss of one thousand men, and the imperial army returned to its camp at Wilsdruf.

Prince Henry, having been misinformed at first as to the result of the action, took up his march on the 28th, to join Fink; on the 29th, he arrived at Elsterwerda, and there learned the result of the combat, delivered eight days previous, and of which he ought to have had information in twenty-four hours. He persisted, however, in his plan of junction, and concluded to pass the Elbe between Meissen and Strehlen; the army then encamped the 2d of October opposite Torgau with the advance-guard at Belgern.

Meanwhile Daun, relying upon reaching the Elbe before Prince Henry, had left his camp at Bautzen to march upon Dresden, where he arrived on the 29th. The army of the Circles was retired behind the valley of the Plauen; the Austrians were encamped near Kesselsdorf, where they halted the 30th, to await or shield its parks and the detached corps. Meanwhile, Daun daily reconnoitred Fink's position, as he wished to overwhelm him before the arrival of Prince Henry. The attack was fixed for the 2d of October; but when the Austrians were put in motion there was no army to meet them; Fink had drawn off his corps in the silence of the night, and had been posted at Strehlen some seven hours.

On the 3d, Daun moved in seven columns to Lomatsch; Brentano disturbed the camp of Strehlen. On the same day Prince Henry crossed the Elbe at Torgau, encamped at Belgern, and arrived on the 4th of October at Strehlen, where he was at last united to Fink's corps; the army then comprised fifty-three battalions and one hundred and three squadrons. General Bulow was posted at Eulenburg with his division, for the purpose of communicating with Leipsic.

Daun came the same day to Heyda; his army was not less than sixty-four battalions and seventy-five squadrons of heavy cavalry, without counting the hussars, the Croat infantry, the corps of Brentano, that of Gemmingen, nor the army of the Circles. Gemmingen, with eight battalions and ten squadrons, covered the left at Seerhausen; Esterhazy with the light troops was at Hof; Haddick's corps was united with the army, and the general had retired.

The Austrian marshal had at length received orders to attack Prince Henry; but little caring to risk the chances of a battle, he preferred to bring about the evacuation of Saxony by his manœuvres, rather than by force of arms. He thought that by threatening the magazines of Torgau, he would force the Prussians to abandon the position of Strehlen, and that he might easily cut them off from Wittenberg and Magdeburg. These trifling and insignificant measures appeared to him in keeping with his favorite maxim, which was: *to move slowly but surely*, and he formed the plan of insensibly extending his position to the left, in order to gain the extreme right of the prince and afterwards to attack him in reverse. It was that which he had in view when he executed the following movements.

Oct. 5th. Esterhazy was moved to Ratzen.

Oct. 6th. The army at Hof in presence of the prince; the posts of the two armies separated by the brook which runs from Schönewitz to Borna.

Daun calls a council of war to deliberate upon the question, whether it be best to attack the Prussians in position? Opinions were so divided, that the council was dissolved without coming to a conclusion.

Oct. 8th. Esterhazy encamps at Lampertswalde.

Oct. 12th. Gemmingen and Brentano, reënforced by the grenadiers-à-cheval under the command of Buccow, march to Dahlen and endeavor to capture the corps of Rebentisch, who had replaced Bulow, and who was at Schilda on the morning of the 13th. Brentano was transferred to the vicinity of Sernewitz, and cut him off the road from Strehlen to Torgau.

Oct. 15th. Buccow moves upon Schilda; Rebentisch, too feeble to encounter him, falls back in time upon Wildschutz, whence, at nightfall, he marches upon Torgau.

By these operations, slow most undoubtedly, but much more prudent, the Austrian general insensibly approached his object. However, his combinations had the defect of always allowing his adversary time to oppose efficient counter-manœuvres. Daun might have reached the same point on the 7th which he did on the 15th, by marching by lines and by the left, encamping at Dahlen and pushing Buccow upon Schilda; for Prince Henry would have been forced to attack him or to retire upon Torgau. The marshal was afraid to risk such a movement, although there was no difficulty attending it.

On the morning of the 16th, immediately on hearing that Rebentisch had been forced to retire upon Torgau, Prince Henry started from Strehlen, to take a position of great strength near the first village, called Siptitz. The prince, fearing an enterprise against Leipsic, detached Fink, with fourteen battalions and twenty-five squadrons, to Eulenburg, to keep up the communications. This corps encamped on the 19th at Groisch, beyond the Mulde.

Daun halted on the 17th. The carbineers occupied the Prussian camp, and General Esterhazy followed them with the light troops. The Austrian army encamped on the 18th at Strehlen, and on the 19th at Belgern.

Prince Henry established the brigade of Schenkendorf astride the Elbe, near Werda, for the purpose of covering and clearing up the front of the army. Hearing that Daun was disposed to attack him, he recalled Fink, and only left in Eulenberg two battalions and twelve squadrons. It seems impossible to think that the Austrians did not oppose this movement, as it was very easily done, since it only required that the strong division of Buccow should be sent from Schilda, by the left, to the vicinity of Strehlen, and that it should be replaced by the army.

Daun's slowness ought to have counteracted his own plans, and have defeated even those best conceived. However, still pondering upon the idea of dislodging the Prussians from the formidable position of Siptitz, he put in movement the army of the Circles, which, for a long time, had been stationed at Dresden. On the 18th, the light troops of Kleefeld and Ried drew nearer to Torgau; the duke of Deux-Ponts arrived on the 21st at Grossenhain.

On the 22d Daun marched from Belgern to Schilda, in six columns.* He replaced Buccow with the duke of Ahremberg, whom he ordered to move his division upon Strehlen, in order to cut off the communications of the Russians with Eulenburg and Leipsic. On the 23d, Gemmingen moved upon Eulenburg, with six battalions and ten squadrons.

Daun then conceived the plan of enveloping Prince Henry. For this purpose, on the 25th, he moved the duke of Deux-Ponts to Peritz, General Ried to Rosdorf, and Palfy to Ubigau. A bridge was laid across the Elbe at Leuwitz, to complete the communications of these corps with the grand army. On the other hand, on the 26th, the duke of Ahremberg was directed upon Dommitsch, and Gemmingen was transferred to Duben, in rear of the Prussians. General Guasco, with five battalions and five squadrons, was established at Schilda, in order to complete the communications of the duke with the army.

This parceling business had the effect which ought to have been expected. The duke of Ahremberg, in moving, on the 25th, to Malitsch, fell in with the corps of Fink, which Prince Henry had detached upon that point.

On the morning of the 26th, the prince, having reconnoitred the position of Ahremberg's corps, decided to turn it. General Wunsch, with five battalions and ten squadrons, was ordered upon Wittenberg, passing along the right bank of the Elbe, afterwards crossing to the left, to rally from Rem-

* This mode of marching by a great number of columns in order to deploy, is contrary to the orders of march pointed out in Chapter V. It requires a great deal of time, and it always rendered the Austrians fearful of being attacked during a movement.

berg the corps of General Rebentisch, and to attack the enemy in reverse, in concert with Prince Henry, at the moment Fink's corps should gain its front.

Meanwhile Odonell, with five battalions and fifteen squadrons, reënforced the corps of Guasco, intended to sustain the duke of Ahremberg, who was to leave Wittenberg on the 28th, at eight in the evening, and who did not commence his march until the morning of the 29th, with his own troops and those of Gemmingen and Odonell.

This day had been designated by Prince Henry for the execution of his plan, and when he heard of the departure of the enemy, he sent Fink and Wunsch in pursuit. The former could not overtake him; Wunsch was more fortunate, and came upon the posts of General Gemmingen in the defile of Merckwitz. The sudden appearance of the Prussians upon his rear turned the head of the duke of Ahremberg, who retired hastily upon Duben by the forest of Torgau. Gemmingen, seeking only to follow him and reach Duben, detached two thousand grenadiers to the heights near the forest of Sackwitz, to secure the retreat, which was conducted in disorder. The grenadiers were not yet more than half way up, when the Prussian cavalry appeared on the summit, charged them impetuously, captured Gemmingen, with one thousand four hundred men, and sabred and dispersed the rest.

Generals Wunsch and Rebentisch encamped at Mairo, and, on the 30th, were united to Fink's corps. Ahremberg was joined by Odonell at Duben, who came to his rescue too late. They afterwards retired to Eulenburg. The Prussians were encamped at Duben on the 31st.

Marshal Daun was greatly exasperated at the conduct of his generals, although he himself was assuredly the prime cause of these disasters, employed as he was in fortifying his own camp, and at the same time detaching large divisions into the midst of the Prussian army. How shall we reconcile such timidity with the audacity of throwing twenty-eight thousand men at a distance upon the rear of an able general? This corps found itself separated four leagues from the main army, and between the two lay the forest of Torgau; what is still more inexplicable, it was left in such a position three days, though not ignorant that the Prussian army was ready to crush it.

Marshal Daun missed an excellent opportunity to attack the prince, when the duke of Ahremberg arrived at Dommitsch; he should then have assailed him from the side of the heights of Siptitz towards Leswig, and should have combined his efforts with those of the duke, who would have taken the enemy in reverse; every chance was in his favor, since nothing could have prevented him from retiring under the cannon of Dresden without loss, whilst the prince would be exposed to great risk, having no retreat except upon Magdeburg or Berlin; but his inactivity deprived the results of this combination of any importance, since it demanded a vigorous execution.

Before giving a history of the operations in Saxony, let us resume those of the Russian army and that of the king upon the Oder.

CHAPTER XIX.

SUCCESSIVE OPERATIONS OF THE KING AGAINST THE RUSSIANS; SOLTIKOF RETURNS TO POLAND; THE PRUSSIANS CONCENTRATE IN SAXONY; AFFAIR OF MAXEN; WINTER CAMPAIGN.

By his march upon Sagan, Frederick formed an interior line of operations, which enabled him to connect his movements with those of Prince Henry, and thus dissolved whatever unity had existed thus far in the operations of his adversaries, and very nearly threw them into positions diametrically opposite to their original ones; for each one becoming isolated, they all concluded that the safest plan would be to approach quickly their several bases.

Soltikof, not having found at Christianstadt any of the supplies of provisions which Daun had led him to expect, did not attempt to hide his dissatisfaction. In answer to the announcement that funds had been provided to purchase provisions, he remarked "*that his soldiers did not eat silver*," and that he would recross the Oder at Crossen. The marquis of Montalembert having demonstrated to him that he would quickly approach his depots by taking the road of Karolath, the marshal was induced to march thither, for the purpose of awaiting the arrival of the trains from Poland, which were given this direction. The army was put in motion on the 22d of September, and encamped, on the 23d, at Freystadt. Laudon was at Windisch-Borau near Neustadtel.

Frederick marched on the same day to Suckan, to be ready to defend the defile of Neustadtel. This hardy movement inducing the Russians to think that the king had received large reënforcements, they laid a bridge across the Oder in the vicinity of Wartenberg, and on the 24th, the army marched to gain Karolath by that road. Laudon was directed upon Beuthen.

As soon as the king got information of this movement, he resumed his march by lines and by the right, and went to occupy the heights between Zobelwitz, Baune, and Milkau, with the view of shutting up the road which led by Beuthen to Glogau. The Russians were filled with astonishment to find the heights of Kleinwirbitz crowned with Prussians. They passed the night on their arms, and encamped the next day, the 23d, a little in rear. Whilst the bridge was laid at Karolath, the king, whose inferiority would have rendered a surprise disastrous, assembled his troops under arms before daylight each morning. On the 27th, Fouquet sent him a reënforcement of three battalions and three squadrons, and the next day General Queiss brought him six battalions, so that his army was increased to about thirty-six thousand combatants.

The misunderstanding between the enemy's generals was increased each day by slight incidents; between the passion of Soltikof and the Austrian pride, there could be but little in common, on which to base a reconciliation; Laudon having demanded on the 26th from the Russian marshal what he could rely upon his undertaking, the latter answered him in a very bitter and disobliging manner, and would have departed instantly for Poland, if the judicious mediator, Montalembert, had not persuaded him to defer passing the Oder until the 30th of October.

The king pursued their rear-guard without success, and marched on the 2d of October to Glogau, where he sent twelve battalions and nearly all his cavalry across the river, which took position at Kleinzerbau, and by their excellent position were to prevent the bombardment of the place.

The Russians marched on the 2d to Kuttlau and on the 4th to Schwusen.

Frederick has been blamed for not having passed the Oder with all his forces, for the purpose of seizing the defile of Hundpass, which covers Herrenstadt and Gurau, which might perhaps have forced the Russians at once to take the road to Poland; this reproach has no good foundation, for it was not his desire to bring the Russians to a state which should necessitate a battle in order to enable them to open a passage, since they were about to return voluntarily, and he would soon be rid of them. Nevertheless, when Soltikof took the direction of Schwusen, and appeared to desire to prolong his stay, the king determined to pass the remainder of his army over the Oder, and detached only seven battalions and ten squadrons under the command of Schmettau to Golgowitz, on the left bank, in order to cannonade the enemy's camp and prevent incursions upon that side.

Having then received information that the Russians meditated a movement upon Breslau, Frederick, with a view of being before them, caused a bridge to be laid at Koben, on the 7th of October, marched to Klein-Gafron on the morning of the 8th, crossed the Oder, and encamped at Sophienthal.

The Russians were to leave on the 20th, and the camp equipage was already on the road since evening, when a courier arrived from Saint Petersburg, ordering Soltikof to continue his operations against Breslau. In consequence ot this, the army marched on the 22d to Sandeborschke oppo site Herrenstadt; Laudon was at Babiele.

The Prussians arrived the same day at Rutschen-Borwitz, under the command of General Hulsen, to whom the king had turned over the command during his sickness. The enemy summoned the battalion, which was at Herrenstadt, with the threat of burning the village in case of refusal. The commandant replied bravely; the bombardment began, and the city was quickly reduced to ashes, and that too without obliging the garrison to abandon its post.

This futile undertaking terminated the campaign of Soltikof. A council of war, convoked the same day, declared that the order of the court of Saint Petersburg could not be executed. The Russian army marched on the 24th of October for Tribusch, where Soltikof received notice from Daun, that despairing of getting an opportunity of attacking Prince Henry with success, he was about to go into winter-quarters; this information brought the marshal's irritation to its climax, and he immediately directed his march on Posen. Laudon fell back upon Kalisch.

As soon as the Russians had departed, Frederick detached Generals Gablentz and Schmettau with nine battalions and twenty squadrons towards Trachenberg, to watch the movements of Laudon upon the frontiers of Silesia. General Meyer, with five battalions and ten squadrons, went to relieve the troops of Fouquet at Hirschberg and Landshut. Hulsen was sent into Saxony with nineteen battalions and thirty squadrons; the king remaining sick was transported to Glogau.

OPERATIONS IN SAXONY AFTER THE ARRIVAL OF HULSEN; AFFAIR AT MAXEN.

We have previously left Daun encamped at Schilda, Prince Henry at Torgau, and Fink at Duben. The departure of the Russians and the arrival of Hulsen at Muska led Daun to fall back upon Dresden; on the 4th of November, he moved to Naundorf, where he was rejoined by the corps of Ahremberg. The 5th, he took position at Lommatsch, and the 6th at Heinitz. The corps of Esterhazy and Brentano preceded this march.

On the other side, Prince Henry encamped on the 5th at Belgern, and the following day at Strehlen; Fink with thirteen battalions and thirty-five squadrons was at Mutschen. The 8th, the army comprising upwards of forty battalions and sixty-three squadrons was established at Altsattel; General Aschersleben at Naundorf, on the Elbe, with four battalions and seventeen squadrons; a strong division under Wedel was posted near Hirschstein; Schenkendorf at Karschitz, intermediate between the latter and Fink, with two battalions and eight squadrons; General Dierke was at Grossenhain with four battalions and as many squadrons.

These reënforcements placed Prince Henry in a condition to assume the offensive; but the position which the Austrians then occupied being too strong, he resolved to dislodge them by turning their left flank, and cutting them off from the mountains of the Erzgebirge. With this view, Fink was posted at Etzdorf on the 9th; Brentano, who flanked the left of the enemy, retired to Nossen on the approach of the Prussians.

The prince, noting with pleasure Daun's immobility, reënforced Fink with six battalions and twenty squadrons, and on the 13th ordered him to dislodge Brentano from Nossen; to occupy Freiberg, and to push parties upon Dippodiswalde and Dohna.

At the first sound of the cannon, the marshal sought his lieutenant at a gallop, and divining the object of the enemy, he withdrew his troops, and a part of his left in the form of a crochet, toward Deutsch-Bohra, in order to cover his flank and rear. Fink was then established upon the heights which extended between Zelle and Siebenlehn, in such a manner that without effort he was situated upon the extreme left of the Austrians, and cut off their communications with Freiberg. Meanwhile, the king arrived at the head-quarters of the army.

The marshal could not hide from himself the danger of his position, and withdrew his army in the night upon Wilsdruf, where he took post between Sohra and Blanckenstein; the reserve and the carbineers upon the heights of Polentz; the marquis of Ainse was at Batzdorf, on the Elbe, opposite Meissen; Brentano was at Herzogswalde.

As soon as the king discovered the departure of the enemy, he ordered General Wedel to pursue him, and placing himself at the head of three battalions of grenadiers and the small corps of Aschersleben, he came up with General Sincere near Korbitz, and caused him considerable loss. The army set out on the 14th, at noon, to go into camp at Krogis; the corps of Wedel at Korbitz; that of Schenkendorf at Deutsch-Bohra.

Nevertheless, Fink had dispatched General Wunsch in pursuit of the enemy, and sent Sydow with four battalions to Freiberg. Frederick, thinking that Daun had retreated to Bohemia, did not wish him to do so in quiet, and ordered Fink to move in all haste to Maxen. That general arrived on the 16th at Dippodiswalde, occupied for two days by a division of the army of the Circles, which was not able to effect its retreat upon Possendorf without loss. The advance-guard under Wunsch halted for the night at Maxen, and pushed a reconnoissance upon Dohna.

The 17th, Fink joined his advance-guard. General Lindstedt, who had remained behind with four battalions and six squadrons to escort the parks, occupied Dippodiswalde to cover his communications.

The arrival of such a strong corps in his rear alarmed Marshal Daun, who quitted Wildsruf the 17th, and came to fix his camp in the valley of the Plauen. This valley, formed by the Weistritz, is not over four hundred paces in width from Plauen to Postchapel; in the course of a league it widens sensibly, but narrows again, and so continues until it reaches Dippodiswalde in the midst of a string of defiles, formed by various groups of steep heights, or rocks.* From Dresden to Plauen extends a perfect plain; the Austrian cavalry was there united; the infantry occupied the heights from Plauen to Windberg. The corps of Sincere was posted upon the heights of Hainchen to cover the rear and guard the defiles of Possendorf, where passed the road from Dresden to Dippodiswalde. Brentano was established at Strehlen on the Pirna road, and afterward at Niekern. Finally, the army of the Circles quitted the camp of Dresden, and took post between Cotta and Gishubel; its light troops under Ried marched to Glashutten and Lipstadt; Count Palfy was with the hussars at Zehist; and General Kleefeld with the Croat and Hungarian infantry at Zaschendorf.

Fink perceived from the heights of Maxen the movement of the army of the Circles and moved Wunsch to Dohna.

Whilst these events were transpiring, the king arrived on the 18th to establish himself at Wilsdruf, with the advance-guard under Ziethen at Kesselsdorf. Frederick informed of the dispositions of Fink caused him to withdraw the detachment from Linstedt, since it was too feeble to prevent a numerous corps from attaining him. Fink obeyed and merely left at this post three squadrons of hussars to watch the movements of the Austrians; but at the same time he wrote to the king to inform him of the danger to which he was exposed, and to point out to him the position of the enemy's corps. This dispatch was probably intercepted as he received no response.

Fink received a letter soon afterwards from the king,

* See the special map of the environs of Dresden by Petry, or that of Bakenberg.

which left him master of his own actions, enabling him to act according to circumstances; but Frederick had added, in his own hand, a postscript, "*You will probably have an affair with the Circles or with Sincere,*" and Fink inferred from this that the king desired that he should defend his post. He therefore remained in position, expecting, besides, that the king, who ought to have received his preceding letter, would make a movement in his favor, when he discovered that Daun was operating against him.

However, the marshal, perceiving that Fink obstinately maintained his post, resolved to capture him. On the 18th he had a conference with the Duke of Deux-Ponts, and agreed that the army of the Circles should take the enemy in reverse by Dohna, whilst Brentano attacked his front, and the grand army, united to the corps of Sincere, should attack him upon the left to cut off his retreat upon the army of the king. For this purpose the corps of Sincere, of which Odonell assumed the command, was reënforced by twelve battalions and ten squadrons, which raised it to thirty thousand men. That army left Rupchen at seven o'clock on the morning of the 19th, and marched direct upon Dippodiswalde, under the lead of Marshal Daun. At first a thick fog prevented Fink from discovering the movement; but when it lifted he would still have had time to reach Dippodiswalde before them, if he had not thought his honor and his duty required him to wait. General Platten occupied Reinhardsgrimma and the heights of Hausdorf, with five battalions and five squadrons. The Austrians encamped with their right upon the heights of Maltern, their left at Oberhaselich; the prince of Stolberg, with seven battalions and five squadrons took post at Buckardswalde.

Fink, no longer doubting the plans of the enemy, began his preparation for defense. General Wunsch, with five battalions and three squadrons, was on the heights of Plaschwitz, towards Dohna, in order to hold in check the army of the Circles, and to prevent it from crossing the ravine. The rest of the troops were arranged in battle, in a crescent form, about Maxen, the line running in the direction of Muhlbach was extended upon the heights in rear of Witgendorf; General Linstedt covered the cavalry and the right with three battalions upon the heights in front of Schmorsdorf.

On the 20th the Austrian corps was put in march in four columns, with the cavalry upon the wings, leaving at Maltern only the brigade Schenkendorf to protect its rear. Daun had his troops formed in two lines, near Reinhardsgrimma, and reconnoitred the position of the Prussians.

Fink also was out reconnoitring, when it was announced to him that the enemy was forming at the same time about Bohrsdorf and behind Reinhardsgrimma. He ordered General Platten to fall back in rear of Hausdorf. That measure appears to have been precipitate, for the defile of Rheinhardsgrimma presented obstacles difficult to overcome. Between Hausdorf and the wood of that village is a very elevated height, which marked the issue of the Austrian columns. The grenadiers having gained the height, Daun established there a battery, whose fire protected the deployment of his troops, which were formed in line of battle, with their right on the heights in rear of Muhlbach, and their left near Hausdorf. (Plate XXIII., No. 2.)

Immediately after, General Ziskowitz, at the head of five battalions of grenadiers, supported by the brigades of Ainse and Dombasle, attacked the Prussians upon the heights in front of Witgendorf and Maxen. These grenadiers were doubled up a little to the right and left; but they threw themselves forward with such impetuosity that they broke the battalions of Grabow and Zastrow, thus pierced the line, and threw themselves into the village of Maxen. General Fink sent the dragoons of Platten and the regiment of

Rebentisch to check them, but these troops were carried away by the fugitives. The battalions of Billerbeck, Kleist, and Fink were thus enveloped and taken between two fires; a charge of the battalion of Willemai saved, it is true, the two latter. Nevertheless, as this wing could not operate in concert with the right, since the enemy held the centre *en masse*, it was forced to cut its way through in order to retreat upon Schmorsdorf.

From the other side Brentano extended more and more in rear of the Prussians. Some moments before the capture of the heights of Maxen, Fink endeavored to charge with all his cavalry, in order to disembarrass himself, and afterwards to oppose his infantry to the marshal; but the artillery fire held the squadrons in check, and this movement only served to paralyze them by their becoming isolated from the rest of the division. Daun re-formed his line, and joined his left to Brentano's corps.

Fink withdrew with the remnant of his battalions to the heights in rear of Falkenhain and Blochwitz, where Wunsch still held out, after having repulsed all the attacks which had been directed against him; they were here soon enclosed. As no recourse was left but to cut his way through, Fink reconnoitred all the roads towards Burckardswalde, and assembled a council of war. The council, considering that the corps was reduced to less than twelve thousand combatants, despaired of forcing the defile held by an enemy five or six times as strong, and he was obliged to capitulate.

Wunsch, whom nothing intimidated, proposed to cut his way through, during the night, with all his cavalry, in the vicinity of Sillen; and Fink having consented to it, that general set out, on the 21st of November, at three in the morning; but it is probable that he would not have succeeded. After he had departed, General Rebentisch was sent to Daun, who would not entertain any proposition until

General Wunsch was recalled. The Prussians were not in a condition to dictate terms. After some discussion they were obliged to accept Daun's propositions, and upwards of fourteen thousand men surrendered prisoners; three thousand had been disabled.

The king, dissatisfied with Fink, brought him before a court-martial, which cashiered him, and condemned him, together with Generals Rebentisch and Gersdorf, to two years' confinement.

Fortune now seemed to exhaust all her spite against Frederick; he had detached to Fink's relief, by the forest of Tharandt, General Hulsen with nine battalions and twenty squadrons. But the latter hearing, on the 21st, near Dippodiswalde, of the fate of his colleague, retired to Freiberg. The king then established four battalions at Mohorn in order to communicate with him.

Daun, reposing upon his laurels, cantoned his army about Dresden; that of the Circles went into Franconia to take up winter-quarters.

The king also took up compact cantonments in face of the Austrians; the advance-guard of nine battalions and twenty-four squadrons was established in the neighborhood of Kesselsdorf; the first line, of twenty-three battalions, was near Wildsruff and Limbach; the second, of eight battalions, was not far from Blankenstein and Meissen; the third, of twenty-eight squadrons, was near Herzogswalde; the reserve, under Hulsen, of eleven battalions and thirty-five squadrons, in the vicinity of Freiberg; six battalions and one thousand horse were established at Koln, opposite to Meissen upon the right bank of the Elbe, in order to prevent the imperialists from foraging the country. Considering the proximity of the enemy, the battalions on picket guard built barracks, notwithstanding the extreme rigor of winter; this trying service cost the army a great number of men.

Daun, encouraged by the success of his operations at Maxen, resolved to capture the corps at Koln; for this purpose, he drew to him Beck's division, which had lain so long at Zittau, reënforced it with five battalions and, on the 3d of December, pushed it before that post. General Dierke, who commanded it, could not reëstablish the bridge on account of the enormous blocks of ice floating on the Elbe; with incredible efforts, before morning, the greater part of his corps was boated across; the next day, those that remained were attacked with fury, and made prisoners to the extent of fifteen hundred men.

After such multiplied and overwhelming reverses, it did not seem possible that the king could hold out a great while against the forces under Marshal Daun; however, they led to no important changes in his affairs; his presence of mind and genius was only equal in extent to the weakness of his conqueror, who intrenched himself under the cannon of Dresden as though he had been defeated, and left the beaten army master of the field.

MOVEMENTS IN SILESIA.

Whilst events were thus crowding each other on the banks of the Oder and the Elbe, the greatest tranquillity reigned in Upper Silesia, where the Austrians had left thirty-three battalions and fifty squadrons before a feeble Prussian line. General Beck covered the environs of Zittau with thirteen battalions and thirty squadrons, and was observed by only four battalions and four squadrons under General Goltz. Harsch and Janus with twenty battalions and thirty squadrons covered Bohemia towards Trautenau and Schatzlar. Fouquet opposed them at Landshut with thirteen battalions and six squadrons.

After the Russians had departed for Poland, and the king

had reënforced Fouquet with five battalions and ten squadrons, the latter with one division rejoined the corps of Schmettau, left at Militsch to observe the movements of Laudon. Hence he directed his march towards the frontiers of Poland; but ascertaining that the Austrian general had returned directly by Galicia upon Moravia, Fouquet started again, November 9th, for Kosel; after harassing the march of Laudon, he went, the 30th of November, to encamp at Ratibor. The Austrian general arrived the same day at Teschin, after having marched incessantly through Cracovia, Bielitz, and Plessen; he united himself to the corps of Draskowitz, which Harsch had sent to Troppau to communicate with him.

Laudon, whose regiments were reduced to half their original number, tired of warring in the midst of winter, asked for an armistice in order to go into winter-quarters; the proposition was acceded to with joy by Fouquet, who sent Schmettau to canton his troops in Lusatia, in the vicinity of Gorlitz.

CAMPAIGN AGAINST THE SWEDES.

The operations in Pomerania hardly merit a place in history. When Kleist was obliged to conduct his corps to the king, after the battle of Kunersdorf, the Swedes were relieved from the presence of the enemy, and amused themselves foraging and levying contributions in the Marche, where they occupied Prentzlow.

Immediately after the departure of the Russians for Poland, the king detached thither the regiment of hussars Belling, and ordered General Mantenfel, who had been slightly wounded at Kunersdorf, to form some battalions of convalescents, which were sufficient to restrain the Swedish army and make them recross the Peene.

CHAPTER XX.

GENERAL OBSERVATIONS UPON THE CAMPAIGN OF 1759; THE OPERATIONS OF THE KING COMPARED WITH THE ACTUAL SYSTEM OF WAR.

FREDERICK concluded the campaign of 1758 by a series of operations which repaired most gloriously the defeat of Hohenkirch. He had succeeded in banishing all his enemies beyond his frontiers; had placed his army in good winter quarters, and three months were sufficient to recomplete his regiments. By his apathy at the opening of the campaign of 1759, he committed a grave error, which became the origin of all his reverses, and each one of them having been justly merited, we can scarcely recognise in him at that time the conqueror of Rosbach and Leuthen. The battles of Jägerndorf and Zorndorf ought to have convinced Frederick that the Russians were dangerous enemies, and as such were not to be despised. By a combination without example in the lines of operations of the coalition, every year, for six months, this Russian army was transported far enough from the scene of operations to suffer it to be omitted in the calculations. It required each time two months to arrive again at the theatre of war, and with all its magazines, equipage, and baggage, the time of its arrival depended upon the condition of the roads in Poland; for whenever it thawed, and in the spring, they were ordinarily impassable to such trains.

It could therefore, with certainty be assumed that the

Russians would not accomplish the passage of the Oder before the month of June. *Thus Frederick not only possessed the enormous advantages of an interior line of operations against two isolated lines at immense distances; but also the certainty that one of these armies would be paralyzed for half the year.*

He did not endeavor to extract the slightest advantage from this state of affairs, and his inaction was unaccountable.

The king had one hundred and fifty battalions and two hundred and eighteen squadrons, divided into three corps, upon this interior line. The Austrians were less numerous, and occupied an immense front; Daun had not more than fifty thousand men in one body. What, therefore, prevented Frederick from assembling his masses rapidly, though the Swedes and the army of the empire gained thereby some temporary success? This concentration might even have been brought about in eight days, without the enemy having any time wherein to take advantage of the movement. Was it not important to attack Daun after the end of February, and force him, by taking the initiative against his communications, to receive a battle which would have decided the quarrel before the Russians dreamed of moving? Leaving eight battalions and ten squadrons to observe the Peene during the winter, and seventeen battalions and fifteen squadrons in Saxony, in front of the troops of the empire, to act conjointly with a detachment from the army of Duke Ferdinand in Hesse, the Prussians could have united, in eight marches, one hundred and twenty battalions and one hundred and eighty squadrons for the purpose of striking a decisive blow, which would have laid open the road to the walls of Vienna.

After gaining a battle there would have been time to unite Prince Henry, with twenty-five battalions, to the eight battalions opposed to the Swedes, and thus form an army of thirty thousand men, to amuse and occupy the Russians on the Oder, whilst the victorious army was following up its success. In case of a check, the Prussians would only have lost the enemy's own territory, and their defeat would have been followed by consequences less fatal than a battle lost when sixty thousand Russians were on the Oder, and eighty thousand Austrians in Upper Lusatia, and only five marches asunder. If it were true that the Russian army gave as much trouble, and did the king as much damage as one hundred thousand Austrians, why did he wait, before commencing his operations, until their arrival just doubled the force of his enemies?

This is not one of those criticisms said to be made after the event, for such are only applicable to errors of combat; always when there is a fault in the plan of campaign it belongs to the one who has drawn it up.

What would not Napoleon have accomplished with the advantageous position of Frederick? How widely different would have been the results of the application of his principles in this position! Glance at his campaigns, and see with what skill, in 1796, he knew how to isolate the Sardinians from the Austrians for the purpose of beating them successively at Millesimo, Mondovi, and at Lodi; with what incredible activity he availed himself of the double line of Wurmser at Lonato and Castiglione, as at Roveredo and Bassano. However, at this period, a simple general, he could only command a few battalions, which were always greatly inferior to those of the Austrians.*

Applying the system of Napoleon to the position of Frederick in 1759, it will be seen that instead of an unfortunate

* Since this chapter was written, the campaigns of 1805 and 1809 have left nothing to be added to the other proofs. It is well known with what rapidity Napoleon could avail himself of the separation of his enemy's forces.

and unproductive campaign, the imperial army should have been destroyed while the Russians were still cantoned about Thorn and Dantzick. Nothing is risked in saying that he might have united his one hundred and twenty-five battalions and one hundred and eighty squadrons about Lignitz at the end of February; pushed light troops towards Glatz, while he reached Zittau and Jung-Buntzlau by forced marches, for the purpose of isolating Daun from his secondary corps, and establishing himself upon the left of his army posted about Gitschin. By executing this march, the Prussians would have acquired the line of the Elbe; Gemmingen, Haddick, and the commander of the army of the Circles, thinking themselves cut off, would have decamped as far as Nuremberg, as they did in a situation less dangerous. Marshal Daun turned by his left would have been in a condition to be forestalled everywhere, and thrown back upon the chain of the Riesengebirge, or upon the Oder and the fortresses of Silesia.

It is not to be concealed that a skillful and active general, well informed of all the movements of his adversary, might have retreated upon Königgratz, and thence upon Olmütz; but if he lost a single day in this first position, the king would have anticipated him at Chrudim; from that time it would have been impossible to reach Olmütz, and the loss of a battle then would have annihilated the Austrian army. Moreover, this hypothesis of the possibility of a retreat, rests upon a contingency which had no existence, namely *Daun's activity*.

Had the king preferred to operate by the left against the extreme right of the enemy's line, it was necessary for him to march from Glatz and Schweidnitz concentrically toward Jaromirs and Königgratz, for the purpose of afterwards constantly gaining the Austrians by the left bank of the Elbe, either toward Chrudim or Nimburg; three or four forced marches would have decided the operation. This plan, perhaps, appeared preferable to an attempt against the left by Zittau and Buntzlau, since it presented a surer base of communication; but on the other hand, as it did not offer the advantage of cutting the middle of the enemy's line of operation, which was too extended, for the purpose of preventing the union of the Austrian forces, it seems that the former was the more desirable.

As it was, whichever plan had been adopted, if founded upon the general concentration of all the forces, and upon vigorous and rapid movements against Daun alone, the most brilliant results would have followed. Frederick lost four months in camp without any known object, confining himself to the insignificant secondary object of pushing the army of the Circles into Franconia. That army was not to be feared, not even when under the very walls of Dresden, for it would have evacuated Saxony at the first news of the king's march against Daun. He might have made better use of the forty-three battalions and sixty squadrons under Prince Henry, by uniting them to that army which was to decide the grand question. Their employment could very well have been changed when the Russians operated upon the Oder, and it would not have been difficult to decide then whether the favorable moment had arrived for abandoning the fate of Saxony to that of the fortress of Dresden.

We can not account for Frederick's obstinate tenacity of Silesia, remaining, as he did about Landshut or Schmotseifen for four months, when Daun was menacing Lusatia, and had separated his army from that of Prince Henry. There was little use in covering all the villages of Silesia; was it not sufficiently protected by its eight fortresses? What he should have done was, to expel Daun from Marclissa towards Olmütz or Prague, whichever appeared more practicable.

A fault of still greater magnitude was that of remaining

during the months of July and August in the camp of Schmotseifen when Daun's force was scattered; he having detachments on the Oder, about Dresden, at Marclissa, and at Pribus. The king says, in his works, that the camp was capable of resisting eighty thousand Austrians; but how could he face an army marching in the direction of Frankfort, while he remained quietly in Upper Silesia, upon the confines of Bohemia? The fact was, that the camp of Schmotseifen, fronting towards the mountains, interposed no obstacle to the movements which Daun might be disposed to undertake to effect his junction with the Russians.

The conduct of Frederick in the operations relating to the latter does not appear in a more favorable light. Instead of sending Count Dohna a simple reënforcement from the army of Saxony, which was not large enough to secure the battle of Kay, he should have sent Prince Henry with the larger part of that army to deliver the first battle to Soltikof. In five marches the Prince could have united upon the Oder his thirty battalions and forty squadrons to the twenty-seven battalions and fifty squadrons of Dohna, for the purpose of attacking the Russians between that river and the Wartha, before the Austrians could have joined them. Frederick, dissatisfied with the operations of Dohna, and making arrangements to concentrate his forces against the Russians, ought not to have partially engaged Wedel at a moment when Prince Henry and Fink were marching towards him, promising to operate in a few days a simultaneous and decisive effort against them. It was most necessary to effect this movement before the battle of Kay; why, then, not have done it?

It was a reprehensible error to have allowed the Russians and Austrians to unite, when it might have been so easily prevented. There are occasions in war when a general may be misled or deceived by the movements and designs of the enemy, and in regard to the means which he will employ to arrive at his end; but this was not such a case; the king himself acknowledges that he had divined them all from the beginning; that Haddick's corps was destined for the Oder, and the direction which he was to take announced to him. Prince Henry was at Sorau when the Austrians were lying in rear of Pribus; how well he might have forestalled them at Sommerfeld and at Guben! The long halt of that prince at Bautzen, the corps which he left there and recalled immediately afterward, confirm the inference that the Prussians did not understand how to adopt a decisive and vigorous course of action. It is not in such cases that ten or a dozen detachments are made upon one line of operations; they should have been concentrated; have marched against the enemy, and beaten him as he was approaching from the Oder in a similar manner.

We shall say nothing of the battle of Kunersdorf, which has been heretofore examined at the end of Chapter XVII. Though the king was loser, his combinations will always be creditable to his sagacity; his spirit, tempered by misfortune, resumed all its wonted energy. His manœuvres after his defeat, as well as those of Prince Henry, are justly worthy of a tribute of praise; not because they succeeded, for that was due to the endless errors of Daun; but for the reason that even in the case where the Austrians thwarted their measures, as was easy to do, they were in conformity to true principles. *They, in fact, reëstablished the interior direction of the lines of operation of the Prussians, and, on the contrary, isolated their enemies.*

The end of the campaign exhibits still more astonishing contrasts, in the turn of events, as well as in the application of the art. *After a most bloody battle, and a total defeat, Frederick heaped success upon success, because his enemies unnecessarily committed faults. When the Russian army was retired into Poland, and his position was become as advantageous as it had been critical, he met with constant reverses.*

The affair of Maxen should be attributed in a measure to the errors of Fink; a circumstance which militates against the firmness and presence of mind of that general, was his order to General Wunsch to return with the cavalry which had already escaped; he ought rather to have followed this corps; for let the result be as it might, he could at any time have surrendered the battalions which could not be saved. Fink ought also to have attempted to retire by Glashutte and Frauenstein, or have thrown himself into Bohemia by Gishubel, and afterward moving to join the army by Basberg or any other road. It seems remarkably strange that Frederick, who has a long chapter in his instruction to his generals on the danger of large detachments, should have sent one himself of eighteen thousand men, upon the rear of the enemy, without taking steps to sustain it. This corps, not sufficing to cut off Daun's communications with Bohemia by the right bank of the Elbe, failed in its mission. Without dispute, it would have been better to have covered that river, encamping opposite Pirna; some bridges should have been laid down, and Fink's corps ought to have crossed and formed on the road from Dresden to Gishubel; for then without being exposed to any risk, Daun's direct communications would have been intercepted, and he would have been anticipated in his others.

Supposing that the king had decided to operate upon the left bank, and to send Fink's corps to Dippodiswalde, he should at least have encamped upon Daun's extreme left towards Tharandt and Rabenau, where he would have covered his detachment, and threatened to inclose the Austrian army; besides, in that position, Fink would have been at hand to combat simultaneously with the king, had the enemy undertaken anything serious.

The details of this battle can never be understood; Fink did all he could to secure his own defeat, since he confided the defense of one of the heights to some hussars, as if cavalry were capable of defending positions. He also committed the error of facing outwards and accepting a decisive combat, instead of taking the initiative for the purpose of overwhelming one of the enemy's columns. A general, who in an open field takes up a position, and allows himself to be surrounded by a triple force, and confines himself to opposing a feeble division to each column of the enemy, and thus awaits a combined effort of all the enemy's forces, violates the first and every principle of the art; for it is only by concentrating and rushing upon one of the columns of attack, that we may hope to bring about an equilibrium of forces and an equality of chances, thus breaking the unity of attack, and the simultaneousness of the shock. Principles so evident require no proof; still, let us open the history of the campaign in 1796, in Italy. The battles of Lonato, Castiglione, and especially Rivoli, demonstrate clearly that Bonaparte was victorious over Wurmser and Alvinzi, by bringing together all his means, and falling in succession upon the Austrian columns which attempted to envelope him.

Passing to the examination of the management of the Austrians, we shall have to admit that though Daun's combinations possess nothing grand, his plan was better arranged than those of his preceding campaigns; since it was based upon a concert of movement, and a general concentration of the forces of the allies. The first operations were more judicious than those of Frederick, and still their execution was not in exact accordance with true principles. The Aulic council concluded, with prudence, that it would be better to await the arrival of an army of sixty thousand Russians before attempting decisive measures. Daun's project of preventing the union of Frederick's forces by marching upon Marclissa, would have done him great credit, had he not divided his army into thirteen isolated divisions. In place of so acting, he should have allowed the army of the Circles to take care of itself, and have profited by the expedition of Prince Henry into Franconia, to unite ten of his divisions and attack the king in Silesia, who had become greatly embarrassed by the arrival of the Russians.

Undoubtedly it was more prudent to wait for the Russians; but could they really expect that Frederick would remain inactive for four months? and ought it not on the contrary to have been feared that he would unite his forces and fall upon the isolated Austrians? It was not therefore proper to divide the troops.

To prevent Frederick from communicating with Prince Henry a sufficient force had to be employed; communications are not menaced by simply maintaining a position, since there will always be a way to pass to the right or the left; if the king failed to make use of the faults of his enemies, it was an error, since in that way he lost in the defensive all that the Austrians gained.

Marshal Daun at Marclissa had detachments from Troppau in Upper Silesia, as far as Culmbach in Franconia. This miserable system of covering everything ought not to have been the one pursued by a power like Austria, in operating against a king nearly deprived of all his real resources. A war of invasion is advantageous, especially when directed against a country of small extent, and whose principal resources are found upon the very theatre of operations; Frederick's enemies misunderstood this truth, for otherwise they would have made but one campaign.

Daun deserves severe censure for not reaping any advantages from this fine position after the battle of Kay. On the 28th, the Russians were at Crossen; Haddick at Pribus; the Austrian army at Marclissa; Prince Henry was lying near Sagan with a feeble corps, and Wedel was retired to Logau. The marshal should have moved upon Sagan by forced marches, and there have attacked the prince, whilst Haddick was reaching Sommerfeld or Christianstadt. The concentration of sixty thousand Austrians upon this point would have enabled him to push Prince Henry before him, and throw him upon the Russian army, by cutting him off from the king. This movement would have been half finished before the king could have heard of it, and an Austrian division should have remained at Lauban to mislead him and retard his march. Somewhat later Daun executed his movement upon Pribus very well without disquieting the Prussians encamped at Schmotseifen.

We have now arrived at the examination of the most extraordinary period of the entire war; *the sequence of the battle of Kunersdorf.* Whilst the Russians were fighting with such fury, Daun halted at Pribus, and Haddick was at Guben; these two corps, forming above fifty thousand men, remained inactive instead of marching upon Mulrose and Frankfort, to strike the last blow against the king; the remnant of the Prussian army might have been cut off from its base, thrown upon the right bank of the Oder, and successively pushed to the sea towards Stettin. Daun and Haddick had greater inducements to act thus, since in case of a reverse, they might cover the retreat of the Russian army along the Oder, and have effected a junction with it to reëstablish their affairs.

If the inactivity of the Austrian general at this period be blamable, it became unpardonable after the battle of Kunersdorf. Since Frederick had begun the war, he had been beaten at Kollin, surprised at Hohenkirch, but had not been completely beaten except at Kunersdorf. The force of his remnant was known. Daun, in three marches, might have joined Haddick, towards Lubben, and marched directly upon Berlin, in order to gain the rear of the Prussians. By this manœuvre the king would have lost all means of salvation, for the mass of his victorious enemies would have been established in the heart of his small states, the fate of which would not have been long doubtful.

This fact proves that Daun, instead of waiting at Pribus and Tribel until the 2d of September, ought to have marched to Mulrose, or at least to Guben, in order to have been ready either to join the Russians, or to deal the last blow to the king, whichever way affairs might have turned.

Soltikof's inactivity after the battle was pardonable, because his army had done everything, and it had become a scandal that Daun's had not burned a cartridge. The dissension and misunderstanding which existed between them was due to the coalition, *which did not recognise a chief*. From this it followed that Frederick gained time, and in war time is everything. It is by losing a few hours an army may become only partially engaged; that it may be overwhelmed by the masses of the enemy, and thus lose its communications and great chances; finally, the conquered may be able to repair the disasters of defeat. Genius does not always preside over victories, but it alone can gather the fruits of one. Napoleon might be cited as an example. What a distance exists, in reality, between the combinations which led to the results of Bassano, Marengo, Ulm, Jena, and Friedland, and the feeble conceptions of those mediocre generals, victorious by chance alone! After all, it is not combinations guaranteeing success to which the talent of great captains is limited. It extends to the vigor with which they gather up the fruits of their original plans. The manœuvres which proved so fatal to Wurmser, Melas, Mack, and the duke of Brunswick, would have been only useless menaces, had not the genius which originated them presided over their execution. Napoleon never delivered a battle simply to gain it, but in order to complete the destruction of the enemy's organized corps. It is true that the force of an army resides no less in the unity of plans and movements than in its physical constitution. After a defeat this unity does not exist; the beaten generals are often without objects, uncertain as to the direction of their columns, and their disorganized corps without communication with their chiefs, who gave them impulsion. This is the favorable moment to attack them, particularly if we have a good base. It is absurd to rest quietly before the vanquished, and give time to an adversary to reorganize his means of resistance.

The army of Frederick II. would have been destroyed if Daun had manœuvred like Napoleon after the battle of Jena, in 1806, and Frederick III. would have saved the *débris* of his, had he been allowed as much time after the battle of Auerstedt as the Austrian marshal allowed to the remains of the Prussian army at Kunersdorf.*

Thus far the faults of the Austrian general show his want of resolution, but his retreat upon Bautzen is unpardonable. Having succeeded, in consequence of a good original plan, and the false manœuvres of the king, in uniting the combined armies in a central position in the heart of the Prussian states, there remained nothing more to do but to direct a decisive effort against one or other of these separate bodies. It was of little consequence that Prince Henry menaced

* Since the first edition of this work was published, Napoleon has been overthrown by the application of the same principles; the vigor developed by the Russian armies in 1812, broke his empire, and the pursuit after the battle of Leipsic made it fall to pieces. If Daun and Soltikof had acted with similar energy, Frederick could not have withstood their attack one month. Those who wish to institute a parallel between these two wars, and judge of the resistance of Frederick from the events of our times, will be greatly deceived.

Upper Lusatia; he should have been allowed to proceed, for he separated himself more and more from the secondary line which he had to maintain, and to which he would be obliged again to return. On the other hand, that excursion of his afforded facilities for crushing the feeble corps of Frederick at Furstenwalde. But, instead of rejoicing at the movement of the prince, Daun became frightened, and abandoned all the advantages of concentration, and went into camp at Bautzen to protect some flour. *That incomprehensible conduct afforded his enemies, in their turn, a chance to form an interior mass, which thwarted all his subsequent movements, discouraged the Russians, and was more useful to the Prussians than the victory of Kunersdorf had been to the confederates.*

Daun might have more certainly disquieted the prince, had he moved by forced marches upon Luben and cut off Frederick's communications, who was already hard pressed upon his front by the Russian army.

Notwithstanding all his errors, praise is due to the marshal for the affair at Maxen; he skillfully availed himself of the large detachments imprudently pushed out without support. His conduct on this occasion is another proof of *what may be accomplished by a central mass against isolated parts of an army, by taking the initiative of the movements and so concealing it for some time.* Fink was destroyed, and the king, who could have had no doubt of it, remained tranquil in his camp at Wildsruff.

Daun, however, made no use of his success; the capture of the corps of Fink and Dierke had restored the confidence of his army; he had a place of arms at Dresden where he could repose in case of a check. He neither dared to march against the king nor attack him vigorously by manœuvring by his right, in order to cut him off from the Elbe and his base of operations. It has been said that the season was advanced; but fighting has been carried on since in Poland, with a greater degree of cold; besides, amid the sands of Saxony and Brandenburg, the roads are better in winter than in summer. Lastly, he afforded Frederick time to repair the loss of half his army, and was thoroughly punished for it in the succeeding campaign.

We will not enlarge upon the operations of Soltikof; he manœuvred very skillfully against Dohna, and extricated himself honorably from the battle of Zulichau; he received that of Frankfort in a position, strong it is true, but of which the communications were held by the enemy, and he thus exposed his army to total destruction. The courage of his soldiers, and the attack of Laudon made at the decisive moment, happily relieved him from this bad position. The marshal committed a graver fault before the battle in not patrolling in the direction of Bischofsee, towards the forest by which the king was to come out. This fault enabled Frederick to conceal his first movement, and to surprise with all his forces an extremity of the enemy's line, which would have been destroyed had the Prussians made vigorous use of this great advantage.

Soltikof's inactivity in the period which followed the battle of Kunersdorf is so much the less excusable, since he had numerous cavalry, and might have vigorously pushed the Prussians, already in disorder, without fear of meeting much resistance, and with the certainty of overthrowing them at the Oder. After the king had passed that river, he might still have destroyed him; but if his conduct was contrary to the rules of war, it was excused, if not justified, by well-founded political dissatisfaction.

CHAPTER XXI.

CAMPAIGN OF 1760; GENERAL PREPARATIONS; OPERATIONS OF THE FRENCH AND ALLIED ARMIES.

WHILST the armies were resting somewhat from their labors, Frederick employed the spare time in negotiating, for the purpose of detaching some of the powers from the formidable league which was arrayed against him; and took occasion, at the same time, to reorganize and fill up the higher grades of his army. The disaster of Maxen had swept away entire corps; and so few of the officers were left, that many of the regiments had not more than half of their complement; for Frederick, although he affected, to such an extent, a philosophical turn of mind, and crushed under foot a thousand prejudices, respected those of the nobility, and dared not throw open the career of arms to the competition of all of the citizens. The recruiting service did not furnish soldiers of a hardy constitution, but only battalions which served to swell the *numbers* of the forces. The material of artillery was repaired and completed. The cavalry was remounted.

Meanwhile, the negotiations commenced by the king miscarried, both at Versailles and at St. Petersburg; the French cabinet was sincerely attached to Austria; that of St. Petersburg was controlled by a favorite devoted to the interest of Maria Theresa.

The English, who feigned a desire for peace, affixed, without doubt, a price too high, and continued their subsidies to their auxiliaries: the army of Duke Ferdinand was raised to seventy thousand men, including the English troops, with those of Hanover, Hesse, and Brunswick.

The cabinet of Versailles, on its side, placed the French armies upon a respectable footing, and confided the chief command to the duke of Broglio. The grand army numbered eighty thousand men; the count of St. Germain commanded, upon the Lower Rhine, a corps of thirty thousand men, and the Prince Xavier a reserve of fifteen thousand.

Austria and Russia had reënforced their armies, and settled a plan of concentration upon the Oder, which was better conceived than that of the preceding campaign. Laudon was sent to command a considerable corps in Silesia, and to operate upon the Oder, in conjunction with Soltikof. Daun, with an army of one hundred thousand men, was to retain the king in Saxony, or to follow him, in case he should march to the relief of Silesia.

Everything augured the approaching ruin of Frederick, and the first occurrences of the campaign would have removed all doubt upon this subject, had not the allies committed their previous faults.

The plan of Marshal Broglio was to seize upon Hesse and Hanover. His intention being to operate with the grand army against the left of the allies, whilst the corps under the Count St. Germain should enter Westphalia. The preparations for the campaign consumed a great deal of time; for, according to the custom of the age, the army did not commence its movement until all of the magazines, which were to subsist it, were provisioned—an operation in itself most difficult when we consider the exhausted condition of the country.

At last, on the 16th of June, the Count St. Germain passed the Rhine, and was in position on the 20th at Dortmund.

On the 22d the army encamped at Gruneberg, and on the 24th near Homberg, behind the Ohm; the light troops took post at Dillenburg and Stauffenberg. Prince Xavier quitted the episcopate of Fulde, and joined the duke of Broglio at Homburg.

As soon as Ferdinand learned of the departure of the French, he moved from Fritzlar to Neustadt. This was on the 24th. All the detached corps were drawn in, the duke's object being to attack; but finding his adversary too well posted, he retired on the 26th to Ziegenhain, behind the Schwalme, followed step by step by the French army, which went into camp at Neustadt on the 27th.

This rapid movement secured for Marshal Broglio the capture of Marburg, a fortified place, which would assure his communications. However, it was necessary to dislodge the allies from their positions, which still covered Hesse. For this purpose he resolved to manœuvre so as to cut off the duke from Lipstadt, and from Sporken's corps, which was near Lunen, watching the Count St. Germain, stationed at Dortmund.

The two armies occupied very strong positions, against either of which an attack would probably have failed, and they therefore contented themselves with skirmishes of light troops, over whose fruitless exploits we will pass in silence.

When Marshal Broglio had arranged his subsistence department, he directed the count of Saint-Germain to join him, by way of Minden and Corbach. The army was put in march during the night of the 7th and 8th, to move on Frankenberg; Prince Xavier formed the rear-guard, and was to sustain the three advanced corps under Stainville.

The duke was tardily advised of this movement; but as he could not mistake the object of it, he detached the hereditary prince with the advance-guard, and ordered General Luckner to occupy the heights of Sachsenhausen and Corbach; he followed with the rest of the army, which took post at Wildingen, on the morning of the 9th; General Kielmanseg was directed upon Frankenberg.

The French army had repassed the Eder at this point the same day. The marquis of Poyanne was to occupy the heights of Imminghausen, where the army was to be established in position, and General Klosen was to cover the march. The latter, encountering Luckner's corps near Corbach, was ordered by Marshal Broglio to dislodge it at once, and sustained the attack by a brigade of infantry and the carbineers.

Meanwhile the corps of Saint Germain, consisting of thirty-three battalions and thirty-eight squadrons, arrived at the abbey of Fritzlar, and there received orders to quicken its march, and at the same time the brigade of Klosen was directed towards the woods at the left of Corbach; the marshal himself arrived at daylight, at the head of six brigades.

During this time the hereditary prince, reunited to the corps of Kielmanseg, took possession of Corbach, and the army passed the defile of Sachsenhausen, two leagues in rear of that place. Ferdinand, who supposed that he had in his front merely the corps of Saint Germain, led himself the brigades of Bock and of Marsbourg to the attack of the woods, and dislodged the enemy therefrom.

Surprised at this vigorous action, the duke of Broglio was at first induced to suppose that all the allied army was present; but observing the weakness of the columns which followed the first, he ordered the Count Saint Germain to retake the woods, and sustained him with four brigades. This attack was impetuous. Outflanked and repulsed by superior forces, Ferdinand was obliged to charge at the head of two English regiments in order to cover his retreat, which he effected with the loss of eight hundred men and fifteen pieces of cannon. General Sporken, however, was not cut off; he retired by Buren and Stadtbergen to Landau. The hereditary prince avenged himself for this slight check by surprising, on the 16th of July, the brigade of Glaubitz, near Amenebourg; but he was less fortunate in the enterprise which he attempted against the magazines of Marburg, saved by the duke of Stainville.

The French marshal felt the absurdity of such a war, and determined to cover his communications with depôts. The corps of Prince Xavier was left at Frankenberg; that of Stainville at Marburg, and the army was extended to the left as far as the Dimel. Lieutenant-General Dumuy took command of the corps of Saint Germain, which occupied Mengerinhausen and the defile of Stadtbergen. On the other hand, the allied army was spread to the left, from Eder to Warburg; and to the right, along the Dimel, the bulk of it towards Sachsenhausen.

Meanwhile Dillenbourg surrendered to the French, on the 15th. The marshal, after providing for the security of his magazines, resolved to expel Duke Ferdinand from his position. On the 24th, he directed three considerable corps against the division of Sporken, which they menaced both in front and rear, but which, nevertheless, retired without loss upon Wolfshagen, where Ferdinand followed it the next day. The French army went into camp near Freyenhagen; with the corps of Dumuy between Volkmarsen and Marburg.

The allies moved on the 26th to Hohenkirchen, on the 27th, to Kalde near Imminghausen; the hereditary prince moved to Oberwemar; Wangenheim to Munchof; Kielmanseg upon Cassel; Luckner near Zweeren; Sporken remained at Westufeln.

The duke, in these positions, awaited his adversary, who moved on the 27th, to Volkmarsen; the reserve of Prince Xavier went to Naumburg, the corps of Stainville besieged the fort of Ziegenhain, that of Dumuy descended the Dimel upon Marburg. The object of these movements was to cut the allies off from Paderborn and Lipstadt, and to crowd them between the confluence of the Dimel, and the Weser, in order to force them to evacuate Hesse, and withdraw into Hanover.

In this false position, after having weighed the inconveniences on each side, Ferdinand moved the hereditary prince and General Sporken, with twenty-four battalions and twenty-two squadrons, to Korbeck, with the intention of securing the passage of the Dimel; but informed that Marshal Broglio had, on the 30th, taken inadvertently the direction of Zierenberg, and increased by one march the distance which separated him from the corps of Dumuy, he resolved to crush that isolated division.

Consequently, on the evening of the 30th, the army was put in march, in order to pass the Dimel, and sustain the hereditary prince in that enterprise. When, on the morning of the 31st, the heads of the columns had arrived upon the heights of Korbeck, the hereditary prince and General Sporken were seen in motion. The troops of the first were conducted, by General Zastrow, through Korbeck, Klein Eder, and Menne, in order to form three lines to the left, towards the latter village; the right to be at Ossendorf; the corps of the second was to pass, by a long detour, between Eissen and Gros Eder, crossing the woods near Narde, and forming in three lines upon the heights behind the enemy. By these dispositions the hereditary prince turned the left flank of the enemy, and, at the same time, took him in reverse. The army was to be formed with its right near Menne, and its left in rear of Warbourg, for the purpose of attacking, at the same time, in front.

Dumuy, who had notice of this movement, detached the marquis of Castries with the grenadiers and chasseurs, to observe it; but a thick fog entirely concealed it. The heads of columns of the prince arrived about two o'clock, P. M., and commenced the attack. Its success depended upon the taking of the heights of Ossendorf, and Dumuy immediately detached thither the brigade of Bourbonnais, but it was anticipated at that point by the English infantry, which sustained at once the Hessian grenadiers, and the artillery.

The combat was warm; the French successively reënforced by the brigades of the Couronne, and of Rouergue, with the Swiss regiments of Jenner and of Lochmann, opposed a fierce resistance, and did not give way, until the column of Zastrow debouched upon the right flank of the Bourbonnais, and was established upon the disputed height; an opportune charge of cavalry expedited the retreat of the Swiss and French. At this moment, there arrived on the field, the cavalry of Duke Ferdinand's army, sustained by a numerous artillery; at its approach, the French cavalry slipped away, and abandoned the infantry. Zastrow, seeing himself so well supported, redoubled his efforts, and repelled those in his front, to the bridges of Dimel. The retreat was executed under the protection of the brigades of Touraine and Latour-Dupin, formed upon the heights in front of these bridges. The French showed a disposition to hold the opposite bank of the river; but retreated upon Wolfshagen, when they saw Ferdinand send across the river twelve battalions and ten squadrons. This affair cost them four thousand killed, wounded, or taken prisoners, and twelve pieces of cannon; the loss of the allies was about twelve hundred men.

It will be remembered that the division of Kielmanseg guarded the intrenched camp at Cassel; Ferdinand, judging it impossible for him to cover at the same time Hesse and Westphalia, ordered that general to retire upon Munden, and thence to Imsen. Prince Xavier occupied Cassel, and advanced himself as far as Dransfeld. On the 4th, he encamped at Goettingen, and doubled up the enemy's corps upon Uslar and Beverungen. The French then established posts upon Nordheim and Eimbeck. Their army encamped upon the right bank of the Dimel, with the corps of Dumuy at Stadtbergen, and a division under Castries at Wolfshagen covering the convoys; the duke's division was on the left bank of that river, between Scheferde and Warburg.

The month of August passed, without any striking events. The duke of Broglio had wished, at first, to manœuvre by his left, and to push the corps of Dumuy on the right of the enemy, with a view of threatening his communications with Lipstadt; but Ferdinand promptly opposed him with sufficient forces. On the other hand, General Kielmanseg having been reënforced, and menacing Prince Xavier's corps, Broglio abandoned his first object, and determined to extend to his right, so as to support that corps, which was destined to invade Hanover; on the 20th of August, he dispatched Dumuy to Volkmissen, and went into camp with the army at Immenhausen. Dumuy then took post at Heckerhausen, upon the left flank; the duke de Stainville was transferred from Corbach to Frankenberg, covering the communications with Frankfort.

Ferdinand, with a view of parrying the effects of this movement, recalled the corps which was on his right, encamped at Bune, near Borentrick, and moved several divisions toward Bodenhagen, Beverungen, and Deissel. He was better able to defeat the projects of the enemy, on account of a reënforcement to his army, at this time, of a corps of ten thousand English, recently disembarked. On the 5th of September, the hereditary prince surprised the post of Zierenburg, where he made several hundred prisoners.

Each army was now so well established, that neither could abandon its position, without giving the other great advantages. Duke de Broglio renewed his attempts against Hanover, by the right bank of the Weser; Prince Xavier reoccupied Goettingen and Nordheim, on the 5th of September, and encamped at Eimbeck; but General Wangenheim having been reënforced by the allies, the prince, in order not to expose himself to being cut off, retired on the 12th to Witzenhausen. Ferdinand, wishing to alarm the enemy in regard to his communications with the Mein, pushed a corps upon Marburg. Marshal de Broglio secured them with the division of Stainville, which thwarted his projects, attacked the Marburg detachment towards Raden, and made four hundred prisoners.

It has been remarked that this campaign was only an imitation of war; the opposing forces amused themselves by manœuvering and threatening, making detachments and surprising them; thus setting at defiance the first principles of the art. Finally, the duke de Broglio resolved to force General Wangenheim to retire, by still further extending himself to the right. To carry out this design, he went on the 13th to Cassel, leaving General Dumuy towards Wallerhausen, and again pushing Prince Xavier upon Goettingen. Ferdinand then repassed the Dimel, moved on the 14th towards Geismar, and ordered Wangenheim to quit Uslar, and take up a position on the Werra; this general was on the 15th established at Dransfeld, and attacked unsuccessfully the post of Munden.

However, Broglio had found means to sustain Prince Xavier. He caused him to be reënforced on the 17th by eight battalions *d'élite* under General Rougé; the French grenadiers, under Saint-Pern; the carbineers, and the reserve commanded by the marquis de Poyanne, whilst Count Chabot occupied the attention of the allies, by manœuvering towards Wolfshagen on their right flank. On the 19th, the marshal joined Prince Xavier, whose corps was swelled by these reënforcements to from twenty-five to thirty thousand men, and arranged the plan of attack; but Wangenheim had time to gain without any great loss, the woods between Hameln and Ellerhausen. Although this enterprise did not meet with entire success, the French army gained ground by it; and in order to secure possession of the country during the winter, Goettingen was placed in such a state of defense, as to secure it against assault.

These operations did not accomplish their object. Ferdinand appreciated better the importance of his position than to resign it to a mere threatened danger; on the contrary, he resolved to concentrate about it all of his forces. The Marshal de Broglio, finding himself deceived, resolved to reunite the scattered troops in Flanders, and joining thereto some regiments under the command of Castries, to march them by Wesel upon the enemy's rear. Ferdinand, having been informed of this project, determined to anticipate the French near Wesel, and to make such a diversion as should force them to quit their position. The hereditary prince set out on the 22d of September from Warburg, with a corps of fifteen thousand men, whilst the duke moved the army towards Libenau.

The former arrived on the 29th at Dorsten, and blockaded Wesel on the 3d of October; his light troops passed the Rhine on the 1st, and beat up the country as far as Clèves, where they captured four hundred men. The fortress of Wesel had a feeble garrison and lacked cannoneers; it would probably have been taken, but for the obstacles encountered in the march of the siege-train, on account of heavy rains which had rendered the roads impracticable; partisans meanwhile were pushed as far as Gueldre and Ruremonde. This diversion, which would have proved fatal to its originator, had he been opposed by a skillful adversary, plunged the French generals into infinite embarrassment. This accessory became the principal object of the war, and the grand armies continued to observe each other, as if the operation of a detachment were to decide the fate of Europe.

Castries quickened his march in order to save Wesel. His corps assembled on the 13th of October at Nuys, and consisted of thirty-two battalions and thirty-eight squadrons, forming upwards of twenty thousand men; on the 14th, he marched to Meurs, and the advance-guard to Rheinbergen. As soon as the hereditary prince heard of this movement, taking the wise plan of leaving a few battalions for the service of the trenches, he flew to meet the enemy, in spite of the inferiority of his forces, and marched on the 15th to Ossenberg. Marshal de Castries was established in the rear of the Eugenienne ditch, with the right at Rheinbergen, and the left in the strong position towards Clostercamp; but after reconnoitering, the prince thought the enemy less watchful there, and resolved to surprise their left. After leaving three battalions and four squadrons opposed to the right towards Rheinbergen, he moved at eleven o'clock in the evening, with eighteen battalions and twenty squadrons upon Clostercamp. The advance-guard, at three o'clock in the morning, rushed upon a French post, situated a half league in advance of that village. They fired, contrary to the prince's order, in carrying the post; but the silence and darkness, giving rise to the belief that it was only a patrol, the army gained the canal without accident. Fischer's corps was cut off and dispersed; but the musketry alarmed the brigade Auvergne, and caused it to occupy the woods near Clostercamp, and all the outlets of that village.

The prince, still marching in the greatest silence, passed the canal at Kampen, and seized the village of Kumpenbrock. Castries' corps would have been lost, but for the devotion of the Chevalier d'Assas, a captain in the regiment of Auvergne. This officer, who commanded a post in the thickets in front of Kumpenbrock, had gone forward to learn the cause of the firing which had taken place in the direction of the convent. Suddenly surrounded by the English grenadiers, and threatened with instant death should he make the least noise, he inferred that it was a surprise, and collecting all his strength, he cried, "Come on, Auvergne, it is the enemy!" and was instantly killed. Lieutenant-General de Segur ran into the village, with a battalion of Auvergne, and was wounded and taken.

In the meantime the alarm was given; the French discovered their danger. Castries conducted the regiment of Alsace to support that of Auvergne. A Swiss brigade was moved to the flank gained by the allies, and the combat was waged with fury. The Auvergne regiment held the enemy in check until daylight, whilst the rest of the French troops were concentrating on the point of attack. After a desperate conflict, which lasted until mid-day, the allies fell back upon Alpen in good order, under the protection of a reserve, which was established in echelon. The loss of the French was about two thousand men, and that of the allies one thousand eight hundred.

Had the duke de Castries known how to profit by his advantage, the prince would have been lost, for a flood had carried away his bridge over the Rhine, and it could not be reconstructed before the 18th; but the French general allowed himself to be intimidated by the good countenance of the allies, and connived at their escape. The prince, after raising the siege, retired to Brune, and went himself, on the 27th of October, to Klein-Reckum, and the duke de Castries to Drevenich. Both sides, after watching each other for a month, went into winter quarters.

Whilst these events were transpiring on the Rhine, the principal armies were reposing on the Dimel. At length the duke, wishing to take Goettingen, passed the Weser, on the 21st of November, and invested it; but the incessant rains, the want of provisions, and the movements of the duke de Broglio, decided him to raise the blockade on the 13th of December, and to go into cantonments.

Thus ended the barren campaign of 1760. In it the opposing armies manœuvred without fighting, and fought without manœuvring. *The combats took place upon secondary points, whilst the main armies only threatened each other, by means of detachments, upon those points at which every effort should have been concentrated for the purpose of delivering a general battle.*

Tempelhof endeavored to show that the duke de Broglio adopted a bad plan in seeking to manœuvre by his right, in pushing corps upon Goettingen and Hanover, and states that it would have been better to have marched to the front by Westphalia, to have taken Lipstadt and Munster, without which his manœuvres would be merely incursions. It is easy to see that these arguments are based upon the old system. This second part of Broglio's plan, therefore, coincided with that of Contades in the preceding campaign. It consisted in manœuvring by the right, for the purpose of gaining the extreme left and rear of the enemy, thus cutting him off from the Weser. It promised, like the other, great chances of success, and, like it, failed, on account of its faulty execution, for, instead of delivering a great battle, the army remained in front of the enemy, only pushing detachments to the right.

Whilst the duke de Broglio was in possession of Cassel, and the allies were encamped upon the Dimel, it was necessary to turn them by their left near Robeck, to change direction upon Warburg, and to establish the French army perpendicular to, and with its left resting upon, that river, pushing the allies upon Lipstadt. Broglio might have accomplished all that by leaving a corps at Kalenberg and at Hochenburg; but it had to be carried out without giving the enemy time to manœuvre. *It is not by taking up positions upon their communications, and there remaining, that armies are destroyed. Had Napoleon stayed upon the Lech in* 1805, *and upon the Saale in* 1806, *he would not have prevented Mack from effecting his retreat by Donawerth, nor the duke of Brunswick from retiring upon the Elbe.*

The sieges of Lipstadt and Munster, of which Tempelhof speaks, were only secondary operations, and brought nothing to pass; one movement of Ferdinand's would have compelled the French to raise them. There is always time to look after the fortresses after deciding the question with the armies which are to succor them.

It is scarcely worth while to waste time in useless reflections upon the extraordinary expedition of the allies against Wesel. It could only withdraw extensive forces from the decisive point, for the purpose of using them in a hazardous enterprise, compromising not only the corps so employed, but also the main army. Had the duke de Broglio operated according to the rules of the art, he would most probably have made Ferdinand pay dearly for this absurd expedition.

CHAPTER XXII.

PRELIMINARY OPERATIONS IN SILESIA AND SAXONY; THE AFFAIR OF LANDSHUT AND THE SIEGE OF DRESDEN.

Without detailing the slight affairs which took place during the winter, we will confine ourselves to those operations which seem to demand our attention.

The Swedes, annoyed in their cantonments, desired to seize the bridge of Anclam, upon the Peene, to secure themselves from the hazard of a surprise. Their enterprise succeeded. They got possession of the suburbs on the 28th of January, surprised the guards, and entered pell-mell into the city. General Manteufel, bewildered in the darkness, was wounded and taken prisoner, with one hundred and fifty men. This exploit was the last one of this unfortunate army. It did not reappear upon the theatre of war until the middle of August, and then only to act a part as insignificant as heretofore.

The armies in Saxony were quiet. A few affairs of outposts occurred. Beck's corps surprised the Prussian General de Zetteritz, in the vicinity of Kosdorf, and took him prisoner.

Laudon, after having denounced the rupture of the armistice which had been concluded with his corps, endeavored to capture the one commanded by Goltz, which was cantoned in Upper Silesia, at Neustadt, and thereabouts; but that general assembled a portion of his troops in time, and concentrated them on the 14th of February at Ober-Glogau;

nevertheless, Laudon reached these with all his cavalry, and attacked the Manteufel regiment, which guarded the parks. That brave regiment was formed in a square, and continued its march, repulsed five or six charges with undaunted bravery, and arrived safely at Steinau, after having lost one hundred and forty men.

All these occurrences produced nothing decisive. The grand armies remained in their places; that of Daun, in consequence of an incredible system, after having gained most signal advantages, continued to bury itself under intrenchments in the valley of the Plauen, and fairly seemed to tremble in the presence of an adversary whom it ought to have crushed. A strong corps, commanded by Lasey, was cantoned upon the right bank of the Elbe, and pushed Beck's corps upon Zittau. The Prussian army was cantoned in their front, with its right towards Freiberg, its centre at Wilsdruf, and its left in the vicinity of Meissen. Schmettau occupied Gorlitz, with seven battalions and fifteen squadrons; Fouquet was in Upper Silesia, and was opposed to the corps of Laudon. Finally, the army of the Oder, under the command of Prince Henry, *was to make head against the Russians whenever they should appear upon the scene.*

The plan of operations on both sides differed but little from that of the preceding campaign; the coalition did not wish to strike a decisive blow in Silesia until after the arrival of the Russians; Laudon commanded an army of fifty thousand men; Daun was to keep the king in Saxony. The affairs of Frederick appeared more desperate than ever; having lost the key of Saxony, and not being able to abandon that country without leaving his own to the mercy of the enemy, it appeared as though nothing could prevent the junction of the armies of the coalition.

On the 18th of May, Prince Henry's army took up its cantonments along the Bober and the Oder to the Baltic Sea;

the bulk of it, which was between Lowenberg and Sagan, connected his right with Fouquet's corps, which was cantoned as far as Landshut. The king's army had made a slight retrograde movement upon Korbitz and Meissen. Daun remained in his position, merely sending General Berlichingen to Wilsdruff; Laudon had retired into Bohemia, leaving Draskowitz in Upper Silesia, and Wolfersdorf at Trautenau, in front of Landshut.

OPERATIONS IN SILESIA.

Whilst awaiting the arrival of the Russians, Laudon resolved to open the campaign, by the siege of Glatz, and also to seize the post of Landshut, which was necessary to secure his communications with Bohemia. He assembled his army at Kosteletz, and started on the 29th of May, encamping, on the 31st, at Frankenstein, whilst Draskowitz occupied Weidenau, and Wolfersdorf was marching to Teutsch-Prausnitz. Fouquet, hearing of these movements, moved immediately to the vicinity of Freiberg, and reported his situation to the king and Prince Henry, and demanded reënforcements. Charged with the double duty of observing Laudon and his movements against Upper Lusatia, and of covering Silesia, it was most difficult for him to carry out his objects with such a slight corps, on so vast a theatre, and that, too, in the presence of an army commanded by Laudon. Having no reënforcements to expect, he fell back, on the 4th of June, to Wurben, near Schweidnitz.

Laudon himself moved, on the 5th, in two columns, to Nimptsh and Reichembach. Fouquet established himself, on the 6th, at Romenau, for the purpose of covering Breslau. This retrograde movement enabled the Austrians to blockade Glatz, and to occupy Landshut. Laudon returned, on the 7th, to Wartha, and caused Glatz to be invested.

While these things were in progress, the king having ordered Fouquet to retake Landshut, that general left Ziethen with seven battalions upon the Ziskenberg near Furstenstein, and set out, on the 16th, for Hartmansdorf and Forste, and there learning that the enemy still had five regiments at Friedland, he resolved to attack Landshut immediately. The Austrians made a weak defense of those almost inaccessible heights, and then gradually retired to those of Reichennersdorf. Fouquet was then reënforced by three of Ziethen's battalions, and took his old post, which he strengthened by an intrenchment. The position being too extended for his corps of seventeen battalions and fourteen squadrons, he was obliged to scatter them along it. He had four battalions upon the heights of Blasdorf, two battalions and five squadrons upon the plateau of Reichennersdorf, three battalions upon the Galgenberg, two battalions and two squadrons upon the Kirchberg, two battalions and three squadrons upon the Buchberg, two battalions and two squadrons upon the Mummelberg, and two battalions at Landshut (V. Plate XXIII.).

No sooner did Laudon hear of this movement, than he resolved to attack Fouquet. With this object in view, he marched, on the 17th of June, with the reserve to Schwartzwald, and ordered the remainder of the troops before Glatz to rejoin him there, with the exception of a few battalions, which were left behind to observe the place. The corps which was at Friedland joined the army on the 18th. Nauendorf with the advance-guard took post near Forste and upon the Ziegenruck, whilst Janus still remained encamped at Reichennersdorf. General Wolfersdorf occupied Mount Nimchefsky and the bridge of Faulebruck. Lastly, Beck's corps, which was at Friedberg on the Queiss, received orders to march by Hirschberg to Schmidberg.

General Fouquet was in a critical position; he reported these movements to the king, foreseeing from them, that he could attempt nothing without risking the loss of the post he had been ordered to maintain. He promised the king to defend it to the last extremity, and solicited that a diversion might be made in his favor. On the 21st, Laudon, having been joined by the troops coming from Glatz, had forty-two battalions, seventy-five squadrons, and forty companies of grenadiers, with which force he deemed himself able to effectually crush his adversary, who had not more than twelve thousand combatants.

On the 23d of June, at two o'clock in the morning, the cannonade began, and at the same time the Austrians were seen in motion, in four columns. The first, under Laudon himself, marched by Vogelsdorf, in order to turn and attack in reverse the left wing of the Prussians. The second, under Muffling, was to carry the Mummelberg. General Campitelli with fourteen battalions was to sustain these two columns. The third, under General Geisruck, attacked Buchberg. Finally, the fourth, conducted by Generals Janus and Wolfersdorf, was to attack the right of the enemy towards Blasdorf.

The first two columns were opposed by three battalions only, which covered altogether too much ground. Laudon's regiment crept between the heights, dispersed the battalion which defended the left of the intrenchment of the Mummelberg, and fell upon the second battalion of Fouquet at the same instant that they were attacked in front by the Austrian grenadiers. The second column only encountered the battalion Mosel, which it outflanked and dispersed; then all began to give way; the two detachments which defended the Buchberg, seeing themselves attacked in turn by General Geisruck, and being menaced upon their left, abandoned their post. The left wing sounded a retreat. Fouquet sent a battalion of grenadiers to its assistance, but in spite of the bravery of the chiefs, who were killed or wounded, it was impossible to restore the battle; it retired with loss; the rest of the left fell back upon the Kirchberg; the cavalry escaped and gained the left bank of the Bober.

Whilst these events were passing on the left, the four battalions on the right, under General Schenkendorf, were attacked by the fourth column, consisting of sixteen battalions and thirty squadrons. After a good defense, the Austrians carried the heights of Blasdorf and Reichennersdorf. The discomfited battalions were re-formed, under the protection of the Galgenberg, from whence Fouquet ordered them to retake their position; this attack was executed with courage; three flags were taken from the enemy, who was thrown back upon Hennersdorf. Things remained thus on this point, while the Austrians moved a brigade of infantry, and all the cavalry of their left, beyond the Bober, in order to cut off from Fouquet his last chance of retreat. The latter, not wishing to quit his post, sent three squadrons to observe this movement.

Thus far the enemy had only gained possession of secondary points; the principal corps still held the heights of the Galgenberg and the Kirchberg, whither all the routed battalions had rallied. Laudon then made his dispositions to storm those heights. The cavalry of his right became useless, owing to the steepness of the heights and the intrenched position of the enemy. He therefore detached it to the left bank of the Bober, for the purpose of falling upon what might remain of the enemy, after they should be driven from their post. He established a battery of twelve-pounders upon the Ziegelberg, in front of Kirchberg, and divided his infantry into two columns, the first of which went round by Landshut, for the purpose of gaining the left of the Prussian position; the second passed through the village of Zieder and attacked the Kirchberg in front. This latter preceded the other some little time; but it was repelled in disorder upon Zieder. However, Laudon, having seized Landshut, passed through the village and carried the redoubt on the Kirchberg, when the first column returned immediately to the charge. The Prussians, who defended this height, although nearly surrounded, effected their retreat with firmness to the Galgenberg.

Fouquet had but two courses left, either to sell his life dearly on the Galgenberg, or cut his way through: he chose the latter. He sent to General Schenkendorf the order to repass the Bober; the officer who carried it was killed. Fouquet then sent a second order by his son, and commenced the march himself with two battalions. On arriving at Leppersdorf, the enemy's cavalry was found in possession of all the passes. Not wishing to give the Austrians time to close upon him, he formed his troops in a square, and harangued them. The Austrian cavalry then attacked him fiercely. Lowenstein's dragoons were several times thrown upon the Prussian bayonets; a well sustained fire made them pay dearly for these efforts. However, their attacks afforded time for a battalion of grenadiers to arrive to the assistance of the imperial squadrons. The combat was then very unequal; Fouquet's horse was killed under him; the infantry were broken and thrown upon their general; the bravest of them making a rampart for him of their bodies. The struggle was horrible, Fouquet was mutilated by three sabre cuts, and was finally saved by the colonel of the Lowenstein dragoons, to whom he surrendered his sword.

On his side, Schenkendorf was defending himself bravely when he received the order to cross the Bober. In making his retreat he had his horse killed under him, and thus fell into the hands of the enemy. Major Arnin, Adjutant Treskow, and some other officers, placed themselves at the head of the troops, safely repassed the Bober, and formed a square which repulsed two charges of cavalry, and gained the heights of Reisdorf; but seeing, in the ravine, several battalions deployed, and on the point of attacking them, in concert with the cavalry, they desired to hasten their march, in order to reach the woods of Reisdorf. This movement caused disorder, and the Austrians quickly profited by it. They fell furiously upon the broken infantry, and sabred a great part of it. The Prussian cavalry, which had also passed the Bober, fought a long time against superior forces; the bravest escaped, and the rest were made prisoners.

Thus ended the unfortunate affair of Landshut, where Fouquet fought with all the courage of a brave man; near fifteen hundred men succeeded in escaping; seven thousand five hundred were made prisoners, of whom half were wounded. The Austrians had more than three thousand men disabled.

General Ziethen, hearing of this event, quitted the Ziskenberg, retired upon Breslau, and collected the remains of the army of his colleague.

Fouquet seems to have been clear of all blame, since he foresaw the disaster, and apprised the king of it, but did nothing to avert it, manifesting a blind obedience.

Still, his position appears to have been too much extended; the camp of Landshut was a known military position; Frederick, it is true, attached to it as much importance as Leonidas did to Thermopylæ; but Fouquet should have known that the occupation of the heights of Blasdorf and the Mummelberg scattered his troops too much. The position, properly speaking, is that of the Galgenberg and of the Kirchberg, shut in by the ravines which run to the right by Hennersdorf, and to the left by Zieder. Since he concluded to give battle, he should have concentrated his troops with his left at the Kirchberg, and his right at Hennersdorf, in order to shorten his line. It is true, he ran the risk of being turned; but this was unavoidable, whatever position he might have taken up; and in fact, it did happen, notwithstanding the occupation of Mummelberg. Besides, he would thus have preserved the *morale* of his troops, and his presence of mind, and might have taken the initiative, and fallen upon one of the enemy's corps before becoming shut up too closely. But it is beyond dispute, that if he did not wish to retire without fighting, his best course was to throw himself *en masse* by Vogelsdorf, upon the column of Laudon; for he could not deceive himself as to the fate of his scattered detachments. Manœuvring in this manner, he would have been certain to have seized the road to Schweidnitz. It was a grievous error in the king to leave this corps without sustaining it, whilst Prince Henry was lying idle with forty thousand men, within three marches of Landshut. In such a position, Fouquet should, at least, have been given the alternative of seeking refuge under the cannon of the fortresses near at hand, or of joining the Prince. Further on, these remarks will be extended, adding the considerations which follow from the general condition of affairs.

Laudon did not know how to gather the fruits of his victory. Silesia was laid open, and should they desire to await the Russians, before invading it, there were some fortresses, at least, which might be taken; but the Austrians did not even begin the siege of Glatz, because their arrangements were so badly made that they had not the necessary provisions.

OPERATIONS IN SAXONY.

Whilst Prince Henry's army lay idle on the Bober, Fouquet's corps only three marches distant was crushed, and the king appeared undecided, as to what course he should pursue.

We have already seen, that having made a retrograde movement, on the 25th of April, he was then encamped near

Meissen, with a portion of the army, leaving the rest cantoned in rear of that place.

Tempelhof has presented a multitude of combinations which were then occupying the king's attention, for the purpose of succoring Silesia, and at the same time protecting Saxony. He contends that his plan was to draw away Daun into Silesia, from the fear that he might undertake something formidable towards Saxony. It was difficult to understand what interest the king had in *concentrating the mass of the enemy's forces, upon the point where he himself desired to operate, thus bringing about the junction of the Austrian and Russian armies, the very thing of all others, from which he had the most to fear.* Whatever may have been the foundation for such an opinion, it will be observed in a chapter of general observations, that it was only by a course directly the opposite of this, that he could hope to avert the storm which was ready to burst upon his head.

However, Frederick prepared to march into Silesia on the 4th of June. On the 6th, he caused a strong battery to be established on the heights of Sedlitz, and on the 11th, detached General Krokow with thirty squadrons by Torgau to Kosdorf, for the purpose of covering the passage, by observing the corps of Lascy, which was encamped upon the heights of Boxdorf. This passage of the Elbe was effectuated on the evening of the 14th, by the first line of infantry in boats, and by the cavalry on a bridge of boats. These troops encamped at Broschof. The second line, commanded by General Bulow, remained at Schlettau, and Hulsen at Katzenhauser, to cover the operation. The bridge was transferred to Meissen, and one was established at Kohlhof.

Daun was promptly informed, that the enemy had passed the Elbe, with only a part of his forces: it rested with him alone, whether one of these isolated bodies should be destroyed, for he could accomplish it by moving his army in the evening of the 15th, by lines and by the right, from Grossenhain to Radeburg, in order to arrive at daylight at Gros-Dobritz, upon the extreme left of the king, whilst Lascy's corps should move along the Elbe, to attack his right towards Meissen. The Austrian general had every incentive to deliver a battle in a position possessing so many advantages; he was now able to strike a decisive blow, without running the least risk, having a secure retreat upon Dresden. Instead of operating in the manner pointed out, Daun feared that Lascy was to be attacked, and moved the first line of the right wing to Wilschdorf, to assist him in case of need. On the 17th, and not till then, he followed with the remainder of the right wing, to Boxdorf, and replaced the corps of Lascy, which was sent to Bernsdorf. In a short time, this movement was followed by the left wing, and the detachments scattered thereabouts, and the camp of Boxdorf was intrenched.

On the other side, General Bulow also, on the 17th, quitted the camp of Schlettau, where he had halted with the second line, and rejoined the king.

At the opening of the campaign Frederick reminded his generals, that it would be more necessary than ever to make rapid and long marches, and to endure fatigues with constancy and courage. No sooner was he informed of Lascy's movement upon Radeburg, than he went there himself on the 18th, marching in three columns, and encamped with his left resting on that village, and his right at Barbisdorf. Lascy appeared to hold on to his position, and Frederick ordered General Hulsen to join him with all his force, except seven battalions and five squadrons. He assembled his generals, and gave them the dispositions he had made for the attack, which was to be made in two lines of infantry, with the cavalry on the wings, and with a third line as a reserve. Early on the morning of the 19th, the army was in motion;

but the patrols announced that Lasey had retired. In fact, Daun, having been informed of the king's march upon Radeburg, had drawn in all of the troops remaining on the left bank of the Elbe, and ordered Lascy to take position at Laues, for the purpose of covering the right flank of the Austrian army, which was under arms an hour before daylight in its camp at Reichenberg.

Nothing could be attempted against an enemy so well prepared, and in a position which was almost unassailable. The king returned to camp, merely occupying Bernsdorf, and posting Hulsen towards Gros-Dobritz, to sustain the corps of Linden, which was left at Schlettau; he also posted nine battalions upon the heights of Beerwald.

On the 22nd of June, the army of the Circles arrived in the neighborhood of Dresden, to form a connection with the Austrian army under Daun, encamped in the valley of Plauen; this reënforcement raised the imperial army to more than eighty thousand combatants. Daun failed to make use of this superiority to strike any decisive blows, and confined himself to annoying their posts with General Lascy.

It would seem that the projects attributed by Tempelhof to Frederick, existed only in his imagination; for it is extremely improbable that Frederick would have remained eight days at Radeburg, when even minutes were so precious. On the contrary, this fault would have appeared inexplicable.

On the 25th the news arrived of the destruction of Fouquet's corps; the Austrians received it with demonstrations of joy. The king was terribly depressed by such a severe blow, but soon regained his usual serenity. It was necessary to put a good face on the failures or abandon the contest. It was under such difficulties that Frederick ever showed himself a great man. Though his genius did not always enable him to adopt combinations which would inevitably lead to great results, yet it is acknowledged that his character lost nothing of its elevation. Each day his situation became more critical. For eighteen months reverse had followed reverse, and but for the unskillfulness of his adversaries his doom had been sealed. Accurate plans, rapidly and fearlessly executed, could only extricate him from his difficulties; but, under circumstances so decisive, his talents shone less than his courage.

Frederick now abandoned the idea of going into Silesia, and determined on an enterprise against Dresden. If this enterprise promised anything like success, it should have been contemplated and executed at the commencement of the campaign, as has been constantly pointed out; but the time chosen was a bad one. Besides, it presented most unfavorable chances, since everything was to be feared in case of failure.

Without stopping to calculate the obstacles which might be thrown in his way by an army superior to his own, the king sent an order to Magdeburg to have a siege-train got ready immediately. He endeavored also to oust Daun from his position, in order to get a chance of bringing him to battle. For this purpose, on the morning of the 26th, he quitted the camp at Radeburg, and retired, in three columns, to Gros-Dobritz. But these manœuvres were ineffectual. The imperturbable marshal multiplied the intrenchments of his camp about Boxdorf. A Fabius when he should be an Alexander, he made, most inaptly, a war of positions, merely pushing detachments upon Schoenfels, Blockwitz, and Grossenhain, to observe and scour the roads of Ortrand.

On the 29th, the king learned that Lascy had quitted Laues, reënforced by a portion of Daun's army, and had moved by Radeburg upon Krakau. At first, believing that he was about to have an engagement with the enemy, he detached General Ziethen to follow him by Lampersdorf, and to observe his movements; but, deceived anew, he despaired of making him accept a pitched battle. Herein Tempelhof contradicts himself. At one time the king is preparing for the siege of Dresden, at another he affirms that it is his intention *to gain a march to carry him into Silesia.* As it was, Frederick moved, on the 2d of July, into the camp of Quolsdorf, whilst Hulsen returned, by the left bank of the Elbe, to that of Schlettau.

When Daun was informed of the enemy's march upon Krakau, he ordered Lasey not to lose sight of them. Consequently that general took up a position at Lichtenberg. The Austrian army was directed on the 3d to Hartha. Frederick rested at Quolsdorf, and only placed an advance-guard at Pulsnitz, from which he learned the movements of Lasey. He resolved to attack; and more perfectly to mislead the enemy, he gave out that the army would march to Hoyerswerda. Daun, fearing that the design of the king was to gain the road to Silesia, hastened to secure those of Bautzen and Gorlitz, by moving, during the night, into the first-named village, the second line, commanded by General count de Wied.

The Prussian army, on the contrary, started at midnight to form on the heights of Neuendorf; but Lasey's outposts informed that general in time, and he fell back upon Daun's army. The Prussians were not able to overtake his rear-guard, owing to the difficulties of the ground. The king bivouacked this side of Pulsnitz, towards Ohorn, and took up his line of march on the morning of the 5th of July, to go into camp near the convent of Marienstern. After the departure of the Prussians, Lasey again moved to the front, and took position at Bischofswerda.

Daun, still uneasy in regard to the road into Silesia, started on the 4th, at noon, with the rest of his troops, to follow the count de Wied to Bautzen. He continued his movement on the 6th, going into camp at Reichembach, and leaving at Bautzen a body of troops intended to communicate with Lascy's corps. The Austrian army made this march of eight leagues very rapidly, in spite of heat so excessive that more than two hundred men fell dead upon the road.

On his side, Frederick proposed to pass the river Spree in three columns, and to encamp in front of Leichnam; but when he arrived near Pannevitz, with the head of the first, he learned that Daun was marching upon Reichembach, and that far from anticipating him there, he would scarcely come up with him. This induced him to take advantage of the isolation of Lascy's corps, and try again to attack him. Instead of marching upon Leichnam, he changed his direction to the right, passed the Spree at Jurke, and went into camp towards Doberschutz, upon the heights which he had occupied after the battle of Hohenkirch. On the morning of the 7th, at the head of a body of cavalry, he beat up the enemy's posts. Carried away by his excitement he was immediately engaged with all of the cavalry of Lascy, and was only relieved from this awkward position by the arrival of a battalion of grenadiers, which covered his squadrons while they rallied.

The next day was named for the attack of Lascy's corps. In spite of all the little ruses employed by Frederick to spread the rumor that he had returned to Reichembach, he was unable to prevent Lascy from discovering that he had passed the Spree on the evening of the 6th. The Austrian general commenced his march about one o'clock in the morning, and retired successfully from Bischofswerda upon Weissenhirsch. The king vainly launched his cavalry in pursuit of them, and took post himself at Bartha, in which place he, for the first time, broached to the commandant of the artillery his project of the siege of Dresden.

On the 10th, Lascy crossed the Elbe, and encamped at

Gros-Sedlitz; the king was at Durrenbuhlau. On the 12th, the first line was sent to level the intrenchments of Boxdorf, which Daun had so carefully constructed; the second line remained at Weissig, under the duke of Holstein. General Hulsen encamped at Mohschatz, upon the left bank of the Elbe, and covered the passage of that river, which took place on the morning of the 13th. The king wished to march by Dippodiswalde, for the purpose of obliging the army of the Circles to fight or evacuate the camp of Plauen; but he was saved from the difficulties of this extensive movement by the army abandoning its camp during the night of the 12th and 13th, and falling back upon Dohna, where it joined Lascy, after throwing a reënforcement of ten thousand men into Dresden, which raised that garrison to fifteen thousand combatants. The king, hearing of these movements during his march, directed himself on Dresden by Plauen and Lubnitz. The duke of Holstein left Weissig, and invested that place on the right bank of the Elbe.

On the morning of the 14th, the commandant was summoned; he replied, as is customary, in the negative. The Prussians effected a lodgment in the Pirna suburb, and established there mortar and ricochet batteries behind the ruins of the buildings burnt in the last siege. During the night they threw up a battery for eight guns and two howitzers in the Mozinsky garden; during that of the 15th and 16th, a small parallel was opened opposite the new city, and a battery for ten pieces was finished, to play against the bridge of the Elbe.

Daun, who was expecting that the king would show himself at the passes into Silesia, was not a little astonished when he heard, on the 10th of July, that he had turned against Dresden; he detached General Reid to follow him, moving his advance-guard to Bautzen, and before undertaking anything, waited to receive more accurate intelligence as to the plans of the Prussians. At last, learning, on the 13th, that Frederick had passed the Elbe, and marched against the place, he sent forward the next day, at two o'clock in the morning, the corps of carbineers, and directed Buccow's corps, which had been stationed so long at Gorlitz, to march upon Dresden; following himself with the army on the 15th, and taking post near Gorlitz.

The king pressed forward the siege works with all possible vigor. On the 18th, the breaching and mortar batteries were finished, and the firing commenced on the morning of the 19th. The same day, he heard of Daun's advance to relieve the place, and that he was already near Weissig. He sent a regiment to reënforce the duke of Holstein, whom the Austrians would be able to attack with most advantage. The Croats having seized the post of Weissenhirsch, the duke thought that they were sustained by Daun's advance-guard, and fearing a serious engagement, he repassed the Elbe without delay, leaving general Tettenborn with a brigade to protect the movement. This general, engaged in front with the Croats, was near being taken in reverse by a regiment which sallied out of the fort, and he was obliged to retreat with a loss of seven hundred men. The duke of Holstein effected his passage without annoyance from the numerous garrison. However, General Maquire caused several sorties on the following days. On the night of the 20th of July, the Austrian cavalry surprised the outposts, and penetrated even to the king's quarters, who came near being carried off by them.

Frederick, having concentrated his forces on the left bank of the Elbe, presuming that Daun desired to attack him, resolved to anticipate him. But it would seem that this campaign was to exhaust itself in projects and plans; the enemy remained quiet, and the Prussians confined themselves to occupying the heights of Rupchen and Gopeln, with eight battalions and eighteen squadrons. Daun took post on the 21st, between Boxdorf and Dresden.

The bombardment continued; the Austrians made a grand sortie at midnight, surprised the regiment of Bernburg in the trenches, and carried a battery; reënforcements arrived and repulsed them. The king, dissatisfied with the regiment which was surprised, took away their sabres.

Convinced at last of the futility of his efforts, he decided to raise the siege; the removing of the material commenced on the 27th, and the king set out with the army on the 29th, at ten o'clock in the evening; the guard of the trenches forming the rear-guard. On the 30th, General Hulsen was detached with a division to Kesselsdorf, and General Wedel to Kienast near Meissen, in order to protect the construction of a bridge. The king encamped at Unkendorf. On the 31st, he went to Meissen, and Hulsen to Schlettau. After the departure of the Prussians, Lasey went on the 30th to establish himself in the valley of Plauen. Daun marched on the 31st to Bischofswerda. Lasey passed the Elbe, and took post at Ubigau.

The Austrian general did not doubt that the king would march into Silesia, but as the operation against Dresden had taught him a lesson, he concluded to wait until the designs of the Prussians were better developed, and limited himself to measures, which were taken to harass their march. Brentano and Reid, with a multitude of light troops, burned the bridges of the Rader and the Spree, and closed all the roads. Beck did the same on the Spree, the Neisse and the Queiss, and protected by abatis, the great forests of Pribus, Muska, etc.

CAPTURE OF GLATZ.

It has already been remarked that Laudon, after the destruction of Fouquet's corps, undertook no other enterprise, and that even before Glatz, which had been a long time invested, trenches were not opened until a month afterwards. This inaction was the more reprehensible, since, on the 26th of June, General Stampa had left the grand army with a reënforcement for him, and General Beck's corps was also to rejoin his army. With such a large force he should have been able not only to cover the siege from the army under Prince Henry, but also, at the same time, to have operated vigorously in concert with Daun against the king.

The preparatory movements of the king, for commencing his march into Silesia, had disconcerted Daun; and the pusillanimous misgivings which beset him caused him to leave Laudon in observation at Landshut, and to direct him afterwards upon the Bober, in order to hold the communication with Breslau. On the 5th of July, Laudon was encamped towards Lahn, where he was apprised that Daun was at Bautzen, and that the king was on the road to Silesia. He then hastened to gain, by a forced march, the heights of Hochkirch (two leagues from Lignitz), where he feared that Frederick would arrive before him. The marshal encamped the same day at Ottendorf; Laudon had an interview with him, and the siege of Glatz was at last resolved upon. His corps remained at Hochkirch, in order to cover the siege, and the blockading division, reinforced by twelve battalions and five squadrons, was placed under the command of General Harsch.

The artillery arrived from Olmütz on the 16th, and the trenches were opened on the 21st. Laudon went himself, on the 25th, to join the siege corps, and had the batteries open fire the next day. The slowness of the Austrians was counterbalanced by the negligence of the Prussians. The videttes of the besiegers, who occupied an abandoned *flèche*, thought that they discovered that the covered way was not guarded, and slipping up there, they found the sentinels all asleep. Laudon at once sent three battalions thither, which quickly routed the guard, and entered the old town along with them, without the officer who commanded there knowing it. The new fortress could still have been well defended, but Colonel Oo surrendered it at discretion. Thus fell the important key of Silesia. Frederick asserts in his works, that Laudon had here gained intelligence, through the assistance of the Catholic clergy, and especially by the aid of the Jesuits, who were sworn enemies of the Prussian name. Be this as it may, this event, which was one of the most extraordinary in military annals, secured to the enemies of the king a base of operations against Silesia, as Dresden had furnished them one for their enterprises against Saxony.

CHAPTER XXIII.

EARLY OPERATIONS OF PRINCE HENRY AND THE RUSSIANS; SIEGE OF BRESLAU; THE THEATRE OF WAR CENTRES IN SILESIA; BATTLE OF LIGNITZ.

WHILST Frederick was sunk in apathy, experiencing all the reverses of fortune, without forming any of those great resolutions which secure her favor, the Russian army was making preparations to open the campaign, and Prince Henry, who was left to observe it at a distance of one hundred leagues, was cantoned, as has been stated, in the direction of Sagan.

This prince, observing at length that operations would commence before long, concentrated his troops near Frankfort, and moved, on the 19th of June, to Landsberg, on the Wartha. He had thirty-seven battalions and sixty-six squadrons, of which seven battalions and twenty squadrons, under Forçade, covered Pomerania, and were advanced to Dramburg, in order to cut off General Totleben, who was ravaging the vicinity of Belgard and Koslin with some Cossacks.

On the 12th of July, Prince Henry crossed the Wartha, and encamped at Gleissen, forming, on the 14th, a long cordon of posts, to protect the country from the incursions of the enemy.

The Russian army was entirely assembled at Posen, on the 17th of July, and numbered in its ranks sixty thousand regular troops and seven thousand Cossacks. After many difficulties, which were greatly diminished by the marquis de

Montalembert, Soltikof decided to march, on the 24th, directly to Breslau; and, in order to render the depôts secure, they were established on the line of Siradin and Kalisch.

The bad understanding existing among the generals, which had exercised such an influence over the preceding campaign, began again to manifest itself. Laudon having inquired of the Russian marshal on what day he expected to reach the Oder, in order that he might thereby regulate his own movements, Soltikof, deeming himself insulted by this very natural question, returned an angry reply. He would not have moved an inch, had not the indefatigable and adroit Montalembert finally induced him to start on the 26th.

The Russian army marched in six columns to Moszinna; the advance-guard, under Czernischef, remained at Winkowitz, where it had been since the 20th. On the 28th, the army encamped at Dollevo, with the advance-guard at Korkow; it moved in three marches, on the 1st of August, to Kobelin, from whence the advance-guard pushed ahead to Rawitz, on the frontier of Silesia. Here Soltikof halted to rest his troops, though he had only marched at the outside, from four to seven leagues a day.

Prince Henry having learned that the Russians were to start on the 24th for Silesia, went on the 26th to Starpel, ordering the detached corps to follow him, and pushed that of Werner to Meseritz; Goltz moved on the 28th from the convent of Paradis to Riedschutz. All the army was united on the 29th at the camp of Padligar, where it rested the next day. The prince was here advised that the Russians were moving by Polnisch-Lissa, upon Glogau, which decided him to detach General Werner to Slawe, with nine battalions and twenty-two squadrons, while he marched himself, in three columns, upon Linden. He then learned with certainty that Totleben's corps of light troops alone, was coming by way of the plains of Lissa, and that the army would continue its route by Gosthyn upon Breslau. This news, coupled with that of the fall of Glatz, led the prince to think that everything was to be feared from an enterprise of Laudon against Breslau, and from the junction of the Russians with that corps. He therefore determined to pass the Oder at Glogau, on the 1st of August, and take a position at Gramschutz, where he heard on the same day that Laudon had already invested the place.

The fact was, that no sooner had that general taken Glatz, than he directed General Draskowitz upon Breslau, and ordered Nauendorf, who was at Neumarck, to pass the Schweidnitz at Lissa, and to complete the investment of the place; which was carried out on the 31st. The same day Laudon uselessly summoned Major-General Tauenzien, and on the next day addressed him a long memorial, the object of which was to prove, that it was wrong for him to attempt the defense of a bad place, against an army of fifty-five battalions, which was about to be joined by seventy thousand Russians, and that he was deprived of all hope of succor. He threw upon him the responsibility of such a defense, which would compromise the inhabitants of a flourishing city; one which could hardly be regarded as a military fortress, and one which could be surrendered without loss of honor. This summons was backed, that same evening, by the fire of three batteries, which caused numerous conflagrations.

The truth was, Tauenzien had but three thousand men to guard an immense *enceinte*, with dilapidated works, and containing a numerous population, but very little inclined to favor the Prussians. Still, he replied with firmness, that not being charged with the defense of the houses, but with that of the ramparts, if General Laudon thought it best to commence the attack by burning the unfortunate inhabitants, he would become himself responsible for a proceeding so barbarous, which would, besides, have no influence upon his own resolution. He took all possible measures of defense, and animated the courage of his garrison.

On the 2d of August, the Austrians again tried, but ineffectually, to induce the commandant to change his mind. Laudon, learning of the approach of Prince Henry, who had started on the 2d of August, and had bivouacked in the vicinity of Parchwitz, was obliged to raise the siege, and repass the Oder on the 4th, and marched to take up a position at Kanth, behind the Schweidnitz-Wasser.

The prince marched on the night of the 4th and 5th to Neumarck, and sent General Werner with a battalion and fifteen squadrons, in the direction of Kanth; this detachment fell accidentally upon Caramelli's corps, at Romolkawitz; this corps was about joining that of Neuendorf, for the purpose of observation towards Neumarck. The Austrians lost nearly all of the fine dragoon regiment of the Archduke Joseph, and were forced to halt. Werner continued on to Lissa, where he joined the prince; the Prussian army went into camp on the 6th under the cannon of Breslau.*

In the meantime, Soltikof having heard that that place was invested, and that the prince had marched to its relief, started on the 4th from Koblin and encamped at Militsch, where he was advised of the raising of the siege, and of Laudon's movement upon Kanth. He marched on the 5th to Kolcharka, and on the 6th to Grosweigeldorf, at two leagues from Breslau; Czernischef, with the advance-guard, moved to Leubus. On his arrival, he was greatly astonished to find neither bridge nor any means of communication with the Austrians, nor was there to be obtained any intelligence as to their army; he turned about and took post at Auras.

* Tempelhof says the 8th, but this must be a mistake.

Laudon had retired on the 6th to Saewitz, and on the 7th to Strigau.

No sooner was the prince informed of the approach of the Russians, than he moved through Breslau five battalions and fifteen squadrons, which encamped under the command of General Platten, between the fortress and the old Oder, to secure the city from a bombardment. Thus did Prince Henry, by a movement based upon good principles of combinations, and well executed, extricate himself from a difficult position, save Silesia, and perhaps rescue the fortunes of the king; for it is now impossible to calculate the results which might have followed from the junction of the enemy's armies, at such a critical and decisive period.

Surprised to find the Prussians there, where he had expected to find the Austrians, Soltikof gave vent openly to his disappointment; in fact, the first plan of operations was a failure. Time was necessary to concert a new one, having the necessary unity, and the season favorable to such operations was fast slipping away; besides the Russians had expected to make Breslau a new base of operations, and a depôt of magazines, had it been captured. However, Montalembert had gained sufficient influence over their general, to induce him to hold on to the position of Weigeldorf, which compelled the prince to remain at Breslau, and put a stop to the manœuvre intended to facilitate the junction of his army with that of the king, who had arrived at Buntzlau, on the 7th of August, and had opposed to him all of the Austrian forces, as will be seen hereafter.

FREDERICK'S MARCH FROM SAXONY INTO SILESIA.

The firmness exhibited by the king was severely put to the test, by the fall of Glatz; this event consolidated the establishment of the enemy upon two strong points of his frontiers, and seemed to bring to a climax of misfortune the disasters of the last twenty months. Still, that force of character, which appears to have been one of his greatest qualities, soon restored his wonted serenity, and his calm self-possession again inspired confidence. *We will recover Glatz at the treaty of peace*, said he: *Now we will march into Silesia, in order not to lose everything.* Let us recall the defeats of Kay, of Kunersdorf; the important capture of Dresden; the destruction of the corps of Fink, Dierke and Fouquet, and finally, of the loss of Glatz, and we shall be able to form some idea of the actual state of his affairs. His partisans trembled for him; but so far from the moral forces, the influence and the audacity of his enemies, tending to crush him, it has been remarked, that they all operated to enlist fortune in his favor, and insure success to his flag.

We left Daun at Bischofswerda, securing all the passes into Silesia, and the king encamped on the 31st of July at Meissen. Wedel passed the Elbe, the same day, for the purpose of protecting the passage of the army, which followed the next day, the 1st of August, and went into camp at Wantewitz. The king waited on the 2d for the arrival of his parks; he drew up a memorandum regulating the order which was to be observed throughout the march during the expedition. Here is an extract from it:

"The army will march in three columns by lines. The first will be composed of the first line; the second, of the second line; the third, of the reserve.

"The military chests and the ambulances of the regiments will follow their corps. The batteries of heavy artillery will follow the brigades of infantry to which they are attached.

"When passing through woods, the regiments of cavalry will march between two corps of infantry.

"Each column will have a volunteer battalion, and

ten squadrons of hussars, or of dragoons for its advance-guard.

"It will be preceded by three wagons, carrying planks for bridges.

"The rear-guard will be charged with the care of taking up and bringing off these bridges, when the army shall have passed.

"Trains will be distributed through the columns, in order to avoid the embarrassment of a great number of wagons in a body.

"Should anything happen to the second or third column, it will be immediately reported to the king, who will be found at the head of the first column. If anything happens to the rear-guard, it will be attended to by Lieutenant-General Zeithen, who will be found with the rear-guard of the first column.

"The officers will see that the soldiers march with an equal step, not running to the right and left, and uselessly fatiguing themselves and losing their distances.

"When the army is called on to form, the wagons will wheel out of column to the left, and file to the rear to be parked, etc."

On the 3d of August, the army marched in the order above mentioned, and encamped at Königsbruck.

So soon as Daun learned that the enemy had passed the Elbe, he sent off his luggage and equipage on the 2d, and moved on the 3d from Bischofswerda upon Bautzen. Lasey went himself to Lichtenau, and caused Reid's light troops to harass the king's march.

A table of the marches made by the two armies in order to gain Silesia is presented below.

PRUSSIANS.	AUSTRIANS.
Aug. 3d, The *king* went to Königsbruck.	Aug. 3d, *Daun* went to Bautzen. *Lascy*, to Lichtenau.

PRUSSIANS.	AUSTRIANS.
General *Hulsen* remained in Saxony, opposed to the imperial army.	
Aug. 4th, The *army* marched to Ratibor and Lugau.	Aug. 4th, *Daun* went to Reichenbach. *Reid*, from Bautzen to Weissenberg. *Lascy*, near Bischofswerda.
Aug. 5th, The *king* to Dobschutz.	Aug. 5th, *Daun* moved to Neukretscham. The *reserve*, under Prince Lowenstein, remained at Reichenbach. *Reid*, to Lobau. *Lascy* followed the Prussians and camped at Geblitz.
Aug. 6th, To Ober-Rothwasser.	Aug. 6th, *Daun* crossed the Queiss, and occupied the famous camp of Schmotseifen. The *reserve* at Haugsdorf, behind the Neisse. *Lascy*, to Gorlitz. *Reid*, to Bernstatdel.
Aug. 7th, The *king* to Buntzlau.	Aug. 7th, *Daun* halted. The *reserve* closed up with him. *Reid*, to Haugsdorf. *Lascy*, to Marclissa, and left *Brentano* at Steinkirch on the Queiss. *Beck*, who, up to this time, had watched Prince Henry between Buntzlau and Glogau, now joined the army, and formed the advance-guard.
Aug. 8th, Rested.	

At last, after having made forty leagues in five days, crossed the Elbe, the Spree, the Neisse, and the Queiss, with the heat most oppressive, and with a large train, the Prussian army rested on the 8th at Buntzlau. This march presented a new spectacle. The king seemed to be escorted by Marshal Daun, who was in his front; by Lascy, who followed him; and by the light troops, who kept along his flanks. It was more like a military procession than like a warlike march; nevertheless it decided the fate of Prussia.

The king learned at Buntzlau that Daun was encamped towards Lowenberg; the two armies were then at an equal distance from Lignitz and Breslau. The marshal, fearing above everything else the junction of the king's and Prince Henry's armies, resolved to take a position on the Katzbach, in order to cut off the king, at the same time, from Schweidnitz and from Breslau, and ordered Laudon to join him. That general started from Strigau on the 8th of August, and went into camp at Seichau; General Beck occupied the heights of Goldberg. The Prussians thus lost their direct communications with Schweidnitz, and there was only left them that of Lignitz. Still Laudon solicited Soltikof to lay a bridge over the Oder at Leubus, to enable him to join Czernischef if necessary. It was not long before he was disquieted.

The king, wishing to continue his march by Adelsdorf upon Lignitz or Jauer, sent, on the 8th, his baggage and equipage to Haynau. On the 9th, he began his march, in three columns, for Adelsdorf. The advance-guard arrived near that place when they discovered Beck's corps and the grand Austrian army *debouching* in three columns from Pilgramsdorf. Frederick was too weak to arrest their march, and he could not repass the Katzbach to reach Jauer, neither could he think of remaining at Adelsdorf, since Daun, by extending his right, could thus cut him off from the route to Lignitz. The Prussian army then changed its direction, and went into camp towards Kroitsch, on the left of the Katzbach, fronting on Goldberg. Daun, on his side, moved along the right bank of that river, and took post, with his left, on the heights of Goldberg, and his right, which was extended by the corps of Brentano, towards Conradsberg. Laudon was established at Arnoldshof, and General Lascy at Lowenberg.

On the 10th, the Austrian army was in motion. Laudon opened the march, and went into camp near Greibnig, and pushed Nauendorf on to Parchwitz. Daun passed the Wuthende-Neisse in three places, and encamped between Wahlstadt and Hochkirch; Beck and Reid formed the rear-guard, and took post at Cossendau and Dolmau. General Uhyazi flanked the march on the side of the Katzbach. Lascy replaced the army at the camp of Goldberg. Daun thus hoped to prevent the king from clearing the Katzbach; but fearing that Prince Henry would arrive at Breslau before him, and that he might attack him in reverse, he imparted information of his position to Soltikof, and also of his design of giving battle to the king, and, at the same time, desiring him to oppose the movements of Prince Henry.

Soltikof had started, on the 9th of August, from the camp of Grosweigeldorf, for the purpose of occupying one near Auras. That general was greatly dissatisfied at the departure of Laudon, for it seemed to him that Daun ought to be strong enough to hold his own against Frederick. *Since he has allowed the king to come as far as Buntzlau,* said he, *he will not be able to stop him from crossing the Oder, and attacking me, in concert with Prince Henry, and it will be impossible for him to sustain me, separated from me by that river.* Nevertheless, the Russian general concluded to reëstablish the bridge at Leubus, and to throw across two others near Auras, and to detach the corps of General Plemenikow to the left bank of the Oder, to prevent the junction of the king and Prince Henry. As soon as Frederick learned that Daun had begun his march, he set out in four columns, in order to anticipate him in the passage of the Katzbach and at Lignitz, and encamped near that city in four lines; his left at the suburbs of Goldberg, and his right at Schimelwitz. He had only thirty thousand combatants, while the Austrian army united had nearly ninety thousand. Obliged as he was to make all of his movements under their eyes, he changed his position daily, for the purpose of preventing Daun from concerting a combined attack at the same time, without losing sight of the object in view, that of effecting a junction with Prince Henry. Not knowing that Lascy was between Seichan and Goldberg, the king resolved to turn the left flank of the Austrians, in order to recover his communications with Schweidnitz. For this purpose the army began its march on the evening of the 10th. At daylight, when his advance-guard arrived in the vicinity of Hohendorf, he was informed of Lascy's position at Prausnitz, and his corps was distinctly seen extended along the heights beyond the Katzbach from Goldberg to Niedergrain. The king ordered the head of the column to change direction to the right, in order to turn the enemy's left by Goldberg: the long curve described in this movement gave Lascy time to retire to Kolbnitz near Jauer. The Prussians passed the Katzbach under a fire of artillery, and took with them the greater part of their baggage. Nevertheless it was impossible to come up with their columns. The Prussians encamped at Seichau on the 11th, and Bulow, with nine battalions and thirteen squadrons, on the heights of Prausnitz, to cover its defiles in case of retreat.

Daun having reconnoitred the position held by the king at Lignitz, and finding it abandoned, started for Arnoldshof, where he expected to unite with Lascy's corps; but learning there that Lascy had retreated, he halted his army and formed it behind the Wuthende-Neisse, and sent the corps of carbiniers and the reserve across the river. The first occupied Breitenberg; the second took post on the heights of Hermsdorf and of Hennersdorf. This enabled the Austrians to close the road to Schweidnitz, and disarrange the king's plans. Daun afterwards encamped at Peterwitz, with Lascy covering his left. Laudon replaced Lascy behind the Neisse, Beck was established towards Buschmüle, and Reid at Weinberg.

Frederick, seeing the impossibility of executing his first plan, resolved to gain Landshut the next day, the 12th of August, by passing through Pombsen and the mountains; but the position of General Beck, who guarded the defile, deprived him of the means of carrying it out. Besides, Daun, fearing an enterprise against Landshut, had sent Lascy there. Frederick, inferring from these movements that the Austrians wished to attack him, drew to him Bulow's corps, ordered the camp to be struck and arms taken. Soon after, perceiving his error, the camp was again pitched. The king blamed himself for committing a great fault in making the last three marches upon Goldberg and Seichau, instead of moving by Lowenberg and Hirschberg, expecting that Daun had all his depots in this latter village, and that their loss would force him to retire into Bohemia. Tempelhof thinks differently, since Lascy, who was then at Lowenberg, might have prevented this movement. The fact was, that Frederick was always very badly informed as to the position of his enemies, for the reason that he expended no more money in the employment of spies.

Now he had no time to lose; his provisions being about exhausted, he contemplated approaching Glogau or Breslau, and of repassing the Katzbach during the night, in order to evade the enemy. General Bulow set out at nightfall to reöccupy his old position at the defile of Prausnitz, and at half-past eight in the evening started all of the baggage, with General Ziethen bringing up the rear.

On the 12th, at half-past eight o'clock in the evening, the cavalry of the wings moved off in two columns; the infantry left at half-past nine o'clock in the same order; twenty squadrons of hussars kept up the fires and outposts until one o'clock. All of the troops were established beyond the Katzbach. This hazardous march was successfully performed by deceiving a column of cavalry which lay near by. If Daun had known how to make use of it, the Prussian army would have been lost; but he remained tranquil, although notified the same evening that Frederick had sent off his baggage.

On the 13th, the Prussian army continued its march, and encamped at Lignitz (Plate XXIII., No. 4). Scarcely were the tents pitched before the Austrian army was seen arriving at Hochkirch. Lascy was established between Goldberg and Niedergrain; Laudon towards Jeschkendorf; Nauendorf at Parchwitz.

Whilst the Prussian and Austrian armies executed all these movements, Prince Henry steadily remained at Breslau; finally, when he heard that Soltikof had marched to Kunzendorf, he ordered his rear-guard to be followed by the generals, Goltz, Platten and Thadden, who took position behind the Weida. The Russians opposed General Totleben, who was reënforced by ten battalions and ten squadrons, and who, notwithstanding this increase of force, dared not undertake anything against them. The prince, not wishing to leave his detachments exposed, passed the Oder, on the 12th of August, for the purpose of occupying a position between Mahlen and Hunern, which he intrenched.

On the 13th, Laudon visited Marshal Soltikof, and it was arranged to move the corps of Czernischef, after reënforcing at Grosbesa on the other side of the Oder, and on the road from Auras to Lissa.

BATTLE OF LIGNITZ.

On the evening of the 13th, the king was informed that the corps of Czernischef was to pass the Oder, and hence concluded that Daun desired to attack him. As the position at Lignitz was not favorable for the defensive, he resolved to repass the Katzbach, to send to Glogau for provisions, and by marching to Parchwitz, afterwards to open communication with Prince Henry.

In consequence of this resolve, he gave orders for the army to march early the next day, but this plan could not be carried out, owing to the close proximity of the enemy, who, discerning the direction of the columns, could have easily crushed the rear-guard; therefore it was necessary to wait until night. Daun made a reconnoissance, which brought the Prussians to arms; it appeared that his plan was to have Lasey turn the king's camp, whilst the main army should attack it in front, and Laudon himself should seize the heights of Pfaffendorf, to cut off his retreat upon Glogau; but this nice combination was thwarted by the sudden departure of the Prussians.

Frederick, feeling the necessity of leaving a position where he was in danger of being overwhelmed by the Austrians, concluded with good reason, that he must take the initiative of the movement, and secure its advantages for himself, besides ensuring the power of falling *en masse* upon a portion of the enemy's army; he reconnoitred the heights of Pfaffendorf, ordered the army to move at nightfall, named the bridges over which the columns would cross the Schwartz-Wasser, and indicated the points on which they should form to await the daylight.

The army began its march by lines, and by the left; some squadrons of hussars replenished the fires and patrolled during the night. The columns crossed the river, and reached the heights of Pfaffendorf without the Austrians discovering their departure. The reserve was formed upon the heights in rear of that village, facing Lignitz, and five squadrons of hussars were sent to Polschildern to reconnoitre.

When the left wing arrived on the Wolfsberg, near Binowitz, the king, seeing more fully the position of the enemy by the fires of their advance-guard, changed his first dispositions. The first line was ordered to move more to the right, and in rear of the wood of Humel, in such a manner that its left was in rear of Panten.

Meanwhile the king lay down to sleep near the bivouac of the grenadiers of Rathenow. He had scarcely shut his eyes when Major Hund arrived at a gallop demanding to see him. Frederick starting from his sleep, and learning what had disturbed him, the major addressed him in an excited manner, *Sire, the enemy is here, he has driven in my videttes, and is not four hundred paces off.* The king, with perfect coolness, ordered this officer to hold the Austrians in check as long as possible, indicated to General Schenkendorf, who commanded a brigade on the extreme left, a line of hills near Binowitz, where he was to form, and directed the second line to extend to the left, to prevent the enemy from turning the flank of the army; and, finally, to throw in front some regiments of cavalry to keep the enemy in play while these orders were being executed. General Schenkendorf gained the hill by a flank march, and established on it a battery of ten twelve-pounders, at a moment when the Austrians were within grape and canister range, when the battery opened on them in such a destructive manner that they were not able to form.

Laudon had commenced his march at nightfall, and crossed the Katzbach in three columns, near Polschildern. Since he was entirely ignorant of the king's movement, and flattered himself that he might surprise the baggage-train, parked near Topferberg, he marched without an advance-guard, at the head of a corps of reserve, which came upon the detachment of Major Hund.

The Austrian general, confirmed in his opinion by this event, and fearing to lose his prey, ordered his columns to take the double-quick step. What was his astonishment, when he found the heights upon which he wished to form, bristling with cannon and covered with infantry! However, with a practised eye, he saw at a glance, that the troops which were engaged, could not be withdrawn without risk; he therefore deployed his reserve corps with as much rapidity as the waning daylight, and the nature of the ground would permit, brought several batteries into position and attacked the height with great courage. The grenadiers of Rathenow and Nimchefsky, with the regiment of old Brunswick, repulsed this attack, and threw back the reserve upon the columns which had not been able to keep up with this rapid march.* These columns were equally surprised at hearing the heavy firing of artillery and musketry, and particularly the one which was to pass through Panten, which came to a halt, and confined its operations to taking possession of the village. This hesitation gave the Prussian infantry time to form. The regiments of Bernburg and Prince Ferdinand were ranged on the left of the battalions mentioned; the reserve hurried up; three of its battalions joined the left of the line; Falkenhein's battalion of grenadiers at the right filled the interval left between the brigade of Bernberg, and the first regiments engaged. The cavalry was formed in the rear of the first line, with the exception of the regiment of dragoons, which covered the left flank. A reserve of three battalions was placed in the rear or the centre. The rest of the line was in order of battle, on the heights extending along the Schwartz-Wasser from Hnmeln, following the course of the river as far as Binowitz, in rear of Lignitz, forming a potence near that city, on the side towards Marshal Daun, and towards Panten and Polschildern on the side of Laudon.

* It must be remembered that the reserve corps was marching ahead with Laudon, and that it had preceded the columns.

Meanwhile the Austrian general, having re-formed some battalions of his centre columns, moved once more against the heights; but being able to deploy only five battalions, he was constantly repulsed. His cavalry on the right at first dispersed the dragoons of Krokow towards Schonborn; but the cuirassiers of the Margrave Frederick charged in flank, and crowded it into the morass of that village. Laudon collected his battalions, and pressed forward once more, endeavoring to turn the left of the Prussians. The latter, by a similar manœuvre, again threw his infantry into disorder. The Prussian cavalry took advantage of it, and charged the three regiments of the right wing, and almost entirely destroyed them. During this time, Laudon had ordered a charge of cavalry against the left flank of the Prussian infantry, from the effects of which, the first battalions suffered a little, but the regiment of Bernburg advancing with closed ranks against the enemy's squadrons, poured into them a murderous fire, and afterwards attacking them with bayonets, repelled them upon the right of their infantry, which was marching in disorder toward Binowitz, where it repassed the Katzbach.

Whilst these events were transpiring on the left, the right wing of the Prussians, commanded by Ziethen and Wedel, remained quietly in position facing Lignitz, the roads from which were enfiladed by strong batteries, and were in readiness to receive the enemy. Quite a large interval separated the two wings in front of Panten. If the Austrian column which was near this front, had taken advantage of it, the left would have been exposed to great risks, but the chiefs wasted their time in deliberations.

No sooner did the Prussian generals discover this, than the seven battalions on the left of the right wing were prolonged toward Panten, to unite more perfectly with the left wing. Colonel Mollendorf, seeing that the enemy showed a disposition to issue from that village, marched there with a battalion of the guard, and set it on fire, thus forcing the Austrians to take flight, and capturing a large quantity of artillery.

After five separate attacks, against as many different lines, Laudon resolved, about five o'clock in the morning, to give up the battle. This action cost the Austrians more than ten thousand men, of which six thousand were made prisoners; they also lost eighty-six pieces of cannon. The loss of the Prussians did not exceed two thousand men, because they had every advantage of ground. The king, foreseeing his need of the victorious troops to sustain his right wing against Daun, and even against Lasey, could not pursue Laudon. The marshal had begun his march on the evening of the 14th, in six columns, in order to approach the Katzbach. Reid's partisans crossed the river at eleven o'clock in the evening, for the purpose of dislodging the Prussians from the village of Schimelwitz, which greatly to their astonishment they found abandoned. Daun heard of this at two o'clock in the morning, and ordered the army immediately to cross the river; but this operation, delayed by the construction of bridges, and the false direction taken by some of the columns in the obscurity, was not completed until five o'clock. It was already too late; Laudon was beaten; everything this day tended to insure his defeat; for the wind prevented Marshal Daun from hearing the cannonade, and accelerating his march.

It was five o'clock when the Austrian advance-guard appeared in the rear of Lignitz; the right wing of the Prussians still occupied the heights behind Pfaffendorf; but to reach it, it was necessary to cross the Schwartz-Wasser, and pass through Lignitz. The marshal caused the city and the suburb to be occupied by Reid's light troops, and sent across the stream thirty squadrons, which he intended to follow himself with the army. Lasey received orders to reascend the Schwartz-Wasser, and to cross wherever he could, and fall upon the rear of the king's army. The result of such a movement could not be doubtful; the cavalry dared not debouch in presence of the Prussian infantry, which protected all of the batteries of the right, and Lasey sought in vain for a bridge or ford by which to cross the stream; its boggy banks rendered it impossible to use a trestle bridge, without first constructing a communication to reach it. His corps therefore remained in its position. The marshal deployed between Weishof and Dornigt, but when he was informed of Laudon's defeat, and saw the countenance of the Prussians, he withdrew to his former position between Neudorf and Cosendau.

This victory relieved the king from his most critical position; but it was necessary for him promptly to take advantage of it, for he had only beaten one of the enemy's detachments; his army was yet intact, and held the direct road from Lignitz to Breslau, and a strong corps of Russians had taken post at Gros-Bresa. Frederick, after firing several salvos in honor of his victory, took immediate measures to carry with him the wounded and prisoners. Fearing that Daun might anticipate him at Neumarck, and reuniting with the Russians, again cut him off from Breslau, he started at ten o'clock in the morning with six battalions and thirty squadrons, passed the Katzbach, and took position on the heights of Parchwitz; the Margrave Charles followed closely with the rest of the wing which had fought; the right under Zeithen marched to that point in the afternoon. The Austrian general Nauendorf fell back from Parchwitz upon Mottigt.

Frederick, hearing at Parchwitz that General Czernischef was encamped towards Lissa, was filled with additional anxieties. The army had but one day's provisions, and none could be had except from the storehouses of Breslau. He therefore wished to remove the Russians from Neumarck, and to do this he had recourse to stratagem; and dispatched a spy with a message to Prince Henry, in which he was informed of the victory, and that he (Frederick) was going to join him, in order to attack Soltikof. Without knowing what would be the result of his ruse, the army was put in motion the next day, the 16th of August, in three columns. The king conducted that of the right, composed of the left wing, and protecting the march on the side of the Austrians; the second column was preceded by an advance-guard, behind which marched the prisoners and the wounded; the third composed of the light cavalry, under the command of the duke of Holstein, and sustained by a few battalions which flanked it on the left, against the Russians and Cossacks, who might pass the Oder at the ford of Leubus. Ziethen, with the right wing, formed the rear-guard.

Meanwhile Daun, recovering from his stupor, had sent on the 16th two officers to Marshal Soltikof, to inform him of what had passed, and of the movements he was about to make to gain Neumarck; the corps of Lowenstein and Beck were ordered there immediately, to unite with Czernischef, whom they still hoped to find on the left bank of the Oder. Laudon was to follow closely this advance-guard, and Daun with the army intended to keep along side of the enemy, in order to arrive at the same time with him.

Whilst this was passing, Frederick's advance-guard fell upon the corps of Nauendorf, near Mottigt, when the latter immediately retired; the Prussian hussars soon after met the scouts of Beck's corps, and drove them back. This corps appeared soon after on the heights of Kumernig, and a good league in rear was seen the entire Austrian army in full march in several columns, but the direction of the columns could not be determined. The situation of the king was very embarrassing; he saw himself in a moment about to lose the fruits of his victory, and to be cut off from his depôts; for he was ignorant of the fact that Czernischef had retired. Such was the case, however, whether from the reception of the supposed letter, whether moved thereto by the report of a Cossack officer, who informed him on the 15th of the defeat of Laudon, or whether in place of the Austrians, he had encountered the corps commanded by the king himself. The general, not having received any news from Daun, had retired that same evening, and repassed the Oder at Auras. Soltikof approved of this thoughtless conduct, and had the bridge destroyed.

Frederick, distressed with uncertainty, and ignorant of this movement, went forward with some hussars, and slipped by the forest, near enough to Neumarck to scan all the neighborhood thereabouts. His fears were soon dissipated, and the army was quietly established at that place, communicating with Prince Henry, to whom a courier was sent, informing him of the victory of Lignitz. General Krokow, with the advance-guard and prisoners, set forward to Breslau, and moved the same day as far as Borna. The Austrian general's design proving abortive, he retired towards Strigau.

On the other hand, Soltikof had exchanged his camp of Obernig for that of Peterwitz, in order to approach the right flank of Prince Henry, and to communicate more perfectly with Militsch. He replied to the officer sent to him by Daun, that he would agree to push Czernischef upon Neumarck, in order to unite with Laudon, and made arrangements to lay down a bridge at Auras, when he learned, on the night of the 16th and 17th, that the king occupied Neumarck. This information brought the dissatisfaction of the Russian marshal to a climax, who, having no positive information of the position of the Austrian armies, was as yet ignorant of what had taken place. At first he wished to fall back upon the frontiers of Poland, expecting that the plan of campaign was broken up, and that nothing now prevented the king and Prince Henry from uniting, and thus crushing the Russian army, by a union of all their forces, before it would be possible to arrange a new system of operations with Daun. However, he did not refuse to concert still further measures with the Austrians; but he did not regard it as prudent to wait until the king should cross the Oder, and therefore he retired, on the 18th of August, to Militsch. These little misunderstandings between the allied generals, their miserable plans, the lack of confidence and concert, their sluggishness and timidity, and the dissemination of their forces altogether, were the causes which saved Frederick. Had he been opposed by a vigorous, though mediocre, commander, and by enemies who understood themselves, he would have yielded in a single campaign.

Prince Henry followed on the 19th, and encamped at Trebenitz. The king set out on the same day for Neumarck, passed the Schweidnitz, and took position at Hermansdorf; a bridge was laid at Auras to communicate with the prince.

The Austrian army moved, on the 17th, in three columns, to Conradswalde, and took post at Hohenposeritz. Laudon established himself at Strigau, and Lasey at Kratzau; the corps of Brentano on the Zoptenberg; that of Beck at Buckau; and Reid at Arnsdorf.

Whilst Frederick moved from Saxony into Silesia, triumphed at Lignitz, and reëstablished the interior direction of his lines of operations, and connected himself with Prince Henry, General Hulsen, with seventeen battalions and twenty-five squadrons, was to cover Saxony and Brandenburg against the army of the Circles, which had united with Haddick's corps. This army, upwards of thirty-five thousand strong, remained buried in the intrenchments of the celebrated camp of Plauen as long as the king was in Saxony; but no sooner had he turned towards Silesia, and thereby indicated his plan of operations, than it was put in motion to drive Hulsen out of Saxony. The battle of Strehla, fought on the 20th of August, was the only remarkable event of this period. It forced Hulsen to fall back upon Torgau. But before giving an account of these operations, it will be well to follow the king into Silesia, to avoid involving the different movements in confusion.

CHAPTER XXIV.

THE PRUSSIAN ARMIES FORM AN INTERIOR LINE OF COMMUNICATION, AND MANŒUVRE WITH SUCCESS; DAUN IS ISOLATED, AND THROWN INTO THE MOUNTAINS OF UPPER SILESIA; OPERATIONS IN SAXONY AFTER THE DEPARTURE OF THE KING.

FREDERICK, after connecting his army with Prince Henry's, acquired a very decided superiority, which could only have been wrested from him by a long series of well-combined movements, and a vigorous and simultaneous attack. The fact was, that the Oder, from its position, enabled him to concentrate the mass of his forces upon a single bank, and thus paralyze one of the two armies of the enemy by putting the river between it and him, and marching quickly against the other.

The allies took just the opposite course from the one dictated by their interests; and it appears that on this occasion Montalembert rendered them little service, by contributing as he did, along with General Blonquet, to the adoption of the plan of an invasion of the Marche of Brandenburg, which totally isolated their armies. Tempelhof justifies this arrangement from political considerations; he contends that the French ministry agreed with Soltikof, that he should march towards Glogau and descend the Oder, for the purpose of disquieting the king in regard to the safety of his capital, and to prevent the execution of that formidable junction. But the name of *diversion* which Tempelhof has given to this project, carries with it its refutation. A diversion is always an *accessory* or *secondary* object, and whilst Frederick operated with all his forces upon the *principal point*, nothing would assist him more effectually than to give the lines of operation of the enemy's armies a divergent direction, which would furnish him an opportunity of striking a decisive blow against one of them; he could have returned immediately to the secondary points, after defeating successively the main armies.

In spite of a deficiency of artillery, it was resolved to besiege Glogau, and at the same time throw forward a detachment as far as Berlin, in order to force the king to separate from Prince Henry. But as it was difficult to provision the army, it was thought best to overcome the inconvenience by making short marches towards the right flank, up to a certain point, in order to prepare in the interval the necessary magazines, and afterwards to fall rapidly on Brandenburg. The Russian army marched, on the 24th, to Trachenberg, and on the 28th, to Hernstadt.

Many circumstances combined to disconcert the views of the Marquis of Montalembert. Soltikof fell sick, and did not wish to give up the command to another; besides, Daun had sent General Blonquet to announce that the Aulic Council demanded two plans of operations, and that, in consequence, it would be necessary to await his reply. The marshal had intended to besiege Schweidnitz, and had collected and prepared the necessary artillery at Glatz.

Frederick, hearing of the retrograde march of the Russians towards Poland, inferred therefrom, that their operations were drawing to a close; and he was strengthened in this opinion by the marshal's sickness. He contented himself, therefore, with causing them to be watched by a corps of twelve thousand men detached from Prince Henry's army, after which he drew the remainder of this army to himself, and proceeded to push Daun into Bohemia. Consequently, Prince Henry, who was sick, retired into Breslau; twenty-four battalions and thirty-eight squadrons, commanded by General Forcade, crossed the Oder, on the 29th, at Pannewitz, and rejoined the army.

On the 27th, General Goltz moved to Sophiental, with seventeen battalions and thirty-three squadrons, which were to observe the Russians, cover Glogau, and in case of extremity, throw themselves into that fortress. This general had the imprudence to leave a cavalry rear-guard unsupported, and separated from the troops by the baggage-wagons. The Cossacks attacked them near Gimmel, dispersed them, and made several hundred prisoners; which would never have happened, had there been with it a single battalion and its artillery. The corps passed the Oder at Koben, on the 28th, and encamped near Glogau.

The king arranged a new order of battle, and organized his army as follows:

Advance-guard........	10	battalions of grenadiers.		
1st Line..............	25	"	48	squadrons on the wings.
2d Line..............	16	"	50	" " "
Reserve..............	9	"	18	" " "
Total......	60	"	116	"

A battery of ten pieces was attached to each brigade; the advance-guard had a battery of horse-artillery of the same number of pieces.

It was with these forces that Daun was to be driven from Silesia. At this time he was encamped between the creeks of Schweidnitz and Strigauer-Wasser; his right flank was covered by Lascy, his left by Laudon, his front by the intrenched heights of Zoptenburg, which were occupied by the corps of Brentano. This somewhat extended position shut up the road to Schweidnitz, and each corps could be promptly sustained.

The king, desirous of opening communications with that place, commenced his march on the 30th, by the great road to Breslau, but when he arrived near Albertsdorf, he discovered that Daun had already anticipated him by prolonging his line to the right, upon Domanze, and by moving Lascy to Zoptenberg. He then resolved to turn this mountain, in order to gain the plains of Reichenbach. The heads of columns, therefore, changed direction to the left, to go into camp at Grunau and Knigwitz. The king ordered the tents to be pitched, and demonstrations of a front attack to be made, to attract the attention of the enemy, and prevent him from occupying the mountains between Nimptsch and Langenseifersdorf; whilst, at the same time, to forestall them in securing this important position, he set out with the army at seven in the evening. The advance-guard had already, by ten o'clock, occupied the heights of Langenseifersdorf, where the army arrived at daylight. Frederick, believing that Daun had taken position behind the heights of Koltschen, went forward himself to the advance-guard, to ascertain the truth of his conjecture, and to cover the march of the army; but the marshal had moved, on the 31st, to the heights of Bogendorf, behind Schweidnitz, extending his position so as to embrace the heights of Hohenfriedberg. The king could then communicate freely with that place, and he established himself at Koltschen, and pushed his advance-guard to Endersdorf.

By this splendid march he destroyed the hopes of his adversaries, and filled them with fears regarding their communications with Bohemia and their depôts. Not only did they abandon the siege of Schweidnitz, and their plans of invasion, but thought of nothing but of protecting their frontiers.

The king marched to Pulzen on the 1st of September, and to Buntzelwitz on the 3d, placing his right upon the heights of Zedlitz, the centre towards Nonenbusch, and the left in the direction from Jauernick to Buntzelwitz. The advance-guard, commanded by General Zeithen, prolonged itself to the right towards Strigau. Several slight skirmishes took place towards the centre. Seeing the close proximity of the Austrian posts, some abatis were constructed in the Nonenbusch for protection.

The armies remained until the 11th of September in these positions, which art rendered still stronger. However, want of unity and uncertainty constantly pervaded the arrangements made by the armies of the coalition. The court of Vienna incessantly devised the most whimsical projects, and such as it was impossible to carry out. Daun had proposed to the Russians to besiege Glogau, conjointly with a force of forty thousand men, to be sent there under Lascy. Soltikof eagerly agreed to the proposition, and sent an officer to Daun to make the arrangement. Scarcely, however, had the latter started when a second messenger arrived from the Austrian marshal, which changed everything, on account of the king's movements against him. This change was concealed from Soltikof, and the marquis de Montalembert succeeded in making him agree to cross his army over the Oder, and to detach thirty thousand men against Berlin, whilst the remainder should encamp between Frankfort and Crossen, to protect the expedition. The army moved on the 11th to Guhrau. But it was necessary to await Daun's reply, and the couriers were obliged to go by way of Poland. Meanwhile the first officer sent by Soltikof came back with a new plan, absolutely different, and which was proposed by Laudon, on the 5th of September. It provided that a portion of the Russian army should pass the Oder, and take up a position on the Katzbach, where it should be joined by Laudon, coming by way of Peterwitz. This everlasting uncertainty could not but displease. Fermor, who had taken command *ad interim*, declared that he would adhere to the first resolution, and besiege Glogau, and that he would move on Carolath, since magazines were already established to operate from that side. He, therefore, began his march on the 13th, and arrived there on the 19th.

Such commanders must necessarily fail in all their enterprises against a king who commanded his army in person, and whose plans were executed without clog or hindrance.

Whilst the allies were exchanging wordy communications, the king was devising means of driving Daun out of the country. This could be effected either by gaining a battle, or by threatening his communications with Bohemia, whence the Austrians drew their subsistence. He preferred the latter course, since it was less hazardous. For this purpose he marched, on the 11th, with his army, by lines and by the right, in order to turn Daun's left by the Strigau, upon Bolckenhain and Landshut. But this kind of war led to nothing. In such strategy Daun was his equal. No one could surpass him in disputing the possession of a country filled with strong positions.

The marshal and Laudon, having been informed in time, defeated this plan by reaching Reichenau before the Prussians. The king saw the impossibility of dislodging them by force, and concluded to remain in his position until the 16th, and to return by his left, defiling along the front of the enemy in order to try the same manœuvre on his right. Daun opposed him with the same thing again, by moving rapidly his reserves of grenadiers upon the heights of Kunzendorf, and by following closely with his entire army. Thwarted once more, the king resolved to open a road towards the defiles by Buckendorf and Hohengiersdorf. To prevent the enemy from reaching that point ahead of him, he marched thither, with the advance-guard, without halting. This rapid movement made the battalions open out, leaving an interval between them, which the enemy's grenadiers-à-cheval took advantage of with boldness. They charged the regiment of Bernburg, and captured a heavy battery; but the neighboring battalions, forming quickly, made them pay dearly for their success by a destructive fire, which drove them back the way they came. Whilst this was passing the advance-guard reached the foot of the mountains of Hohengiersdorf, and commenced the ascent by several footpaths, when, suddenly, General Ferrari showed himself thereon, with eight battalions. The position was embarrassing; but, all at once, General Neuwied succeeded, by good dispositions, in dislodging the Austrians with loss. During this time the king was drawing up his army in order of battle. When he learned the result of the combat, he went into camp upon the heights of Hohengiersdorf, with a part of his forces, the rest remaining in the plain between Schweidnitz and the foot of the mountains.

By these two bold marches, executed in sight of an army superior in number, Frederick turned the enemy, intercepted his communications with Glatz, but exposed himself to sure destruction, had he been contending with generals who had dared attack him in his camp at Reichenau. It was his perfect knowledge of the character and of the motives of Daun, which made his enterprise justifiable. By his new position at Hohengiersdorf, the Prussian army was in a condition to communicate with Schweidnitz, and with the base of operations. It had been able to assume this position since the 3d of September, in making the movement by the left, which was executed by the right in a more extended and more dangerous manner.

On the 18th, the king wished to prolong his movement still further, by the left, in order to gain Waldenburg, where the bakeries of the Austrians were placed, and bordering the road from Friedland and Glatz; but Laudon had already occupied the heights and the outlets of Neu-Reusendorf. Frederick, in consequence of this, established his left upon a hill of Schenkendorf, and his right upon the heights of Nieder-Bogendorf; the cavalry remained in the plain, between Schweidnitz and the foot of the mountains. The Prussians covered this formidable position with intrenchments.

Daun had established his army as follows: the right, towards Schweidnitz-Wasser at Tanhausen, the centre, towards Seitendorf, whence the line extended to the vicinity of Freiburg. Lascy was at Langen-Waltersdorf, in a second line from the right.

The armies remained for several weeks in observation at these advantageous posts, where they could not be attacked without risk. They were so near each other as to be able to exchange shots. The king endeavored to gain time, until the approach of winter, and his adversary hoped to be rid of the king by a diversion operated by the Russian army. However, the generals of the coalition armies never succeeded in understanding each other; Daun wished the Russians to march upon the Katzbach; the latter refused to do it, from fear that the king would crush them with his entire force, and insisted as strongly on the necessity of a diversion upon Berlin, which was determined upon. General Tottleben, with his Cossacks, reënforced by two thousand grenadiers, two regiments of dragoons, and all the light troops, was to march rapidly upon that capital, passing by Guben and Beeskow. The advance-guard, under Czernischef, was ordered to take a position on the Spree, to sustain the movement; a part of the army in a third echelon to Guben; whilst the rest, under Romanzow, were in observation on the right of the Oder, in the neighborhood of Crossen.

Daun, informed of these dispositions, detached General Lascy, with fifteen thousand men, to effect a junction with the Russians through Lusatia.

Before giving an account of this enterprise, we will briefly relate the operations of General Hulsen in Saxony, after the departure of the king.

OPERATIONS IN SAXONY DURING THE ABSENCE OF THE KING; GENERAL HULSEN IS DRIVEN OUT.

Whilst Frederick was triumphing at Lignitz, and separating the armies of the coalition, who were about to unite on the Oder, General Hulsen was deputed to hold in check the army of the Circles, reënforced by a strong Austrian corps, as has been remarked in a previous chapter.

The duke of Wurtemberg joined it soon after at the head of his troops, which formed a separate corps.

As soon as the king reached Silesia, this army ventured forth from its retirement, and encamped at Wilsdruff on the 13th.

It is scarcely worth while to enlarge upon the contemptible operations of this army, which in eight days might have invaded Saxony and Brandenburg, but which only attempted the most trifling projects.

After some tardy demonstrations against Hulsen's little corps, it was forced to retire, and occupied the same camp at Strehla which Prince Henry had in the previous year. The camp was much too extended for such a small body of troops, and it was resolved to attack it on the 20th of August. The corps of Stollberg and Kleefeld were to attack and turn the right of the Prussians, whilst they were to be sustained in echelon by the grenadiers commanded by General Guasco; the army of the Circles, at the same time, was to attack the enemy in front. The movements were not made simultaneously nor with unity; Kleefeld alone attacked the flank of the Prussians, which was ready to receive him; the prince of Stollberg took no part in the action, and the army of the

Circles merely went through the motions of a simulated attack.

Kleefeld was therefore repulsed with a loss of twelve hundred prisoners, and a great number of wounded. This combat, carried on in opposition to all the principles of the art, could have had no other result; the consequences were not very important. The duke of Wurtemberg, joining the army of the Circles, placed it in a decided superiority. Hulsen was then forced to retire as far as Wittenberg, and afterwards to Belitz. Thus entire Saxony fell into the hands of the Imperialists, with the exception of the fortress of Wittenberg, which was nearly shut up.

We will now give an account of the progress of the allies against Berlin, and of the operations of the Prussians to rescue their invaded provinces.

CHAPTER XXV.

THE RUSSIANS BESIEGE COLBERG, AND CAPTURE BERLIN; THE KING AND DAUN MARCH INTO SAXONY; THE BATTLE OF TORGAU.

Whilst Frederick was manœuvring against Daun in Upper Silesia, and Hulsen was struggling in Saxony against the army of the Circles, and the grand Russian army remained inactive, a Russian fleet disembarked, near Colberg, a corps of eight thousand men, to besiege that city, and thus to procure a good base of operations. The place was invested on the 29th of August, by land and sea, and the bombardment immediately commenced; but they had to deal with Major Heyden, who had so valiantly defended it in the campaign of 1758. The burghers emulated the courage of the troops and the governor, who were invincible. At length the king detached General Werner, with a small corps of four battalions and ten squadrons, to the relief of Colberg. This general arrived on the 18th of September, so opportunely, that he surprised the detachments which guarded the bridge over the Persante, sabred or made prisoners all who passed through the city, reconnoitred the Russian camp on the sea-shore, and resolved to attack them the next day. But such was their surprise at the arrival of succor, that they broke up their camp and abandoned the siege. A portion of the besieging army reëmbarked, and the remainder retired upon Koslin; even the fleet sailed away on the 23d.

Thus was terminated this enterprise, for not having been

combined with the movements of the main army, which operated at a great distance off, or which, still worse, remained inactive; it is true, that General Olitz was detached with twelve battalions upon Drossen, in order to sustain, if necessary, the siege corps, BUT HE SET OUT FROM THE ARMY ON THE VERY DAY IN WHICH THE PLACE WAS RELIEVED.

After an expedition which had terminated thus gloriously, General Werner marched by Stetten upon Passewalk, against the communications of the Swedes; the latter had only opened the campaign in the middle of August, and contented with the occupation of Prenzlow and Passewalk, were lying in complete inaction before the little corps placed to watch them.

Werner, after driving in their outposts, on the 3d of October, seized all the redoubts in advance of Passewalk; but General Ehrensward, who commanded in the town, set fire to the barns in the suburbs, and threatened to burn the city also. Werner then retired to Stettin, with six hundred Swedish prisoners and eight pieces of cannon. The rest of the operations of this army, which only began the campaign on the 16th of August, are not worth relating.

THE INVASION OF THE MARCHE BY THE RUSSIANS.

Conformably to the plan which has been previously explained, Tottleben marched upon Berlin, and appeared, on the 3d of October, before that capital, which was immediately summoned. General Rochow, who commanded there, assisted by General Seidlitz, who had not yet entirely recovered from his wounds, received at Kunersdorf, made all the preparations for a vigorous defense, and repelled two attacks made against the gates of Halle and Cottbus. Czernischef encamped the same day at Furstenwalde; the principal Russian army did not move until the 5th, towards Frankfort on the Oder.

The consecutive arrival of the Prussian corps commanded by the prince of Wurtemberg, who had been engaged against the Swedes, and General Hulsen, coming from Saxony, disconcerted for a time the enemies of the king; but General Lascy, detached, as we have seen, with fifteen thousand men from the army of Daun, having also appeared before the capital, at the same time that the prince and Czernischef were cannonading each other on the heights of Lichtenburg, the Prussian generals considered the chances too unequal. Persuaded, that should they be beaten Berlin would be given over to pillage, and that there might be preserved intact a corps of sixteen thousand men, which above all would be exposed to certain ruin; they retired upon Spandau, and abandoned the capital to its fate; the commandant capitulated. The misunderstanding existing between the Austrians and Russians here showed itself in its worst light; the former carried it so far, as to be on the point of forcing the Russian guards, and coming to blows with them. Lascy's troops pillaged the city, and committed the greatest havoc at Charlottenburg. Tottleben ordered all the Russian grenadiers into Berlin, and directed them to fire upon the Austrians, if they still persisted in firing upon the guards. Thus this capital owed its safety to the firmness of the chief of the Cossacks, employed against soldiers who were, so to speak, his compatriots. The city escaped with the ruin of its military establishments.

The stay of the allies in the capital was short. On the 11th, they heard of the king's approach; all the generals were afraid of being cut off. Lascy started in the night of the 11th and 12th, and marched upon Torgau. Czernischef took the Frankfort road on the morning of the 12th, and Tottleben followed in the evening.

FREDERICK MARCHES INTO SAXONY, AND DAUN FOLLOWS HIM.

We left the king at the camp of Hohengiersdorf, in front of Daun's army. No sooner was he informed of the invasion of his states than he ordered the count de Wied to throw six battalions into Breslau, to reënforce its garrison, and to move with all his cavalry to Schweidnitz.* Frederick immediately rid the army of its baggage, and on the 7th of October, at three o'clock in the morning, began his march, for Buntzelwitz, in the greatest silence, whence he pushed upon Strigau his advance-guard, composed of ten battalions of grenadiers and twenty-five squadrons, under the command of Ziethen. The object of the king, at first, appeared to be to move against the Russian army for the purpose of attacking it, and cutting off the corps which was in Berlin; but he learned, during his march, that the capital had been evacuated. He then moved towards the Elbe, and Daun followed him.

Below is a table of the movements of the two armies:

PRUSSIANS.	AUSTRIANS.
Oct. 8th, The *king's army* moved to Brochelsdorf. *Hulsen* and the *Prince of Wurtemberg* left Berlin on the night of the 8th and 9th, and retired to Spandau. The Cossacks captured their rear-guard.	Oct. 8th, *Daun* marched to Lauterberg. *Laudon* remained in Silesia towards Kunzendorf. The *army of the Circles* before Wittemberg. *Lascy* and *Czernischef* before Berlin. The *Russian army* marched towards Frankfort.
Oct. 9th, The *king* to Conradsdorf, near Haynau.	Oct. 9th, *Daun* to Schonewald and Weissenthal, in advance of Lahn.
Oct. 10th, To Prinkenau.	Oct. 10th, To Neulande, beyond Lowenberg.
Oct. 11th, To Sagan.	Oct. 11th, Stationary.

* The count de Wied then commanded the corps of Goltz, of which we have spoken.

Prussians.	Austrians.
	The *combined troops* evacuate Berlin.
	Oct. 12th, *Daun* to Longau, upon the Queiss.
Oct. 13th, To Sommerfeld.	Oct. 13th, To Pansig, behind the Neisse,
Oct. 14th, To Guben. *Frederick* wished to attack the Russian army in order to cut off the retreat of the corps which was in Berlin, but he learned of the evacuation of that city, and marched	Oct. 14th, To Ullersdorf. *Czernischef* joined the Russian army, which retired on Drossen, having no one in its front. The *army of the Circles* took Wittemberg. *Lascy* retired upon Torgau.
Oct. 15th, To Gros-Mockerau. The *Prince of Wurtemberg* advanced too late to the relief of Wittemberg, and withdrew from Belzig to Ziesar.	
Oct. 16th, The *king* to Sikadel, between Liberose and Lubben.	Oct. 16th, *Daun* to Mikel upon the Spree. The *army of the Circles* repassed the Elbe at Bernsdorf, half way on the route from Konisbruck to Hoyerswerda.
Oct. 17th, *Frederick* to Lubben. The *Prince of Wurtemberg* to Treuenbritzen, moving upon Magdeburg.	
Oct. 19th, The *king* detaches Goltz into Silesia, with sixteen battalions and thirty-eight squadrons, for the relief of Kosel, menaced by Laudon.	Oct. 19th, *Daun* to Hermsdorf, near Ruhland.
Oct. 20th, The *king* to Dahme.	Oct. 20th, *Daun* to Frauenheim. The *Russians* cantoned between the Oder and the Wartha, from Soldin to Landsberg.
	Oct. 21st, *Daun* to Martinskirch.
Oct. 22d, To Jessen.	Oct. 22d, To Tritewitz, opposite Torgau. *Lascy* joined the army.
Oct. 23d, The *king* with the right wing to Wittemberg. *Ziethen*, with the left, re-	Oct. 23d, *Daun* threw a bridge across the Elbe, near Torgau, and passed over the re-

PRUSSIANS.	AUSTRIANS.
mained towards Jessen and Schweidnitz.	serves and the grenadiers, who encamped at Dommitsch.
Oct. 24th, The *king* had a bridge thrown over at Roslau. The *Prince of Wurtemberg* was at Calbe, and afterwards marched upon Dessau.	Oct. 24th, The *marshal* crossed with the army, and encamped at Groswig. *Lascy* remained at Tschekau. *Reid*, with the light troops, to Pretsch.
Oct. 25th, The *king*, joined by ten battalions of Ziethen's corps, marched along the Elbe towards Coswig.	
Oct. 26th, The *king* passed the river at Roslau, and encamped at Janitz. The *Prince of Wurtemberg* and *Hulsen* joined him.	
Oct. 27th, The *army* marched to Kemberg.	Oct. 27th, *Daun* moved to Eulenburg, in order to sustain the army of the Circles. The *latter* retired from near Duben upon Leipsic. *Reid* was attacked near Granischen, and repulsed upon Duben.
	Oct. 28th, *Lascy* crossed the Elbe, and encamped at Siptitz.
Oct. 29th, The *king* encamped his right at Duben, his left at Gorschelitz, in order to prevent the junction of Daun with the army of the Circles.	Oct. 29th, *Daun* resumed his camp at Torgau, his right at Zinna, his left towards Groswig. *Lascy* moved in rear of Schilda. *Brentano* to Betaune. The *grenadiers* behind Groswig. The *army of the Circles* towards Leipsic. The *Russians* still towards Landsberg, on the Wartha.
Oct. 30th, *Frederick* marched to Eulenberg, encamped towards Talwitz, between Kultschau and Morlitz. *Hulsen* crossed the Mulde and encamped at Gostevitz, in order to keep off the army of the Circles;	Oct. 30th, *Lascy* retired to Mokrena. *Reid* to Strehlen. The *grenadiers* to Weidenhain.

PRUSSIANS.	AUSTRIANS.
he detached Linden, with nine battalions and fifteen squadrons, upon Leipsic.	
Nov. 2d, *Linden* left two battalions in that city, and rejoined the army. The *king* moved, in order to feel the enemy, and encamped at Schilda.	Nov. 2d, The *army of the Circles* to Vexelburg. *Reid* to Mokrena.
Nov. 3d, *Battle of Torgau.*	Nov. 3d, *Battle of Torgau.*

It will be seen, by this table, that the Russians remained inactive behind the Oder, without enemies in their front; that Frederick, taking a central direction, with the intention of attacking one of the two armies, isolated them in such a manner that they could only unite by fighting. The apathy of his adversaries did not allow them to bring things to this extremity. There existed no concert of action between Daun and the general-in-chief of the army of the Circles, though there was nothing to prevent them from uniting on the 27th of October; and it is to this failure to unite, that we are to look for the principal cause of the battle of Torgau. The army of the Circles did not again appear upon the theatre of action during this campaign.

BATTLE OF TORGAU.

There has arisen a great controversy as to whether the king was right or wrong in attacking Daun in the formidable position of Torgau. Warnery, in the *History of the Campaigns of Frederick*, blames him for having done it, contending that he might have obliged the enemy to retreat by threatening Dresden, or by cutting off his communications with that place, and besides, that this battle could not lead to great results, on account of the proximity of that capital. Tempelhof takes up the gauntlet, and endeavors to refute this opinion. In truth, it would have been dangerous for the king, with an inferior army, to have gone into camp between Daun, with an army superior to his own, and the fortress of Dresden, thus putting his communications with his states at the mercy of the former. But though Warnery is mistaken, it seems to us that Frederick neglected the finest occasions to attack Daun, and that his apologist has fallen into an opposite error, by advancing that a battle was indispensable, and advocating that the Prussians were not in a condition to attempt an enterprise against Dresden, *because they had brought with them but five days' provisions.*

Let these different assertions be founded on what they may, Frederick has clinched his resolutions by informing us, in his works, *that he was informed, on good authority, that the Russians, cantoned between the Wartha and the Oder, intended to pass the winter in the heart of his states, provided the Austrians were able to maintain their position at Torgau.* There then would have been left him no means of recruiting his army. In either case, as the Prussians had neglected such superior chances of success, and since the Austrians occupied a position of such strength, prudence dictated that the attack should be deferred until November; for it was possible that Daun might retire into Bohemia, or the Russians into Poland, according to their custom.

In a measure to carry out this plan, the king left the brigade Roebel near Eulenburg, and moved, in four columns, on the 2d of November, upon Schilda, keeping himself with the advance-guard during the march, in order to discover in what direction the enemy's outposts lay. These all falling back upon Torgau, he concluded that Daun was making preparations to receive him there, and that there were no means of dislodging him from that position but by an attack. The Croats of Brentano were attacked near Schona, and about four hundred made prisoners. The Prussian army encamped with the right on the heights beyond Schilda, and the left beyond Lang-Reichenbach, in the annexed order of battle.

The Austrian army then changed its front, and faced to the rear, with its left moved to the heights of Zinna, and its right on the vineyards behind Siptitz (see Plate XXIV.); the corps of reserve near Groswig; the division of grenadiers of the left wing at Weidenhain; that of grenadiers and carbineers of the right, in rear of Neiden. Lasey was withdrawn from Schilda upon Loswig and Torgau; Reid, with the light troops, on the extreme right, towards Mokrena.

This position was formidable; the left rested on the Elbe; the great tank of Torgau, and the closed city, sheltered it from all enterprises; the front, almost unattaïnable, was covered by the stream of Rohrgraben, narrow and marshy, and also by steep heights, in part covered by vines; the right rested on the forest of Dommitsch, having its flank covered by that forest and extensive abatis. The front of this wing was secure from insult on the heights of Groswig.

Judging from the results of the attacks, and from what Tempelhof has told us, we may believe that the king had formed a design as hardy as it was wise. The front of the Austrians was unattackable, and the flanks could not be turned; but as their camp was very deep, and their lines were formed one behind the other, Frederick calculated that he might easily throw their centre into disorder by bringing it between two fires, by means of a double attack, in front and in reverse. This was not a very prudent plan, and we shall see, in the following chapter, that, in fact, it had more success than could have been hoped for under the circumstances.

To carry out his project, the king divided his army into two parts. He was to turn the enemy with the left, and debouch upon their rear, unperceived, owing to the forest of Dommitsch, which would enable him to conceal this movement. Ziethen, with the right wing, was probably to make demonstrations against the front, and afterwards to attack the centre, at the moment in which Frederick was to attack the rear. It required a rare occurrence of events to secure the success of this movement, subject to miscarriage either by the delay of one column, which might happen from the inequalities of the ground, or from the position of the enemy, who possessed the advantage of holding a central position. But, rather than anticipate here the observations which we wish to make, let us return to the account of the battle.

Frederick, after having dictated special instructions to Ziethen, assembled his generals and gave them the following order:

"The army will set out to-morrow morning, November 3, at six and a half o'clock, in four columns, by the left. The dragoons of Schorlemmer, the hussars of Mohring, of Dingelstadt, and the volunteer dragoons, will remain in observation at Weidenhain. As there may be one of the enemy's corps towards Pretsch, it will be necessary to show front in each direction. Our left wing will attack the Austrians; consequently the generals will see that the battalions keep closed upon the march, so as to be able to disengage themselves from the column in time to support each other. The lines will be extended some two hundred and fifty paces.

"So soon as the enemy shall be driven out of the vineyards, some batteries of heavy cannon will be established there, and the battalions will be re-formed. If cavalry are required, only as many squadrons will advance as will be able to act. His Majesty relies upon the bravery of the officers, and doubts not that every effort will be made by them to gain a complete victory."

In accordance with these dispositions, which, nevertheless, received several modifications, the army was in motion the next morning. The first column, of ten battalions of grena-

ORDER OF BATTLE OF THE PRUSSIAN ARMY AT TORGAU.

ADVANCE-GUARD.

MAJOR-GENERALS .... SYBURG. STUTTERHEIM.

Syburg.
- 1 bat. Young Billerbeck.
- 1 —— Schwartz.
- 1 —— Karlowitz.
- 1 —— Baehr.
- 1 —— Falkenhaim.

Stutterheim.
- 1 bat. Anhalt, grenadiers.
- 1 —— Haake.
- 1 —— Old Billerbeck.
- 1 —— Nimchefsky.
- 1 —— Ratenow.

FIRST LINE.

MARGRAVE CHARLES. GENERAL ZIETHEN.

LIEUT.-GEN'S.... .. ....PRINCE OF HOLSTEIN. BULOW. NEUWIED. PRINCE OF WURTEMBERG.

MAJOR-GEN'S... Acbersleben. Meinecke. Ramin. Gablenz. Butzke. Saldern. Zeunert. Bandemer. Schwerin.

Acbersleben.
- 5 squads. Schmettau.
- 5 —— Cuirassiers of the guard.

Meinecke.
- 5 squads. Margrave Frederick.
- 5 —— Spaen.
- 5 —— Schlaberndorf.

Ramin.
- 1 bat. Old Stutterheim.
- 2 —— Manteufel.
- 2 —— Goltz.

Gablenz.
- 2 bat. Young Stutterheim.
- 2 —— Queiss.
- 1 —— Old Stutterheim.

Butzke.
- 1 bat. Forcade.
- 2 —— Wedel.
- 2 —— Old Brunswick.

Saldern.
- 1 bat. Prince of Prussia.
- 2 —— Guards.
- 1 —— Saldern.
- 1 —— Forcade.

Zeunert.
- 2 bat. Syburg.
- 2 —— Zeunert.
- 1 —— Prince of Prussia.

Bandemer.
- 5 squads. Carbineers.
- 5 —— Prince Henry.
- 8 —— Seidlitz.

Schwerin.
- 8 squads. Guardes-du-corps.
- 5 —— Gendarmes.

SECOND LINE.

LIEUT.-GEN'S. .... FINKENSTEIN. KANITZ. FORCADE. PLATTEN.

MAJOR-GEN'S.

- Mohring.
  - 10 squads. Ziethen, hus.
  - 10 —— Mohring.
  - 10 —— Dingelstedt.
- Meyer.
  - 10 squads. Bareith drag.
- Spaen.
  - 5 squads. Wurtemberg, dr.
  - 5 —— Platten.
- Queiss.
  - 1 bat. Margrave Charles.
  - 2 —— Prince Henry.
  - 2 —— Ramin.
- Grumkow.
  - 1 bat. Hulsen.
  - 1 —— Sidow.
  - 2 —— Dierke.
  - 1 —— Margrave Charles.
- Tettenborn.
  - 2 bat. Lestewitz.
  - 2 —— Wied.
  - 2 —— Hulsen.
- Krokow.
  - 5 squads. Zetteritz, drag.
  - 5 —— Norman.
  - 1 —— Krokow.

RESERVE.

GENERAL HULSEN.

MAJOR-GEN'S.

- Kleist.
  - 10 sq. Kleist, hussars.
  - 4 — Volunteer dragoons.
  - 2 — Volunteer hussars.
- Schlaberndorf.
  - 5 sq. Plettenberg, drag.
- Röbel.
  - 1 bat. Grabow.
  - 2 —— Dohna.
  - 1 —— Hesse-Cassel.
  - 1 —— Salenmon.
- Kleist.
  - 2 bat. Lehwald.
  - 2 —— Kanitz.
- Linden.
  - 2 bat. Bevern.
  - 2 —— Old Schenkendorf.
- Browne.
  - 1 bat. Lubath, grenadiers.
  - 1 —— Bourgdorf.
  - 1 —— Beyer.
  - 1 —— Nessel.
  - 1 —— Lossow.
- Schlaberndorf.
  - 10 sq. Schorlemmer, drag.

DETACHED..

The brigade Röbel of the reserve..........	5 bat.	5 squad., Plettenberg.
The second battalion of Kanitz...........	1 "	0 "
The hussars of Mohring, Dingelstedt, and Schorlemmer, with the parks...........	0 "	30 "
Total	6 bat.	35 squad.

Under the command of the king...................	42 bat.	55 squad.
Under the command of Ziethen...................	20 "	52 "
Detached	6 "	35 "
Total........................	68 bat.	142 squad.

diers, and all of the first line of infantry, preceded by a scouting party of Ziethen's hussars, was to pass between the mills of Mokrena, take the road of Weidenhain, and afterwards to prolong its direction towards Neiden.

The second column, consisting of seven battalions of Hulsen's reserve, followed by all of the second line of infantry, was to keep along the left of the first, taking the road of Losnitz, and afterwards directing itself on Elsnig.

The third column was composed of all the cavalry of the two wings, and of the remainder of Hulsen's infantry, and marched by Robershain, Schona, and Strollen. Its movement was a good deal more extended than were those of the others. It passed by the Hunting-house, leaving to the left the village of Roitsch, and changed direction to the right, in order to move towards Vogelgesang, at the extremity of Elsnig.

The fourth column was made up of the baggage, escorted by thirty squadrons, and was at first to remain at Weidenhain, but was moved by Roitsch to Trossin.

When the heads of the columns arrived at the great road of Leipsic, they halted, and this corps separated from the army; it was composed of four brigades of infantry of the right wing, consisting of twenty battalions, of the cavalry of the right wing, and of the brigade Kleist of the left wing, making in all fifty-two squadrons. This corps, having less distance to march, halted in the woods, and waited until the columns of the king had arrived at their points of attack; it afterwards continued its movement.

The king followed the routes mentioned; his advance-guard pushed back in succession Reid's corps, from Mokrena upon Wildenhain and Groswig. Some prisoners were made, from whom it was ascertained that the dragoons of Saint-Ignon were hidden in the forest, in such a manner as to become surrounded by the first and second columns. The hussars of Ziethen were ordered to beat up the woods, and to fall upon the enemy, who were forming; they were charged, and captured or sabred.

As soon as Daun learned from Reid that the king was passing through the woods, and that he was already opposite the heights of Groswig, he inferred that he was about to be attacked in reverse, and changed his front, by a countermarch by the right, and moved his line, bringing his right towards Zinna, and his left in potence, on the heights of Siptitz. The Austrian army was organized conformably to the annexed table. Lascy was posted between Zinna and the suburb of Torgau; the reserve remained on the heights of Groswig; the grenadiers, under Ferrari, fell back on Zinna; those of Colonel Normann were posted before the left wing, against the woods; all of the artillery reserve was distributed along the front of the army. A long abatis, of which mention has already been made, covered the new position of the left wing in potence; this abatis commenced near Groswig, and extended along the course of the stream of Rohrgraben, and was prolonged as far as in front of Neiden. The Austrians had taken the dry wood away from it for the use of their camp, so that it could be passed in several places.

The head of the column of grenadiers debouched from the forest about one o'clock. The king ordered a halt, to close up the battalions, which, having been obliged to march by the flank, had suddenly become disconnected. The second and third columns were still in rear, furthest of all, the last, commanded by the duke of Holstein. Nevertheless, the king had counted upon his arrival at the same time with the others, since it was made up almost altogether of cavalry, and besides, had started before the others; by an inconceivable fatality, at one o'clock, he had only reached the

ORDER OF BATTLE OF MARSHAL DAUN'S ARMY AT TORGAU.

FIRST LINE.

GENERALS	ODONELL.	SINCERE.		AHREMBERG.	BUCCOW.	
LIEUT.-GENERALS	PELLEGRINI.	DOMBASLE.		ANGERN.	SCHALLEMBERG.	
MAJOR-GENERALS	Lobkowitz.	Mighazzi.	Ellmendorf.	Pellegrini.	Hartenegg.	Voghera.
	5 squads. Zerbst. 5 —— Archduke Ferdinand. 5 —— Darmstadt.	2 bat. Hildburghausen. 2 —— Archduke Charles.	2 bat. Dourlac. 2 —— Kollowrath.	2 bat. Puebla. 2 —— Wied.	2 bat. Emperor. 2 —— Neuperg. 2 —— Geisruck.	5 squads. Savoie. 5 —— Leopold. 5 bat. Daun.

SECOND LINE.

GENERALS	ODONELL.	WIED.	BUCCOW.	
LIEUT.-GENERALS	PELLEGRINI.	HERBERSTEIN.	OKELLY.	BERLICHINGEN.
MAJOR-GENERALS	Zollern.	Brinken.	Phil. Browne.	Wiese.
	5 squads. Odonell. 5 —— Portugal.	2 bat. Sincere. 2 —— Harsch. 2 —— Leopold Daun. 2 —— Harrach.	2 bat. Charles Lorraine. 2 —— Botta. 2 —— Merci. 2 —— Ahremberg.	5 squads. Bathyani. 4 —— Buccow.

CORPS OF LASCY.

Zeschwitz.

Brentano.
- 6 squads Hus. of the Emperor.
- 6 —— Esterhazy.
- 4 —— Dragoons, Croats.

Pr. Lichtenstein.
- 6 squads. Lichtenstein.
- 6 —— Birkenfeld.

Buttler.

Ziegan.
- 2 bat. Henry Daun.
- 2 —— Line.
- 2 —— Lascy.
- 2 —— Old Colloredo.

Meyer.

Pful.
- 2 bat. L. Wolfenbutel.
- 2 —— Thierheim.
- 2 —— Bethlem.
- 2 —— Haller.

Zeschwitz.

Goeswitz.
- 5 squads. Carbineers, Saxons.
- 5 —— Bruhl.
- 5 —— Albert.
- 5 —— Courlande.

Renard.
- 6 squads. Schiebel.
- 5 —— Rudnicke.
- 6 Hulans, Croats.

RESERVE CORPS.

PRINCE OF LOWENSTEIN.

Lieut.-Gen'l............................Stampa.

Major-Gen's.....Baumbach. Bibow. Bettoni. St. Ignon.

St. Ignon.
- 5 squads. Saint Ignon.

Bettoni.
- 5 squads. Serbelloni.
- 5 —— Lampach.

Bibow.
- 2 bat. C. Colloredo.
- 2 —— Tillier.

Baumbach.
- 2 bat. Bareith.
- 2 —— Giulay.

CORPS OF GRENADIERS.

General............................Ayassasse.

Brigadiers..................Norman. Ferrari.

Ferrari.
- 5 sqs. Carbineers.
- 3 bat. Grenadiers.

Norman.
- 3 bat. Grenadiers.
- 5 sqs. Carbineers.

Daun..................................	34 battalions,	50 squadrons.
Lascy..................................	16 "	66 "
Other corps..........................	14 "	25 "
Total..........................	64 battalions,	141 squadrons.

The Croats and Reid's corps not included.

Hunting-house, abreast of Weidenhain, having yet a long distance to march.*

Ziethen's corps reached the Leipsic road at ten o'clock, and at one the bridge which cuts the causeway at the right of Graffendorf. An Austrian detachment cannonaded and fusiladed his advance-guard furiously; Ziethen, presuming from the strength of the defense, that this corps was to be sustained, attacked it with several battalions, and ordered a battery to open upon it. This detachment then fell back upon the cavalry, which Lascy sent to its relief.

When Frederick heard the cannonade and the musketry fire, he exclaimed: "My God! Ziethen has attacked already, and my infantry has not arrived!" In fact, he had in hand only ten battalions of grenadiers, the brigade Ramin, and a single regiment of hussars. He immediately sent his aid to hasten the march, and relying upon the bravery of his grenadiers, he resolved to commence the attack, in hopes that the other troops would quickly arrive. The two batteries of twenty twelve-pounders, which followed the advance-guard, passed the creek of Stribach upon the roadway bridge, and the troops upon small ones thrown over at the moment, or which the Austrians had built to facilitate their communications.

After clearing this stream, the grenadiers were formed in two lines, as seen in the plan; the brigade Ramin, placed in a third line, was successively joined by the others of the first, as fast as they arrived with the left in front. This formation carried with it some disorder; several regiments being faced by the third rank; others were brought *by inversion into line of battle.* The greatest evil of this irregularity of forma

* The count de Retzow states, that this column, bearing too much to the right, met the second, and that General Hulsen pressed forward to sustain the king, who was engaged, and prayed the duke of Holstein to halt until his battalions had passed. If this be true, it seems that it would then have been better to have moved up with this column, than to have made a detour of two leagues.

tion was, that the heavy batteries attached to the brigades were not able to follow in the woods.

The grenadiers being formed under a fire of grape, at eight hundred paces from the enemy, they cleared the abatis, and attacked the centre of the Austrian left wing with extraordinary bravery; but they were received by a shower of grape from the artillery, which covered the front of the entire line. This fire was so destructive, that the brigade of Stutterheim was, in a short space of time, almost entirely leveled to the ground. Its general was wounded; the colonel, Prince d'Anhalt, and a great number of officers were killed, and nearly all the others were wounded. The batteries, which were to be established at the left of the wood, were quickly annihilated; men, horses, and guns disappeared in the twinkling of an eye.

The brigade Syburg, which afterwards advanced, shared the same fate. The fire was so terrible, that the king, turning to General Syburg, remarked to him: "*Have you ever heard such a cannonade? As for me, I never saw the like.*" He was posted on the right, between two lines, and thus witnessed the destruction of his grenadiers, the *élite* of his army. He exhibited in this critical moment as much courage as coolness. When the death of the Prince d'Anhalt was reported to him, he turned towards his brother, who was service aid-de-camp, and said to him: "*Everything goes wrong to-day; my friends leave me; I have just been told of the death of your brother.*" A sublime expression, in which is limned the soul of a hero, and which, pronounced amid the horror of such a conflict, demonstrates the greatness of his character better than all eulogiums and apologetical memoirs.

The Austrian carbineers, viewing the disorder of the grenadiers, charged furiously upon them, sabred some, and forced the rest to seek safety in the woods. The infantry regiments of Dourlach, Wied, and Puebla, believing the victory certain, left the heights of Siptitz to pursue the Prussians.

Meanwhile, the brigade Ramin, sustained by a part of the first line, was deployed. It attacked the victorious Austrians with great vigor, overthrew them, and advanced near the heights of Siptitz. Had there been posted there a strong division of cavalry, the victory would have been decided, but the king had only eight hundred hussars. Daun had time to come to the rescue of his broken battalions. He put himself at the head of two infantry regiments of the reserve, with ten squadrons of cuirassiers, and attacked the Prussians, who, being charged and outflanked on their left at the same instant by two other regiments of cavalry, were cut up, and mostly sabred, the remnant being driven into the woods. It was in this attack that Marshal Daun received a gun-shot.

All of the king's first line was then beaten and dispersed, but the Austrians were not in a much better plight, especially their cavalry. However, the second was not shaken by these bloody reverses, but was formed in the interval, and came to dispute the victory. The regiment of Prince Henry performed prodigies; but surrounded by a numerous cavalry, it was almost entirely destroyed; afterwards, charging the other battalions of the division, they were driven into the woods.

Finally, towards three and a half o'clock, the cavalry of the duke of Holstein debouched from the forest. Its destination was, in the first instance, to sustain the first attacks, but in the present state of affairs, nothing was more pressing than the necessity of, in a measure, restoring the battle. The duke marched slowly toward Elsnig, without taking any notice of what was passing around him; fortunately, the king sent him an order to charge.* The cuirassiers of

* Others contend that it was Colonel Dallwig, who charged with his own accord, with the cuirassiers of Spaen, which he commanded.

Spaen, which were just debouching, were extended to the right, and fell upon the regiments of Wied and Puebla, which were cut up, and almost entirely taken prisoners. Ten squadrons of the Austrian cuirassiers hurried to the rescue of their infantry, and withheld them for a moment, but the regiment of the Margrave Frederick, which followed closely, fell on so opportunely, that they were broken and thrown upon the Austrian battalions. The dragoons of Bareith, which brought up the rear of the column, having also quickly debouched, turned the right flank of the enemy, and in succession, broke the regiments of the emperor, of Neuperg, Geisruck, and Bareith, of which the greater part were captured. (The Imperial army had also an infantry regiment Bareith.)

The first line of the Austrians was then dislodged, and the cavalry of the king was master of the field of battle.

Whilst this was passing, the duke of Holstein, with the fifteen squadrons, forming the head of the column, had pursued his route between the ravines of Zeischken and Wolsan, with the view of turning the right of the enemy, but the ravine separated the two parties, and they confined themselves to skirmishing. Daun had some cannon brought up, and the duke retired towards Neiden.

At four o'clock, the column of reserve, which was with the cavalry, debouched with a battery of twelve-pounders. The Austrian squadrons then disappeared, and were not seen again. This infantry was established upon the ground of the first attack, towards the small hill beyond Neiden. The cavalry was formed upon the wings; they remained in this position until nightfall. At five o'clock, the regiment of Old-Schenkendorf, of this reserve, was ordered to dislodge some Austrian battalions, which were seen on the plateau of Siptitz. This regiment, acting in concert with some battalions of the brigade Butzke, drove the enemy from that height, which was the key to the battle-field. It appears that the success of this decisive attack was due, principally, to the arrival of Ziethen, whose operations will now be given.

This general had at first formed his corps in two lines, with the right on the pond, but when he heard the fire, resulting from the king's attack, he extended the second line from the left of the first, in order to draw off the attention of the enemy, by displaying, apparently, a strong force. Lascy, observing this movement, rested his right towards Zinna; Daun made his second line, or rather the part of it in front of Ziethen's corps, face to the rear, and directed upon him an overwhelming fire from all the batteries, to which the Prussians answered until three o'clock.

When Ziethen perceived that the fire of the king slackened and receded, he resolved to march by his left, across Siptitz, to communicate with him. The columns being in front of this village, the general ordered the regiment of Dierke to attack a small intrenchment which covered the wind-mill. It was seized, but the Austrians being established behind the village, this was only a temporary success, without any particular result. The brigade Saldern attempted to pass the thickets more to the left, and to seize upon the heights, covered with vineyards; but the resistance of the Austrians, added to the difficulties of the ground, rendered all their efforts useless.

Ziethen was still continuing his movement to the left, when Colonel Mollendorf discovered that the enemy had not occupied the dike, which separated the two dams, and that the heights facing it were clear. It was five o'clock in the evening; Daun had, in fact, drawn reënforcements from this point, in order to strengthen the right, which was again threatened by the king, with the rest of the brigade of Butzke, and the regiment of Old-Schenkendorf, as has already been stated. General Saldern then formed two battalions in double columns, on the right and left flank, sent them rapidly across the dike, ascended the heights, and marched on Siptitz, whither he was followed by the rest of the troops.

Ziethen then passed over all his corps, partly by the dike, and partly through the thickets to the left of Siptitz. Some Austrians troops made their appearance, and opposed this movement, causing the two battalions, of which we have spoken, a considerable loss; but they were at length driven away. This combat extended far into the night; from which resulted a good deal of confusion, and some Prussian battalions fired upon each other. The brigade Saldern resisted all of Lascy's efforts to retake the village and heights of Siptitz. On the other side, General Ziethen, joining the corps under command of the king, and the five battalions of the reserve, terminated the battle. These troops formed upwards of twenty-eight battalions, and were in fine condition, drawn up on the position which was the key to the field of battle. Besides these, there were re-formed during the night, upwards of ten battalions from the remains of the left; so that the Prussians were in a condition to renew the struggle in the morning with success.

Facing these troops, were the Austrian regiments of Lorraine, Mercy, Botta, and Staremberg; Lascy's corps had partially changed front, and advanced towards Siptitz. The remainder of the army was in disorder, and suffered greatly.

. Daun, although wounded, only quitted the field of battle at a late hour, to be conveyed to Torgau, and relinquished the command to General Odonell. When the marshal heard, at nine o'clock, of the occupation of the heights of Siptitz by Ziethen, he assembled his lieutenant-generals, and asked for their reports. The intelligence which they gave him, satisfied him that another battle might have fatal consequences; he therefore gave orders to recross the Elbe at midnight, which was carried out in the greatest silence, and with such a preservation of order that the Prussian army did not discover it. Lascy's corps moved along the Elbe as far as Loswig, whence it marched upon Dresden.

This battle was remarkable for the extraordinary scenes which the confusion of the two armies occasioned, during the night. The battle-field was strewed with bewildered companies. The escort which accompanied the king to Elsnig fell upon a battalion of Croats, belonging to Reid's corps, and captured nearly all of them; an instant after, it came into the midst of the Austrian carbineers. This second troop was charged, taken and dispersed. Firing was heard the entire night, occasioned by similar encounters. It has been stated that some battalions, ignorant of the issue of the combat, and recognizing each other at their fires, agreed to surrender to those whose army should prove to have been victorious, on the arrival of daylight.

At last, the wished-for moment arrived; the king had already rejoined his army, and had the satisfaction of seeing that the Austrian army had abandoned the field of battle; but coming daylight discovered all of its multiplied horrors. The cries of the wounded, weltering in blood and dying with cold, smothered every sentiment of pride which the victory inspired. The king encamped, at ten o'clock, with his right at Siptitz, and his left at Neiden. Hulsen was detached with ten battalions and twenty-five squadrons to Torgau, which he occupied without opposition.

The army rested on the 5th of November.

Thus terminated the celebrated and bloody battle of Torgau. The Austrians lost there upwards of eleven thousand killed or wounded, and eight thousand prisoners, together with forty-five pieces of cannon. The Prussians met with an equal loss in killed and wounded, but lost only four thousand prisoners.

The imperial army retired by the right bank of the Elbe,

and on the 8th, crossed it to the left, where it joined Lasey, and was reënforced by the corps of Maquire, who was with the army of the Circles, and came to take up his favorite camp in the valley of the Plauen.

The king followed it closely, and came, on the 12th, to Grumbach and to Reitsch. General Queiss crossed the Elbe on a bridge at Meissen, and moved with nine battalions and eight squadrons to Tschaila, in front of Beck's corps. The prince of Wurtemberg set out with eight battalions and five squadrons to arrest the incursions of the Cossacks in New-Mark.

Whilst all this was passing, the army of the Circles, retired, the 7th of November, by successive marches, upon Chemnitz. The king sent General Hulsen against it, which movement induced it to take refuge towards the end of the month, behind the Saale, where it went into winter-quarters.

The two grand armies, after watching each other up to this time, concluded an armistice, on the 11th of December, in order to take good cantonments. Thus, with the exception of a small party in the neighborhood of Dresden, the king had recovered all of Saxony, and had a prospect of reopening the campaign with success.

We have stated that Laudon threatened Kosel, and that the king had detached Goltz with a corps strong enough to save the place, and cover that province. On the 25th of October, this general arrived in the vicinity of Glogau. Laudon, hearing of his approach, furiously but unsuccessfully bombarded Kosel, and raised the siege on the 30th. He evacuated Silesia, towards the middle of the month of November, and afterwards went into winter-quarters.

Meanwhile, the Russians were still cantoned in New-Mark, and a part of them in Pomerania. General Tottleben, with his Cossacks, even crossed the Oder, and went to ravage Ukeraine-Mark. Werner arrived at the end of October, and forced him to repass that river. Marshal Butturlin at length, on the 6th of November, arrived to supersede Soltikof, whose health was not yet restored. After the news of the battle of Torgau, he came to the conclusion that it would be impossible to maintain his position in that country, already devastated, and, therefore, led his army into Poland, leaving Tottleben with his light troops in Pomerania; but when the duke of Wurtemberg arrived from the king's army, with the detachment of which we have spoken, and which effected a junction with the troops under Werner, the enemy's partisans were forced to retire from the country with some loss.

The prince then marched by Prentzlow upon Mecklenburg, where he went into cantonments.

Such was the issue of a campaign, in which Frederick, who was on the verge of losing everything, reconquered, by his skillful manœuvres, not alone his own states, but a part of Saxony. He now had the same means of raising men, and the same resources for paying and provisioning them, as he had at the opening of the war. The morale of his army, shaken by eighteen months of reverses, was restored by two victories, and raised to a pitch to guarantee new successes.

CHAPTER XXVI.

OBSERVATIONS ON THE CAMPAIGN OF 1760.

WAR is composed of three combinations, and its theory may be divided into three branches, each of which has its principals; from whence follows that the right application of the maxims of these three combinations united constitutes a good operation.

The first of these combinations is *the art of adjusting the lines of operations in the most advantageous manner*, which has been improperly called the *plan of campaign*. We do not really understand what it is intended to convey by this last term, since it is impossible in a plan of operations to see beyond the second movement.

The second, is the *art of placing the masses of an army in the shortest space of time on the decisive point of the original or accidental line of operations;* this is what is generally understood by *strategy*, which is really only the means of execution.

The third, is the *art of combining the simultaneous employment of masses upon the important point of the field of battle.* This is the *art of combat*, which many authors have designated as *orders of battle*, and which others have styled *tactics*.

It may be observed, from the nature of these combinations, that a general may have the talent of applying one of these principles without succeeding in the employment of the other two. Until Frederick's time, but little was known except concerning the last of these arts. Systems and prejudices contributed to their remaining unappreciated. Frederick himself was not able to shake off the yoke. Though he manœuvred with so much skill at Hohenfriedberg and at Soor, though he excited the admiration of all at Rosbach, at Leuthen, and Kunersdorf, though he displayed a great mind in nearly all the events of his life, still it will be admitted that it would seem an exaggeration to present him to his contemporaries as the most profound tactician, and the most skillful warrior that had ever existed. The fact is, that the art of war made but little progress under him; and though he improved the second part, the history of his campaign shows that he entirely misunderstood the first. It is true that he several times placed his greatest mass on the decisive points, but he did not know how to adjust his lines of operations in such a manner as to gather all of the favorable chances to his side.

The truth of these assertions will be admitted, if the statements which have been previously made of the advantages possessed by the king be recalled, and it be remembered that he occupied with a mass, sufficiently great, a central line opposed to isolated armies, which only acted in succession at intervals of three or four months; whose commanders were irresolute, timid, and at variance. Five months' reverses, nevertheless, did not teach him that it was a great error to pass in inactivity the six most favorable ones, instead of crushing the army which was before him, whilst the others were one hundred leagues distant in winter-quarters. From the first campaign to the last, he never originated a movement which was bold and vigorous, in order to strike a blow which should ensure to him the greatest chances of success.

This reproach, which we have brought against him for the campaign of 1759, is still better founded on his acts at the commencement of the campaign of 1760. The king had been overthrown at Kunersdorf and at Maxen; he should have known that the parties of the coalition would seek to operate in concert, and perhaps to effect a junction this side of the Oder, as they had, previously to his disasters, already attempted to do. The reënforcements sent to Laudon's corps afforded a criterion of what was to be undertaken on that line, and the only way to avert it was to take advantage of the scattered condition of the Austrian army, to concentrate his own, Prince Henry's, and the corps of Fouquet, between Daun and Laudon, and then to overwhelm, at a blow, that one of the two which offered the greatest chances of success; then to push the other at such a distance that nothing would be feared from it during the remainder of the campaign, to enable him to move against Soltikof on the Wartha. The system pursued by the Russians, in the three preceding campaigns, showed plainly that they would never have passed Posen, had the Austrian armies experienced any great check before they broke up their cantonments.

It is not necessary to repeat what we have said on this subject in Chapter XX. We will simply observe that circumstances indicated much more plainly, in this last campaign, that success could only be expected by an energetic course of conduct, and that it was most dangerous to give his enemies time to concert measures for effecting their junction, and bringing all of their forces into action against him. Under another view the occasion seemed most propitious, for the Austrian troops were scattered upon a double line, which was not the case in 1759.

As a consequence of the system upon which are founded all the observations offered, it is believed that Frederick should have given his three corps a concentric direction, and have rapidly assembled them at Lobau, or Zittau, in order to operate afterwards, according to circumstances, against that one of the Austrian armies which he should be best able to overcome, and to cut off from its own frontiers. Napoleon once remarked at Warsaw, *That there were but three things to learn in war: to march ten leagues a day, to fight, and afterwards to go into cantonments.* This great truth, which was applicable to the king's position, shows the inconceivable negligence of this prince, with the light he had, and enables us to arrive at the results which he might have obtained, by the application of the modern system, under like circumstances. Recalling, for example, that the same troops, whose threatening attitude in Bavaria and Swabia restrained Austria to the end of September, 1806, entered Berlin victorious a month after, we shall be able to judge whether Frederick, who had many more chances of success, ought not to have disembarrassed himself of the Austrians in the six months which elapsed each year before the allies could appear on the scene. We do not wish to say that the king should have made a war of distant invasion; he was in such a position, after 1757, as to forbid it, as has been observed in Chapter XIV. But it was a greater reason for his profiting by his central position, in order to enable him to rid himself of his most troublesome enemies, whilst he had the means of doing so with every prospect of success. Whatever may be alleged for his justification, it will be difficult to overlook the fact, that he ought to have delivered battle to the Austrians whilst the Russians were cantoned beyond the Vistula, and not have accepted battle at Torgau, when they were upon the theatre of war, only distant a few marches from the field of battle. He committed the same fault at Kunersdorf, where Daun might easily have joined Soltikof.

But if he is not exempt from blame in these combinations, what shall be said of his conduct in Fouquet's affair? It will be recollected that between the months of April and May General Fouquet was cantoned about Landshut, and

Prince Henry on the Bober, between Lowenberg and Sagan, at the time when Laudon was reënforced and preparing to open the campaign. Why should the king leave thirty thousand men upon the Bober, for the purpose of observing an army scattered behind the Vistula, and which it would take three months and a half to reach Posen? Only four days were necessary for the prince to join Fouquet, and to get rid of Laudon for the rest of the campaign. Let me recall again to my readers the affairs of Lonato and Castiglione, of Roveredo and Bassano. They demonstrate what may be accomplished by taking the initiative, by rapidity of movements, united with the successive employments of a mass against isolated corps. These examples are worth more than long arguments; they will show whether or no my criticisms have a just foundation.*

As it was, the Prussians did the very reverse of what they ought. Laudon had manœuvred for thirteen days against Fouquet, when Prince Henry began his march. Perhaps it may be thought that he was about to attempt to overwhelm the Austrian general, and punish him for his offensive demonstrations. Far from it. It was to remove still further from the unfortunate Fouquet, for the purpose of observing, from Landsberg, a Russian army, which assembled at Posen only five weeks afterwards.

Frederick's inaction in front of Dresden is as astonishing as his enterprise against that city. How could he have hoped to besiege a fortress tranquilly which had a garrison of sixteen thousand men, in presence of an army superior to his own? To do this a great battle was necessary, and it would have been a dangerous undertaking to deliver one under the cannon of Dresden. Besides, had he gained one, his affairs had not been advanced, since the junction of Lau-

* Abensberg, Eckmühl, and Ratisbon have given us still more striking proofs; we trust that these may not be lost to the art, as were those which preceded them.

don with the Russians, in Silesia, would soon have made him pay dearly for his victory. On the contrary, a defeat would, to say the least, have carried with it the loss of Silesia and of Saxony.

The army which, above all others, he ought to have destroyed, was that of Laudon. Against it the Prussians should have acted in concert. It was necessary to strike a decisive blow, for, once defeated, the Russians would have remained upon the Wartha, and the Austrians upon the Elbe. But to bring about this result, it was necessary that the three corps of the king's army should make rapid and well-combined marches, in order to prevent Daun from manœuvring to oppose their junction. Had the marshal remained upon the Elbe, the operation had been certain; had he followed Frederick, the latter could have directed himself, concentrically, towards the other masses, have joined them, in order to deliver a battle to Daun, with such a superiority as should make a victory certain. Now the consequences of a victory over an army marching far from its base of operations are incalculable. Laudon would have been forced, in that case, to quit Silesia, and the Russians would have remained upon the Wartha. This plan offered another advantage. Daun, in order to follow the rapid and concentric marches of the king, would have had no leisure to rest, nor to occupy inaccessible camps. Thus he might have been easily forced to accept a battle, or to have abandoned everything.

The king, soon after, wished to carry out a similar operation when he marched into Silesia; but how different the circumstances! Then there were sixty thousand Russians in that province! Although this was executed at an inopportune, and even a dangerous period, it brought him out of all embarrassments. Three months earlier he might have produced much more brilliant results, without being exposed to the same dangers, for then the Russians were a hundred leagues distant from this province.

Tempelhof has advanced the proposition, that the king's interests demanded that he should draw Daun into Silesia; but let us not confound the periods of time. This would have been a good move at the commencement of the campaign, before the Russians were on the Oder; after they had arrived it was dangerous. Undoubtedly it behoved Frederick to open communication with his brother's army, in order to form a central mass; but it did not occur to him that the enemy might manœuvre in the same way. The best thing which could happen for the king's interest was, that Daun should remain in Saxony whilst he operated this concentration, without being shut up too closely. Moreover, the Prussian general, who contended that the duke of Brunswick was not opposed, in 1792, to the junction of Kellermann and Dumouriez, for then *he could beat them both at the same time*, seems to have based his absurd reasoning upon this same ground.

Tempelhof greatly admires the first manœuvres of the king. We have already observed that the real object of these movements was unknown, since they have as much bearing upon a march into Silesia as on the siege of Dresden. The fact is, that these manœuvres appear to me to indicate merely the irresolution of the king. There is no evidence in them of a vast or subtle plan. All that favors the assertion is, that no preparation whatever was made for the siege of Dresden before the beginning of July.

After commenting on the faulty adjustment of the general line of operations made by Frederick, and his bad method of employing masses upon the decisive points, we must do him justice by speaking of the execution of some of the partial operations of this campaign. His determination to reëstablish an interior line with Prince Henry, and, when necessary, to unite with him to strike a decisive blow, is, above all, worthy of eulogium. It was carried out in a critical time, which made it especially dangerous; but, after all, it was the only course left, and Daun threw no obstacles in the way. Frederick displayed great skill in the marches of the 9th and 13th of August upon the Katzbach. We have only to blame him for losing one march, by uselessly halting, on the 8th of August, at Buntzlau. We know, in these days, that it is easy to march seven or eight days consecutively, and it was sufficiently important to gain a march on Daun to have omitted this halt.

The night march which he executed at Lignitz, to escape from his embarrassments, was one of the best combined during his campaigns. It was necessarily successful. A severe critic perhaps might blame him for having at first brought too few troops to bear against Laudon, instead of profiting by Daun's absence, to decide the first attack by employing a part of his useless forces which were facing Pfaffendorf; but he is excusable on the ground that he was nearly surprised. Nevertheless this error might have been irreparable had Laudon been able to maintain his position until the arrival of Daun, after which the situation of the king would have been desperate. It was upon the first movement that all depended. Frederick had a too correct *coup-d'œil* not to have seen it, and it is hardly conceivable that he did not immediately decide to bring a greater mass against the opposing corps which was threatening him. Otherwise this monarch, sleeping by the fire of his bivouac, and awakened by Major Hund with the intelligence that the enemy was distant but four hundred paces, commands our just admiration by his self-possession, and the opportune orders which he gave in this emergency. This act is one of the finest of his life.

The battle of Lignitz has a great similarity to, and approaches very nearly the operations of Bonaparte when he besieged Mantua, and Wurmser debouching at the same time upon Verona and upon Brescia endeavored to surround the French army. The only difference which exists is, that Bonaparte combined his rapid movement against the two isolated bodies, and that Frederick being surprised was deprived of the initiative of the combination.*

The king, joined by Prince Henry, would have been able in a moment to repair all the errors of the campaign. This operation would have been worth as much as a victory, and yet it was not thought of. The Russians commencing to withdraw, Frederick sought to press Daun. This was all well enough, and should have been persevered in until he had taken a direction so decidedly divergent that all concert in their operations would be impossible. But to do this it was necessary to risk a battle. The circumstances were more imperative than at Torgau, and much more favorable. The king had in his favor all the fortresses on the line of the Oder. In Saxony, on the contrary, there was nothing between Dresden and Berlin, and the first-named city was in the hands of the Austrians. The Prussians were able to concentrate seventy battalions and one hundred and twenty squadrons, and might have fallen upon Daun, at Domanza, on the 30th of August, instead of marching upon Schweidnitz. The king had never commanded a finer army. The victory of Lignitz had restored all its moral force. In case of a check he could lose nothing, since he could rally and reform under the protection of eight fortresses. A partial success would have given greater results than a complete victory at Torgau. Lastly, would he not have come out of the struggle victorious? Daun repelled and driven into the defiles of Bohemia, with no retreat except on Prague or

* The affair of Lignitz offers a still greater resemblance to the battles which have taken place since the above was written, at Abensberg and at Eckmuhl, where may be seen the successive defeats of isolated bodies by an interior mass.

Konigsgrätz, would have lost half of his army. The Russians had already established the fact, that a reverse experienced by their allies would drive them to the Vistula.

We have not been able to comprehend the object of the marches and countermarches made by Frederick, when he wished to drive Daun into Upper Silesia. It was necessary, as has been said, to attack him at Domanza, at the same time masking the Zoptenberg. Since the king considered it preferable to menace his communications, the march to turn the Zoptenburg by Langenseifersdorf was very well, but for the subsequent ones, it is difficult to assign a reason. Frederick, seeking to threaten the communications of the Austrians with Bohemia, should have manœuvred by his left, in order to gain a position on their extreme right. From Pulsen, he might in one march have reached Hohengiersdorf, and have rested on Schweidnitz; then Daun's position, extending to Hohengiersdorf, might have been attacked at Bogendorf with success, and the vicinity of Schweidnitz presented far greater advantages for a field of battle than could be found in connection with the fortresses of Brieg, Neisse, and Breslau.

The king's movement on Buntzelwitz, his halt in that camp, and the march by Strigau upon Reichenau, thereby turning the left of the Austrians, are operations which have received the most exaggerated praise from Tempelhof. If it was the object of Frederick to gain the communications of his adversary by Landshut, why did he consume thirteen days in two camps? Besides, he gained nothing by the movement, the marshal having a direct and natural communication with Bohemia by Friedland, Braunau, Glatz, or Politz. In fact, by taking post at Landshut, between Daun and Bohemia, the king would have run no slight risk, if the Austrian general had attacked him; he would have been without depots and without communications; the slightest check would have thrown him upon the defiles of the Riesengebirge, whilst he could have done no damage whatever to the Austrians. The prize was not worth the risk. By operating from Pulzen upon Hohengiersdorf, and by attacking the Austrians at Bogendorf, on the 1st or 2d of September, Frederick might, on the contrary, have succeeded in directing his efforts by the left, so as to gain Freiburg gradually during the attack ; he would thus have established himself on the road from Glatz to Hohengiersdorf, and from Landshut to Freiburg. It will be observed, that after having lost fifteen days, he was obliged to return and resume this march upon Hohengiersdorf ; but then, the aspect of affairs had changed, the Austrians being inclosed in a formidable position, which secured their communications.

We come now to the observations upon the battle of Torgau.

We will not again recur to the question, whether Frederick was right, or no, in delivering this battle. It is true, nevertheless, that owing to the strong position of the enemy, he had little to hope and everything to fear ; he ought, therefore to have deferred the attack until the middle of November ; then, if Daun persisted in his resolution, it might have become necessary for the purpose of preventing Daun from wintering in Saxony. We will, therefore, limit our examination entirely to the arrangements for the combat.

From the definitions which we have given at the commencement of the chapter, we find that the best dispositions for a battle *are those which bring into action at the same instant on the decisive point, all the masses present, excepting only such as are held as a reserve.* On this principle, all double attacks which are executed by extended movements, and upon a multitude of points, appear to us to be dangerous, and if they succeed, it is because the enemy opposes bad movements to them, or that all circumstances unite to effect a miracle. As this case is rare, it is better to avoid such attacks, for their consequences are almost always fatal.

In reading the account of the battle of Torgau, we find in almost every line a confirmation of the truth of these assertions.

At the first glance, it will be seen, that Daun's position could only be attacked by the woods and by the side of Neiden, between the village and the forest, that is to say, near the crotchet formed by the Austrian line. By becoming established upon this point, the field of battle was gained, but this was not an easy thing to do.*

1st. This point could only be reached through defiles, and under the fire of formidable batteries.

2d. In forming a single attack, the head of the column would be crushed before the rest of it could be brought into action.

3d. In operating upon two, or several points, there was incurred the risk of not acting simultaneously, and of exposure to all the dangers of a double attack.

It may be doubted whether Frederick had done all that was necessary to establish his line upon the above-mentioned point. Fortune favored it a good deal, as we shall attempt to show.

In order to judge of his combinations, it will be necessary to know the precise instructions which he gave Ziethen ; but if the first movements of the latter were made in carrying out the king's orders, it is not probable that the monarch desired to unite his troops upon the heights of Siptitz, as did

* The most advantageous strategic point was the one between Zinna and the great pond. A successful attack upon this point would probably have led to the fall of Torgau, and the bridges of the Elbe, into the hands of the Prussians, who were, before the battle, astride of Daun's communications. The Austrian army would then have run the risk of complete ruin ; but such an attack would have placed Frederick's army between that of Daun and the great pond, which would have crippled the movements of the Prussian columns, and in case of check, left behind them a gulf into which they were certain to be driven.

in fact take place; for Ziethen did not take the road thither, when he deployed his troops towards the great pond. It is natural enough to suppose, that the king, thinking that he had troops sufficient with him to decide the battle, had posted Ziethen on this point with the view of attempting an enterprise against Torgau, and of destroying entirely the enemy's army, by charging it, in its retreat, with fifty-two squadrons, on the even ground which separated it from the city of Rohrgraben. For, on a contrary supposition, the position of Ziethen had nothing reasonable to recommend it. So long as the Austrians held these heights in force, Ziethen was kept behind the ravine, and considered as a mass not acting, which, under any circumstances, would have been a great fault, had he been left to carry out such a part.

If Ziethen was to attack the left of Siptitz, then he made a most untimely parade in his deployment towards the great pond, because the movement which he afterwards executed by his left was made in sight of the enemy, who made a show of opposing it, and moved the bulk of his forces between Zinna and Siptitz; besides, by this movement, his attack was delayed three hours.

The object proposed would have been better attained, had some squadrons and cannon been moved into that position, in order to deceive Lascy's corps, and to keep it, as it were, in check, between the pond and Torgau. The rest of Ziethen's wing should then have defiled between Groswig and Siptitz, in order to operate along the forest—the same attack which Frederick made there from the side of Neiden. This was the only way to insure unity of action or of effects between the two attacks, and we feel satisfied that the affair could not long have remained doubtful.

As it was, there was no concert whatever in the attacks, as will be readily seen from the account which has been given. The hurry of the first attempt, made by the grenadiers, was one of the principal causes. In the peculiar situation of affairs it would have been perfectly easy for Ziethen to have opened a cannonade and commenced the attack half an hour before the king. It would have required at least this time for him to become fully engaged. Frederick ought then to have awaited the arrival of his columns of infantry, rather than to have sacrificed his grenadiers alone; for, had he not debouched so inconsiderately, he would very soon have become convinced that this first cannonade of Ziethen's was only temporary, and, of course was merely connected with an affair of posts. This resolution to wait awhile, at least, would have entirely changed the face of affairs, as the king then would not have become partially and successively engaged, as he did, in order to repair his first faults.

After what has just been said, and even following the account given by Tempelhof, it appears that Ziethen had no order to unite with the king; *for he took it upon himself to make the effort when he heard the sound of the firing receding.* Then the combinations of Frederick were dangerous, and Ziethen, by this movement alone, saved the Prussian army, and rendered it victorious.

Though the king, in this plan of battle, did not display that character which we have throughout this work assigned to him, still it may justly be said that he exhibited an admirable courage, and his great soul never shone with more splendor. The coolness and the perseverance with which he maintained the wrecks of his army until the arrival of Ziethen's corps, point out the true hero. He was exposed to great personal dangers, and it is said that on this occasion his breast was grazed by a ball.

We will terminate these reflections by drawing a parallel between this battle and that of Preussich-Eylau, which, in its results, shows a great similarity, though there is a vast difference in the anterior dispositions, and in the ordering of the battle.

At Eylau, as at Torgau, a division was engaged singly and overthrown. In both of these battles, a grand charge of cavalry partially restored the battle; concert of action took place before the last, and the two parts of the victorious army were united on the bloody field. At Eylau, the arrival of Davoust had the same effect as the arrival of the column of the duke of Holstein, and the march of Marshal Ney upon Schloditten was similar to Ziethen's under like circumstances at Torgau. Both occurred towards the close of the day, and were decisive. On both fields, the struggle was bloody, the slaughter dreadful, and the artillery played an important part; and finally, the victorious armies remained masters of the field of battle without knowing it, for the Russians at Eylau, like the Austrians at Torgau, did not abandon it until far in the night.

But these battles differ very much in other points. That of Eylau was brought on by a great movement, necessitated by that of the Russians upon the Lower-Vistula. Beningsen, by adopting a contracted line of operations, between the sea and the French army, had risked, by a movement of the latter against his left, being thrown upon Elbing, and being reduced to the alternative of cutting his way through, or being forced to capitulate. He extricated himself from the position with courage, but this was due to the accidental capture of his adversary's plan, which had been sent to the prince of Ponte-Corvo.

Frederick sought no such great result; his object was to dislodge Daun with the least possible risk to himself. The king was the assailing party, but the French general, on the contrary, was surprised in the midst of a movement. Frederick might have avoided the partial and successive engagement of his forces, which he commanded himself. Napoleon, attacked whilst the corps of Ney and Davoust were in march, took immediate measures to establish unity of action ; in the morning, he sent an aid-de-camp back to Marshal Ney, ordering him to return by his right, in order to form a connection with the left of the army. When the corps of Augereau had been overwhelmed by superior forces, Napoleon succeeded, by means of his courage and coolness, as well as by his good arrangements, in sustaining the combat with a very small active force. He thus passed the critical moment, and gained time to wait for Marshal Davoust's corps to come into action. Frederick, on the contrary, after the destruction of his grenadiers, persisted in his partial engagements ; he took no efficacious measures to concentrate his efforts, and chance alone led Ziethen to his relief.

Though Marshal Ney did not arrive earlier than Ziethen, it was from no fault on the part of Napoleon. The aid-de-camp whom he sent to Ney lost his way, and arrived very late, when the marshal, seeing the flashing of the cannon, had already taken up his march to connect his own with the corps which was engaged, but not, unfortunately, until the arrival of a brigade which had previously been engaged in the direction of Creuzburg. Had the officer who was sent delivered the order in time, the marshal would have arrived on the field of battle at two o'clock, simultaneously with the engagement of Davoust. But still another advantage would have resulted from it, which was this: Ney would have crossed the direction of Lestocq's corps, which then would not have arrived to the relief of the enemy, and thus the latter would have had fifteen thousand men less, whilst the forty thousand fresh men of the above-mentioned corps would have been in action.

It remains to be observed, that these two bloody battles demonstrate how extremely doubtful an attack is, when directed against the centre of a well-concentrated force.

Supposing in such case the victory is gained, it is always at such a sacrifice that little can be made of it. Forasmuch, as there is a great advantage in forcing the centre of a divided army, so is there likewise a great disadvantage in attempting the same thing when the enemy is concentrated; for when the enemy is not united, the centre is the weakest point, and by seizing it, the two wings are isolated and overwhelmed separately, since they can neither effect a junction, nor make a concerted effort. But with an army in line, in close order, the centre is ordinarily the strongest point, since behind it the reserves are generally placed, and since it is more readily sustained by either wing, not only by sending out their unemployed forces, but by a movement doubling from the right and left upon the enemy.

No battle can give a clearer illustration of these ideas and of their truth, than that of Cannae; Hannibal brought his centre into action, and made it fall back in a simulated flight, until the Roman army in the eagerness of pursuit had passed the wings of his army, when the centre facing about, and the two wings closing in on the Romans, they were taken on all sides, overwhelmed with arrows, charged by the cavalry in their confusion, and entirely destroyed. Had the wings of Hannibal's army been beyond attacking distance, the battle might have taken a different turn.

Hence we may deduce the following maxims:

1st. *When it is desirable to make up for our inferiority in numbers, by bringing all our forces into action against a single point of the enemy's line, in case that line is a continuous one, the point of attack should be as far as possible from the centre. Since the centre of a continuous line can be sustained by the two wings, which should attack in concert with it; whilst a point selected upon one of the extremities of the line, can only be supported slowly and successively by the single divisions of the adjacent corps.*

2d. *An attack upon the centre can only be attempted in case the enemy's line should be too extended, and composed of isolated divisions; then the attack ought to succeed on the same principle. Its results are even more brilliant, because the enemy's corps are separated by a great distance, and often not in a condition to unite, whilst an attack upon the wings could only procure the same advantages under peculiar circumstances.*

OBSERVATIONS UPON THE OPERATIONS OF THE COMBINED ARMIES.

We shall not say much about the operations of Daun and Soltikof. It is only necessary to read the account of them to discover their misunderstandings, and, in fact, everything which neutralizes the effects of warlike preparations. The Austrian Fabius, who, in place of attacking the king when he was before Dresden, perched upon the mountains, and there surrounded himself with intrenchments, before an army beaten twenty months before, and inferior in numbers, can hardly be offered as a model to such as wish to understand how best to choose a line of operations, how to adjust it in the most advantageous manner, and to bring our masses by bold and rapid movements upon the most important points of the line.

Some portions of the original plan of the allies were good; the execution was wretched, as were the plans which resulted from these first dispositions.

Laudon and the Russians were to concentrate ninety thousand men upon the Oder; which was well enough. They did not unite, on account of a simple movement of Prince Henry towards Breslau; at the same time, nothing could have prevented it, had they made a concentric march by the left bank of that river, or, at the worst, by the right bank of the same. Laudon showed his weakness, by taking a direction absolutely divergent. We do not here recognize the conqueror of Landshut and Belgrade, the man whom Frederick feared to have in his front.

The Austrian general went to unite himself to Daun, which would have amounted to the same thing, had the allies known how to educe therefrom the possible advantages, and at the same time had acted in concert. We have said that the first movements of the king should have been to concentrate his masses upon an interior line, and this he did not do. Daun ought to have profited by this error, and have attacked him, either before Dresden, or on his march into Silesia. Frederick was isolated, and what was more to the purpose, he was then at a distance from his two bases of operations, and might have lost a decisive battle: we leave to the military reader to say what would have been the consequences.

The moment that Laudon joined, Daun should have attacked the king. He had twice the amount of force necessary to do it. He groped about for seven or eight days, and ended by leaving Laudon to fight the king alone, when he was but half a march distant.

Had the allies desired to arrange a bold and vigorous plan, the Russian army should have been made to cross the Oder at Stadtleubus, between the 10th and 12th of August. It should have been rapidly pushed towards Lignitz to join Daun, establishing thus the mass of their forces in the centre, and separating the king from Prince Henry, delivering battle at once, and overwhelming one of them by an irresistible force. Of the two, the king could have been attacked with the most success; he had no refuge and but few supplies. Dresden was in the power of the enemy; the road to Silesia was closed; no asylum remained to him short of Berlin. Even there he might be anticipated by a movement made during action, which was to extend the right. The allies had an immense advantage, and might have accomplished great things. Their lines of operations being divergent, one of the two armies might have uncovered its communications for the purpose of operating decisively. There would always have been, in case of necessity, a point of retreat open on the frontiers of its ally.

As to the battle of Lignitz, the plan of it was not without merit on the part of Daun, but its execution was indifferent. He elevated an accessory into the principal attack, and the principal was reduced to a secondary affair. Laudon was charged to forestall Frederick, and cut him off from the road to Parchewitz. Since Frederick's object was to gain that road, and unite with his brother, it was clear that he would not remain long at Lignitz, but that he would attack Laudon. That general then should have been sustained by uniting with him. There was nothing to be gained by keeping the entire grand army in front of the Prussians. Again, the Austrian general committed a fault when he arrived on the ground and saw that Laudon was defeated, in not having marched immediately towards Royn, upon the Leisbach, for the purpose of there anticipating the Prussian army. Then the victory would have been barren of results, and the king been prevented from communicating with Prince Henry, for Daun would have been in the central position, which would have secured to him the two roads of Parchewitz on the right, and Neumark on the left.*

Frederick having succeeded, by the victory of Lignitz, in reëstablishing an interior line with his brother, the allied generals should have adopted a very different plan of operations, striking a vigorous blow at Prince Henry, and trans-

* Since this chapter was written, I have seen Royn, which I have pointed out for its strategic importance. That position is extremely strong. Daun could not have found in Silesia a more favorable field of battle.

ferring the theatre of war to the centre of the states of the king. The possession of Dresden secured to Daun both banks of the Elbe, and a sure retreat into Bohemia. The allies might then have undertaken, in concert, one of those movements of which Napoleon has given us so many examples. The allied armies should have marched rapidly and concentrically, the Russians towards Peitz or Guben, and Daun to Luben, whilst a small Russian division, descending the right bank of the Oder, should have moved to Frankfort, simply to secure a direct communication. One hundred and thirty thousand men thus established in the heart of Frederick's states, masters, in fact, of Potsdam and Berlin, would quickly have obliged him to fight upon that disadvantageous point, staking everything on the result, with scarcely a hope of success. In fact, had he been compelled to fight between the Oder and the enemy's army, he would have been destroyed without remedy, and thrown upon the river or upon Poland, whilst the enemy retired upon the Elbe towards Dresden. Had the king adopted a contrary course, and engaged with the allied army in such a way as to place it between him and the Oder, it would then have been able to retreat through Crossen, upon the right bank of that river, whilst, on the contrary, a defeat might have accomplished the ruin of Frederick, for the Russian and Austrian armies would have been in possession of all his states. There would have been left him no resources for raising men or money, and no retreat, except to the Elbe. There would have been time, before winter, to overrun all his states, in every direction, as well as to complete the destruction of an army without allies, without subsistence, and without other refuge than that of Magdeburg or Stettin.

To undertake such an operation, I am satisfied that it was not necessary to have, as Tempelhof has estimated, so many barrels of flour and so many bushels of oats for an army so numerous, for two months, and shall not conclude with him that this affair was therefore impossible, since these stores could not be accumulated in advance. Six or seven marches must be executed to carry out this movement, and the country was fertile enough to furnish ample subsistence for the troops. The expedition should have succeeded in eight or ten days; if not, it might have returned to Dresden without danger.

We have seen that Tempelhof blames Daun for allowing himself to be turned at the Zoptenberg, instead of extending his position further to the right; it appears to us, as we have already said, that this criticism is badly founded. If Frederick wished to avail himself of the divergent direction, which he had given to the operations of the enemy, he ought to have profited by their isolation and his own concentration, and have assailed the Austrians alone. It has been observed heretofore, that a fine opportunity was offered for attacking their centre, towards Domanze, if the marshal had extended his right towards Langenbielau and Reichenbach, and his left towards Strigau, as Tempelhof remarks, for the greater the number of forces upon these points, the less upon the decisive one. It mattered little to Daun, if the king did gain one of his communications with Bohemia through Glatz, provided he preserved the two which remained; besides, there were other than these two, important secondary lines, from which it was not easy to cut him off; the first was that of Dresden and of the army of the Circles; the second was that of the Russian army by Parchewitz, with which he might have united, if the king had been absolutely thrown into the mountains upon the extreme right of his enemies. The marshal should have concentrated instead of extending, and then have attacked; he might especially have done this under the favorable circumstances, from his camp at Adelsdorf, when the king undertook his dangerous movement upon Reichenau. Instead of fearing for his communications, which he did not need, or manœuvring as if he were playing chess, he should have marched rapidly against the Prussians whilst they were entangled in such a dangerous position. By manœuvring so as to gain ground to the right in the action, in case of success, he could have pushed Frederick into the defiles of Bohemia. The Russian army, by driving off the small corps of Goltz, and then returning upon Breslau, to unite with Daun, would have completed the success of this enterprise, in which there would have been nothing risked, since communications with Friedland and Glatz would have been open on one side, and with Dresden on the other.

In general, Daun's conduct, throughout this entire campaign, was similar to what it was in 1759; the same incredible slowness, irresolution, and weakness of character, which can never be replaced by any amount of personal courage. His march, following Frederick into Saxony, and encamping at Torgau, was the best movement he attempted; but still it was not connected with any general views, nor was it combined with the armies of his allies; he even left Laudon in Silesia, with a strong corps, occupied with trifling and secondary objects; whilst his own enterprise, had it been sustained simultaneously by Laudon and the Russians, would have sealed the fate of the Prussian monarchy upon the Elbe.

Let us recall the object of the battle of Torgau, in order to comprehend what would have been the consequences if Laudon, the army of the Circles, and that of Russia, had operated upon that point.

The expedition against Berlin, which Montalembert regarded as a masterpiece, was only a contemptible accessory, particularly at the moment when the armies took a divergent direction. Accessories or diversions are all useless, when employed against a great mind, which cannot be duped, and which makes use of them to decide more important questions. That expedition would have done very well, if, as has already been stated, it had been executed by a concentration of all the armies on the river Spree; then it would have been transformed into the principal object, and an operation against the important points. The result of this showed that an operation upon a larger scale would have entirely succeeded, and at the same time been productive of great consequences.

The account given by Tempelhof of the battle of Torgau, affords but slight opportunity to judge of Daun's conduct during the action; it merely appears that the artillery had greatly more to do with it than the employment of the troops. The marshal, on this occasion, may be blamed for the same thing as the king, that he had had much finer opportunities for offering battle. To convince our readers of this, we will merely sketch the relative positions at different periods of time.

Had Daun attacked the king at Reichenau, as we have said, it would have been much more to his advantage.

1st. Having the initiative, he would have been able to bring all his troops into action, instead of waiting, as at Torgau, until the enemy attacked his right.

2d. He was stronger at this time, by the corps of Laudon, which lay in Silesia, whilst the king was weaker by the corps of Hulsen and the Prince of Wurtemberg, which only joined his army on the Elbe.

3d. Frederick was at Reichenau in a dangerous position, in which a battle lost was destruction; that was the time to profit by great opportunities. At Torgau, by waiting for an attack, nothing more could be done than to repulse it.

4th. That operation, executed towards Adelsbach, could be more easily combined with a movement with the Russian army, which, after a few marches, would have been ready to unite with the victorious one by pushing away, or even leaving on one side, the small corps of twelve thousand men situated in its front.

Instead of combining thus actively and vigorously the greatest possible force, Daun, though able to unite with the army of the Circles towards Eulenburg, failed to do so, and suffered that army to retire without a cause. Thirty thousand men were thus uselessly lying in their cantonments at three days' march from Torgau, when they might have decided the fate of the battle. It is difficult to find examples of dispositions altogether so faulty.

Regarding the battle itself, Daun exhibited, throughout, great courage. He made, opportunely, two fortunate charges; but contenting himself with simply defending the heights, he made none of those manœuvres or dispositions which confer the title of great captain; and had he won the battle, it could only have been said that he did it by chance.

It appears also that Daun, knowing as he did the condition of the Prussian army, might have avoided repassing the Elbe, encamped about Schildau or Oschatz, caused the army of the Circles to join him, and then have delivered another battle. This resolution would have been much wiser, as the Austrians had a secure retreat upon Dresden, and since the king would not have been disposed to follow too closely with an army which was decimated. Supposing that they had gained a victory here, Laudon and the Russians would have had time to march concentrically upon Spremburg, in order to complete the establishment of a formidable mass in the heart of the Prussian states.

Though the nearly undecided battle of Torgau had such fatal consequences for the combined armies, they themselves brought it about. Far from each one trying to secure and save himself, they should have lost two similar battles, and the Prussians would have been ruined. It seems as if their generals had derived pleasure from this singular war, for they benevolently preferred giving the king time to repair all of his losses during the winter, that in the spring they might have a new enemy to deal with. At least it is most difficult to explain this astonishing mania of taking, for six months in every year, a divergent direction for one hundred and fifty leagues, and exhausting the other six in endeavoring to unite.

But enough upon this campaign. We shall not again return to the operations of the French army upon the Weser and the Rhine, the principal faults of which we have pointed out in the brief relation given in Chapter XXI.

CHAPTER XXVII.

CAMPAIGN OF 1761.

GENERAL PLAN OF THE CAMPAIGN; OPERATIONS OF THE FRENCH AND THEIR ALLIES IN WESTPHALIA; OBSERVATIONS.

THE belligerent powers had become fatigued with a ruinous war, the results of which seemed problematical, and opened a congress; but the negotiations were obstructed by diversity of interests, and during the progress of the treaty, the preparations for entering into the ensuing campaign were pushed forward with vigor.

France redoubled her efforts. Hoping to put an end to her maritime disasters by an alliance with Spain, she employed the arguments dictated by a wise policy to induce that power to make common cause with her, no doubt regretting bitterly that she had made this discovery too late. Whilst new activity was infused into the shipyards, her land forces were placed upon a formidable footing. An army of eighty thousand men was assembled on the Lower Rhine, under the command of the Prince of Soubise, to besiege Munster, Lipstadt, and other fortresses, whilst the duke of Broglio, with fifty or sixty thousand men, starting from the line of the Mein, should penetrate by Gottingen into the country of Hanover, thus menacing the communications of the allies.

The army of the Circles, coming from Franconia, was to

operate upon the Saale, in order to connect the right of the French with the left of the Austrians, who, under the command of Daun, desired to conquer Saxony.

In Silesia, Laudon commanded an army of sixty thousand men, which was to unite with the great Russian army under Butturlin, and operate with it in besieging the fortified places of that province, on the safety of which depended Frederick's salvation. Another Russian corps, commanded by Count Romanzow, was to act in concert with the Swedes in Pomerania, to besiege Colberg, for the purpose of securing a more advantageous base of operations.

It will be seen, from this narration, exactly how far these projects, more or less badly conceived, were carried out.

The duke of Broglio had placed his troops in winter-quarters, between the Fulde and the Werra, uniting by Gotha with the army of the Circles, which was cantoned between Erfurt and the frontiers of Bohemia. The object of all his combinations was to preserve Gottingen, the base of all the offensive operations in Westphalia, during this campaign.

The month of January was consumed in a war of posts; these skirmishes having no other object than the provisioning of Gottingen, we have not thought proper to relate them.

At length that place being revictualled, the troops again took their cantonments on the first days of February. They were badly posted, for the mass of their forces, which should have been at the right, in case of attack, were scattered along the entire front; and the left and the centre, opposite to the greater part of the enemy's forces, were stripped of troops, nor was the decisive point any better reënforced. Duke Ferdinand did not let this opportunity escape. He asked Frederick to sustain him towards the left, by the Thuringia, assembled his troops in a few days, and divided them into three corps, in order to fall upon the centre of the

French position, and to cut off their left by forcing it to repass the Mein.

The first of these corps, commanded by the hereditary prince, was collected on the right, between Lipstadt and Rhuden, and took the direction of Fritzlar. General Sporken, with the left wing, was united at Duderstedt with the corps detached to the Thuringia by the king, for the purpose of attacking the right of the French cantonments, commanded by the count de Stainville. The bulk of the army, under the command of the duke, was assembled on the Dimel, passed that river and threatened Cassel. The hereditary prince began his march on the 9th of February, in two columns. The first was commanded by General Breitenbach, in the direction of Marburg; the prince with the other upon Fritzlar. This double enterprise failed; Breitenbach was killed, on the 15th, in the attack of Marburg; the hereditary prince was repulsed, on the 12th, by the viscount de Narbonne at Fritzlar. The duke, with the bulk of the army, crossed the Dimel on the 11th, cantoned his troops in the neighborhood of Westufeln.

Marshal de Broglio, confident that the duke's object was only to disquiet him, at first, merely adopted half measures to oppose him; but when he heard of the success gained by his troops before Marburg and Fritzlar, he inferred that he ought to hold his position, and attempt nothing more than to close in towards Meinungen. Count de Stainville was ordered to pass the Werra, and to join him, as likewise were the Saxons, who were in the miserable camp of Langensalza. This order reached them on the 15th, at the moment when Sporken was about to attack them; Stainville obeyed the order without giving himself any uneasiness concerning the fate of the allies; the count de Solms, who commanded them, not having any knowledge of it, was engaged, and so forced to retreat. This he effectuated with great difficulty; the cav alry of General Syburg and of the allies broke the Saxon ranks, and they lost two thousand men, and scarcely succeeded in joining Stainville at Eisenach. The duke de Broglio was apprised of this event on the 16th, and at the same time of a second attack upon Fritzlar, in which M. de Narbonne had accepted, on the 15th, an honorable capitulation; he then thought it full time for him to disengage his flanks, and he subsequently returned to Hirschfeld; in the hope of forestalling the hereditary prince on his arrival at that place. The French army remained in that position until the isolated corps on the Werra had terminated their retrograde movement.

Ferdinand quitted the environs of Zierenberg on the 17th, and cantoned his troops between Fritzlar and Gudensberg; the hereditary prince marched nearly to Homberg, where the army arrived on the 18th, with the advance-guard at Ziegenhain and the hereditary prince near Hirschfeld. On the 19th, the army cantoned in the vicinity of Schwartzenborn, with the advance-guard at Neukirch and the hereditary prince at Obergeisa; Sporken was between Eisenach and Berka, his advance-guard at Vach, from which count de Stainville withdrew.

These movements alarming the French concerning the communications of Fulde, the marshal concentrated his right corps at Hunefeld, and went there himself with the army on the 20th, after having destroyed his fine magazines at Hirschfeld. But new doubts assailed him, and impelled him successively, on the 21st, to Fulde, and on the 26th, to Bergen; abandoning or destroying his immense subsistence stores, collected with extreme difficulty, and absolutely necessary in ulterior operations. Stainville occupied Budingen and Salmunster; The Saxons were established at Gelnhausen. Lieutenant-General Rougé, fearing that he might be cut off, left a garrison at Marburg, and retired through Giessen upon Butzbach.

The allied army marched, on the 21st, to Hausen; on the 23d, to Grabenau; on the 26th, to Alsfeld, and went into close cantonments upon the Ohm, in the vicinity of Schweinsberg. The hereditary prince covered the left at Lauterbach, Lord Granby with the advance-guard was between the Ohm and the Lahn, Luckner on the Kintzingerbach, and Kielmanseg at Laubach. Ferdinand directed the siege of Cassel, on the 1st of March, and had the other places in Hesse invested. Count de Broglio defended the first-named place with vigor, and in a sortie, destroyed nearly all of the batteries of the besiegers.

On the 8th and 9th of March, the French received a reënforcement of fifteen thousand men from the army of the Lower-Rhine, which placed the duke de Broglio in the ascendant, and authorized him to take the offensive in order to rescue Cassel. On the 15th, he broke forth, with all his forces, and after several marches, he arrived, on the 18th, in the presence of the allies. The latter occupied close cantonments on the Ohm, from the Wetter to Homberg; they had raised the sieges of Marburg and Ziegenhain; the corps of Lord Granby, which formed the covering force between the Ohm and the Lahn, rejoined the army. The hereditary prince, flanking the left towards Budingen, was withdrawn to Laubach and Gruneberg; Stainville cannonaded it on the 16th, and forced it back upon Homberg.

The French army cantoned with its right towards Hungen, and its left between Giessen and Wetzlar; Rochambeau covering the front at Faurbach and Ilshausen; and Fischer with his advance-guard at Hachborn and Erbenhausen; the marquis of Poyanne at Treys and Allertshausen; the Swiss brigade, under Boccard, in echelon at Altenbuseck; the duke de Stainville at Gruneberg; and his advance-guard, under Closen, at Londorf and Udenhausen. Finally, Lieutenant-General Dumuy, after having crossed the Lahn, cantoned on the Salzbott, and sent forward detachments upon Seelbach and Hohensolms.

Ferdinand thought that he might attack successfully the right flank of the French, which had the appearance of being in the air, and removed the hereditary prince, on the 19th, to Gruneberg. On the other hand, de Broglio, on the 20th of March, reënforced the corps of Stainville with three brigades of cavalry and the grenadiers of France, in order to oblige the prince to repass the Ohm. To arrive at this end, the French army made sundry demonstrations, and disturbed the centre and right of the allies, with the view of deterring them from reënforcing the prince through Homberg. With this in view, the brigade Cursay was directed to advance upon the Lahn, as far as Gosfeld, whence it was to send its scouts to Origny, on the Wetter, in order to attack the corps of Scheiter. Rosières, with a detachment, occupied a position upon the heights of Panenburg; Rochambeau formed his corps about Ebsdorf, and threw strong parties upon Schweinsberg. Baron Closen was directed to Stangerode, and it was pointed out to him that he must adopt such measures as would enable him to sustain the principal attack, directed by the duke de Stainville, upon Gruneberg, to hold in check the troops which the enemy might send out through Homberg, and also to take in reverse the position which the hereditary prince would undoubtedly occupy near Gruneberg. Closen's corps was supported by that of the Marquis of Poyanne, who had advanced to Londorf with the carbineers and the brigade of Auvergne, which was also supported by Boccard's Swiss brigade.

Stainville formed two columns, and himself led the attack of Gruneberg; brigadier Diesbach commanded that of Laubach. Marshal de Broglio followed the first attack, and reconnoitred the position of the enemy from a height this side of the village. Several discharges of small arms and of cannon, which came from his right, led him to think that Diesbach had dislodged Luckner from Laubach. Stainville then caused the regiment of Schomberg to advance upon the heights between Gruneberg and Laubach, in order to cut off the retreat of the allies, sent the brigade Royal-German to support it, marched count de Scey-Montbeillard, with the dragoons of the king and of Ferronnaye, upon the heights of Stangerode, and lastly, directed his infantry with its right upon Gruneberg.

When the count de Scey arrived near Stangerode, at his left was the division Closen. At the same time the corps of the hereditary prince was discovered in the village of Alzenheim, surrounded by a pond and several ravines. The quietude exhibited by his outposts showed that he did not anticipate an attack, and had he acted with promptitude and made use of the surprise by precipitating his cavalry quickly into the village and to its rear, it is probable that the hereditary prince would have saved very little of his own corps. But as the French had agreed to announce their arrival, they opened a useless cannonade. The allies quickly abandoned the village and formed upon the heights in the rear. Baron Closen sent his foot volunteers to turn their right flank; from his left, by the woods of Bernsfeld, and placing himself at the head of his cavalry, he passed to the right of the village against their left flank. When he arrived near the pond, perceiving that the allied infantry was neither formed nor supported by many mounted troops, he placed himself at the head of the regiments of Antichamp, Orleans, and the volunteers of Saint Victor, and falling upon the enemy's squadrons, drove them into a scattered brushwood near by. Then turning to the left he charged the infantry, which was sabred at will. Finally the king's dragoons, of the corps of the count de Scey, having also arrived, the allied infantry was pursued through the brushwood as far as the position held by its own cavalry. The latter seeing that the French were pursuing with but little regard to order, charged them in turn, and forced back the most advanced upon the second squadron of Ferronnaye; but that regiment standing fast, and the volunteers of Saint-Victor sustaining it opportunely, the allied cavalry was repulsed. However, this charge allowed the prince time to retire upon Burgmunden, and to repass the Ohm, with the loss of two thousand men, nineteen flags, and ten pieces of cannon. This check would have been much more severe, had the brigade Royal-German, which was to pass through the woods along the Ohm, and form in the plain, carried out its orders; but encountering Luckner, who was retreating from Laubach, through Nieder-Ohm, he halted, and uselessly exchanged some round shot with him, and remained concealed behind a height.

After this affair Ferdinand went himself, on the evening of the 22d of March, to the vicinity of Ziegenhain, the siege of which he raised the next day. He crossed the Eder on the 24th, took up cantonments thereabouts, and caused the siege of Cassel also to be raised on the 28th, that he might be enabled to pass the Dimel on the 31st. All the skirmishes with the rear-guards terminated in favor of the French, who made some eighteen hundred prisoners.

The duke de Broglio was now in full possession of Hesse, but as he had lost all of his magazines during his retreat, and since the country had been gleaned and foraged for fully a year, he did not think himself in a condition to prosecute his operations before collecting a new supply of subsistence stores. This undertaking kept him a long time inactive. The allied army, on the 1st of April, reëntered cantonments behind the Dimel; the duke de Broglio resumed his between the Werra and the Fulde.

The French exhausted two months in strengthening their position about Wesel, and in fortifying the places of Hesse. Their generals corresponded even in folio to establish unity in their operations, without succeeding. The allies, on their part, increased the fortifications of Hameln, Munster, and Lipstadt, and saw them in a respectable state of defense. Never were the evil results of a divided command more strongly exhibited, never were forces more entirely misapplied, never were so many plans arranged as were discussed by the two marshals, and ordered by the French minister of war. The two generals-in-chief exhausted all their talents in discussing what the enemy might do to oppose their reciprocal movements, and ended by allowing the season suitable for operations to slip away, whilst endeavoring to calculate within thirty marches what the enemy might undertake against each one of them. Thus it was that an army of one hundred and twenty thousand men, perfectly organized, and composed of warlike troops, scarcely managed to maintain itself against a collection of sixty thousand combatants of all nationalities, which, so to speak, had no secure means of recruiting.

At length the army of the Lower Rhine was united, early in June, about Wesel and Dusseldorf; that of Broglio near Cassel. The allies were concentrated at Neuhauss, the hereditary prince towards Munster, and Sporken near Warburg.

The prince of Soubise crossed the Rhine, and on the 18th of June encamped at Matten, near Dortmund. Ferdinand informed of this movement, inferred that he would have time to place himself between the two French armies. On the 20th, he sent the hereditary prince to Ham, and on the 23d, encamped himself in the excellent position of Soest. Soubise marched on the same day to Unna, and intended to move the next day, the 28th. to Werle, but he was there forestalled by the duke, who immediately afterwards, on the 29th, took up a position within half a league of the French army. His object was to attack it, but he found it so strongly posted there that he resolved to turn it. For this purpose he set out, on the 1st day of July, at ten o'clock in the evening, in four columns, and after marching thirty-six consecutive hours, he arrived, on the morning of the 3d, in the plain of Dortmund, upon the communications of the French prince, who, filled with astonishment at the manœuvre, immediately struck his camp and retired to Hemmerle. The allies were too tired to follow; but, nevertheless, made a movement, during the night of the 3d and 4th upon Unna. The armies manœuvred in face of each other until the 7th, when Soubise encamped at Soest, and Duke Ferdinand near Werle. The allied army was organized as follows:

Right Wing.

Under the command of the hereditary prince of Brunswick and General Kielmanseg.............................. 27 bat., 24 squad.

Centre.		Bat.	Sqds.	
Under the command of the duke in person:	Division Conway,	8	7	24 bat., 23 squad.
	" Howard,	6	10	
	" Pr. Anhalt,	10	6	
Left Wing.				
Under the command of Lord Granby, and afterwards of the duke in person, between the Asse and the Lippe.	Division Wutgenau,	7	5	26 bat., 27 squad.
	" Granby,	12	14	
	" Wolf,	7	8	

Grand total........ 77 bat., 74 squad.

Not included:

The remainder of Sporken's corps encamped at Hertzfeld, and the other detachments.

Whilst these things were passing, marshal de Broglio, with fifty thousand men, had begun his operations, on the 26th of June, and gradually pushed back Sporken's corps upon Lipstadt, where he arrived, on the 8th of July, in accordance with instructions of the duke. Broglio's advance-guard joined the army of Soubise at Soest on the 7th, and on the next day they had effected their junction and were in line. Ferdinand contented himself with moving his camp nearer the village of Illingen, where his centre was posted, covered by the creek of Salzbach; the left was between the Lippe and the Asse, towards the village of Willinghausen.*

The French generals lost eight days in a council of war. They read, it is true, elegant *mémoires* upon the inconveniences of attacking the enemy in his advantageous position, and exhibited clearly all the resources possessed by the enemy, which it was possible to oppose to the French army, so that far from confirming the French generals in an energetic resolution, they only increased their uncertainty.

Finally, a plan of attack was arranged for the 16th of July. Broglio was in motion on the 15th, in order to pass by way of Oslinghausen, and take a position towards Hultrup, where the corps of the prince of Condé had orders to join him. His advance-guard was to cause two brigades to attack the posts of Nordel and Willinghausen. Soubise went himself from Ervitte to the Saltzbach. This march of two leagues, executed on the morning of the 15th, was intended to bring the troops near the enemy, in order to be ready for an attack the next day, and for the purpose of intrenching the heights in rear of Saltzbach, to protect the retreat of the army in case of a check.

On the 15th, at daylight, Broglio quitted the camp of Ervitte and took his army into camp at Oslinghausen (Plate

* We have merely given a sketch of this battle and of what followed subsequently on this line of operations, for the reason that we have already too many engravings. Amateurs can follow out all the campaigns of Duke Ferdinand upon the atlas of Colonel Bawr, chief of staff of the duke, or upon the maps of Hesse and Westphalia, by Julien; these will suffice for such as have not the beautiful maps of Lecocq.

XXI., No. 3), whence he started at five o'clock in the afternoon, in three columns. That of the right, composed of the advance-guard, under Lieutenant-General Closen, was to attack Willinghausen; that of the left, formed of the division Belzunce, had orders to attack the chateau of Nordel; the centre, which remained in rear, was composed of the bulk of the army, which in case of necessity, was to sustain only the first two columns.

At six o'clock in the evening, the duke was advised of these movements, which threatened the road to Ham; he at once ordered Lord Granby to maintain his position to the last extremity, and directed General Wutgenau to sustain him. The line was prolonged towards the left, in order more effectually to support the left, which was about to become engaged. Anhalt's brigade crossed the Asse, in order to replace Wutgenau, and was joined to his right. Finally, General Sporken, who was encamped at Herzfeld on the right bank of the Lippe, was directed to send to Lord Granby a corps of eight battalions and seven squadrons, commanded by General Wolf.

Meanwhile, Closen attacked the forest of Willinghausen with the foot volunteers of Saint-Victor, sustained by the regiments of Nassau, of Deux-Ponts, and the *élite* battalions of Auvergne and Poitou. The English, under Granby, defended themselves at first with vigor, but were repulsed in the village, and charged with impetuosity. At this moment the corps of Wutgenau arrived, and the French were forced to reënter the woods. Closen then demanded reënforcements from the general-in-chief, who detached to his assistance the brigade Guerchy, and marched himself with the king's regiment to his relief. The attack became more lively; Willinghausen was taken and retaken, and night alone put an end to the combat. The French remained masters of the village, which was occupied by the brigades of Aquitaine and Rougé.

Whilst these events were in progress, the marshal heard from the prince of Soubise, who informed him of his march upon Eimbecke, and notified him that as the enemy was apparently withdrawing all of his troops from the right, he should have to recall the prince of Condé. Broglio had too certain proofs to the contrary to believe this, and then invited the prince of Condé to join him, and advised his colleague to resume his intermediate position.

Ferdinand, on the first intimation of the movements of his enemies, had, as we have stated, ordered a general prolongation to the left, to sustain the engaged wing. Not content with sending thither, during the attack, the English brigades of Pembroke and Cavendish, he repaired to the point himself, whilst the hereditary prince, commanding the right wing, established his troops near Illingen, in the position previously occupied by the centre, and steadily held in check the army of Soubise. On the 16th, at daybreak, the attack upon Willinghausen was renewed by a brisk cannonade. Broglio, considering himself too weak to maintain his position there, directed the prince to resume his former position at Oslinghausen; but already engaged, he could not extricate himself in time to effect his retreat; and reënforcements from all directions joining the allies, Ferdinand was enabled to seize the village of Willinghausen; not, however, without its making a most obstinate resistance. The Rougé regiment was captured. Broglio then decided to retreat, and did so, covered by the grenadiers of France, which thus far had not been engaged. It was conducted in good order, being favored by very broken ground, which prevented the enemy's cavalry from acting.

The dispatch of the marshal, announcing his retreat, reached the prince at the moment when he was commencing the action to force the passage of the Saltzbach, towards Scheidengen. Alarmed by the possibility that he might become engaged alone with the enemy, he recalled his columns to the camp of Closter-Paradise, which he had just left, without considering that his own great superiority, and the presence of the corps of Lieutenant-General Dumesnil near the Werl, would have insured to him the means of overwhelming the hereditary prince by way of Sundern.

This retreat ended the affair of Willinghausen, in which the French lost some five or six thousand men, and the allies above two thousand. Never was there an engagement which more clearly exhibited the fatal consequences of irresolution, of an absence of unity in the movements, and more than all, of a divided command. Here we see an army composed of veteran troops compelled to retreat before an enemy, cut off from his communications, in a hazardous position, and unable to bring into action half the number of combatants. Here, likewise, posterity will find a most forcible example of the influence exercised over the course of events by the art of conducting troops. By a comparison of the operations of the army of Soubise and the means of its adversary with those which we have seen in our day, we are forced to acknowledge, that in this art of commanding lies the true strength of armies and of empires. The military register, presenting a pompous display of regiments, does not give the real force of the army; there might as well be none, when the government does not place at its head a man capable of commanding it under all circumstances.

Though the loss sustained by the French should have affected them but slightly, still this combat of Willinghausen totally changed the face of affairs. The generals renewed their disputes. Soubise desired that the armies should remain united; Broglio, on the contrary, insisted that they should be divided, in order that a strong diversion might be made in the country of Hanover, by the right bank of the Weser. The prince, at length, fell in with this arrangement, reënforced the army of his colleague with thirty thousand men, and encamped with the rest at Herdringen, on the 25th of July, in order to cover Hesse. Broglio immediately took up his march, and arrived, on the 27th, before Paderborn, at the instant when the government, which disapproved of a separation, had sent an order to attack Ferdinand anew. It was too late, for the prince had been on the march since the morning of the 27th, and had gone into camp on the 30th at Buren, between the two French armies, leaving the hereditary prince at Rhuden to observe Soubise.

Marshal Broglio took position on the 28th at Dryburg and Dringenberg. He only awaited a new reënforcement of ten thousand men, which had left the corps of Soubise on the 9th of August, for the purpose of threatening Hameln, whilst the latter was to make a demonstration towards Munster. The duke then resolved to take a central position, which would at the same time prevent these enterprises and interrupt the communications between the two French armies. He set out on the 10th of August, and marched by Detmold, on the heights of Moltmorbergen, where he encamped on the 13th, with his right at Reilkirchen, and his left at Sieghof.

In the meantime the ministry approved of the plan of the diversion, provided that, instead of driving Ferdinand across the Weser, they should turn him by the Upper Lippe. This project encountered the fate of the previous ones, and far from carrying it out, Broglio, after several insignificant movements, passed the Weser at Hoxter, on the 18th of August, threatening Hameln and Brunswick. Ferdinand, without being disquieted, remained upon the left bank of the river, about Hoxter, in order to cover the forts, which gave him a good support, and, at the same time, enabled him to menace the communications of the French with Hesse.

The prince of Soubise, on his part, had marched, in the early days of August, to the Lippe, to threaten Munster; but the duke, giving himself very little uneasiness on account of the temporary success of this secondary corps, withdrew even the hereditary prince, who was opposed to him, and hurled him, by three rapid marches, to Lichtenau, on the 14th, upon Broglio's rear, who was then posted around Dryburg. So soon as the grand French army had passed the Weser, the duke concluded that he might thwart its plans by threatening Cassel, whilst the hereditary prince should counteract, on the other hand, those of Soubise. The duke then threw Granby's corps upon the Dimel, on the 24th of August, in order to attack the duke de Stainville, and went himself, with his army, on the 27th, to Immenhausen. This enterprise succeeded, for the French general hurried to the succor of Hesse with a part of his army, and the duke being satisfied, on his side, with having led him into a false movement, returned to Buhnau on the 1st of September.

Broglio, resuming his plans against Westphalia, returned on the 5th to Sulbeck, and pushed his reserve upon Gendersheim, in order to march upon Wolfenbuttel. But the duke opposed him by the manœuvre which had already succeeded so well. He crossed the Dimel on the 18th of September, pushed forward to Wilhemsthal, and caused the hereditary prince to rejoin him. The French general, on his side, occupied an intermediate position near Munden, reënforced De Stainville, and formed a kind of cordon from Luternberg to Eimbeck.

It is unnecessary to give in detail an account of these petty operations, in which Duke Ferdinand gained all the honor, owing to the contracted combinations of his enemies, who at the least demonstration were alarmed with fears of perishing by hunger in a country both rich and fertile, and who, though trembling for the fate of their numerous detachments, still continued to make others to sustain the first.

Broglio, at last deeming himself secure, returned, on the 3d of October, to Uslar, to push forward detachments upon Wolfenbuttel and Brunswick; the count of Lusatia marched there with the reserve. The first of these forts was occupied on the 10th, the second, which had a weak garrison, was invested on the 11th; but Prince Augustus of Brunswick being, with some battalions, at Hanover, on the night of the 13th and 14th, surprised the post of Selper, and entered the place in full view of the French.

The count of Lusatia, who had no other enemies to oppose him thereabouts, nevertheless, believing that the whole army of the allies was upon him, raised the blockade, evacuated even Wolfenbuttel, and fell back upon Broglio's army.

Ferdinand having determined to stop these incursions, left a small portion of his army to observe Soubise, and caused the hereditary prince, who had returned to Lipstadt purposely, to join him; but the duke falling ill, all the operations were suspended until November. As soon as he recovered, he crossed his army over the Weser on the 4th, and arranged the movements of the several columns for the purpose of cutting off the division Poyanne, which guarded the defiles of Escherhausen; the delay of a solitary one, as usual, defeated this project. On the 5th, the hereditary prince cannonaded Broglio towards Eimbeck, and forced him to concentrate his divisions, so that he changed each month from a most belligerent attitude to one most shamefully defensive. The armies were facing each other, but neither thought best to give battle so late in the season, and each waited for the other to become tired of the war and give up his position. Discovering, however, at last, that his adversary had as much endurance as himself, the duke menaced his left flank and his communications with Gottingen,

This plan succeeded. Broglio, regarding the campaign as terminated, did not consider it best to hold his position, but drew near Gottingen, by way of Morungen, arriving at the former place on the 16th. Soon after his troops occupied the same winter-quarters behind the Werra which they had on the previous winter.

The prince of Soubise was in advance; but after threatening Munster, and sending the Prince of Condé upon Hamm, he fell back from Appelhusen upon Westerholz, because the hereditary prince had seized the city of Dorsten, where the French had their bakeries, and whence was jeopardized the security of the provision trains coming from Wesel. As soon as the prince started to join the duke's army, Soubise revived his old idea of an incursion upon the Ems; but not daring to undertake it himself, for fear of losing his convoys of bread, he threw forward his light troops upon Embden, confining himself to merely taking position at Kosfeld, on the 20th of September. That insignificant war does not deserve even a tabular account of it.

Ferdinand, perceiving that the Weser separated his army from that of Broglio, and that the latter was reduced to the condition of constantly defending Hesse, sent back the hereditary prince to Lipstadt on the 10th of October, in order to restrain Soubise; but the latter had already anticipated him, and concluding that there was nothing more to be done at Kosfeld, nor on the Ems, and also regarding an enterprise against Munster as too hazardous, directed his movement on Borken, near the Rhine. The duke then recalled the hereditary prince on the 15th of October, and Soubise lay quietly in his cantonments until the 10th of November, when his troops began to cross the Rhine, to go into winter-quarters on its left bank.

Thus was terminated a campaign for which the French had made such extensive preparations. It would have been far better for them to have abandoned this impolitic war, instead of sending numerous armies into the field, and thus losing each year thirty thousand brave men, for the purpose of defending a few bags of flour.

We shall not enlarge upon the faults of this campaign. The line of operations was the same as in the preceding year. The only way to succeed was to march *en masse* towards the sources of the Lippe, to oblige Ferdinand to accept a battle upon his communications, and to repulse him to the Rhine. The duke, by his imprudent movement upon Dortmund and Unna, had just placed himself in a most difficult situation, and the French did not know how to take advantage of it. The affair of Willinghausen, as has already been observed, was as badly arranged as it could well have been. A simple glance at a detailed map will show that whatever might have been the position of the duke's army upon the ground, the feeble part of it was his left wing, placed in a corner between the Asse and the Lippe,* exactly where passed the important road to Hamm. The duke, though desirous of turning the French, had taken none of those sage precautions which might render his undertaking free from risk, and, as it appeared, he was more effectually turned than the French army, whose communications with Hesse and the Mein were entirely covered. If, instead of groping along the entire front of the allies' line, one division of light troops had been left upon the heights of Meyerke, before their right and their centre, and as the two French corps of eighty thousand men were approaching in two

* M. de Broglio thought the same. This general composed several memoirs founded upon this campaign, which contain excellent principles; but whether he was not his own master, or whether it arose from want of resolution, the execution did not come up to his views. It is better to act more vigorously, and write less. As it is, it must be admitted that he and the Marshal d'Estrées are the only ones, of all the French generals-in-chief, that even passably conducted this war.

columns, the first along the banks of the Asse, by Kirch-dinken, and the other by following the left bank of the Lippe, by Ultrup and Untrop, whilst a division had marched by the right bank upon Ham, to seize the bridge of boats, it can not be doubted that the left wing of the allies might have been captured on the 15th, and the remainder cut off from Munster, Lipstadt, and all communication would have been annihilated on the following days. But to effectuate all this it was necessary that the march should have been swift and vigorous, that no masses should be deployed without an object, nor should they be drawn up in battle array and lose time by a cannonade. Whether the allies had but one wing of their army upon the ground, or all their forces were assembled to the number of sixty thousand men, it was the only movement capable of bringing about the total destruction of their army, without hazarding more than the loss of a few thousand men, since there was open a safe retreat by Soest upon Cassel, and even upon Siegen. The general positions of the armies on this occasion were the same relatively as were those in which Napoleon placed his enemies at Bassano, Marengo, Ulm, and Jena. From this we may infer what would have become of the allied army had he possessed half the forces under his command which were under Soubise and Broglio.

The general dispositions employed were not exempt from censure; but their execution was wretched. When Broglio saw that he had in front forces nearly equal to his own, it might have been inferred that Soubise would have less of them in front of him, between the Asse and the Salzbach. The latter, far from retiring with seventy thousand combatants before twenty-five thousand, should have forced the passage of the Salzbach, and taking possession of the villages of Illingen and Sud-Dinken, would thus have cut off the duke from the rest of the line, from which he was separated by a river. In the same way he might have seized the heights of Rindern, and should have pushed vigorously the *débris* of the army of the hereditary prince in the direction of Unna. Thrust upon the Rhine, the whole of that wing would have been lost, for Duke Ferdinand was not in communication with it, and he could not have manœuvred for its safety, having before his left wing a corps twice as numerous as his own, and the army of Soubise between himself and the hereditary prince.

The rest of the campaign was conducted upon the best principles, but its execution was contemptible. It is a remarkable fact that Broglio was successful when he fought and manœuvred alone, in the month of March, to reconquer Hesse, and experienced nothing but reverses after having been reënforced by an army of eighty thousand men, superior itself to all the forces of the enemy. His operations upon the right bank of the Weser were incredible. Glancing at the map, it seems a matter of astonishment that a general commanding ninety thousand men, opposed to forty-five thousand, should be alarmed at every demonstration of his adversary, and so make fourteen or fifteen defensive detachments, instead of falling upon him with his entire force. All this was well enough upon the Weser, as it was necessary to prolong it to the right, as was proposed by the duke de Broglio; but this was no place to remain passive. *The art of war does not consist in running races upon the communications of our enemy, but in securing possession of them, and marching thereon, for the purpose of bringing him to battle.*

As soon as Soubise separated from the marshal, his fortunes declined. Although he still had forty thousand men, he did not venture upon an enterprise in presence of the hereditary prince, who opposed him with only fifteen thousand. Ferdinand held him in such light estimation that he ordered the prince three times to the Weser, often leaving in the front of the enemy only three or four thousand men, and yet Soubise himself did not dare move over four marches from the Rhine, for fear of getting out of bread and compromising his convoys. The position, occupation, and operations of the army presented nothing allied to a military combination. So far as that was concerned, his partisans in the Oost-Frise had no end in view connected with the war. After marching and countermarching, for three months, between Munster and Wesel, this army repassed the Rhine, and took up its winter-quarters, at the moment in which Broglio was becoming seriously engaged beyond the Weser. How shall we designate such manœuvres as these?

If, instead of employing such extensive forces as accessaries alone, the prince had occupied a central position at Stadtbergen, on the Dimel, to close the roads of Paderborn, Lipstadt, and Munster, he would have fulfilled two important ends. The first would have been gained by his covering the communications of the marshal, and thus preventing him from decamping at each demonstration of the duke, and enabling him to draw to his support the corps of De Stainville, which then would not have been necessary at Cassel, and with the addition thus made to his strength, Broglio should at once have been able to strike a decisive blow. The second end which he would have accomplished was the completing of the arrangements for holding the communications of the duke, thus throwing him back upon either the Rhine or the North Sea.

Ferdinand accomplished nothing remarkable in this campaign. He committed fewer faults than his adversary, that was all. The enterprise which he undertook during the month of February, against the quarters of Broglio's army, had a useful object; but it was badly conducted. It was undertaken by several small, diverging corps, instead of pushing *en masse* upon the centre and left of the French.

The duke was then much stronger, and it was for his interest to strike a decisive blow upon that isolated portion before the army of Soubise was in a condition to open the campaign. Nothing was risked in case of a reverse; were he to succeed, the campaign would be decided in his favor. To reap no advantage from such a state of things, or at least not to attempt it, was an inexcusable oversight. There could be no reason for his not directing the mass of his troops against the centre and the right of the French, except the fear of losing his communications with the Weser. But was there any foundation for this when, with sixty thousand men, he was able to overwhelm and dispose of the thirty or thirty-five thousand men parceled out, and with their centre pierced? The detachments of the Lieutenant-Generals Saint Pern and Stainville could never have compromised the communications of a victorious army. Then the enterprise of the duke could not have been limited to a partial success, for, from its nature, it would have obliged the enemy to concentrate his cantonments in the rear, which would have been equivalent to a victory. Moreover, it would have been far better to expose his communications, with every chance of success in his favor, than to have compromised them three months afterwards, in presence of three times his numbers, as happened at Dortmund and Unna, so lauded by Templehof, and of which nothing displeased that historian save a misplaced sally. As it was, the duke lost all of his communications, in order to gain one of the three lines of the enemy's retreat. Such a manœuvre, executed by an army inferior by half, would not be justified. The nephew of Ferdinand, who commanded the Prussians in 1806, in imitation of his uncle, made a similar manœuvre by marching upon Gotha, whilst Napoleon was marching upon the Saale. But what was the fatal result? did he not lose the Prussian army and monarchy together?

It has been already remarked in Chapter XV., that the duke, by persisting in his stay in the vicinity of Lipstadt, was exposed to the loss of his communications, and placed himself in the same position in which the Prussians were at Jena. However, his movement upon Dortmund was extremely rash. Abandoning the support of the fortresses of Lipstadt and Munster, and every means of effecting a retreat, he placed himself between the Rhine and a superior army, which possessed two communications. Finally, this march of Duke Ferdinand appears so much the more extraordinary, as his entire system ought to have been, with a central mass, to prevent the union of the isolated portions of the enemy. By going into camp between the Rhine and the corps of Soubise, he left, on the contrary, the latter at liberty to unite his army to that of Broglio, and thus double his force, for, with a little attention, it will be seen that the junction of these two generals was the legitimate fruit of this manœuvre. Is it for bringing about this result that Tempelhof has lavished upon him so much praise?

CHAPTER XXVIII.

GENERAL DISPOSITIONS FOR THE CAMPAIGN; FREDERICK MARCHES INTO SILESIA.

In the preceding chapter, we have seen the vast preparations and endless projects of the enemies of Frederick. The final and great blow was to be given in Silesia, after the Russian army had effected a junction with Laudon, whose corps was to be increased to eighty thousand men, by reënforcements drawn from Daun's army. The king could only oppose to the allies an army worn down by fatigue, supported by a nation so far exhausted as to be incapable of furnishing any more recruits. To add to his embarrassment, the allies had refused to exchange prisoners, since 1760, and they occupied a portion of his provinces, where he would have been able to raise some men.

It may be recollected that in leaving for Saxony, he had left General Goltz in Silesia, with about twenty thousand men, to watch the Russians and Laudon. At the end of the campaign, the two parties took winter-quarters, under a mutual agreement, which was prolonged until the 26th of May.

The Austrians receiving reënforcements, which swelled their army to sixty-four battalions and eighty-five squadrons, Laudon interrupted the armistice with the hope of capturing Goltz's command while the king was still in Saxony. To this end, he entered Silesia, on the 23d of April, in three columns, and established himself at Waldenburg, but Goltz collected his troops under the fortress of Schweidnitz, in the strong positions of Hohenfriedberg and Hohenkunzendorf, in order to guard the defiles. Laudon, finding that he had been anticipated, and being under orders to undertake nothing which might compromise his army until the arrival of the Russians and some reënforcements from Daun, gave up his plan, and halted in the neighborhood of Saltzbrunn.

Before he was informed of this event, the king had deferred marching into Silesia, for the purpose of making use of the last days of the armistice to drive the army of the Circles out of Thuringia and Voigtland in Franconia. When informed of the rupture, he assembled, on the 3d of May, thirty-three battalions, sixty-three squadrons, and eight batteries of heavy artillery, crossed the Elbe at Strehlen, intrusted Prince Henry with the defense of that river, and in nine marches, reached Hohenfriedberg with his army, where he encamped on the 13th. His plan was to manœuvre against the army under Marshal Butturlin, and that of Laudon, in order to delay their union, and to attack the latter before the arrival of the Austrians, should an opportunity be presented.

Daun, hearing of the king's march, put in motion for Zittau, on the 9th of May, from twenty-five to thirty thousand men, commanded by Generals Sincère and Odonell, for the purpose of preserving Bohemia from invasion, and afterwards to join the army of Silesia, which had already been reënforced by the divisions of Argenteau and De Gourcy. On the other hand, Laudon, on the 12th, entered the county of Glatz, where he took up a position at Braunau and Dittersbach. His principal corps, numbering upwards of forty thousand combatants, occupied the intrenched camp at Hartmansdorf; General Ellrichshausen flanked the right of the position at Giersdorf, and General Wolfersdorf the left at Bolich, near Trautenau; a corps of thirteen thousand men under Draskowitz, covered the county of Glatz, in the neighborhood of Silberberg and Wartha; and lastly, General Bethlem with four thousand Croats observed the Prussians towards Kunzendorf. Odonell held Zittau in Lusatia with twenty-five thousand men.

Frederick then recalled a part of the corps of Goltz, and his army thus raised to forty-eight thousand combatants, on the 16th, occupied the positions and cantonments indicated in the adjoining table. General Goltz, with the remainder of his troops, amounting to ten thousand men, occupied the intrenched camp of Glogau, in order to observe the Russians. A reënforcement of two thousand grenadiers was sent to the prince of Wurtemberg, who, with twelve thousand men, held the intrenched camp of Colberg, in order to cover Pomerania; lastly, Prince Henry, with thirty-two thousand men, was established, on the 4th of May, upon the heights of Schlettau and Katzenhausern behind the Triebsche, between Militz and Nossen. That position, which was already formidable by nature, had been fortified during the winter, and placed in a strong state of defense.

Daun's army, which was opposed to Prince Henry, consisting of fifty-four battalions and more than one hundred squadrons, remained tranquil in the vicinity of Dresden. The marshal might also have drawn to him Lascy, who commanded a separate corps at Reichenberg and Boxdorf, the division Guasco, which covered Eger, General Haddick, detached to Dippodiswalde, and lastly, the army of the Circles, upwards of twenty thousand strong, which guarded Voigtland. All these forces, after the departure of the corps sent to Laudon, would have swelled his army to more than seventy thousand combatants; in spite of this great superiority, Daun did not attempt a movement during the entire campaign, and Prince Henry was careful not to disturb him.

TABLE OF THE ORGANIZATION AND POSI-

FIRST

MARGRAVE CHARLES.

LIEUT.-GEN'S .... PLATTEN.

MAJOR-GEN'S..Schmettau. Flans. Gablens. Browne.

Schmettau.	5 squads. Spaen. . . . . 5 —— Prince Henry. . .	Cantoned at Wilkau, Gersdorf, Pulsen, Graditz, and neighborhood.
Flans.	5 squads. Bredow, cuirass. 5 —— Vasold, cuirass. .	(same)
Gablens.	2 bat. Lestewitz . . . At Bogensdorf. 1 —— Falkenhain . . . . 1 —— Nimschefsky. . . .	At the camp of Kunzendorf.
Browne.	2 bat. Thadden. . . . . 2 —— Bernburg.	At the heights dorf.

SECOND

MAJOR-GEN'S.........Bulow. Prince Bernburg. Wangenheim.

Bulow.	4 squads. Old Platten. . . 10 —— Bareith, drags. .	Cantoned at Poln-Weistritz, Burckerdorf, Leutmausdorf, and neighborhood.
Prince Bernburg.	2 bat. Ziethen, at Boyndorf. 2 —— Thiele, in second line at the camp of Kunzendorf.	
Wangenheim.	2 bat. Gablenz. . . . . 2 —— Prince Ferdinand. 2 —— Wied.	At Zirlau.

RE-

MAJOR-GEN'S..Saldern.

1 bat. Saldern, at Kumerau.	
1 —— Salenmon, vols. 1 —— Wunsch. . .	Upon the Kolberg towards Tanhausen and Pantenau.
10 sqs. Mohring, hussars, at Leutmansdorf.	
1 bat. chasseurs, near Nimptsch.	
2 —— Lindstedt. . . 2 —— Forcade. . .	At Arnsdorf.

-TION OF THE KING'S ARMY, MAY, 1761.

LINE.

GENERAL ZIETHEN.

Wied.

Zeunnert.
- 2 bat. Ramin. . . . .
- 2 — Margrave Charles. . .
- 2 — Schenkendorf. . .

camp on the of Kunzen-

Knobloch.
- 1 bat. Anhalt. . . . .
- 1 — Haak. . . . .
- 1 — Schwartz. . . . .
- 2 — Old Brunswick. . . .

At the camp upon the Ziskenberg.

Platten.

Lentulus.
- 5 squads. Seidlitz. . . .
- 5 —— Horn. . . . .

Schwerin.
- 8 squads. Gardes-du-corps.
- 5 —— Gendarmes. . .

Cantoned in the neighborhoods of Wurben, Buntzelwitz, and Jauernick.

LINE.

Ramin.
- 2 bat. Maurice, at Hohenfriedberg.
- 2 — Prince Henry, at Freyburg.
- 1 — Young Brunswick, at Zirlau.

Pomeiske.
- 5 squads. Pomeiske. . .

Zastrow.
- 5 squads. Zastrow, drags.
- 5 —— Zetteritz. . . .

At Schwaiwitz, Ullersdorf, Thomaswalde, and Halbendorf.

-SERVE.

Mollendorf.
- 2 bat. Pr. of Prussia.
- 2 — Guards. . . .

Schenkendorf.
- 2 bat. Zeunert. . . .
- 2 — Syburg. . . .

At Kunzendorf.

10 sqs. Hus. of Ziethen, at Schweidnitz and Hausdorf.

Total, without including the corps of Goltz, 52 battalions, 87 squadrons.

OPERATIONS IN SILESIA.

The different armies retained their relative positions until June.

On the 22d, General Goltz sent word to the king that Marshal Butturlin had arrived at Posen, on the 13th, marched into Silesia on the 24th, 25th, and 26th, with four divisions, estimated at sixty thousand men, and proposed to attack them before they again united, provided a reënforcement was sent him. Frederick consented, and detached eight thousand men; but on the 28th of June, as Goltz was about to commence his march, he was attacked with a violent fever, of which he died two days after.

The king sent Ziethen to replace him; that general arrived on the 29th, and commenced his movement the next day, but it was already too late; the Russian army having reunited on the 29th, had just been established at Czempin at the head of the defiles of Zartsch. The Prussian general took a good position, on the 1st of July, at Kasten. Hearing that the Russians were about to march to Dolsk, he went into camp, on the 3d, near Kopkowa. Notwithstanding all his efforts, it was with the greatest difficulty that he obtained news of the enemy, inasmuch as the Cossacks swarmed over the country, and masked all their movements. Having learned, on the 9th, that Marshal Butturlin was to have arrived at Borke, he marched immediately for Boyanowa, taking the direction by Trachenberg upon Prausnitz, where he was enabled to cover at the same time Glogau and Breslau.

Frederick had the strongest motives for not attacking the Russians, and, in fact, there was nothing to be gained by it there; he therefore ordered Ziethen to divide his corps into two divisions, and encamp them separately at a short distance from Breslau, on the left bank of the Oder, with the view of placing one of the corps under Breslau, in case the Russians threatened it, and to protect Brieg with the other.

On the 15th, the Russian army entered Silesia, and encamped at Tschirnau.

During the execution of these changes, the king and Laudon were stationary in the mountains; but so soon as the Russians approached Breslau, the latter formed some magazines in Upper-Silesia, where the corps of Bethlem was found, and on the 3d of July, transferred his light troops from Brentano to Michelsdorf. Frederick at once presuming that the enemy desired to advance upon Reichenbach and Nimptsch, to cut him off from the Neisse, determined forthwith to abandon the mountains, so as to reach Pulzen near Schweidnitz on the 6th. As it was, the Austrian light divisions had made their appearance at Heidelberg and Reusendorf; but the main army remained fixedly in camp, where it was joined, on the 15th and 16th of July, by the corps of Odonell, which had arrived from Daun's army. Laudon then had seventy-five thousand men in hand, and received from Maria Theresa full and complete authority to direct the operations according to the dictates of his own judgment, for the glory of her arms. This individual mark of the queen's confidence determined him to issue from the defiles where he was posted, for the purpose of fixing upon the attention of the king, and by misleading him, to protect the movements of the Russians. He came to Frankenstein to encamp, on the 20th, at Baumgarten. A chain of small corps guarded the mountains towards Habensdorf and Hohengiersdorf; General Bethlem threatened Neisse.

Although these movements were carefully hidden, they did not escape the vigilance of the king; he saw that the Austrians wished to operate their junction with the Russians towards Oppeln. Although he might anticipate his enemies at that point by Grottkau, it was still more important to reach Gros-Nossen before them, in order to preserve at the same time his communications with Neisse; he therefore commenced his march before daybreak on the 21st, that he might take a position at Siegenroth near Nimptsch.

The unexpected arrival of the king at Siegenroth somewhat deranged Laudon's plans, who had pitched his camp at Stolz near Muncheberg, with the intention of drawing nearer to Oppeln. He resolved to take, on the morning of the 22d, the camp of Gros-Nossen. Frederick, fearing above all that he might be cut off from Neisse, the pivot of his movements for the purpose of preventing the junction of the enemies' armies, and where he had extensive depots, adopted the course of going to Karlowitz and attacking Laudon, if he made his appearance in that direction. He opened his march before daylight, in three columns; the Austrian general was likewise in motion, but the Prussians gaining his right flank, his camp equipage was seized at Gros-Nossen. The stream of Ohlau alone separated the two armies, and this sudden apparition caused no little disorder among the Austrians; of which the king failed to take advantage. However, he pushed forward to Gros-Carlowitz, where he established himself.

This bold and skillful march, executed in the presence of the enemy, and under the fire of his outposts, was a complete success. On account of it, Laudon abandoned the hope of effecting a junction with the Russians in Upper-Silesia, and went into camp, on the 22d of July, at Pomsdorf; at which point he proposed to Butturlin, who, meanwhile, had advanced as far as Namslau, to accomplish their junction by Lower-Silesia.

On the 23d, Frederick established his army on the heights of Woitz and Ullersdorf; a bridge of boats was laid across the Neisse, near Gumpiglau. General Ziethen, with his two corps, quitted Breslau; his own marched at first to Zultz and then rejoined the army; Knobloch's marched to Steinau. The king, after some movements against the enemy's detached corps, having heard that Laudon had withdrawn to Weidenau, reassembled his army, on the 1st of August, at Opersdorf.

It is hardly worth while to give a detailed account of the marches and countermarches which took place, on one side to unite the two armies, and on the other to prevent it.

This junction it appeared impossible to effectuate without a battle, and the king impressed them too favorably for the Austrians, notwithstanding their superiority, to wish to risk one. The circumstances were such, that it behooved the allies not to fight until they had reunited, and for similar reasons, it was important for the king to bring on a decisive action with one of them, if possible. Laudon took the best of measures to secure his object, and he was seconded marvelously by his allies. Count Czernischef, after making demonstrations against Breslau, was to throw some bridges across the Oder and pass it, at Leubus; the Russian army would follow him by Lignitz and Jauer, whither Laudon was to come from his side to meet them. The plan was good, but in order to carry it out, it was necessary either to fight the king or deceive him; the latter seemed the wiser course. To accomplish his purpose, the Austrian general employed every possible ruse; he continued to sustain his detachments towards Oppeln by larger corps; sometimes he made demonstrations to take the same direction, sometimes he indicated a determination to fight the king.

Frederick was in the dark, and moved first to Strehlen, whilst General Knobloch debouched from Breslau, in order to observe the Russians. But Laudon, returning quickly upon Schweidnitz, and taking post on the heights of Hohenfriedberg at the same time that Beck's corps, which thus far had lain at Zittau, was directed upon Lignitz, the king was obliged, on the 10th of August, to take up the central position at Kanth. Meanwhile the Russian army had advanced, on the 5th, from Bernstadt to Hunefeld; on the 6th, to Hochkirch; on the 9th, to Trebnitz, and Czernischef's corps to Auras. On the 10th, the latter encamped at Wohlau, and caused three bridges to be laid across the Oder at the convent of Leubus. On the 11th, whilst the army marched to Kreidel, Czernischef passed the Oder, and encamped at Damm. On the 12th, the army crossed the Oder and encamped near Parschwitz.

The multitude of Cossacks spread over the country prevented the king from obtaining any knowledge of these movements.* However, there was no longer any doubt involving the subject, as the Russians sought to cross the Oder towards Breslau, wishing to unite with their allies by Lower-Silesia. It then appeared evident to the king, that in order to favor this movement, Laudon would forsake his position at Hohenfriedberg, thus affording him an opportunity to attack him with advantage, and decide the campaign. With this view, he endeavored to mislead the Austrian general in regard to the strength of the corps which was posted at Kanth. The third line marched upon the heights, with the right at Schimelwitz, and the left at Polsnitz. The cuirassiers were in reserve behind it. The remainder of the army took up a concealed camp between Schimelwitz and the faubourg of Kanth, which was masked by the timber bordering the banks of the Strigaur-Wasser. On the 11th, the army rested in this position; innumerable false reports confirmed the king in his error. On the 12th,

* The journal of Thielke assures us that the cannon of Breslau apprised the king, on the 12th, that the Russian army had passed the Oder, and it was this which led him to march from Kanth to Lonig.

he moved to Lonig, believing that he should fall in with Laudon, who was said to be marching upon Strigau.

General Schmettau, who had been sent forward upon the route from Neumark to Breslau, reported that he met only parties of Cossacks, and that from all the information he could gather, the Russians had not yet cleared the Oder. However, as has been already stated, Czernischef had then been on the left bank since the evening, and the Russian army was crossing at the very time that Schmettau made his report. The king, thinking that the latter general had been deceived, immediately detached General Mollendorf upon Dombritsch, with orders to push forward his patrols upon the Katzbach. This measure was more successful, for a Russian corps of ten or twelve thousand men was discovered towards Polschildern. Mollendorf, in giving an account of this to the king, on the 13th, added that all the rumors afloat confirmed the passage of the Oder by the Russian army; but Schmettau, by a new report, contradicted it, and thus prolonged this unfortunate state of uncertainty. Finally, at five o'clock in the evening, a second message from Mollendorf made known definitely that Butturlin was on the left bank of the Oder, and was marching upon Panten. The camp was immediately struck, and the army put in march in four columns, upon Lonig, not to attack the Russians, but to impress that belief upon Laudon, and draw him into the plain. In the course of this march, Frederick received the further information, that Laudon was moving on Jauer; this information was untrue, but probable. We are easily led to believe what we wish to be true; and the king had motive for supposing that his adversary would remain in such inactivity all of this time. Consequently, he halted the infantry of the advance-guard near Jenkau; the hussars pushed a reconnoissance upon Behrsdorf; the army, which at first was to encamp at Lonig, went on further, and took position as follows: the first column towards Mertzdorf, the second at Dromsdorf, the third at Tschinwitz, and the fourth at Plomnitz, where Frederick awaited the return of the hussars. His object was to cross the little stream of Weidebach at daybreak, by brigades, and to form his army unexpectedly on the heights of Jauer, to receive the heads of the Austrian columns; who would thus have encountered the centre of an army deployed in line, and would have been overthrown, as were those of Soubise at Rosbach. The hussars returned at three o'clock on the morning of the 11th, announcing that they had not encountered the enemy, but had distinctly seen the fires of the main Austrian army, in its camp at Hohenfriedberg, and those of Brentano at Strigau. The truth was, that the Austrian general had remained immovable in his camp, without being drawn therefrom by any uncommon solicitude for his allies.

The Prussian army then made a half turn to the right, and returned to Lonig; some detachments were sent to Kanth to communicate with Breslau, and to Merschutz to beat up the roads and country on the side of Jauer. General Platten, on the 15th, went upon the heights of Walstadt, in order to reconnoitre the Russian army. He discovered several thousand Cossacks attacking the hussars of Ziethen towards Jenkau, without being able to break them, and also perceived upon the heights of Wandris a division of regular cavalry which was coming to their assistance; he quickly opened a cannonade upon these squadrons, but the king directing General Ziethen to march upon Nicolstadt in order to turn them, they withdrew.

During this skirmish the outposts reported that clouds of dust were raised on the road to Jauer. The king immedi ately detached Mollendorf to Dromsdorf, and General Ramin to the heights of Mertzdorf. Fifteen squadrons were soon observed deployed between Dromsdorf and Rudern, and behind them a column of cavalry, which passed through the village of Bartsdorf at a trot, and was moving upon Proten. It was General Laudon, who, inferring from the reports of the cannon which were heard, that the Russians were approaching, had placed himself at the head of forty squadrons, for the purpose of sustaining them, and opening the long-desired communications with them. The king, who was ignorant of the true state of the case, put himself at the head of a brigade of infantry, and a division of cuirassiers, and thus advanced upon Klein-Polwitz, by Skule, to sustain Ziethen, who, after having evacuated Nicolstadt, found himself between this column of Austrian cavalry and that of the Russians.

Laudon then took the left, by Walstadt, and joined the cavalry of his allies, near Strachwitz. From the other side Platten was directed upon Wandris, and the king, after uniting with Ziethen, formed his cavalry, and moved at first to Nicolstadt, and then in the direction of Walstadt. This brought about a cannonade and a slight combat. The Prussian cavalry, which formed the head of the column towards Strachwitz, overthrew some Austrian regiments, became too eagerly engaged, and was taken in flank by some cuirassiers, and surrounded by a swarm of Cossacks, through whom they had to cut their way. The king having sustained it, the enemy's column was obliged to fall back upon the Russian army, which was in full march for Parchwitz and Klemerwitz. Butturlin encamped in this latter position with his cavalry and upwards of ten thousand foot, which had taken the advance. The remainder of his army did not arrive until the next day. The king, causing the troops with him to be reënforced by a brigade of infantry under Mollendorf, and Colonel Lottum's brigade of cavalry, remained at Mertzdorf, and during the night intrenched the heights of Walstadt with twenty-four battalions and fifty-eight squadrons, being ignorant that the Russian army was in the rear, and thus losing the opportunity of crushing the corps of Butturlin.

That general had most reasonably depended on the advance of Laudon, on the 15th, and expected that he would be supported in his march upon Klemerwitz if he were attacked; but the Austrians desiring that the junction should take place at the convent of Walstadt, their allies saw nothing of them, and had the king attacked them with all his forces, they would have been seriously compromised upon their left. At length Butturlin insisted and decided the Austrians to advance towards Jauer. Laudon marched, on the 17th of August, to Gerlachsdorf, Luzinsky upon the Streitberg, near Strigau, Beck to Lignitz, and Brentano near Jauer. Janus guarded the heights of Kunzendorf. The Russian army did not stir from Klemerwitz. The king rectified his position on the night of the 16th. He posted his right at Gross-Wandris, his left towards Strachwitz, and his headquarters at Nicolstadt.

Frederick, thus having the Russians in his front and the Austrians behind him, had no other point of retreat than Schweidnitz; he caused the remainder of the army, which had halted at Lonig, under command of the Margrave Charles, to join him, assigning his corps a position with its right upon the heights of Granowitz, and its left at Dromsdorf. The two parties remained in each other's presence until the 19th; the allies thus lost forever their most favorable opportunity for overwhelming Frederick. Instead of profiting by the time which elapsed between the 15th and 18th, they held councils of war, in which it was resolved that the Russian army should be brought nearer on the 19th, with its right at Eichholz, and its left towards Lignitz. In this embarrassing situation, there still remained for the king the possibility of his concealing a march and gaining the heights of Kunzendorf before Laudon, and cutting him off from all his magazines. He eagerly took advantage of this on the morning of the 19th, but the vigilant Laudon divined his object, and started himself at once for Kunzendorf, so that the king found him, on the morning of the 20th, master of those heights and of all the defiles.

Frederick then, looking about him for a post where he could, at the same time, prevent the siege of Schweidnitz, cover Breslau, and be within striking distance of his magazines, marched and established himself, on the 20th of August, between Buntzelwitz and Tscheschen, with the right of his army on the heights of Zedlitz, and its left at Jauernick. The approach of the Russians compelled him to rectify this position.

The camp of Buntzelwitz was formed by a chain of elevations, separated by several streams of water, of which the principal ones were the Freyburger-Wasser and the Striganer-Wasser, which protected the front and left but few points of attack. The lines were so arranged as to form a kind of oblong figure, the right side of which was towards Tscheschen and Zedlitz; the front extended from Zedlitz to a point in rear of Jauernick; the left side from Jauernick to the rear of Wurben, whence the line extended until it joined the right side towards Tscheschen. (See Plate XXIV.) There were six salient angles, forming real bastions, which swept all the ground around, and flanked the interior intrenchments. All these hills were strongly fortified, especially those of Wurben, which dominated over the camp, and might be regarded as the citadel. One hundred and eighty pieces of cannon, without counting the artillery of the battalions, defended the approaches to the position. The camp was surrounded with *abatis*, *trous-de-loup*, and *fougasses;* the army labored there during ten days and nights with ceaseless and extraordinary activity. Every advantage was taken of the nature of the ground to combine and employ thereon the different arms, or to dispose of suitable works. In a word, this camp, which formed an epoch in the annals of the art, was long considered a masterpiece of field-fortification. The two attackable fronts were found between Jauernick and Buntzelwitz, and between Peterwitz and Neudorf.

The allied generals having regulated at length, on the 21st of August, the important affair of their subsistence-departments, Marshal Butturlin moved, on the 24th, to Jauer. Laudon caused the corps of Beck and Brentano to occupy the heights of Strigau. On the 25th, the Russians marched to Hohenfriedberg; Laudon at last issued from the mountains, and encamped, on the 26th, with his right at Bogendorf, and his left at Zirlau. Luzinsky's corps seized the heights of Arensdorf, and maintained that position in spite of all the efforts of the Prussians to dislodge them.

This sudden appearance of the Austrians led the king to fear a general attack. He ordered the tents struck, the artillery harnessed, and the army to pass the night under arms. This painful condition of things lasted for several days without the enemy showing himself. Still he might be expected the very day that any of these precautions were neglected, therefore they had to be continued.

On the 28th, the Russian general yielded somewhat to the urgency of Laudon, and shut up the Prussians a little closer by shifting his right to Oelse and his left to Strigau. Czernischef's corps replaced Brentano's at the Streitberg, and the latter took position at Nicolsdorf. The next day Czernischef placed his right in camp at Muhrau, and his left towards Jerichau; he detached his light troops, under General Berg, to the heights of Laasen, whence they drove the Prussian outposts from Conradswalde.

Laudon, perceiving that the labors of the Prussians increased daily, came to the conclusion, though rather late, that they ought to be attacked. He made use of all his eloquence to incline Butturlin to coöperate with him in this attack, on the 1st of September, but his efforts were ineffectual, as the Russian declared distinctly that he would take no part in it, and the council of war which he summoned, enlarging upon his sagacity, concluded that it would be imprudent to attack such a formidable position, which the king would soon be forced to abandon by the want of provisions. All the persuasions of the Austrian general, the array of incalculable advantages which the assailants would reap from the superiority of the initiative, and finally, the honor to be gained by this operation, seemed to have no effect upon the spirit of the Russian general, who thought himself doing a great deal when he offered to furnish a corps of twenty thousand men, in case the Austrians should be attacked.

Laudon would not allow himself to be thwarted, but arranged an attack for the 3d of September, and went on the 2d to the headquarters of the Russian general to discuss it. This plan was well combined, and consisted in a general effort against the centre by echelons. (See Plate XXIV.) The centre, which formed the head of attack, was composed of chosen troops and volunteers formed in column, who were to seize the village of Jauernick. The divisions of the right wing, disposed in echelon, at the same distance, were to penetrate by this point, and be formed in line as they arrived, so as to give a divergent direction to the wings of the enemy, which would thus be beaten and separated. These dispositions do honor to the judgment of Laudon. They were communicated to all the lieutenant-generals, and the Austrian troops were even assembled, on the night of the 2d and 3d, at the places of rendezvous indicated, but Butturlin was immovable, and held fast to his first resolution. Laudon, greatly affected by this occurrence, fell sick, and the troops returned to their camp. In fact, this result is not difficult to explain; it must be attributed to the slight consideration which Laudon showed for his ally. He sent to Marshal Butturlin, by Giannini, his chief of staff, a plan already arranged, and in which the part to be performed by his allies was fixed in a manner as little honorable as it was little conformable to the decision arrived at a few days before by the council of war. It appeared very remarkable to the Russian general that, after the deliberation of the council, at which Laudon was present, he should have brought him without any further consultation, a project of attack, already prepared, in which had been determined what should be done both by his army and the corps of Czernischef.

Frederick was ignorant of all these events, which were so favorable to him; but, nevertheless, he concluded that his enemies did not yet consider themselves competent to attack him, and ordered that, in future, but half of each regiment should take arms during the night. On the 4th of September, he caused the heights of Sabischdorf to be occupied by the division Gablenz; a post and a battery were established in the old Swedish intrenchments which had been restored.

On the 9th of September, at nightfall, the Prussians perceived that Butturlin's camp was in flames, and, at the same time, Brentano was descending the heights towards Grunau. In fact the Russian army was moving upon Jauer, where it repassed the Oder, leaving General Czernischef, with a corps of twenty thousand men, to reënforce the Austrian army. Laudon then gave up the hope of attacking the king with any prospect of success, and, on the morning of the 10th of September, he resumed his position at Kunzendorf. Frederick thus fortunately escaped the greatest danger to which he had ever been exposed. We see, moreover, that the misunderstandings between his adversaries contributed as much to this result as did his own genius.

POSITIONS IN SAXONY AND POMERANIA.

During the progress of these events the Saxon army was still in the greatest state of inactivity, scarcely relieved by a few trifling affairs of posts, which are unworthy of a description. Daun encamped with one portion of his troops in the valley of Plauen, under Dresden; the remainder cantoned towards Dippodiswalde, and Lascy at Dobritsch. The army of the Circles did not leave Voigtland until near the end of July, under pretext of the lack of provisions. This was the first time that it was ever urged that the lack of subsistence kept troops stationary; heretofore it had compelled them to abandon a country, but it was reserved for General Serbelloni to prove the contrary. At length this army encamped, on the 21st of July, near Ronneburg, pushing some posts as far as Gera and Naumburg. The prince of Wurtemberg defended his intrenched camp at Colberg, as we shall see hereafter, and the Swedes, who had commenced their movement in the *month of August*, penetrated into the Ukeraine Marche, until the small reënforcements joined Colonel Belling, which being perceived by them, they were induced to reënter within their line of demarkation.

FURTHER OPERATIONS OF THE KING. LAUDON CARRIES SCHWEIDNITZ BY ASSAULT.

It is probable that Frederick was ignorant of the cause and the object of the march of the Russians towards the Oder. He presumed that, having found his positions unattackable, they had formed the project, as in the last campaign, of a diversion upon Berlin, for the purpose of facilitating the operations of Laudon in Silesia. To thwart this design, and to disable the Russians for the remainder of the campaign, the king resolved to destroy their magazines upon the line of the Posen. He gave General Platten charge of this expedition, and placed under his command fourteen battalions and twenty-five squadrons, with orders to march afterwards upon Frankfort or Glogau, and in case of meeting with obstacles, to move to Landsberg on the Wartha. As this general was about to operate on the rear of a large Austrian army, he was not fettered by instructions, but only directed to do the enemy all the mischief he was able. He crossed the Oder, at Breslau, on the night of the 11th, encamped at Sabisch on the 14th, and destroyed a magazine at Kobielin. Learning that a great convoy was parked at the convent of Gostein, he took the advance with the cavalry, and ordered General Knobloch to follow him. He reached the convent on the 15th, and found the park barricaded and defended by five thousand infantry, which obliged him to await the arrival of his own. When they came up he ordered four battalions to take the convent and the barricade, whilst the rest formed in readiness to support them. The barricade was stormed and the convent taken. They killed six hundred men, took fifteen hundred prisoners, and dispersed the remainder in the woods. More than five hundred wagons were destroyed. This corps encamped on the 16th at Czempin, and on the 17th at Stenzewa, whence a detachment was sent to Posen. General Dalk had retired from there, taking with him the public stores. Platten continued his march to Neustadt, where he remained some days. He marched by Birnbaum and Golmitz to Landsberg, where, on the 22d, finding the bridge over the Wartha cut, he threw one across with some pontoons and rafts, which were very fortunately found in the river.

The king had thus far remained in his camp of Buntzelwitz, but the reduced state of the magazines of Schweidnitz obliged him to approach the Neisse; he therefore transferred his army in three columns, on the 26th, to Pulzen, on the 28th, to Siegroth, and on the 29th, to Gros-Nossen. Colonel Dalwig flanked his march on his left with twelve hundred horse and a battalion of light troops, to ascertain the movements of Laudon on the side of the mountains. The king expected that the Austrian general would follow him in order to cover the important road to Glatz, and was a good deal surprised to get no report of his movements. Each detachment sent out for that purpose having made no discovery, the king, on the 2d of October, dispatched General Lentulus for the purpose of reconnoitering as closely as possible Schweidnitz and the old camp of the Austrians. That general was not more fortunate, but announced that according to the rumors pervading the country, Laudon had carried Schweidnitz by assault.

As it was, Laudon was no better informed of the movements of the Prussians, and hearing nothing of them, he resolved to attempt the escalade; whilst Brentano, posted at Ludwigsdorf, and Draskowitz at Wartha, were to guard the communications of the mountains of Glatz. In preparation for the attack, he drew in his outposts around the works, on the 30th of September, and established a second chain outside of these, and at the same time collected ladders in all the neighborhood.

The attack was made by four columns directed against the four forts (see Plate XXIV.); these columns were led by cannoneers, sappers, workmen with shovels, axes, picks, and men carrying ladders, with their arms slung over their shoulders. Engineer officers who knew the place were made use of as guides for each of the columns. The commandants of the columns of attacks were summoned to head-quarters, and the following is the substance of the instructions which they received:

1st. The attack will be made with the bayonet without a

musket-shot being fired. 2d. As soon as the leading battalions arrive upon the glacis, they will jump upon the covered way and into the ditch, erect the ladders, and quickly penetrate into the body of the work to let down the drawbridges. 3d. The troops will preserve the ladders with care, that after the capture of the fort, they may be used to escalade the city. 4th. The battalions of grenadiers attached to each column will be the first to attack; they will be followed by a battalion of fusileers; the latter will carry the curtain which connects the forts with the lunettes; the other two battalions will remain in rear with the pieces of artillery until they may be required. 5th. Immediately after the exterior forts are carried, the battalions of reserve attached to each column will move forward and take possession of them; those which shall have executed the attack will be immediately reformed for the purpose of attacking and carrying the body of the place.

The commandant received information of the contemplated attack, but gave it little credit. However, he got his little garrison under arms, and assigned the several parties their different posts; twelve hundred men guarded the interior enceinte of the town, one thousand were disposed in the forts and in the curtains joining them; eighty were stationed in the ditch to overturn the ladders, and the remainder, fourteen hundred men, were held in reserve between the enceinte of the detached forts and that of the town; but this reserve was not instructed as to which of the numerous points its several detachments should repair in case the enemy succeeded in any of his attacks, nor were they informed of the probable incidents that would attend enterprises of this nature. From which it followed at the moment of escalade, that a part of the reserve withdrew into the village, and the remainder ran hither and thither, from one side to another, without knowing what they ought to do.

The columns attacked with vigor, and after a combat of four hours' duration, more or less obstinately maintained at the different forts, the Austrians gained possession of the place, with the loss of fourteen hundred killed and wounded, compensated by thirty-four hundred prisoners. Laudon then garrisoned the place with ten battalions, repaired the works, and sat down in his camp upon the heights of Kunzendorf. The news of this unforeseen and disagreeable event obliged the king to give up his manœuvres in Upper Silesia, and to move, on the 6th of October, to Strehlen to cover Breslau.

The Austrian general could undertake nothing without the orders of his court.* The Aulic council, which made war at the fireside, directed him, notwithstanding his superiority of forces (they being double the strength of the Prussians), to remain on the defensive in the mountains, and to send to Marshal Daun the troops he had received from him in the beginning of the campaign, should the king direct himself against him. On the 11th of November, the Austrians went into winter-quarters, as well as Czernischef, who remained with his corps attached to them in the county of Glatz. The Prussian army did the same early in December, and thus terminated most happily, without combat or battle, a campaign in which the Prussians might have been crushed a dozen times.

Whilst everything was thus brought to a close in Silesia in such a pacific and unhoped-for manner, Frederick was exposed to another danger of a very different nature. A Silesian gentleman, named Warkotsch, whom Frederick had loaded with benefits, resolved to seize him, conjointly with one Captain Wallis, and deliver him to the Austrians. This

* Thielke states positively that Maria Theresa had given full power to Laudon to direct his own operations. In the end it matters little to the reader whether it was a council of war or the general-in-chief to whom honor should be given for a success, or upon whom blame should fall for an error. We should seek only the principles on which they rest.

plan was disclosed by a domestic of Warkotsch, at the moment when the Croats were in their advanced position in readiness to receive him.

END OF THE CAMPAIGN IN SAXONY.

As we have before stated, the army of the Circles was posted towards Ronnenburg in the end of July. Daun and Prince Henry held all their positions, and aside from the slight sparring of the light troops on either side, their camps might have been mistaken for camps of instruction. Prince Henry was obliged to send some battalions to Berlin, as the Swedes menaced it, and others towards the frontiers of Halberstadt, to protect them against the incursions of the French light troops belonging to their army, which had passed the Weser on the 19th of August. Notwithstanding these detachments, the Austrian general did not become more bold. He allowed Prince Henry to send eight battalions and twenty-four squadrons, on the 2d of September, against the detachment from the army of the Circles. Seidlitz advanced upon Ronnenburg, and after having repulsed various parties, attacked the right of that army resting at Rensterberg, when it changed its position. He then took post at Altenkirch, where he menaced the left. Lieutenant-General Serbelloni, considering it altogether useless to fatigue the troops by constant watching, concluded that it would be better to retire into the camp at Weida. Seidlitz then rejoined the army, on the 15th, by way of Altenburg and Borne.

Prince Henry detached that general a second time, on the 12th of October, to the neighborhood of Magdeburg, to brush away the small parties of the enemy infesting that vicinity. Daun did not appear to be any the less tranquil in his camp, though he separated from the army of the Circles.

On November 1st, there arrived at his camp a reënforcement of twenty-four battalions and forty-two squadrons, sent by Laudon after the capture of Schweidnitz; Daun's forces were thus raised to seventy-six battalions and one hundred and forty squadrons; more than sufficient to crush Prince Henry and march to Berlin. On the 5th of November, the marshal started out of the camp, and attacked all the line of the enemy's advance-posts; but the laboring mountain brought forth a mouse; Daun took some villages on the left side of the Mulde, from which the Prussians annoyed their cantonments, and in which he established his army on the 19th of November. The army of the Circles did the same thing on the same day of the month, and both of them retired early to rest from the toils and fatigues which they had experienced.

CHAPTER XXIX.

AFFAIRS OF POMERANIA; SIEGE OF COLBERG.

We have already remarked that the Russians, being desirous of establishing a base of operations which would permit them to place their depots near the sea, undertook the siege of Colberg. Lieutenant-General Romanzow was put in charge of this operation with a corps of eighteen thousand men, which was to be protected by the combined fleets of Russia and Sweden. The prince of Wurtemberg, having orders to cover Pomerania, sent General Werner to the environs of Koslin and Belgard, and encamped on the 4th of June under Colberg; his left at the farm of Bollenwinckel, his right at Persante. In advance of his front, which was covered by a deep ravine, was the village of Neckin; on his left, extended impassable swamps. This strong position was further strengthened by thirty-eight redoubts, comprising those on the heights of Pretmin; the space between the left and the sea, though little practicable on account of a marsh, was nevertheless connected with the hill by three redoubts and an advanced work.

When the prince of Wurtemberg learned that Romanzow had at first sent forward but ten thousand men, he made a proposition to the king that he should attack them, so as to get rid of them during the rest of the campaign; but Frederick, who was then giving his whole attention to the plans of General Goltz against Butturlin, thought this would suffice to relieve Pomerania. On this account, he declined acceding to the proposition of the prince. It will be remembered how the latter enterprise failed from the sudden death of its author. Frederick regretted when it was too late having refused to listen to a proposition which would have been most useful in any event, as it was founded on the principles of the art.

The Russian general was reënforced, on the 5th of July, and took post about Koslin, awaiting the arrival of the fleet, which anchored on the 30th, and disembarked some troops and artillery. His corps was thus raised to twenty-four thousand men. On the 22d of August, he established his right on Quetzin and his left at Dejow; the fleet arrived before Colberg two days after, and immediately began a bombardment, which lasted nearly fifteen days. On the 4th of September, the Russian army shut up the Prussian camp; but Romanzow, finding, no doubt, that it was too strong to be attacked by open force, resolved to regularly besiege it.

The prince of Wurtemberg adopted the best measures for the defense of his works, and drew up instructions which might answer for a model of their kind. Wishing to make use of his cavalry, he detached them in the night of the 11th of September, with a volunteer battalion under the command of General Werner, towards Belgard, in order to destroy the depots of the Russians and threaten their communications. Unfortunately, Werner cantoned his corps, on the 12th of September, in the neighboring villages of Treptow, where he was surprised by Colonel Bibikow, who took him prisoner as he came out of the village, with all his infantry and a hundred dragoons. The rest of the cavalry being doubled back upon the other squadrons, found time to retire, after having overthrown a portion of the enemy's troops into the Rega, towards Kletkow, and made a hundred prisoners.

Romanzow, in the meantime, continued his approaches against the Bollenwinkel, which was the key of the enemy's camp. On the night of the 17th and 18th of September, he caused an attack to be made on the intrenchment on the beach and the green redoubt; the first was carried, the second withstood the assault. The following night the attack was renewed unsuccessfully, and that point became from that moment the object aimed at by the besiegers. The prince of Wurtemberg had a redoubt constructed upon the highest point of the Bollenwinckel, hoping that General Platten would not delay in bringing him subsistence and reënforcements.

That general, whom we left at Landsberg, after his expedition against the depots at Posen, started from there on the 25th of September, and was joined, on the 27th, at Freyenwalde, by the cavalry which had been surprised at Treptow, and took up a position, on the 2d of October, at Prettmin, upon the left bank of the Persante; which raised the forces of the prince to sixteen thousand men; but his embarrassment on account of subsistence was undiminished; in fact, was increased, for he had to bring his supplies from Stettin through to Golnow, over a thousand obstacles. A large convoy was expected from that village, but Romanzow multiplied his efforts to prevent its arrival. On the other hand, the grand Russian army, after leaving Silesia, had encamped successively at Driesen and at Dramburg, detaching Generals Berg and Fermor upon Greifenberg, with orders to push forward to Treptow.

Nevertheless, Colonel Kleist was sent to meet the convoy, and joined it at Golnow. General Platten was detached with six battalions, in order to draw to him all the small corps near Greifenberg, and afterwards to move on Golnow, for the purpose of facilitating the march of Kleist and his convoy. At the same time Knobloch was posted in rear of

Treptow, and sent a detachment into that place to draw therefrom one battalion and the provisions left there. The officer who carried this order, either gave it erroneously, or it was not understood; the general marched with his detachment, on the 20th, to Treptow, where he was surrounded and cut off on the next day, by a Russian corps, which Romanzow had conducted himself by Garrin for that purpose.

Platten encamped on the 19th at Schwanteshagen, and on the 20th he sent Lieutenant-Colonel Courbières with two battalions and a regiment of hussars on a foraging expedition towards Baumgarten and Zarnglaf. This detachment was captured by General Dolgorouky at a short distance from camp, without the possibility of giving it any succor. At the same moment the grand army of Butturlin arrived in the neighborhood of Regenwalde, and detached General Fermor for the purpose of attacking, in concert with the light troops of Berg, the corps of Platten, and cutting him off from Stettin. But he decamped during the night of the 21st of October, passing through the forest of Kautreck in the midst of the enemy's sharpshooters; and as Fermor had committed the error of halting at Glewitz, the Prussians rejoined at Golnow the convoy which they were to protect on its march.

On the 22d Fermor attacked Golnow, which obliged the train to return to Stettin, and on the 23d Platten fell back upon Damm. This event had the most fatal consequences. Knobloch was shut up in Treptow from the 21st, and was forced to surrender on the 25th, with eighteen hundred men; the communication between the camp of Colberg and General Platten was interrupted, and it was necessary to abandon the idea of the convoy of provisions.

Further, the Russians, on the 22d, captured the redoubt of Spie, and compelled the troops which occupied the heights of Prettmin, on the left bank of the Persante, to reënter camp. This mishap did not discourage the prince; he determined to delay until the last extremity, before cutting his way through, trusting that the severity of the season would oblige the Russians to retreat. He also fortified the passage of Colberger-Deep,* the only point by which he could effect his retreat. A vessel, loaded with grain, by accident dropped anchor near the port, and was towed in by some boats, and furnished bread for five days.

On the 2d of November, the grand Russian army started for Poland, leaving with Romanzow a strong reënforcement under the command of General Berg.

Platten's corps, which the king had at first destined to cover Berlin against the invasion threatened by the Austrians, was united, on the 9th, at Berlinchen, to that of General Schenkendorf, who led, for the same purpose, eight small battalions from the army of Silesia. These two divisions marched to Naugarten, where they arrived on the 14th, pushing before them the small corps of Berg, which fell back upon Freyenwalde. By a happy chance the prince of Wurtemberg was, at the same time, making his preparations to quit the intrenched camp by the Colberger-Deep. After collecting, on the night of the 13th and 14th, all the boats necessary to throw a bridge over the Rega, and having them transported from Colberg to the rear of the sandhills of Kamper Lake, the prince began his march at seven in the evening of the 14th, leaving only the guards of the most advanced trenches at their posts to conceal the retreat. The corps arrived an hour before daylight at the Colberger-Deep, and as the trestle-bridge, over which they were to pass, was not ready, the advance-guard crossed in canoes. The corps

* Colberger-Deep is a village situated near the sea and Lake Kamper; a road runs between the sea and this lake to the harbor entrance which closes it, so that this passage forms a narrow defile in which, besides, is the obstacle presented by the harbor entrance, which requires a long bridge.

followed when the bridge was finished, passed the marsh on an old dyke, which had been neglected by the Russians, and arrived on the 15th at Treptow.

General Platten marched on the same day from Naugarten, in the direction of Koldemantz, where he was informed of the fortunate retreat of the prince, and of his plan to move, on the 16th, to Greifenberg. In fact, the prince ordered this general to move to Plathe, to repair the bridge; and on the 17th the two corps were united at Greifenberg. The prince of Wurtemberg resolved to try again the plan of operating upon the rear of Romanzow, and moved, on the 18th, to Falkenberg, pushing before him Berg's light troops. But the Russian general was not deceived. He invested the fort of Colberg, and took post himself, with a strong corps, at Gostin, for the purpose of covering the siege.

Under these circumstances nothing could be done by the Prussians, unless it were to approach their great convoy coming from Stettin. For this purpose they marched by Naugarten and Schwusen to Treptow, where the convoy arrived on the 10th. After having provisioned the troops, the prince returned, on the 12th, to Colberg, and found Romanzow's corps drawn up in line of battle between Prettmin and Rehmer, on the left of the Persante. A cannonade was immediately opened from each side. The Prussians seized at first the intrenched passage of Spie; but they could succeed in gaining nothing more, and the weather becoming too cold to continue operations, the prince was compelled to abandon the place to its fate. On the 15th, a portion of his troops were distributed through Saxony and Lusatia, and he himself went to Mecklenburg. The brave Colonel Heyden, who commanded, surrendered the place on the 16th of December, for want of provisions. Romanzow's corps, which had made this conquest, took winter-quarters in Pomerania.

CHAPTER XXX.

GENERAL OBSERVATIONS UPON THE CAMPAIGN OF 1761; OPERATIONS OF DAUN COMPARED WITH THOSE OF 1809.

After analyzing the operations of four or five active campaigns, it is very difficult to say anything new upon another, conducted on the same theatre without fighting. The errors have always been the same; the forces of the coalition have embraced the lines of operation in the manner least conducive to their interest. Frederick, whose strength diminished daily, did not know which system he ought to adopt. A war of invasion did not suit him, neither did it consist with his interests to fly alternately against the Austrians and the Russians, since a war of such vigor would have exhausted his last soldiers, who had escaped from the bloody fields of Zorndorf, Kunersdorf, and Torgau. Prudence counseled him to leave them undisturbed, until an opportunity should present itself of attacking one of their armies alone. This was a certain means of causing the other to return to its own frontiers. Perhaps he may be justly blamed for not having fought a battle with Daun before he left Saxony to march into Silesia.

It seems to me that inasmuch as Frederick had a mass of troops in Saxony, and wished to take the greater portion of them for operations in Silesia, he ought to have attacked the marshal before leaving, in order to diminish his desire of profiting by his enormous superiority over Prince Henry.

Could it have been foreseen that Daun would remain inactive, it would have been policy to let him alone; but nothing less than a treaty between the marshal and himself, either should or could have led him to suppose it. Daun had thus far shown a sort of intimidation, due to the superiority of genius which he recognized in the king; nevertheless he had attacked him twice with success; he had never been opposed to any other general, and the inference was natural that he would not fear Prince Henry so much as Frederick, and that he would not lose the opportunity of fighting thirty thousand men with sixty thousand.

Once arrived in Silesia, it seemed useless to leave the corps of Goltz at Glogau, for the Russians were still between Posen and the Vistula. Had Frederick joined the army, it would have been sixty thousand strong, and, without doubt, able to attack Laudon, who did not command over fifty thousand. The Austrians held good positions, but they were not inaccessible, and it would have cost nothing to have sought to dislodge them by manœuvres. Had the king succeeded, in the month, in forcing them back by Glatz into Bohemia, their junction with Butturlin could not have taken place, and Frederick would have gained possession of the defiles of the mountains, which insures great advantages to the defensive. Instead of preventing this junction, Frederick did all in his power to facilitate it, by allowing himself to be deceived by the movements of the enemy. He has been blamed justly for not having attacked Laudon on the 22d of July, at Beerwalde near Munsterberg, for he had much better have delivered a battle there at that period than to have shut himself up, six months afterwards, in a camp, surrounded by armies superior to his own.

So soon as the enterprise contemplated by General Goltz was defeated, and the Russians had advanced to the Oder, either their army or General Laudon's should have been attacked. Every motive and interest pointed to it, for a victory would upset their plan of campaign, and there were greater hopes of a victory over a corps separated by a river from the one which was to succor it, than over two armies united and capable of falling on simultaneously. No military grounds would furnish justification to the king for allowing the time between the 1st and 15th of August to pass without an attempt to overwhelm either the Russians or the Austrians; he could not and ought not to have supposed that such formidable forces would effect a junction merely for the purpose of making a grand parade.

There can be no doubt that the idea of the camp of Buntzelwitz was a happy stroke of audacity; but to me it appears that more valuable results would have followed from the exhibition of a portion of it, in delivering battle to the enemy on the 22d of July, during the march upon Munsterberg. As it was, a check would have involved no loss to the king, but had his camp at Buntzelwitz been forced, he would have lost everything. It appears very certain, at all events, that if the plan of attack which was conceived by Laudon had been carried out on the 3d of September, the Prussian army must have been totally annihilated, provided that general had known how to profit by his victory.

In a word, *if it be admitted that an army, occupying a double interior line of operations against two armies, separated at a great distance, should not go too far out of its way to seek them, it is also indispensably necessary that it should be precipitated vigorously upon that one which it is the most important to overwhelm, for the purpose of keeping them at a suitable distance, and to prevent them from moving simultaneously.* Frederick acted altogether contrary to this principle. Possibly he had some secret motive for believing that were the armies even to unite they would not act simultaneously, nor even operate in concert. This would furnish the only justification for such an oversight.

Finally, it seems to me that Frederick committed an error which cost him dearly, when he refused to give permission to the prince of Wurtemberg to attack Romanzow in Pomerania, when he was superior to that general. The pretext of awaiting the result of the attack undertaken by Goltz is not defensible. Goltz had not enough troops to strike decisive blows against an army three times his strength. We believe the employment of Wurtemburg's corps would have been much more convenient had it been first posted at Landsberg, in order to enter afterwards upon the expedition, whilst Romanzow was awaiting in his cantonments the arrival of the siege-train and stores; but if the king preferred to leave it in Pomerania, there was everything to be gained by causing the attack to be made on Romanzow before the latter had received his reënforcements.

The king lost, by this delay, a place which became very dangerous in the hands of his enemies, and the conquest of which might have given a decisive turn to the subsequent campaign, had not events of a different nature totally changed the complexion of affairs.

The errors of the Austrians in this campaign arose from a bad choice of their lines of operations, and the calculating and dilatory system adopted by Daun.

The conduct of Laudon, without being indicative of a lofty genius, was often worthy of praise; and in that war this was a great deal. According to the plan of campaign which had been adopted, he had no motive for action before the arrival of the Russians, and he manœuvred well in order to unite with them. As has been already observed, the scheme of attacking the camp of Buntzelwitz, was founded upon the employment of masses upon the decisive point; the direction which Laudon desired to give them would undoubtedly have produced the greatest results, had he succeeded, as there was every reason to believe that he would do. Finally, the capture of Schweidnitz by escalade sealed the success of his operations; an enterprise well-conceived, ably conducted, and which paved the way for a fine opening to the succeeding campaign. This was the only place where Laudon had the chief command, and that he accomplished no more is to be attributed to his original instructions, and to the trifling assistance which he received from the Russian army, upon which assistance were based all the combinations of the cabinet of Vienna.

But, although there is a bright side to his operations, he is somewhat exposed to blame. And first, for not taking advantage of his superiority to attack Goltz in the month of April, and for confining his action merely to demonstrations. He should have undertaken the attack, since he risked only the loss of a few men, which, in the numerical proportion then existing between the two armies, was no great evil. Had he succeeded, that corps would have been annihilated or driven into some fortress, where, perhaps, it could not have been sustained; in any event, it was a result to be desired. In the second instance, his error was more grave; in not having attacked the king at Nicolstadt between the 15th and 18th of August. It is incredible that two armies, separated by two hundred leagues, which required half of a campaign to connect their operations; and which succeeded in placing between them an enemy without support and without retreat, and divided into two corps, in order to present a front to each of their masses; and when nothing interfered to prevent both armies attacking at the same instant, should pass four days without attempting anything, and then suffer the king to escape from these embarrassments. How could Laudon, who had planned the attack against the Prussian army when it was posted in a strongly intrenched camp, backed by Schweidnitz, justify himself for having allowed that army to lie tranquilly in a position commanded from all sides, without intrenchments, and with no possible line of retreat in case of reverse?

If we can believe Thielke, Laudon cannot lay his faults to the Aulic Council, for he had received, at the beginning of the campaign, a letter in the handwriting of Maria Theresa, which accorded him complete freedom of action, and liberated him from the instruction of that famous council, to which Austria owes all her reverses since the time of Prince Eugene of Savoy. If the fact is as stated, we should also demand of Laudon why, after having escaladed Schweidnitz, he did not unite his ninety thousand men, including the corps of Czernischef, and then attack the king and march upon Breslau? The marshal might have easily overwhelmed Frederick, who had only forty-five thousand divided combatants, whose defeat would have assured the conquest of Silesia. Instead of delivering these important blows, he reënforced Daun, who then had twice the amount of his adversary's forces, and made not the slightest use of them.

Those who conceived the general plan of the campaign, and Daun himself, were much more reprehensible than Laudon. By transferring the scene of the leading operations to Silesia, they forced the king to repair thither. Now this, according to an old proverb, was taking the bull by the horns. That province presented to him the line of the Oder, on which, from Stettin to Neisse, were eight strongly fortified places, which offered him inestimable support in case of defeat, of depôts, magazines, and, above all, the facility of manœuvring upon either bank of the river. On the contrary, in Saxony and upon the Elbe, the Austrians had Dresden in a first line and Prague in a second, whilst the king held only the post of Wittemberg. He was some six or seven marches from the centre of his power, and a victory or two would have terminated the struggle, by cutting him off from his communications with the Oder.

Every possible motive should have induced the Austrians to strike their heaviest blows in Saxony, because a single one there would have crushed their enemy; whereas, in Silesia, it would have but slightly disabled him. Besides, by operating in the first-named province, they had the advantage of a salient frontier, formed by the mountains of Bohemia, in the centre of their operations towards Bautzen and Zittau, between Dresden and the county of Glatz. Daun had there, in the month of April, including the army of the Circles, a force of from ninety to one hundred thousand men; Laudon then numbered forty-five thousand. Had they left twenty thousand about Glatz, until the arrival of the Russians, giving to Butturlin the siege-operations, whilst Laudon and Daun rapidly formed their armies, the first from Dresden to Bautzen, with some light troops at Pirna, the second from Bautzen to Hoyerswerda, and had two masses of sixty thousand men, under the command of a single chief, attacked Frederick simultaneously, crowding him steadily to the left, he would have been cut off from all his resources, and a battle lost would have been his destruction. If, contrary to every probability, Daun had lost one or two battles, what would have followed? Did he not have behind him Dresden, the defiles of Bohemia, and, in the last extremity, Prague. A single march of the Russian army on Breslau would have amply made up for these two battles, the losses of which could have been replaced in fifteen days.

This is nearly the same direction that Daun gave his operations in 1760, when he wished to prevent the king from going into Silesia; and he certainly manœuvred much more skillfully in that campaign. His position would have produced the greatest results, if, at that time, he had attacked Frederick during his march, as has been already observed in

Chapter XXVI. But it is not by occupying positions, by halting often, and fearing to march too near an army, inferior in number, that an adversary is prevented from opening his communications and succeeding in his attempts. If the marshal, after the month of April, had sent his one hundred and twenty-five thousand men to the Elbe, taking Torgau and Wittemberg, and attacking the Prussians wherever they might be encountered, upon either bank of that river, or even had he manœuvred in such a manner as constantly to keep the right of his army reënforced, and prolonged to the left of the king, it would have precluded the possibility of his retiring anywhere except upon Magdeburg, which would have placed his states in the power of his enemies. Frederick, feeling that such a conquest would tend to the destruction of his means of recruiting, would most assuredly have sought to deliver a battle among the first movements; but what would have been the consequences, since, in case of reverse, a point for rallying and support existed under the walls of Dresden, which would have enabled the Austrians, eight days after, to renew the attempt. Two battles gained by the king would have destroyed his army, without his having acquired a foot of ground upon this line of operations.

It is more natural to impute these greater faults to the Aulic Council than to the marshal, but at the bottom there is no difference. It matters little, in the demonstration and application of principles, whether it be the cabinet or the general who has made bad combinations. We are not writing for the purpose of praising or censuring individuals. What did undoubtedly depend upon the marshal was the wretched employment of masses, of which he had the exclusive command. When the king set out for Silesia, on the 2d of May, only thirty thousand men remained with Prince Henry. Daun had eighty thousand combatants, the army of the Circles and the corps of Odonell included. Why did he not endeavor to force the king upon Wittemberg on the 6th or 7th of May? What motive could have induced him to detach Odonell to Zittau, and defer marching upon the capital, for the purpose of destroying the resources of the king; or upon Buntzlau, in order to connect his operations with the Russians and Laudon? After the departure of Odonell, he would still have possessed sixty thousand men, with which to pursue an army reduced to twenty thousand by the probable loss of a battle. Tempelhof, for the purpose of excusing the marshal, has not hesitated to put forward the idea that the king, who was but four or five marches off, would have returned again. This is false reasoning. At Lignitz Laudon was beaten at two leagues from Daun, without the latter being able to sustain him. The battle of Prague was lost because the Austrians left an interval of some yards between the troops, at an angle which formed their centre. How then should Frederick, at forty leagues from Prince Henry, and hurrying to Schweidnitz, have been able to prevent his brother from being beaten near Meissen, on the left bank of the Elbe?

To appreciate the arguments of Tempelhof at its just value, let us examine the operations of Napoleon upon Ratisbon in 1809, and about Mantua in 1796. We see in the memorable battles of Eckmühl, Abensberg, and Ratisbon, two grand armies successively beaten, broken, and overthrown, at two days' march from each other. In Italy the two columns of Wurmser were annihilated in twenty-four hours, not forty leagues apart, but on the same ground, at Lonato and Castiglione. Let us, for an instant, substitute Napoleon for Daun, with his one hundred and twenty-five thousand men, in the month of April, and let us assume the ordinary train of enterprises which this great captain pursued, and it will be conceded that, by the month of June, there would have been no troops in Prussia, except those that were shut up in the fortified places.

These observations, joined to those which we have already had occasion to present at times on the advantages of the initiative in warlike operations, seem to require that we should recapitulate those maxims which they serve to confirm.

1st. *It is undeniable that an army taking the initiative of a movement may be able to conceal it until the instant of its complete execution; thus, when the operations take place within the interior of his line, a general may gain several marches upon his enemy.*

2d. *It is of the greatest importance in judging clearly of military operations, to exclude from all the combinations those precise calculations which presuppose that a general will be informed of a movement, and that he will oppose it by the best manœuvre at the very instant when it shall be begun.*

3d. *Whenever two army corps shall combine their operations so as to bring the enemy between two fires at the distance of several marches; they will form a double line of operations against a single one, and thus expose themselves to be beaten separately, if the enemy makes full use of his central position. It is with this manœuvre, as it is with a movement from a distance against an enemy's flanks; and both should be embraced in that class which includes all operations wherein a simultaneous effect cannot be produced at the moment of their execution.*

4th. *The experience of several centuries and the maxims adduced in Chapter IX. have proved, that a general compels all the chances in his favor when he assumes the initiative of the movement, whether in his strategical combinations or his dispositions for combat.* Let us suppose an army of forty thousand men be required to defend a country against one of sixty thousand; if it anticipates the enemy, it will be able by strategic movements to bring into action the bulk of its forces at a point where the enemy cannot oppose so great a force, and he will therefore be obliged to engage under a disadvantage, or employ counter manœuvres which will retard his progress.

By the application of this system to the dispositions for battle, the advantages will be doubled, since there will only be a portion of the enemy's corps occupying the points designated, against which a general effort is to be made.

The part performed by Daun, compared with what he might have accomplished, convinces us how little he deserved the enormous reputation which he enjoyed so long in the Austrian army. To know how to encamp troops and bring them into action is not sufficient to constitute a great captain.

Let us grant, as Tempelhof has proposed, that Daun did not fight Prince Henry, on the 6th and 7th of May, from fear of bringing the king back upon him; the object might have been secured by deferring the attack until the 10th, and not detaching Odonell's corps until the 15th; since, at that date, the king was already in Silesia, and hence there was no longer any fear of his return. Odonell's presence in that province was not urgent, for he remained an entire month at Zittau, watched by a single regiment of hussars. Thus the marshal cannot be regarded as justifiable in his course, whatever may have been the instructions of the Aulic Council, which governed his conduct; besides, since his panegyrists agree that he possessed a great military character, why did he not do as Prince Eugene did under like circumstances, when he defeated the Turks contrary to, and in spite of, his orders. A general who has a reputation to sustain, proves himself without genius when he consents to marshal eighty thousand men against thirty thousand, without firing a shot during the campaign, when active operations are in progress upon every other point. Daun did not commit a fault less grave at the end of the year, when he failed to strike a decisive blow with the fifteen or eighteen thousand men which Laudon sent him. He confined himself to taking several villages, in order to give more comfort to his winter-quarters. Was this the proper way to employ a mass of seventy-five thousand men, that had to combat only thirty thousand, in order to conquer a kingdom and terminate the war? It was not intended that he should remain upon an absurd defensive, when he was reënforced by withdrawing troops from Silesia, after the departure of the Russian army. This last stroke brought to a climax the blunders of this campaign. It has been said that the Austrian generals were embarrassed by their regiments; they detached them, they made them march and countermarch, and all for no reasonable object.

By considering this faulty employment of forces, the results which it furnished, and those which would have been brought about by a system founded upon modern principles applied with celerity and vigor, we shall be convinced that the Austrians were incapable of devising a worse combination, and that they would have received a merited retribution if the king had not been exhausted.

It is unnecessary to comment upon the Russians. They accomplished nothing because their policy required it. The conduct of Marshal Butturlin only proves that two armies under different commanders, and having to act in concert upon the same line of operations, will execute everything with difficulty and nothing well, and that a single one will do more than both, aside even from the misunderstandings that may exist between their chiefs.

CHAPTER XXXI.

CAMPAIGN OF 1762.

CAMPAIGN OF THE FRENCH AND ALLIED ARMIES IN 1762; BATTLE OF WILHEMSTHAL; GENERAL OBSERVATIONS UPON THE LINES OF OPERATIONS IN WESTPHALIA.

Before recounting the operations of the land army, it may not be amiss to take a glance at the condition of maritime affairs. The year 1760 passed unmarked by a single event of importance. That of 1761 began in the same way. It was not yet known that Lally, shut up in Pondicherry, had capitulated on the 21st of January, and that Martinique was about to be invaded. The death of George II. raising up a dangerous rival to Pitt, in the person of Lord Bute, governor of the young Prince of Wales, who succeeded to the throne, the friends of peace began to hope for a more favorable turn of affairs.

The duke de Choiseul at length found the only remedy for the evils with which Europe was threatened, in the alliance with Spain ; however, it was now too late ; the Spanish fleets and commerce deprived of the support of the French navy, which was then broken up, did nothing but add to the trophies of the enemy. No sooner had Pitt heard of the negotiations in progress between the two courts, than he proposed to fall upon the commerce and colonies of Spain, as was done in the case of France in 1755. Being opposed in his policy, he preferred to abandon the reins of government rather than to hold them with a feeble and uncertain hand ; he therefore gave in his resignation. Lord Bute succeeded him; but the impulse given to the English navy by his predecessor outlived his ministerial career: the elements of superiority existed; they did not forestall the enemy, but were fast becoming rich with spoils. Martinique surrendered in the beginning of 1762; the island of Cuba was invaded; the Philippines conquered, Havana and Manilla sacked; many rich convoys belonging to Spain were seized; even Acapulco and Vera Cruz, on the American continent, furnished an immense booty to the bold English cruisers. A bloodier transaction was the taking of Belle-Isle on the coast of France, in spite of the honorable defense made by the chevalier of Saint-Croix, but which could not be prevented, inasmuch as France possessed no fleet strong enough to keep the sea.

In the mean time, Lord Bute, making an application of the Roman maxim, consented to conclude a peace during prosperity. The duke de Choiseul has been accused for gratuitously compromising the resources of Spain, by uniting too late with her, or for having too quickly concluded an onerous peace, provided the union of the two nations rendered possible the reëstablishment of affairs. However, it cannot be denied that the family compact, retaining all of its vigor during peace, the treaty of Versailles was very advantageous to France. A temporary humiliation may be endured, in hope of future vengeance, and the two countries, so soon as their exhausted resources were recruited, might repair their losses and concert a good plan of operations. Under this point of view, it would be so much the more unjust, since the fortunate issue of the American war, which broke out fifteen years afterwards, enabled them to gather most glorious fruits from their former treaty. But not to anticipate in point of time, we must return to the recital of the military operations.

The extraordinary efforts of France in the preceding campaign ended in the miserable affair of Willinghausen, the consequences of which, more pitiable still than the combat, had reëstablished matters upon the same footing which they occupied at the beginning of the campaign. The plan of the cabinet of Versailles, opposed to that of 1761, was based upon the actual position of the troops and a knowledge of past errors. It was resolved to bring into action the principal mass of eighty thousand men against Hesse by the right, while a corps of thirty thousand should operate by the lower Rhine. This latter was confided to the prince of Condé. The government took the astonishing resolution of dividing the command between the Marshals d'Estrées and Soubise, and of recalling the two brothers Broglio to their rendezvous.

The allied army closed up somewhat in the early part of May. The Hanoverian corps, under Sporken, cantoned about Blumberg; the English, under Lord Granby, in the vicinity of Bielefeld; the remainder at Holzminden and Eimbeck. The last-mentioned troops passed the Weser, and encamped, on the 15th, at Reilkirchen and Horn. Headquarters were transferred from Pirmont to Corvey, on the 6th of June. General Luckner and Prince Frederick of Brunswick remained on the Weser, at Eimbeck and Hoxter, for the purpose of covering Brunswick and Hanover.

The French army was cantoned upon the banks of the Fulde, as far as the vicinity of Corbach; the Saxon corps of Prince Xavier occupied Thuringia; the light troops ran as far as Halberstadt; the fortress of Gottingen, at the head of their range of quarters, had a strong garrison. Lieutenant-General Chevert was to cover it with a corps of eighteen battalions and twenty-eight squadrons. All remained quiet on both sides until the 18th of June. Ferdinand concentrated his army on the 18th of June, and took post with it at Brakel, at Borckholz, and on the 21st, between Korbeck and the heights of Teischel. The light troops passed the Dimel and occupied the woods of Rheinhardswalde, as well as the château of Sababurg. Prince Frederick transferred himself to Trendelburg in view of sustaining that post. General Waldegrave occupied the heights of Libenau, and the brigades Walmoden and Zastrow encamped upon the heights of Everschutz. On the 23d, all the advanced posts crossed the Dimel to cover the construction of some bridges, which was accomplished during the night.

At the very time that Ferdinand was beginning the offensive, the French generals were apparently combining to favor his movements; they undoubtedly thought that in approaching the Dimel, the duke had nothing further in view than defending the passage. Consequently, the French army, after being assembled at Cassel, was moved, on the 22d, towards Dimel, and went into camp at Burguffeln, between Immenhausen and Meyenbrechsen (Plate XXI.); the reserve of the right wing, commanded by Castries, was advanced towards Carlsdorf, and took position with its right at the woods of Rheinhardswalde. The count de Stainville was upon the heights which border the creek of Westufeln.

This position was very badly chosen; for it was too far from the Dimel to enable the French to dispute the passage of that river; but a greater imprudence arose from resting the right upon a wood, the issues from which were neither guarded nor examined, and which, in fact, were occupied by the enemy without its being known; this might have brought upon the French the most fatal consequences.

The duke did not allow these errors to escape his observation, and resolved to attack the French the next day. With this view, he ordered General Luckner, who was posted at Sulbeck, to cross the Weser at Wambeck during the night, and thence to march to Gottesburen. Lord Granby was to pass the Dimel, on the 24th, at two in the morning, near

Warburg, and arrive by a long detour upon the rear of the French, in order to seize Durrenberg.

The bulk of the army received the following order:

"To-morrow, on the 24th of June, the army will assemble under arms, ready to cross the Dimel in seven columns.

"The first on the right, composed of the English cavalry, will cross at Liebenau.

"The second, composed of the English infantry and artillery, will cross below that village.

"The third, composed of the infantry of Brunswick, will cross at Hemmern.

"The fourth, or the heavy artillery of Hanover, at Ewer schutz.

"The fifth, composed of Hessian infantry, between Ewerschutz and Sielen; it will be followed by sixteen squadrons from the left.

"The sixth, composed of the infantry of Hanover will cross at Sielen.

"The seventh, composed of the remainder of the cavalry of the left wing, will effect its passage below Sielen.

"The regiments will arrange their departure from the camp in such a way that the columns may arrive upon the ground indicated exactly at four o'clock. Kingsley's English regiment will cross the Dimel at two o'clock, near Liebenau, and will take position upon the heights fronting Zwergen, in order to cover and protect the passage of the columns. The chasseurs of Lord Cavendish, those of Hanover, the pickets of the army, and the regiment of Riedesel, will form the advance-guard.

"So soon as the English troops, with those of Brunswick and the Hessians, shall have reached the heights near Kelse, on this side of the ponds, they will be formed with their right resting upon the woods and the ravine Niedermeissen, and their left on the river Asse, in the direction of Carlsdorf.

The village of Kelse, the ponds, and the ridge of heights of Langenberg, will be in their front; the cavalry of the fifth column will be formed in echelons on the left, a little in rear of the Hessian infantry.

"The chasseurs of Cavendish, and those of Hanover, will endeavor to seize the ridge of heights called Langenberg, and take possession of the passes in the direction of Westufeln and Call. Lieutenant-General Sporken, who commands the sixth and seventh columns, will pass through Hunme, afterwards moving between Beverbeck and Hombrecksen, arranging his march so as to arrive at the same time upon the heights of Kelse. He will there form his troops, fronting Grabenstein, and giving his left a direction towards the corps of Luckner.

"General Luckner will begin his march from Gottesburen at three o'clock in the morning, going by Sababurg to Mariendorf. He will there form his troops near the woods, so that the latter village shall be on the left flank, and the right be prolonged in the direction of Hombrecksen. He will expedite his march, so as to be in position at seven o'clock precisely, with his infantry in the first line and his cavalry in the second. Major Specht, with his detachment of light troops, will set out at three o'clock from Sababurg, and leaving his infantry in the woods near Holzhausen, will advance himself with his cavalry upon Hohenkirchen.

"When the army shall be formed, General Sporken will attack the right flank of the enemy's corps, posted near Carlsdorf, and General Luckner will endeavor to take it in reverse. Should the enemy retire to avoid becoming engaged, these two generals will pursue him vigorously, in such a way, however, that the first shall remain upon his right flank, and the second maintain his position upon the enemy's rear.

"All the baggage wagons and company horses will be left

at the tower of Warth, situated between Bogentrick and Buhne."

These dispositions were carried out with sufficient exactitude. The French were as quiet in their camp as if the enemy had been twenty leagues distant. Undoubtedly it never occurred to them that a river could be crossed in broad daylight, in presence of an army so superior as theirs, for the purpose even of giving battle on the same day.

General Sporken reached his position between seven and eight o'clock; but he was discovered and cannonaded by the corps of Castries, which was posted at Carlsdorf. That general then decided to attack the enemy, and seize the heights of Hombrecksen, without waiting for the arrival of General Luckner. He afterwards posted his artillery there, and replied fiercely to that of Castries. This uproar roused the French army from its slumbers; the long roll was beaten, and all flew to arms. The disorder always attending these alarms might, nevertheless, have been fatal to the army, for the generals had no knowledge of what they ought to do, and were in doubt whether to beat a retreat or engage in a battle for which nothing was prepared. Meanwhile Castries made use of every effort to interrupt the march of Sporken's corps, and threatened it with several battalions thrown out against its right flank, which, however, were obliged to return. He attempted the same manœuvre with his cavalry against the left flank of the Hanoverians; but General Luckner arriving at this instant in position, the French were obliged to abandon that project. They continued, however, to defend their post.

The cannonade continued furiously for more than an hour, without Sporken's demonstrations producing the slightest effect. However, the heads of the third, fourth, and fifth columns having at length appeared in his front, General Castries concluded that it was time to commence his retreat, which he conducted with considerable order upon the right wing of the army. He re-formed his troops immediately in the ravine, near Grewenstein, and threw a part of his infantry into that small village.

Whilst Duke Ferdinand, with several columns was approaching the front of the French army, slowly on account of the difficult nature of the ground, General Granby was arriving also by Zierenberg, having turned the enemy's left and taken him in reverse. The Marshals d'Estrées and Soubise were not expecting the arrival of this corps, and its sudden appearance alarmed them. They inferred that no time was to be lost in effectuating their retreat, and immediately sent all of the baggage to Cassel, escorted by six battalions, and ordered the retreat of the army by several columns. Nevertheless time was pressing, for the duke was deploying at the foot of the Langenberg, between Meyenbreckse and Kelse, whilst Lord Granby was advancing by Ershen and Furstenwalde. The retreat became difficult, and Stainville's corps, posted, as before stated, in advance of the left wing, along the heights of Schachlen and the Westufeln brook, absolutely ran the risk of being cut off. In this hazardous position Stainville changed front perpendicularly to the rear, threw himself in potence in the woods between Meyenbreckse and Willhemsthal, and covered thus the march of the columns, whilst Marshal d'Estrées drew the cavalry from the left wing, and advanced at the head of it against that of the Duke Ferdinand.

Stainville's corps was composed of the grenadiers of France, the regiments of Aquitaine and Poitou, and the two Swiss regiments of Waldner and Eptingen. These troops became engaged with the English infantry under Lord Granby, in a furious combat, which lasted several hours. Nevertheless the allied army was continually gaining ground, and at length reached and occupied the heights of Calle, upon Stainville's rear, at the same time that a detachment assailed his right. This movement, executed at a moment when the corps of Lord Granby was gaining some success by the vigor of his attack, became decisive; a portion of the French infantry was broken and dispersed with a heavy loss. Stainville was thus induced to begin his retreat, and although he was nearly surrounded, he conducted it with so much order that the allied army could merely follow him quietly as he retired from one position to another, without meeting other loss than that which he had experienced in the action in the woods.

The French army took up a position on the heights of Tannenwalde. Duke Ferdinand encamped his own, with its right at Weimar and its left at Hohenkirch; General Luckner encamped at Holzhausen, and Lord Granby upon the Durrenberg, at the right of the army.

The French lost four or five thousand men killed, wounded, or made prisoners; the loss of the allies was very small.

The Marshals d'Estrees and Soubise crossed the Fulde, above and below Cassel, during the night of the 24th and 25th, and encamped between Landwershagen and Luttern-berg. A division occupied the intrenched camp of Kratzenberg, in advance of Cassel, where they remained until the 17th of August. The enemy having thus abandoned the left bank of the Fulde, the duke detached a brigade to occupy the heights of Tannenwalde; Granby's corps took position upon those of Karlsberg, and in the woods of Habichtswalde.

The result of the combat of Wilhemsthal upset the plans of the French marshals, and threw them upon the defensive, although the possession of Gottingen and the superiority of their forces authorized them to resume their operations. On the other hand, the duke was afraid to follow up his success upon the Main, because his left wing and his communications were directly threatened by that fortress. He therefore confined himself to the observation of the enemy's army, in order to profit by the first misstep it might make.

The marshals hoped everything from the diversion made by the prince of Condé, upon the Lower Rhine, against the corps of the hereditary prince. While awaiting this result they were joined by Prince Xavier of Saxony, who had come from the neighborhood of the Thuringia, to aid in the defense of the Fulde. The army then took up a more extended position on the 26th of June, its left being placed near Durrenhagen and Berghausen, and its right on the heights of Heilegenrode and Lutternberg, with a strong garrison in Munden, at the confluence of the Fulde and the Werra. Lieutenant-General Chevert was at Dreyrode, near Gottingen, with eighteen battalions and thirty-eight squadrons.

The position of this corps induced the duke to reënforce General Luckner at Holzhausen, and to post at that point twelve battalions and twenty-four squadrons. Several other movements were made for the purpose of disquieting or protecting communications. Count Rochambeau was detached with a brigade of infantry and three regiments of cavalry, for the purpose of dislodging Cavendish's brigade from Fritzlar, which withdrew upon Homberg at the approach of the enemy. The duke, perceiving that the enemy would undertake nothing more serious, directed Lord Granby, on the 2d of July, to join the brigade of Cavendish, and drive them off. Rochambeau, thus attacked, fell back to Treisa, and Lord Granby established himself at Homberg, from whence he detached parties to seize the depôts of Rothenburg and Melsungen. These little occurrences determined the French to make a forward movement on the 4th of July; the allies retired at their approach to Fritzlar. Rochambeau encamped first at Homberg and afterwards at Wabern.

Until the 15th of July nothing occurred worthy of notice.

The allied army gradually prolonged itself to the right, from whence it disquieted the French army. It took position on the 16th, upon the heights in the woods of Habichtswalde, with its right resting on the ravine near Hof, and its left on the Durrenberg fronting Cassel.

The marshals, thinking that they had discovered the duke's plan, and desiring to thwart him, recalled Chevert's division, which had lain so long near Gottingen. On the 21st their left wing was pushed forward as far as the Eder. The better to observe these movements, the duke established himself between Niedenstein and Kirchberg, with four brigades at Gudensberg, Granby's corps at Gerstenhausen, upon the Schwalm, and Luckner, with a new division, upon the heights of Wabern; his old detachment, under the command of General Waldhausen, was transferred from Holzhauzen to Wilhemshausen in the Rheinhardswalde, and afterwards to Hombrexen, in order to cover Marburg and the Dimel.

As the corps of Prince Xavier of Saxony was too greatly extended between Lutternberg and Munden, the duke determined to derive some advantage from this error, so common and so frequently punished in war. General Waldhausen was reënforced with three brigades, and given the direction of this operation. He set out from Wilhemsthal on the 23d of July, at nine o'clock, and arrived in the night on the banks of the Fulde, effecting the passage of it, at daylight, at four points. Colonel Schliefen left Uslar and passed by Hedemunden upon the Werra.

The banks of that river were lined with Saxon grenadiers, who defended themselves with courage, but were overthrown. Waldhausen, detaching two battalions to restrain the garrison of Munden, attacked the heights of Lutternberg, drove off the enemy, and pushed the Saxon cavalry upon that of Colonel Schliefen. The remainder were repelled in disorder against the right wing of the French army, after having lost one thousand prisoners, thirteen pieces of cannon, and five standards. The allies returned to the other side of the Fulde, and encamped near Hohenkirch. During the above attack, Prince Frederick of Brunswick had held in check the intrenched camp of Kratzenberg by a fierce cannonade.

On the 24th, after midday, Frederick established himself in the woods of Oberstenholz; Lord Granby upon the heights of Borken; General Waldegrave replacing him at Gerstenhausen; Luckner crossed the Schwalm, and took position upon the right bank of that river; Generals Zastrow and Gilsa were directed on the wood of Habichtswalde; the corps of Bock, Waldhausen, and Holdenberg were moved to Niedermessel, and Colonel Schliefen to Geismar, in order to cover the depots on the Weser.

On the other side, General Rochambeau joined the French army, and encamped near Melsungen. Ferdinand, observing that that wing was isolated upon the left bank of the Fulde, while the rest of the army was upon the right bank, resolved to attack it. He moved his right wing as far as Elfershausen and Mostheim, and General Sporken with the remainder of the army was advanced to the vicinity of the Eder, in the neighborhood of Feldsberg; but when the duke discovered that that portion of the French army was intrenched upon the Heiligenberg, he abandoned his project, and, on the 26th of June, returned to Gudensberg. The French profited by this lesson, and withdrew their troops to the left bank of the Fulde. The rest of the month was exhausted in skirmishes about the magazines.

Whilst they were trifling away their time in Hesse, the hereditary prince was watching the corps of Prince Condé from the vicinity of Munster; who, after having concentrated his troops at Wesel on the 21st of June, gradually pushed forward his light troops upon the Ems, with the intention of destroying the depots of the allied army. The hereditary prince, feeling too weak to secure everything, remained about Munster for the purpose of saving at least that place and Lipstadt. The course of events in Hesse having determined the French Marshals d'Estrées and Soubise to recall the prince of Condé, he departed, on the 16th of July, leaving Lieutenant-General d'Auvet with several thousand men upon the Rhine. He directed his march upon Dusseldorf, traversed the duchy of Berg, passed the Lahn at Giessen, on the 6th of August, and took position at Alten-Buseck. The hereditary prince followed up this march by Corbach, arrived, on the 2d of August, in the neighborhood of Warburg, and encamped at Ober-Weimar.

The duke's design heretofore had been to compel the French army to quit the vicinity of Cassel, which could only be accomplished by preventing the junction of that army with the prince of Condé; and to do this, it was necessary to fight. It is evident that two corps in communication, able to choose a place of junction in rear of their central point of assembling, can only be kept apart by a combat. The duke therefore resolved to attack the bulk of the army, which still occupied almost the same position behind the Fulde, extending from Munden to Spangenberg. Stainville, who was stationed at Bebra, had the corps of General Luckner in his front at Rothenburg.

All the dispositions for attacking were completed on the 8th of August. Luckner received orders to leave a corps of light troops in front of Stainville's corps, and to file off with the remainder of his troops by Heimbach upon Spangenberg and Bergenheim. General Freytag was to cross at Neumorschen, and march to Morshausen. The instructions addressed to Lord Granby required him to take arms and form in front of his camp, this side of Melsungen; General Conway, with twelve English battalions and the corresponding artillery, crossed the Eder in three columns at Brunslar, and took possession of the woods between that village and Wagenfurth. Sporken with twelve battalions and twenty-nine squadrons occupied the high ground between Baunerherberg and Baldorf; twelve battalions and the Hanoverian artillery were joined to Bock's corps, and marched to Brand, where they joined the hereditary prince, who was, besides, reënforced by twelve squadrons and the brigade of Gilsa. The brigade Marburg and four squadrons were ordered to move into the Habichtswalde. Prince Frederick, with the corps of Waldhausen, started at daylight on the 7th, crossed the Weser, and ascended the Werra, with the intention of marching by Eschwege and Wanfried upon the enemy's rear.

Each corps having reached its post, Lord Granby cannonaded the enemy at one in the afternoon, and detached General Wangenheim to Mansfeld with two battalions and four squadrons, to lay a bridge across the Fulde. General Conway from that side drove in the French posts between Grabenau and Buchwerra, and placed his artillery upon Ellenberg, in order, under the protection of its fire, to throw a bridge across near Buchwerra. Sporken occupied the mills of Grifse, General Malsburg Nieder-Zweeren, and the hereditary prince the defiles of Wilhemshausen, Spelle and Wohnhausen.

At six in the evening, the French camp was furiously cannonaded by all the batteries; General Wangenheim passed the Fulde at Mansfeld, and took position in the woods upon the left of the enemy. Conway crossed the Fulde near Buchwerra with two hundred men, for the purpose of driving the enemy from the right bank, and intrenching himself there. The cannonade was kept up until ten in the evening. Tempelhof does not state why the attack did not take place on this day, nor the following. It appears to have been intended that the hereditary prince should turn the right wing of the French army whilst Prince Frederick should arrive by the Werra upon their rear, and that the other corps should support the attack upon their front and left, but the heavy rains causing all the rivers to overflow their banks, frustrated the execution of the plan; for, on the 10th, the different corps reoccupied their former positions. The army encamped with its left on the Baunerherberg, the centre near Haldorf and Ellenberg, and its right near the woods of Melsungen. The corps of the hereditary prince lay at Homberg, on the Ohm, before the prince of Condé, who was at Stangerode.

The position in which Ferdinand had shut up the French army deprived it of nearly all resources, and especially those derived from foraging; the two marshals, likewise, feeling the necessity of operating their junction with the prince of Condé, resolved to march upon Friedberg. In view of this, the garrisons were withdrawn from Gottingen and Munden, and the defense of Cassel was confided to General Diesbach, under whose command was placed for this purpose sixteen battalions and three hundred horse. On the 17th of September, at daylight, the army broke through between the Fulde and the Werra, and marched upon Hirschfeld. Stainville's corps formed the advance-guard, and the count of Guerchy flanked the right of the column.

The duke readily concluded that his enemies were about to join the prince of Condé's corps, delivering Cassel and resuming the offensive. Therefore, leaving enough troops in that place, he marched with all haste by Homberg and Schwarzenborn to the vicinity of Grabenau. Generals Luckner and Bock were to reënforce the hereditary prince, remaining in front of Condé. The duke remained two days in his camp, in order to learn the direction taken by the grand French army.

So soon as this information had been obtained, which was

on the 26th, he moved to Ulrichstein; but it was then too late, for the French had reached Hitzkirchen; and since Stainville's corps with Guerchy's preceded it by one day's march, and occupied Windecken, the junction with the prince of Condé became almost impossible to prevent.

The hereditary prince, on his part, made every effort to frustrate it. After receiving his reënforcements under Generals Luckner and Bock, he determined to attack the prince of Condé, who was encamped with his corps at Rheinersheim, and for this purpose he crossed the Ohm, on the morning of the 22d, in four columns, and repulsed the advance-guard of the French. Unhappily, his good resolution was defeated by one of those casualties which almost always accompany multiplied attacks: two of the columns did not arrive at the time fixed. On the 23d, new efforts were made, but the French had abandoned the position; he established his infantry at Gruneberg, and followed it with his cavalry. Condé drew up his troops in order of battle, and resolved to maintain his position. The prince was taken aback at this attitude, and considered it prudent to return to Gruneberg, for the purpose of arranging his plan of operations for the next day. He was well started on his march at daylight, but notwithstanding his diligence, he found the position evacuated; profiting by his experience of the day previous, he followed the enemy with all his forces; but he had missed the favorable moment, and when he was ready to attain his object, the enemy occupied an excellent position near Gruningen. On the morning of the 25th, he endeavored in vain to dislodge him from his position; which failure induced him to repass the Wetter, and return, on the 26th, to Gruneberg.

Ferdinand, who had marched to Schotten, and thence to the river Nidda, arrived just in time to see the prince of

Condé enter camp at Pohlgons, and upon the Johannisberg, whence he communicated with the grand army.

Early on the morning of the 30th, this advance-guard was dislodged, after a sharp combat, by the hereditary prince, who was marching on Assenheim. However, the prince of Condé got information, about eleven o'clock, of the departure of the latter, and was then in full march to sustain his advance-guard, having been reënforced by five battalions of grenadiers, drawn from De Stainville's corps. The heads of his columns arrived at the moment when the duke of Brunswick was forming his troops in the position recently occupied by Condé's advance-guard. The brigades Boisgelin and Berry, with the gendarmes, immediately attacked the right of the allies, and De Stainville the left. Then commenced a furious and bitter conflict, in the progress of which, the French, who were constantly receiving accessions of fresh troops, succeeded in turning the right of the enemy. The hereditary prince was finally forced back across the Wetter, after losing ten guns and near fifteen hundred men.

When Ferdinand learned the unfortunate issue of this affair, he detached, the same evening, the troops constituting his second line upon Bingenheim and Staden, and followed them himself, on the morning of the 31st of August, with the rest of his troops and those of the hereditary prince. The concentration of the French army was finally consummated during the night of the 30th and 31st. It was encamped with the right at Nidda, and the left upon Johannisberg; the Saxon corps was between Bergen and Vilbel; that of the duke of Castries at Karben.

After this consummation, so long desired, the French turned their attention to the relief of Cassel, which was blockaded by Prince Frederick of Brunswick. The shortest way of doing this was to deliver a battle; but the fear of losing it restrained the marshals, and they endeavored to arrive at the same happy result by manœuvring by their left upon the Lahn, and opening for themselves a communication with Cassel through the principality of Waldeck. The prince of Condé opened the march on the 4th of September, and moved through Giessen to Grosenbuseck. The army followed, and was established, on the 9th, at Burkardsfeld; Prince Xavier with his Saxons remained at Bergen.

Ferdinand promptly divined the intention of his adversaries, and took up a position, on the 9th, on the banks of the Ohm, between Schweinsberg and Homberg; in this skillfully chosen position he was prepared to anticipate the French at all points.

On the 10th, the French advance-guard, under the duke de Stainville, crossed the Lahn, and was directed on Krosdorf. The army followed, on the 12th, and encamped near that village; on the same day, the advance-guard moved on to Frohnhausen, which was also reached by the prince of Condé. In order to oppose this movement, Ferdinand left Granby's corps upon the heights of Homberg, and went himself, on the 14th, to Schwarzenborn, whence he detached Conway's division to Roda, to take possession the next day of the heights to the right of Wetter, where the army went into camp on the 15th. By this movement the plan of the French generals was again thwarted, for it was their design to have encamped themselves at Wetter. The fact was, that on the 16th, they had taken the direction of Marburg; but being informed that they were forestalled by the duke, they established themselves in a very strong position, with their right at Marburg, their left at Michelbach; Stainville's corps, covering their front at Cosfeld, and the prince of Condé at Werda. The Lahn and the Ohm separated the two armies.

The marshals, convinced that all their manœuvres were ineffectual, devised others from their right. The corps of

Prince Xavier and of Castries were transferred from the environs of Bergen, on the left bank of the Lahn, to the vicinity of Ameneburg; their light troops, which beat up all the country between the Ohm and the Fulde, already disquieted the communications of the allies with the Cassel blockading corps and its supplies. By pushing these divisions across the Ohm, to act in concert with the light troops, it was probable that they would insure the raising of the blockade of Cassel, or compel the duke to make a movement. The allies guarded the crossings of that river indifferently. Wangenheim was at Homberg, with seven battalions and seven squadrons; Zastrow was at Langenstein, with six Hanoverian regiments, and Lord Granby near Kirchhain. The bridge at the Ameneburg mill was barricaded and protected by a large redoubt; the citadel contained a garrison of six hundred men.

Suddenly the Franco-Saxon army had become established in front of Homberg, with its left near Ameneburg. At daylight, on the 21st of September, the chateau was battered in breech, and the redoubt at the bridge assaulted. The garrison defended itself bravely until eight o'clock, when Zastrow's corps came to its relief. This general caused the troops in the redoubt to be relieved, posted his artillery upon the right bank of the Ohm, and scorched the French troops, who were attacking the head of the bridge. This uproar drew Ferdinand to the spot. He immediately recalled Granby's corps, which relieved at four o'clock in the afternoon the weary troops of Zastrow. Finally, after a continuous combat of five hours, the French abandoned their enterprise with a loss of eleven hundred men disabled; the loss of the allies was about the same. The garrison of the chateau Ameneburg surrendered after a gallant defense to the duke de Castries. The two armies maintained their respective positions. The extraordinary rains which fell at this period rendered the roads impassable, and suspended the operations of both armies.

In the middle of October, Ferdinand reënforced the corps blockading Cassel by eight battalions, and began the siege on the 16th, under the direction of General de Huth. The commandant of the fortress at first defended it with vigor, but for lack of provisions surrendered it, on the 1st of November, on condition that the garrison should be permitted to join the army.

On the 7th of November the news of the preliminary treaty of Fontainebleau, between France and England was received. It ended, at an opportune moment, those scenes which were the inconceivable accompaniments of this campaign, without any reference to the scandal caused by the miserable conduct of the maritime war. The shameful compact concluded at Versailles, by the duke of Nivernois, ceded Minorca to England, and thus opened the Mediterranean to that power. They acquired Senegal, Acadia, Canada, and Cape Breton. To the English were guaranteed the not less important possessions of Florida and Pensacola, upon which depended the command of the Gulf of Mexico; also the islands of Granada, Dominique, Saint Vincent, and Tobago, advantageous stations in the Antilles, on the coast of South America. Finally, it included the right to cut logwood, which, in such hands, secured an opening, through the facile means of commerce, for stronger pretexts, and a broader basis for their extravagant pretensions to Spanish America.

OBSERVATIONS UPON THE LAST CAMPAIGN IN HANOVER.

The faults of the preceding campaign were so obvious that they were the cause of an entire change in the choice of the primitive line of operations. If it were contrary to every principle of the art to establish two lines in 1761, upon a single frontier, it was still more absurd to employ one hundred thousand men in subordinate operations, such as the sieges of Munster and Lipstadt, while the army, to operate effectively from its advantageous position, need not have exceeded forty-five thousand men. It was then resolved to return to the plan of 1759, and to establish the principal mass in Hesse, for the purpose of operating by the right; but the forces were again isolated, and a second army, absolutely useless, was formed upon the Lower Rhine. Can there be anything more astonishing than to see a government incurring incredible expense, and raising formidable armies, merely to leave them inactive; placing them at enormous distances, and employing three months to concentrate them again, to cancel the folly of their isolation, when that concentration might have been effected at the beginning of the year by a single scratch of the pen of the minister of war? They fell into the old errors of 1759 and 1760, in having in view no great object as the end of their operations, as has been observed in Chapter XV. (see page 49). In glancing over the theatre of this too famous war, it is observed that it nearly forms a square, as stated in Chapter XIV. (see page 44).

The face A C will be found formed by the Rhine and the Ems; the face A B, by the North Sea; the face B D, by the Weser; the face C D, by the line of the Mein, which was the natural pivot of the offensive movements of the French army.

It would be impossible to find a more favorable theatre of war. The French army had for its use three sides of the square, for the line of the Rhine belonged to them. Holland formed an obstacle by its neutrality; the North Sea was worth more than an army, since, if the allies were driven upon its shores, they would be obliged to surrender or embark. In such a case, were this to occur subsequent to one or two vigorous battles, it is easy to see that but a small

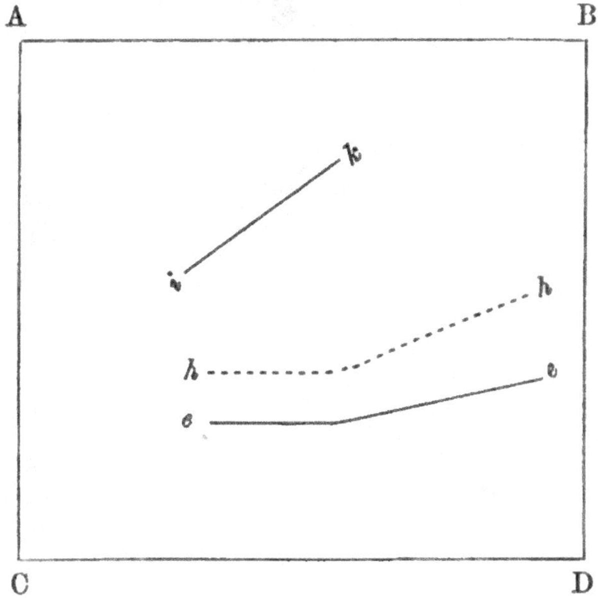

portion would have escaped; for it is no easy thing to embark sixty or seventy thousand men. Besides, at that period the English navy was employed on distant voyages, and it may be assumed that half of such an army would have been destroyed.

To secure this great object, it was sufficient to gain the oblique central position of Paderborn, or of Lipstadt and Minden, by operating with such celerity that the duke would have constantly remained on the left of the army, towards Munster and Osnabruck, in the angle C A B, line *i k*. This would have been easier of accomplishment, inasmuch as the French, by the possession of Gottingen, formed already the broken line *e e*, which it was only necessary to extend rapidly a little to the right in order to form the line *h h*, which could have been effected by three or four marches. It was also much more natural to have given this direction to the operations, and to have pushed them forward with energy, since, in case of reverse, it was always easy to fall back upon the line *h h* to that of the Main, indicated by the side C D.

The campaign in which the operations came the nearest to those pointed out, was that of 1759. The French were then, by a single stroke, masters of half the theatre of war, and afterwards, had they acted with more vigor, the war ought to have been terminated in two months.

We know that that direction, though decisive, could not have destroyed an army without fighting. It was further necessary, in place of remaining quiet in camp for six weeks, *that the French should march swiftly against the enemy, in order to conquer and destroy him; and if repulsed that they should make use of their numerical superiority, and of the advantages which resulted from the general direction of their operations, in order to renew the conflict, and to continue fighting until the end in view should be obtained.*

The campaign of 1806, against Prussia, exhibits the best confirmation of the truth of their assertions, as we have already stated in Chapter XIV. The theatre was the same as the one above given; it was bounded by the Rhine, the North Sea, the river Elbe, and the Main. The march upon the Saale would produce the line *h h*, and cause the Elbe to be gained ahead of the Prussians, which was the only side of the square which they controlled. It was the same combination even which placed the army of Melas in such an unfortunate position at Marengo, since the Austrians having against them the line of the Alps, that of the Mediterranean Sea, and the Adriatic Gulf, Bonaparte had merely to seize the only point of retreat for this army, on the Po, in order to overwhelm it. Finally, it is precisely the same line of manœuvre which Napoleon was intending to take against the Russians, in his expedition to Eylau, and which would have obtained the most splendid results, had not the officer sent to the Prince of Ponte-Corvo been captured, thus enabling General Beningsen to escape from the angle formed by the Vistula, the Baltic Sea, and the line from Thorn to Konigsberg.*

In the campaigns from 1758 to 1762, the French had the strongest inducements to adopt this same system. Their army, though already numerous, might have been reënforced at will by the provincial militia; it had merely to contend with the petty princes of Hesse and Brunswick, backed by about twenty thousand English. This allied army, once driven from its depôts by the movement which we have endeavored to point out, would have been deprived of all resources and means of recruiting.

In fact, it will be a lasting reproach to the reign of Louis XV. that his generals were allowed to be repulsed, during four consecutive campaigns, back to the Rhine and the Main, by an army inferior by half, composed of the troops of two or three petty princes, that a single battle would have annihilated for ever. Surely the blame rests upon their miserable combinations and irresolution, since the army which they commanded was brave, inured to war, and composed of the same troops which had covered themselves with glory in the affairs of Bergen, Wilhemsthal, and Ameneburg. These indisputable truths should impress those princes and ministers who are called upon to nominate the commanders of armies, with the vast weight of responsibility towards posterity which rests upon the wisdom of their choice.

It is not proposed to present a long dissertation upon the operations of this campaign; it bears the stamp of the mediocrity of the generals who directed it.

* This was published in 1809. Since then, the Emperor Alexander executed the same movements when directing the march of the Russian and Prussian armies by Bohemia in 1813.

The French army began its offensive movements at the end of June, having the strong corps of Chevert and Prince Xavier detached to its right, independently of the army of the prince of Condé upon its left, sixty leagues distant; thus only half their forces were disposable. What was the use of these strong detachments as accessories? Like the army of Soubise, in the preceding campaign, Condé's corps would have been much better placed at Stadtbergen than at Wesel, inasmuch as it would have connected his operations with the grand army, and would have secured its communications by cutting off altogether those of the enemy. In fact, it would have formed the base or important crotchet of the line *h h* indicated in the square.

If the position of the French army on the Dimel were a defensive one, it was badly chosen, as has been already remarked. If, on the contrary, it had an offensive object, why should the marshals permit themselves to be disconcerted by the multiplied columns of Ferdinand, who presented himself for combat with a river at his back? Instead of retiring precipitately upon Wilhemsthal, they should only have made a general change of front against Sporken's corps as soon as the affair was begun, for by this manœuvre Sporken would have been overcome, and the duke anticipated on his communications at the same moment in which the division of Granby was marching to its destruction. The same manœuvre might have been executed by the wing opposed to that division, whilst marching against it, and, isolated, it would have been overthrown, whilst the rest of the army was deploying its columns upon the Dimel.

The affair of Wilhemsthal presented exactly the same general dispositions as were employed in the battle of Creveldt: the left wing was turned and a corps was hastily placed in potence, whilst the army decamped from the position. The only difference is this, at Creveldt the movements were more strongly combined, as the allies turned the wing with a larger mass of troops, which was the more dangerous for the French army, inasmuch as their right was threatened with destruction in the Rhine.

At all events this action should have been undecided, as half of the French army was not present, and of those present the greater portion took no part in the combat. Nevertheless, a slight check administered to one division decided the success of an entire campaign, although the army, not counting its immense detachments, was superior to that of the enemy. From this may be inferred the quality of the manœuvres, and of the military ideas of the generals commanding.

It can never be understood why the marshals, after recalling the corps of Chevert and Prince Xavier, and thus having acquired a decided superiority, did not determine to effect their junction, by a march in advance, with the prince of Condé. It was more honorable, and, at the same time, more advantageous, to attack Ferdinand and to effect that junction by main force, instead of sneaking to the river Mein in order to bring it about. But what was far more surprising was their timidity after their concentration. They commanded one hundred thousand combatants against fifty-five thousand. It was their first duty to rescue an important fortress and the sixteen battalions which it held. Nevertheless it was allowed to fall at the distance of a few marches off. The history of the wars of the revolution presents few similar examples; on the contrary, it exhibits more striking contrasts. The successive raisings of the blockades of Dunkirk, Maubeuge, and Landau, in 1793, conferred as much honor upon the inexperienced generals of the Republic, as did the shameful abandonment of Cassel contribute to the disgrace of the learned captains of Louis XV.

Ferdinand's idea of marching to the front of the French

army and taking the initiative was profoundly wise; but his attacks were more scattered than at Creveldt. It is difficult to discover the object of the attack made by Sporken against Castries' corps, whilst Lord Granby was dealing the decisive blow upon the opposite wing. It is certain that had Sporken been connected with the duke's centre, and had the latter detached a corps of equal force to the assistance of Lord Granby, all the principles of the art would have been complied with; the allied army would then have concentrated its efforts against the left of the French army, which assailed in front, flank and reverse by superior forces, could not long have disputed the victory. This was the place to apply the maxims contained in Chapter XII.; for, if the French army lost a decisive battle upon its left, the corps of Castries, which was too distant to take part in it, would have been perfectly cut off by the attacks from the centre of the allied army. *But the duke deprived himself of the use of a strong corps, at the decisive point, for the purpose of bringing into action a greater mass of the enemy's forces; which is one of the greatest errors.*

The plan of crossing the Fulde was conceived upon principles less secure in their foundation; the duke must have had a supreme contempt for his adversary to have extended himself by his wings during three days, and to have moved against the right of the French, one corps which was obliged to pass three great rivers before it could turn the enemy. This system of enveloping the wings at a distance has been sadly dealt with in the later wars, whenever there has been an affair with a general who understood the employment of central masses; it caused the loss of the battle of Neerwinden to Dumouriez, that of Fleurus to Coburg, that of Lonato to Wurmser, that of Stockach to the army of the Danube, that of Marengo to Melas, and that of Hohenlinden to the Archduke John. It was that which ruined the Austrians at

Montenotte, Rivoli and Austerlitz; it insures the miscarriage of every combination made upon principles so erroneous. The only excuse which may be offered on the part of the duke, is the character of the men who were opposed to him; and this excuse is hardly available, for it would have been equally practicable to have acted in mass upon one of the extremities, with as many chances in his favor, in case of success, and fewer against him in case of failure.

CHAPTER XXXII.

GENERAL ARRANGEMENTS FOR THE CAMPAIGN OF 1762; OPERATIONS IN SILESIA.

FREDERICK found himself, in 1761, in a far more critical situation than in the preceding year; it seemed altogether probable, that in spite of all his exertions, and the absurdities of his enemies, he must eventually succumb to his adverse fate. In fact, the capture of Colberg not only established the Russians in the heart of his states, but it also enabled them to begin their operations early. On the other hand, the capture of Schweidnitz, the occupation of Upper-Silesia, of the rich electorate of Saxony and of Pomerania, left the king no means of recruiting his army, which diminished daily; and as a climax of evils, England withheld her accustomed subsidies. The house of Austria was so sure of concluding the war, that five hundred officers and twenty thousand men were furloughed out of the best troops which the army contained, and this subsequently proved a sad blunder. Providence, who holds in his hands all the elements of human combinations, disappointed the hopes of the king's enemies; the empress of Russia, the most implacable of all, died on the 8th of January, and was succeeded by her son, Peter III.

This prince had long been a sincere friend of the king, and scarcely had he assumed the reins of government, than he announced to the belligerent powers his pacific intentions, and ordered Czernischef's corps to retire into Poland, which was carried out in the course of the month of March. His individual treaty of peace was signed at St. Petersburg on the 5th of May, and Sweden did not hesitate long in following suit.

Frederick having gotten rid of his most formidable enemy, felt his hopes revive. His army was fitted out as if by enchantment, and reënforced, besides, by the corps of Pomerania and the Marche, and was immediately ready to begin the campaign.

The defection of Russia and Sweden disconcerted the allies, and destroyed their first plan. Daun had just taken command of the grand army of Silesia, which was raised to one hundred and six battalions and one hundred and forty-nine squadrons. It appears that the base of his plan was to preserve what he had gained without dreaming of extending his conquests. Serbelloni commanded the Austrian corps, which was to act on the defensive in Saxony with the army of the Circles. France adopted a plan of campaign the direct opposite of the preceding year, of which we have already given an account.

Daun reached the army on the 9th of May, and caused it to issue from the defiles in six columns, in order to establish it in the plain of Kratzkau, between the mountain of Zoptenberg and the stream of Schweidnitz-Wasser; its right was at Kaltenbrunn, and its left near Stephanshain.

The Prussians, without greatly disquieting themselves, reënforced their outposts, and remained shut up in their cantonments, near Strehlen, and upon both banks of the Lohe. On the 20th of May Frederick having received the information that Czernischef was to join him, as an auxiliary, resolved to await his arrival; and the Austrian general, who had already begun to entertain fears for the future, waited complacently until he should be disturbed. The two armies therefore held on to their positions during the entire months of May and June, without other event than some skirmishes, in all of which the Austrians came out with discredit, which reminded them of the folly of furloughing their excellent light troops.

Frederick desired to begin by opening the siege of Schweidnitz. Now this could only be undertaken by displacing Daun from his positions, either by a battle or by manœuvring upon his communications. To do this General Werner assembled a strong corps at Cassel, and marched himself, on the 13th of May, to Ratibor. This diversion failed to accomplish the desired object. Daun made no large detachments, but confined himself to strengthening Beck's corps, which covered Moravia, to nine thousand men. There were none but insignificant movements until the 24th of June, when the duke of Bevern arrived with a small reënforcement at Eichlau, and took the command of a corps of twenty-one battalions and thirty-six squadrons.

At length, on the 1st of July, Czernischef joined the Prussian army with twenty-three battalions and sixteen squadrons, which raised it to eighty-two battalions and one hundred and thirty-five squadrons, with three hundred and sixteen guns, not including Bevern's division.

The king, with the intention of turning Daun, cutting him off from the defiles, and forcing a battle, gave the command of twenty-five battalions and twenty-six squadrons to General Neuwied, who moved, during the night of the 1st and 2d of July, to the neighborhood of Kostenblut; whence he was to march on the following night to seize the mountains of Ziskenberg, in rear of Freyburg, passing by Weicherau and Bertelsdorf. The army, which was concentrated on the 1st, at nightfall, was posted in the greatest silence upon the heights of Sachwitz, whence it was to start, in the night of the 2d and 3d, in four columns, in order to gain Freyburg by Ossig, Rauske, Preilsdorf, Tscheschen, leaving Zirlau to the left; but Daun was informed by a deserter of the departure of Neuwied's corps, and put his army in motion on the same night, reëntering the defiles, where he encamped, with his right at Oberbogendorf, his left at Pulsnitz, and his centre in rear of Freyburg. Frederick, having been informed of their movements, on the morning of the 2d, sent his light troops on the trace of Daun, and went himself with the advance-guard to the heights of Wurben near Schweidnitz, where, on the morning of the 3d, the army reëntered its old camp of Buntzelwitz. Neuwied's corps moved, on the 2d, to Strigau.

Frederick knew that Daun's position was unassailable in front, but he was not ignorant of the fact, that in manœuvring by Hohenfriedberg its left would be turned, and at the same time, Braunau, where Daun had his magazines, would be menaced. Daun, on the other hand, inferred from a reconnoissance made by the king that this was the course which he would adopt, and immediately sent Brentano's corps from Burkersdorf to the heights of Adelsbach, which protected the road from Friedland to Braunau.

Daun was not deceived; since the 4th, the king had resolved to send Neuwied's division, and a corps of twenty-two battalions and thirty-three squadrons, commanded by General Czernischef, for the purpose of operating against the Austrian army, whether it might still be in its old position of Kunzendorf, or in any other. But Frederick having been severely indisposed, the execution of this movement was deferred until the 5th.

On the same day, Neuweid began his march at nightfall, upon Hohenfriedberg, and thence upon Reichenau, where his army encountered the outposts of Brentano's corps, which were driven in. At midnight, the king quitted the camp of Buntzelwitz with Czernischef's corps. As soon as he heard the sound of cannon on the side of General Neuwied, he hastened to join him with the cavalry, and at its arrival, he ordered the enemy's troops to be dislodged from the heights between Reichenau and Adelsbach; but the Austrian posts fell back upon the peaks, which formed an unassailable plateau in rear of the latter village, where Brentano's entire corps was drawn up. The Prussian infantry, nevertheless, passed through Adelsbach, under the fire of the batteries, and began to ascend the mountains. But the king perceiving the difficulties of this attack, recalled his troops. All of the troops returned except five leading battalions, which had become too much engaged to be extricated. After ineffectual efforts, they arrived out of breath at the summit of the mountain, where they were charged and overthrown into the ravines by fresh troops and superior numbers. This affair, which might possibly have succeeded had it been sustained, cost the Prussians seven hundred killed or prisoners, and six hundred wounded; but the worst features of it were, that it retarded Neuwied one day, and afforded Daun time to secure his depots at Braunau.

Nevertheless, Frederick pursued his operations by endeavoring to turn Brentano's corps, in order to gain Friedland; Neuwied was directed to continue his march; but the extrême fatigue of his troops would not permit of their being pushed beyond Witgendorf. Daun, who for some time had divined the schemes of the Prussians, having no further information of this movement, concluded to send Brentano's corps to Friedland, and to change his front to rear; he then repassed the ravine of Weistritz, and encamped with his right at Breitenhain, and his left upon the heights of Charlottenbrunn: a corps under General Okelly, stationed on the heights of Burkersdorf, connected the right with Schweidnitz in such a manner, that this excellent position covered at the same time the fortress and the depots of Braunau.

Meanwhile, Ziethen, who commanded the half of the army

which remained in the camp of Buntzelwitz, having discovered, on the 7th, that the Austrians had evacuated their position, put the troops in motion, and occupied it himself, with the right of his army resting at Furstenstein, and his left at Bogendorf. The king passed through Adelsbach, and encamped between Altwasser and Seifersdorf.

As Neuwied approached Friedland, he was astounded at discovering Brentano's corps, which he supposed still remained upon the rocks of Adelsbach. As Brentano was posted in an awkward position, and was inferior in numbers, he should have been immediately attacked; but Neuwied, instead of ordering it at once, called a council of war, which was taken advantage of by his enemy to make his escape into the old camp of Dittersbach, where he was secure from all attack, and at a distance to be readily supported by Daun's army. Finally, Haddick's corps, which up to this time had remained at Wartha, joined Brentano's corps, and the king was constrained, for the present, to renounce his enterprise against this point.

That all the stratagems might be tried which could induce Daun to leave his strong position, Frederick undertook a diversion into Bohemia. Neuwied's corps was moved to the heights of Trautenbach, and his patrols were sent forward as far as Konigsgratz; but the marshal limited his actions to throwing some troops into the forest of Konigsilva, to disquiet his adversary, and sending Brentano's corps to Politz, and Ellrichshausen's to Steingrund; however, he took the precautions to remove his magazines from Braunau to Scharfeneck, in the county of Glatz.

The king perceiving that the right of the position near the heights of Hohengiersdorf and Burkersdorf, occupied by the army of the Imperialists, was somewhat deprived of troops, formed the resolution of seizing upon it with the intention of cutting them off from Schweidnitz. The execution of this plan was dangerous; it was no less than taking up a position between a fortress and a superior army which covered it. To carry out the king's resolution, General Ziethen was ordered to march in two columns; the first of which encamped with its right upon the steep heights of Hohengiersdorf, and its left resting upon the woods of Ameisenwalde; the second column took post with its right resting upon the road which leads from Schweidnitz to Hohengiersdorf, and its left at Bogendorf, fronting Schweidnitz. On the 15th, Neuwied returned to Rosenau.

The army remained in position during the 16th. The king was devising means to compel Daun to decamp from before the place that he might lay siege to it; and sent a column to Kunzendorf, and Neuwied's corps to Gablau and Altreichnau; at the same time making demonstrations to occupy Daun's left.

On the 18th, Neuwied's corps repaired to Buntzelwitz through Hohenfriedberg. Everything portended events of a decisive character, when Czernischef communicated to the king the news of the terrible catastrophe which had precipitated Peter the Third from the throne of Russia, placing thereon the celebrated Catherine, and at the same time exhibited to him the order which he had received to return to Poland. All that Frederick was able to obtain was that his Russian corps should remain three days longer in its present position, preserving a strict neutrality; and he availed himself of this opportunity to arrange the attack upon the heights of Leutmansdorf and Burkersdorf, which commanded the Austrian position, and whose loss would have forced them to fight under a disadvantage or withdraw from it.

On the morning of the 19th, the king transferred his headquarters to Bogendorf, and Neuwied's corps with the Mollendorf brigade began the movement at nightfall. At daylight, on the 20th, all the troops had reached their destination, passed the stream of Weistritz upon trestle bridges, and encamped between Bogendorf and Esdorf, facing towards Schweidnitz. The enemy was reconnoitred. The heights of Leutmansdorf and Burkersdorf were very steep, broken, woody, and of extremely difficult ascent; they were protected by strong redoubts thrown up on the borders of the ravine, through which ran the Weistritz, protected by palisades and extensive abatis. General Okelly occupied the position of Burkersdorf with nine battalions; the heights of Leutmansdorf having only four battalions, Daun sent thither, at midday, Brentano's division, which occupied not only these heights, but also those of Michelsdorf and Ludwigsdorf. At the approach of the Prussian troops, the enemy's outposts fell back upon their lines, excepting the one which guarded the chateau of Burkersdorf. The king caused the chateau to be seized, and, in the night, established there a battery of forty-five howitzers and twelve twelve-pounders.

On the 21st, at daylight, the king made another reconnoissance, but discovered no more troops than on the previous evening; he was ignorant of the arrival of Brentano's corps. The troops, who were gotten under arms before sunrise, were put in motion. Neuwied's corps was charged with the capture of the heights of Leutmansdorf, and for this purpose it was formed in three divisions; the first two were ordered to escalade the heights and the redoubts, whilst the prince of Bernburg should cover the left flank of the attacks on the side of the Austrian army, and take possession of Leutmansdorf. This prince arrived near that village, drove out of it the enemy's posts, the troops of which fell back upon the six battalions stationed upon the mountain of Bergseite; after receiving some reënforcements, he attacked them with impetuosity, and repulsed them as far as the woods of Michelsdorf.

Whilst this was passing upon the left, General Neuwied seized upon the first level of the heights, and had put all his artillery in battery against the intrenchments. The Austrians sustained this fire with firmness, although it was greatly superior to their own. General Neuwied then ordered the attack. Colonel Lottum with one of the right divisions marched against the intrenchments, and became involved in a furious combat; but discovering a ravine which led to their extreme left, he crossed it at the head of the regiment of Mosel, re-formed his troops upon the heights, and carried the intrenchments almost without a shot. The enemy fled in disorder, leaving eleven pieces of cannon in the hands of the victors.

The enemy's right was not so easily dislodged from the mountains of Leutmansdorf; the prince of Bernburg had successfully stormed the first height, but their intrenched position remained still to be taken; he sent against it the regiments of Wunsch, Moritz, and a battalion of Finck. These troops encountered such prodigious obstacles of ground, and such an obstinate resistance, that they lost five hundred men without making the slightest progress. Finally, a way was discovered of turning the redoubts by a ravine at a moment when Colonel Lottum, disengaged from the right, was threatening to cut off their defenders from another quarter. These latter then fell back upon the corps of Brentano, who, perceiving his wings turned and his retreat menaced, abandoned the heights of Michelsdorf, and fell back, under a continual fire of artillery, as far as Wustwaltersdorf.

The attack upon Okelly's corps, which guarded the heights of Burkersdorf, was not less successful. Neuwied directed against that point the first column, protected by the fire of the great howitzer battery, which we have previously mentioned; General Mollendorf was to sustain this attack, and at the same time restrain the troops of the garrison of

Schweidnitz, which was formed on the glacis for that purpose. The tremendous roar of the battery, if the German historians are to be depended upon, had no other effect than to drive off in disorder the cavalry of Okelly.*

The troops of the garrison of Schweidnitz having reëntered the works, Brigadier-General Mollendorf found means to assail the Prince of Ligne, who was intrenched behind an abatis, and covered by a redoubt at the left of the ravine of Weistritz. The Prussians dragged up their artillery by hand through a by-path called the Schaafsritt, and played furiously upon the enemy, whilst some battalions of the guards, ascending the steepest heights and penetrating the thickets, arrived at last before the abatis, which they endeavored to clear. At that instant, Marshal Daun, seeing the troops of the Prince de Ligne compromised, ordered him to retire; the Prussians then seized the redoubt, in which the enemy had left a force to cover his retreat, and established themselves upon the heights.

When Daun discovered, at ten o'clock, that Neuwied's corps was at Michelsdorf, in his rear, and that Mollendorf's brigade had possession of the Burkersdorf heights, he resolved to abandon his camp that evening for the purpose of placing his right at the Falkenberg, his centre at Giersdorf, and his left at Tannhausen. When Daun's movement began, Czernischef's corps ceased to form a part of the Prussian army, and began its march into Poland. Frederick, having at length attained his object, made preparations for the siege of Schweidnitz, and for this purpose established his army in

* It is difficult to say why this cavalry was obliged to endure a fire of shell, in a position where it could be of no use. In the campaigns of 1805 and 1806, we have often known the French cavalry doomed to this same sad experience. To place it in line under a heavy fire of artillery at a moment or on ground where it can not manœuvre, is a fault against every principle of the art of war. Such a thing is only allowable in a great battle, in which we desire to impose upon the enemy by a given line, or to conceal or protect a decisive manœuvre.

the following positions, already strong by nature, and which he caused to be intrenched with the greatest care:

General Gablenz, with five battalions and ten squadrons, near Hartmansdorf; five battalions at Altwasser, under General Ramin; Neuwied's corps, consisting of nineteen battalions and eighteen squadrons, upon the heights of Taschendorf; Colonel Lossow, with two battalions and twenty squadrons upon the Kolberg, near Waldichen; the brigade Mollendorf, with five battalions, fronted Schweidnitz, near Weistritz; nine battalions, under the command of Manteufel, on the heights of Barsdorf; General Bulow commanded fifteen squadrons at Seitendorf, and twelve battalions and fifteen squadrons at Bogendorf; the prince of Wurtemberg was moved from Lowenstein to Peterswalde, with thirty-three squadrons, and, finally, three battalions remained at Wurben with the bakeries.

Before recounting the details of the siege of Schweidnitz, and the operations which immediately succeeded it, we will resume the thread of events in Moravia. The duke of Bevern was endeavoring to turn the right flank of General Beck, and to threaten that province by the Troppau road. His corps was divided into two divisions; the first, commanded by General Werner, consisting of ten battalions and fifteen squadrons, was one day in advance of the other, which was composed of eleven battalions and twenty-one squadrons. The former was ordered, on the 2d of July, to Troppau, and on the 9th to Misteck, from which point parties were dispatched in all directions to levy large contributions. General Beck, not considering his force sufficient to prevent this practice openly, marched from Freudenthal to Baehrn, and spread the report over the country of the arrival of Laudon with fifty thousand men. This ruse succeeded perfectly. Werner, fearing to be overwhelmed, returned on the 12th to Matzinnau. Beck, on the same day, took position at

Bautsch and at Schwansdorf, where he intended to throw himself between the two Prussian divisions, and to cut off that of Werner, which immediately returned to Gratz.

The Austrian general, satisfied with having attained his object, returned to Guntersdorf. The two parties maintained the same positions until the beginning of August, at the time when Czernischef's corps departed. This obliged the king to call in Bevern's corps, which encamped on the 25th at Kosel. The division Werner took position towards Neisse on the 28th. Beck then returned to Zuckmantel.

Frederick, presuming that Daun would recall Beck's corps to succor Schweidnitz, ordered the duke of Bevern, in case the latter should march to Wartha, to direct himself rapidly upon Neisse, in order to replace Werner's corps, which at once proceeded to join the main army before Schweidnitz. On the contrary, should this not happen, the duke was to time his movements so as to arrive at Neisse by the 25th of August.

SIEGE OF SCHWEIDNITZ; COMBAT OF PEILE.

On the 4th of August, the place was entirely invested by the corps of General Tauenzien, consisting of twenty-one battalions and twenty squadrons, making altogether about fourteen thousand men. The garrison was eleven thousand strong, and commanded by General Guasco; the celebrated Gribeauval commanded the artillery and directed the defense.

This siege was one of the most memorable in modern history. A wretched place, which some time previous had been taken by escalade, sustained two months of open trenches. But matters had changed; the place was defended by a skillful man and a chosen garrison, whilst it was attacked by Major Lefèvre, a very weak man, and badly supported, for the art of conducting sieges was then most backward in Prussia.

Whilst the siege works were commenced before Schweidnitz, Daun remained in his camp at Giersdorf, and, instead of endeavoring to succor the place, he threw up intrenchments around himself for fear of being attacked. However, the marshal subsequently resolved to advance upon the heights of Klotschen, to try and raise the siege; but he awaited the arrival of Beck's corps, which set out on the 6th of August from Zuckmantel, in Moravia, for Closter-Camenz, where, on the 10th, he effected a junction with the right of the army. No sooner had the duke of Bevern received notice of his departure than he crossed the river Neisse, and endeavored to anticipate him at Nimptsch, by a night march, for the purpose of reaching Oberpeile on the morning of the 13th, where he was ordered to take post. As it was, the duke encamped with his right near Reichembach, and his left upon the Fichtelberg (Plate XXIII., No. 6). When Beck heard of the departure of this corps, he began his march for the purpose of occupying that same post; but there was no longer time, and he was obliged to return, on the 14th, to Schonwalde. The Prussians drove off his rear-guard, and established their advanced-posts at Ellguth and Pulzendorf. The king sent to the duke of Bevern's corps several batteries of heavy cannon, and intrenched his position.

This event thwarted Marshal Daun's plan, which could only be executed by beating the duke of Bevern, thereby running the risk of becoming involved in a general action, contrary to his system; notwithstanding which it was very necessary that this attack should be made. He arranged his dispositions to crush the duke, with the greater part of his forces, whilst the remainder were to stay in position, in order to deceive the king. In consequence of this Lasey's and

Brentano's corps set off at daylight to form a junction with Beck upon the heights of Kleitsch.

The Austrian generals caused the tents to be pitched in the morning, in the position of Lang-Bielau; but at three o'clock in the afternoon their columns were seen in motion. Brentano's corps and the cavalry, under the command of Odonell, were formed in advance of Niederpeile. Lascy went through Mittelpeile with several battalions, placed a strong battery in advance, and two others in rear of this village, whilst Beck's corps, in two columns, was sent against the left of the duke of Bevern, through Oberpeile, and was deployed in two lines between that village and Girlsdorf.

As soon as Odonell's cavalry issued from Niederpeile, General Lentulus, with eighteen squadrons, crossed the woods behind the infantry, for the purpose of attacking it. Several changes were made on each side at this point, without any result, but the fire of the enemy's cannon forced the Prussians to retire.

Meanwhile, Lascy, Brentano, and Beck's first line were wasting time in cannonading, while this latter general, at the head of his second line, had passed through the thickets of Girlsdorf, taken possession of the adjacent heights, and caused his grenadiers to attack the Fischtelberg; the ground over which they had to pass was marshy, and was exposed to a plunging fire from the Prussian artillery, which played upon them incessantly; it was seven o'clock before Beck was able to extricate himself from the woods and issue into the plain in rear of the enemy's position. The other Austrian divisions were waiting only for this moment to commence the action. The duke of Bevern then attacked vigorously with two battalions the head of the column which had begun to debouch, and threw it into the swamp. Meanwhile, fifteen squadrons were detached from the left by the king, which overthrew the enemy's cavalry towards

Niederpeile, and before it was scarcely reformed again, it was charged by General Lentulus of Bevern's corps, and thrust upon the infantry near that village, where the duke of Wurtemberg completed their disorganization with fresh reënforcements. Finally, General Mollendorf arrived also, after sundown, with six battalions; and the Austrian generals, witnessing the failure of the enterprise, withdrew with their troops from the field to the camp of Haberndorf, after having more than a thousand men disabled in the combat.

This affair gained the duke of Bevern much honor; for he had only eleven battalions and five regiments of cavalry opposed to thirty-three battalions and fourteen regiments of horse; it is true, that nearly two-thirds of the enemy's infantry merely paraded to the sound of the cannon; but that portion paralyzed half of the duke's corps, and it must be conceded that he seized with infinite judgment the decisive moment to strike the blow which was to extricate him from his embarrassment.

It is difficult to account for the inaction of Lascy's and Brentano's corps, especially when the Prussian artillery, which opened its fire upon Beck's column, must have announced to them that the grenadiers had reached their destination, and were becoming engaged. They exposed Beck's corps to destruction. Under any circumstances it was better to attack the front too early than too late; they had abundant forces for storming the position. We are also tempted to blame Frederick for having hesitated so long to sustain the duke; but it is certain that the camp pitched at ten o'clock in the morning, upon the heights of Lang-Bielau, had deceived him to such an extent that he was not disposed to credit the report of the attack. Had his troops marched at once, the corps of Lascy and Brentano would have been totally defeated.

On the 17th of August, the enemy remained encamped at

Haberndorf; the next morning he resumed his positions, and afterward moved by Wartha, between Patzdorf and Oberstein; Beck occupying the intrenched camp of Wartha, and Brentano taking post at Schonwalde.

It appears that the ill success of this enterprise disgusted Daun with all engagements, for he undertook no more of them for the salvation of Schweidnitz. The siege works before it were pressed vigorously; the attack was directed against the fort of Jauernick, in the defense of which Gribeauval employed with great success the subterranean warfare of mines. The works of the sap were pushed forward with activity until the 22d of August. The parallels and the batteries were established to within one hundred and fifty paces of the covered way, by means of counter-mines. But here it was necessary to feel the way, and to destroy by means of globes of compression, the system of defense of the besieged. This peculiar war lasted six entire weeks; Major Lefèvre, who directed the siege, lost his mind, and the king gave orders, good or bad, for the continuation of the siege. Finally, on the 8th of October, a grenade, thrown by chance, blew up the powder magazine of Fort Jauernick, and a mine was let off the next day which blew away a part of the covered way and some of the palisades. Although the besieged had repulsed the attack which succeeded it, and had promptly repaired the damage resulting from these accidents, General Guasco, who had been parleying for more than a month, capitulated and surrendered himself a prisoner, with eight thousand six hundred men. We cannot conceive what could have induced him to sign this disgraceful compact after so fine a defense, which it was easy to prolong still further. The garrison had lost men, it is true, but the place had not been breached, and was not likely to be soon; before they had crowned the covered way, and effected the descent into the ditch, much time would have elapsed, and the season was far enough advanced to lead to the belief that the cold weather might have suspended the labors of the besiegers. The loss of the Prussians reached three thousand two hundred and twenty-eight men killed and wounded; that of the garrison was two thousand eight hundred.

As soon as the place had surrendered, the king, wishing to provide Prince Henry with the means of occupying Voigtland, detached General Neuwied, on the 15th of October, into Saxony with twenty battalions, fifty-five squadrons, and sixty pieces of cannon. The remainder, under the command of the duke of Bevern, were cantoned at Schweidnitz and in the neighboring mountains. Daun remained quiet on his side, and, on the 24th of November, an armistice was concluded, which enabled the two armies to go into winter-quarters.

CHAPTER XXXIII.

OPERATIONS IN SAXONY; BATTLE OF FREIBERG.

The Prussian army, deprived of the finest part of the Electorate of Saxony, and of the Voigtland, after passing the winter in want of everything, in a distressed and exhausted country, which never was known to be fertile, numbered, in the opening of the campaign, forty-eight battalions and ninety-three squadrons, making upwards of thirty-five thousand men.

The Austrian army was commanded by Marshal Serbelloni, and comprised fifty-seven battalions and one hundred and eight squadrons. Its main body was posted around Dresden; Macquire's corps occupied the intrenched camp of Freiberg; finally, a chain of posts covered the cantonments from Nossen as far as Roswein and Dobeln. The army of the Circles, consisting of thirty-eight battalions and forty-seven squadrons, which was intended to reënforce the Austrians, was cantoned around Altenburg and Naumburg.

In spite of this marked superiority, it would appear that the commanders of the allied army had determined not to depart from the plan pursued in the preceding campaign, for everything remained in the greatest tranquillity until the 12th of May.

At this period Prince Henry, after making various movements, in order to lead the Austrians to think that he desired to concentrate in the capital position of Katzenhauser, near Meissen, suddenly fell upon the enemy's posts in four columns, between Roswein and Leisnig, pierced their chain, and carried off several cantonments, making more than one thousand eight hundred prisoners. Manœuvring afterwards with a view of penetrating into the Voigtland, and to establish his own army between the armies of Austria and the Empire, for the purpose of preventing their junction, he marched, on the 13th of May to Hanchen, whilst General Hulsen, who had remained with a part of the army in the position of Katzenhauser, made a demonstration against Nossen, which obliged General Brunian to evacuate it and retire to Freiberg. On the 14th, the prince was in presence of Macquire, whose position was unattackable in front. That general was trembling at the presence of the Prussians, and did not feel himself justified in waiting to see whether they made an attack or not, but fell back in the night upon Dresden, which led Prince Henry to establish himself where he was. Seidlitz having scoured the immense ravines of the Weistritz, from the forest of Tharand as far as Frauenstein, the prince moved, on the 16th, to the heights of Pretschendorf, and General Hulsen to Gros-Sohra, near Wilsdruf. The Austrian corps under Macquire occupied the intrenched camp of Dippodiswalde, another division the heights of Rabenau, and the rest of the army lay in the Val-de-Plauen under Dresden.

The army of the Circles was advanced as far as Chemnitz. When the prince of Stollberg, who commanded it, ascertained that the Prussians had separated him from the Austrian army, he began to fear an attack, and retrograded to Zwickau; but Marshal Serbelloni ordered him back to Chemnitz. Prince Henry held him and his force in such contempt that he sent only four battalions and five squadrons to watch him, which took post at Oederan, with the Lohfluss behind him. This detachment, having been attacked suddenly by General Luzinsky, lost seven hundred men, which obliged the prince to give the command of it to General Kanitz, and to reënforce it with one battalion and five squadrons. The army of the Circles, overcome by this success, was reposing upon its laurels at Chemnitz. The two other armies observed each other in their respective positions without firing a shot.

If Marshal Serbelloni had instructions to venture nothing, Prince Henry had much stronger inducements to act in the same way; consequently, the whole month of June wore away without any event worth noting. The Austrian army, reënforced by several regiments from Silesia, limited its operations to the capture of General Kleist's post at Reichstadt, which was somewhat of an annoyance.

Prince Henry on his side, having been reënforced by a battalion and fifteen squadrons, which came from Pomerania, resolved to rid himself for a while of the army of the empire, and, on the 20th of June, he detached Seidlitz with three or four thousand infantry and upwards of four thousand horse, to threaten its right flank. Scarcely had the patrols from the corps shown themselves in the neighborhood of Penig, upon the Altenburg road, than that army fell back successively upon Zwickau and Reichembach; but the Prussians following closely, it did not feel secure until it had reached the Monchberg mountains near Bareith, where it perched itself on the 27th of June.

Serbelloni, hearing of this strange retreat, ordered the army to advance, and felt obliged to make some demonstrations to facilitate this operation. He meditated a plan of attack upon Hulsen's position, and arranged, it was said, very excellent dispositions for an attack upon his left. But timidity was the incurable disease of the Austrian army; four columns presented themselves before Constapel, Weisdrup, Hundorf, and Braunsdorf. The first two, whose success was to decide the affair, returned as soon as the redoubts of Pinkwitz fired upon them. Therefore, after an exchange of cannon shot at a distance of over fifteen hundred paces, hurting nobody, the retreat of the two columns terminated the day.

It has been stated that Hulsen became aware of the uncertainty of the enemy; for he did not make the slightest disposition to repel the attack against his left; he had not even sent enough artillery, which, in that position, ought to have been the principal arm; the rest of the line remained quiet.

In fact, this enterprise of Serbelloni's, so extolled by Tempelhof, was badly planned. *When an army occupies a position perpendicular to a river, with one of its wings resting thereon, it is necessary to be careful in attacking that wing, because the attacking body is exposed to being thrust into the river, should the enemy execute a change of front in mass from the opposite side. By attacking the other wing, on the contrary, with nearly all our available force, we embrace all the favorable chances; for if this wing be vigorously assailed in flank, and turned by superior forces, it will be inevitably captured or driven upon the rest of the enemy's army, thrown into disorder, crowded into the river, and placed in a position to be completely destroyed.**

Now Serbelloni had double the force necessary to execute such an attack upon the right of Hulsen's corps, which ought to have been thrown into the Elbe, or obliged to cut its way out.

* The battle of Wagram may be cited as an example, in which the Austrians imprudently pushed their right along the Danube, when Napoleon had transferred and established the mass of his troops on their left. Had not the corps of General Hiller been speedily withdrawn, Napoleon had only to abandon his communications by Vienna, destroy his bridges, and change his front to the extreme left of the Austrians, in order to crowd them into the Danube. A battle lost by the archduke, in that position, would have terminated the war, and the emperor would have risked nothing. He might have opened a line of communications through Franconia, or have reëstablished it upon Passau. This was the same movement which Wurmser should have made at the lines of Wissemburg, and of which we shall speak in the wars of the French Revolution.

Meanwhile, Prince Henry had removed the corps of Kleist to Oederan, with orders to effect a junction with the troops stationed there, and to prosecute the invasion of Bohemia. The latter advanced in the night of the 1st and 2d of July, through Marienberg upon Einsiedel, where they broke up the enemy's posts, leaving a reserve of grenadiers in the intrenched positions, and pressed forward as far as Brix and Ossek, whence he withdrew, on the 7th of July, upon Oederan. Prince Henry reënforced him, and ordered him to drive off the corps of General Blonquet, which had advanced from Toplitz to Dux. Kleist then moved upon Einsiedel, on the 17th and 18th; attacked the Croats and the dragoons posted in the Johannisdorf woods, expelled and pursued them to Herrlich, with the loss of three hundred and forty prisoners. This corps returned a second time through Brix, Comotau, and Pasburg, to Oederan.

During these events, as has been previously stated, the army of the Circles was ordered to make a forward movement, repulsing Seidlitz, and joining, through Bohemia, the Austrian army which lay at Dresden. This movement was undertaken early in July, in two columns; the army commanded by the prince of Stollberg went to Hof, and Luzinsky's corps to Eger. The former was transferred to Oelsnitz on the 14th, and the latter to Auerbach, whence they expelled the outposts of General Belling toward Zwickau. The two columns were reunited on the 17th; and marched to Schneeberg, thinking to greatly disquiet Seidlitz, who still lay at Zwickau; both sides remained in position until the 20th. On that day the prince of Stollberg ascertained that Seidlitz, far from being disturbed by his manœuvre, was calmly maintaining his position, and that General Kleist had arrived at Marienburg in Bohemia upon his right flank; a panic seized him; he conceived that the rules of the art forbade him to hold any position where his flank might be disturbed by the enemy, whatever might be the insignificance of his forces; and to avoid a defeat, he decided to operate a second retreat, more precipitate and more shameful than the first. On the 21st, Belling went in pursuit of the van-guard, and captured three hundred men. This check entirely demoralized the army, which only took breath at Monchberg, preparatory to establishing itself in the mountains in the vicinity of Bareith, where it was buried in intrenchments.

That retreat offered too good an occasion to the Prussians for attacking the Austrian corps posted at Toplitz, to be allowed to pass unimproved. General Seidlitz marched, on the 29th of July, from Zwickau through Annaberg upon Schervina, where, on the 1st of August, his hussars surprised the corps of Prince Lowenstein. Everything resulted in the most favorable manner, but he did not improve his good fortune with his usual intelligence; he waited for his infantry, which allowed the prince time to effect a change of position, so that the next day he lost upwards of seven hundred men without dislodging him.

As soon as the army of the Circles was apprised of the advantage gained over Seidlitz, it took up a position at Hof on the 11th of August. The prince of Stollberg was ordered to join again in Saxony; and for this purpose he put his troops in march on the 18th, and reached Dresden through Eger by the 6th of September. Belling profited by his absence, and made an incursion into Bohemia, which succeeded perfectly, during which he surprised the fortress of Eger.

While this was passing, Marshal Serbelloni, who had been severely reproached for not covering more effectually the frontiers of Bohemia, resigned the command to General Haddick, and retired to his estates.

OFFENSIVE OPERATIONS; BATTLE OF FREIBERG.

At this period, the imperial troops occupied the following positions:

	Batts.	*Sqds.*
Post on the right bank of the Elbe, near Dresden.........	1	6
General Reid between Briesnitz and Bennerich..........	9	16
Upon the Windberg and in the Val-de-Plauen...........	11	7
Upon the heights of Rabenau.........................	5	0
At Dippodiswalde....................................	18	34
At Altenberg and Schellerau.........................	8	14
At Toplitz in Bohemia	10	38
The army of the Circles.............................	23	42
Torreck's corps of light troops.....................	1	10
Total.............	86	167

On the other hand, Prince Henry still occupied the camp of Pretschendorf; Hulsen's corps was at Wilsdruf, and Seidlitz had been ordered, on the 2d of September, to withdraw from Porchenstein to Burkersdorf, that he might be nearer Prince Henry. Haddick conceived the plan of driving the enemy from Voigtland, and of establishing himself in the position which he held at the termination of the preceding campaign. To accomplish this, he had two courses open to him; he could deliver battle, contrary to the system pursued by the Aulic Council, or could turn the right of Prince Henry, threatening his bakeries at Freiberg, and even his communications, whilst a part of his army should disquiet his front, and the front of Hulsen's corps, to prevent him from opposing the contemplated movement. The latter plan was preferred; but at the moment of its execution a Prussian corps appeared in Lusatia, and caused its suspension until the return of the detachment which Haddick had seen fit to dispatch to meet it.

At length, on the 27th, this movement commenced. The different corps which were posted at Toplitz and Altenberg, were directed upon Freiberg. Prince Lowenstein conducted the first through Bohmisch-Ensiedel, against the corps of Kleist, which was pushed upon Voigtdorf, with the loss of three hundred men. The prince took post at Porchenstein; Campitelli, with the other corps, at Clausnitz. At the same time Haddick made demonstrations against Prince Henry's corps, whilst General Ried repelled the posts of Hulsen towards Weistrup, and seized the intrenched heights of Kunzendorf. On the 28th, everything was tranquil along the front, but General Campitelli forced Kleist to withdraw to the village of Mulde.

On the morning of the 29th, the combined army was gotten under arms, and commenced serious demonstrations in order to draw off all the forces of Prince Henry and Hulsen, by attracting their attention, whilst Prince Lowenstein should push Kleist's corps before him, and gain the extremity and the rear of the Prussians by Mulde and Nassau, on the left bank of the Mulde. General Ried, debouching from Tharandt, bordered the forest on the right, crossed the ravine of Weistritz, and gained possession of the redoubts which connected the communications of Prince Henry with the post held by Hulsen at Grumbach. But these redoubts were again taken towards evening, and Ried was thrown back upon Tharandt.

Nevertheless Lowenstein and Campitelli already menaced Freiberg, in which were stored the supplies, and which also contained the bakeries, which might effectually compromise Prince Henry were he to be attacked the next day by Haddick. These considerations induced the prince to pass the Mulde, during the night of the 30th of September, and on the following day to go into camp behind that river, his right resting at Brandt and his left near Tuttendorf. Hulsen was ordered to resume his position at Katzenhauser, behind the ravine of Tribsche. Haddick took position upon the heights of Satisdorf and Frauenstein, placing his advance-posts at Pretschendorf.

The 2d of October Kleist was vainly attacked, the enemy was repulsed, and that general then occupied the heights of Mudigsdorf. Belling's corps moved towards Gros-Waltersdorf. Various posts were established to keep up the communications between Chemnitz and Zwickau.

Haddick did not adhere to the first part of his plan, and to expel the Prussians from the Voigtland he resolved to drive them from Freiberg by the same manœuvres which had obliged them to abandon the position of Pretschendorf. He called to him the corps of Prince Lowenstein, on the 4th of October, and detached General Campitelli to the left bank of the Mulde, at Dorf-Chemnitz. The prince of Stollberg moved with the army of the Circles to Frauenstein, and General Luzinsky took post at Burkersdorf.

On the 13th of October, Ried's corps was directed towards Molitsch, in order to hold in check Hulsen's corps. The Prince of Lowenstein was established between Limbach and Birkenhain. Macquire went into camp at Niederschone, between the forest of Tharandt and Mulde. A brigade which preceded the march drove the Prussian posts beyond Conradsdorf. General Luzinsky, who was established at Burkersdorf, strongly threatened the right by way of Weissenborn. Finally, on the 14th, the Prince of Stollberg effected a junction with Campitelli at Dorf-Chemnitz, in order to operate by the left bank of the Mulde upon Mudigsdorf, against the right flank of Prince Henry. Kleefeld was detached, at the same time, to dislodge Belling from the heights of Erbisdorf, which was attempted without success.

On the 15th, the enemy began a new system of demonstrations against the left wing of Prince Henry's force, near Tuttendorf, and against the corps of Hulsen. The prince of Stollberg likewise renewed his attempts against Belling's corps with more success than in the previous evening. General Campitelli directed this expedition whilst the army was forming at Weidmansdorf; he seized the heights of Langenau, and sent General Kleefeld to dislodge the Prussians from Monchfrey. Belling having begun his retrograde movement somewhat late, was unable to retire through Monchfrey, upon the extreme right of the army, and was forced, in consequence, to pass through Kleinhartmansdorf, upon Langenau. Reaching that village, he found Campitelli occupying it with his corps, which compelled him to file between Galentz and Reichembach, in order to join General Syburg, and afterwards to countermarch upon Linda. This mishap had most unfortunate results, inasmuch as the enemy took advantage of it to attack General Syburg at the village of Erbisdorf and at the Kuhberg, whilst his cavalry held Seidlitz in check at Berthelsdorf. Campitelli being unable to debouch under the fire of artillery from the Kuhberg, took the resolution of seizing the heights of Erbisdorf, which Belling was obliged to cover. Syburg, it is true, detached the regiment Salmuth, hoping to reach the heights before the enemy; but it was surrounded and captured the moment it reached the village. Not satisfied with this error of his, he still wished to carry Erbisdorf with the two battalions which were left him, and caused them all to be entirely captured. Such dispositions, in presence of an enemy six times as strong as himself, could have no other result. It is astonishing that the person who made them, should have been able to retire to the heights of Brandt, with several pieces of artillery. General Belling did not arrive until the evening at Linda, where he went into camp near Kleinschirma.

The position of Prince Henry was already turned. At nightfall he sent off his parks and stores, and retired with the army in two columns through Losnitz upon Reichembach and Kleinvoigtsberg. The army of the Circles took possession of the camp of Freiberg, and intrenched itself there.

Prince Henry, getting information that the king was sending him a reënforcement of twenty battalions and fifty-five squadrons, persuaded himself that he might be able to maintain his communication with the Voigtland, and took position upon the heights of Marbach and Augustenburg for the purpose of approaching General Hulsen, and closing upon him more perfectly; but hearing that the Austrians were waiting for a much stronger reënforcement than his own, he took the resolution of making immediate use of his central position, by attacking the army of the Circles and beating it separately.

The right wing of that army, which was formed of the Austrian corps under General Campitelli, had its front covered by the defiles of Kleinwaltersdorf, and by the works which were extended to the woods of Spittelwalde, which was in front of the centre and the left, having a vast extent of abatis, and even of intrenchments, at its outlets into the plain of Kleinschirma (See Plate XXIII., No. 7).

From the best intelligence, it appeared that the left rested in the air; in consequence of which, the prince determined to conduct the bulk of his forces by Brandt and Berthelsdorf upon that extreme left and its rear, whilst the rest of the troops should vigorously attack the front as soon as affairs indicated a favorable turn towards the left.*

To carry out this plan, the army was divided into four corps, as follows:

	Bats.	*Sqds.*
1st, Advance-guard, General Kleist	7	12
2d, Right wing, commanded by Seidlitz:		
Brigade Diringshofen	5	0

* If it really was the intention of the prince to convey the bulk of his forces against the enemy's left, his plan was a good one; but we have more reason to believe the contrary, as Tempelhof's barren assertion alone sustains it.

	Bats.	Sqds.
Brigade Young Stutterheim	4	0
" Bandemer	0	10
" Manstein	0	10
3d, Left wing, under Stutterheim:		
1st Brigade	5	5
2d Brigade Belling	3	12
4th Division, commanded by General Forcade	7	10
Grand Total	31	59

The prince of Stollberg, apprised of this movement, could hardly believe that the Prussian general desired to give him battle; but to be prepared for whatever might happen, he got his troops under arms at midnight.

On the 29th of October, at daylight, Prince Henry, who found himself on the right, gave the order to march. General Kleist directed himself upon Oberschone, as he had been instructed, in order to seize the heights of Saint-Micheln, between Brandt and the woods of Spittelwalde. Seidlitz, with the brigades Diringshofen and Manstein, followed him. The brigade Young Stutterheim and General Bandemer, with his cuirassiers, were formed at their left towards Kleinscherma, to keep up the connection with Belling, and to attack the Spittelwalde whilst the right should be arriving at its destination. General Belling went in person upon the Nonenwalde and the woods of Struth, whence he drove out the Austrian light troops. The division Stutterheim was advanced upon the heights of Gros-Schirma, until Belling should issue from the woods of which he was to take possession, and afterwards occupied the heights in rear of Kleinwaltersdorf, where he established his artillery for the purpose of playing upon Campitelli's corps, which held the intrenched heights beyond that village. Finally, General Forcade remained in reserve with his division in rear of Gros-Schirma; he was to disturb the retreat of the enemy upon the right bank of the Mulde.

During the progress of these movements, Prince Henry had debouched from Oberschone, dislodged Torreck's light troops, placed to the left of the wood of Spittelwalde, between Linden and Saint-Micheln. After these first successes, the volunteer battalions of Heer and Luderitz entered the woods and expelled the Austrian sharpshooters, establishing themselves along its border. The remainder of the column continued its march, and finally attained the heights at the left of Saint-Micheln, between Brandt and the Spittelwalde. Prince Henry then, for the first time, saw a corps of six thousand men which flanked the left of the enemy's position upon the heights of Erbisdorf and Kuhberg, on the other side of Brandt.

This discovery, it should seem, ought to have dissuaded the prince from his undertaking; all his dispositions having been originally made to turn the extreme left in such manner, that the column detached for that decisive operation, would not find itself subjected to an attack in reverse, and be overwhelmed by superior forces; but on the assurance of General Kleist that the column in view was commanded by General Meyer, from whom nothing was to be feared in any emergency, the prince determined to continue his march with five battalions of grenadiers and fifteen squadrons, leaving only the Brigadier Diringshofen with four battalions and five squadrons in potence upon its right in order to observe him; at the same time expediting the order to the corps Young Stutterheim to attack the Spittelwalde immediately.

When the enemy perceived that his posts upon the Spittelwalde, and in the direction of Saint-Micheln, were hard pressed, he became alarmed for his left, and extended his line in that direction, in order to rest it upon the hill of the Three Crosses.

Nevertheless, Prince Henry steadily advanced from that

side; General Seidlitz attacked the hill at the head of the grenadiers, whilst Kleist and Manstein covered their right against the Austrian cavalry. As soon as Stutterheim got the order to carry the Spittelwalde, Captain Pfuhl was thrown forward against the redoubt placed at the outlet towards Kleinschirma, and a battalion marched to the left against the intrenchment of Kleinwaltersdorf, the artillery protecting these two attacks. The imperialists evacuated the works, and the troops were withdrawn behind the abatis in the middle of the woods, where they were reënforced by several battalions. The Prussians who first made their way through the abatis, did not long hold out against forces so unequal, and they were, in consequence, repelled to the very outlets of the forest. It was in vain that their general caused them to be sustained by a new battalion; this slight reënforcement did not reëstablish affairs; the Old Stutterheim also detached a battalion and drew its artillery from Kleinwaltersdorf, without accomplishing anything.

Meanwhile, the attack made by the grenadiers on the right seemed to take a favorable turn, in spite of the efforts of the cavalry. When the Old Stutterheim became sure that they were well engaged, he resolved to attack the enemy's left, and passed through the village of Kleinwaltersdorf at the head of the regiment of Bevern, supported by the grenadiers of Baehr and the first battalion of Manteufel. Schmettau's cuirassiers and Belling's hussars followed this infantry. Lossow's grenadiers and the volunteer battalions of Schach and Lenoble preceded it, swept the village, and then turning suddenly to the right, threatened to cut off the retreat of the troops, which defended themselves so obstinately in the Spittelwalde, that the Young Stutterheim attacked again with his united brigade.

This simultaneous effort of three divisions became decisive. As soon as the troops of the left wing had cleared

Kleinwaltersdorf, they marched swiftly against the enemy. The Austrian cavalry, shaken by the fire of artillery, fell back before them, but the infantry stood fast and repelled a charge of Schmettau's cuirassiers. At length, however, Belling's hussars and the two squadrons of detached cuirassiers renewed that charge with so much impetuosity, that the infantry regiments of Nicholas, Esterhazy, and Giulay were overthrown and almost entirely destroyed. The regiments of Wied, Wurtzburg, and Salm were likewise broken, and lost many men. At the same time Generals Seidlitz and Kleist had repulsed the cavalry of the left wing, thereby favoring a new attempt against the Austrian grenadiers, who defended the hill of the Three Crosses. These latter, seeing themselves abandoned by the squadrons of cavalry which supported them, retired also through the suburbs of Freiberg upon Hillersdorf. The troops that defended the woods of Spittelwalde, discovering that they also were compromised, drew back upon the heights of Tuttendorf, where the prince of Stollberg halted to reassemble the scattered corps of his army, and to cross the Mulde in some order. General Meyer's division, which might have decided the affair by descending from the heights upon the right flank of the Prussians, withdrew by Bertelsdorf upon Sussenbach, after having sent a few cannon shot after the prince.

The loss of the imperial army amounted to some four thousand five hundred prisoners, and about three thousand disabled; the Prussians lost fifteen hundred; they took twenty-eight pieces of cannon and nine flags. This affair was the more honorable to the prince, as he had but twenty-nine battalions and sixty squadrons against forty-nine battalions and sixty-eight squadrons.

Hulsen's corps took no part in the action, and its operations were confined to furnishing a detachment of seven battalions and twenty-five squadrons in the morning, which were sent to occupy the heights of Hirschfeld and Neukirch, in order to observe the Austrians towards the forest of Tharandt. It would have been a sad day to the beaten army, had he known how to profit by the advantages of his position; but, on the 31st, he returned to camp.

The prince of Stollberg fell back to Frauenstein. The Prussian army resumed its position at Freiberg; Belling's corps went to Pretschendorf.

On the day of the battle, reënforcements for each party arrived on the Elbe from Silesia; the one intended for the Prussians, commanded by General Neuwied, crossed that river on the 30th, and replaced General Hulsen's corps the next day at Katzenhausen and Schlettau; that corps, thus relieved, afterwards joined Prince Henry. The Austrian corps under the command of Prince Albert of Saxony, rejoined Haddick on the very evening of the battle. This general then detached a reënforcement of six regiments to the beaten army, and remained cantoned between Dresden and Dippodiswalde.

Prince Henry was not a man to sleep on his laurels. Scarcely had his reënforcements reached him, when he instructed Kleist, on the 2d of November, to undertake, with six battalions and twenty-five squadrons, to destroy all the depots of the imperial army in Bohemia, in order to oblige the prince of Stollberg to leave the strong position of Frauenstein. To support this movement, he detached six battalions and seventeen squadrons to Dorf-Chemnitz, under the orders of General Platten, and caused demonstrations to be made towards Pretschendorf and Wilsdruff, to attract the attention of Haddick, and fill him with apprehension. The prince of Stollberg concluded to abandon the position; which he did in the night of the 3d and 4th of November, and fell back to Altenberg, whence he went soon afterwards to Pirna. Prince Henry then moved General Platten to Porchenstein;

the army took the place occupied by his corps at Dorf-Chemnitz, whilst Kleist, marching through Brix to Saats, destroyed one of the principal magazines of the enemy. This general having returned to Oederan on the 11th, the prince retook his camp at Freiberg.

Frederick, having reached the army on the 6th, conceived the plan of availing himself of the victory gained by his brother, Prince Henry, over the troops of the empire, to open negotiations with the smaller princes who desired neutrality, thus getting rid of a part of his enemies, who, though little dangerous by themselves, obliged him to oppose them with forces of which he could make a far better disposition. Terror being one of the surest remedies for diplomatic delay, the king directed General Kleist to march into Franconia with six thousand men, and put the country under contribution. This general set out from Oederan on the 13th of November, and reached Nuremberg on the 29th; this place opened its gates to him on his arrival. The Prussian patrols were thrown forward to the vicinity of Wurtzburg and Ratisbon, where they greatly alarmed the members of the Diet. The prince of Stollberg desired to obtain permission to fly with his troops to the succor of the Circles, but Haddick refused it on the plea that he awaited instructions from Vienna.

During the progress of these events, Frederick brought to a conclusion, on the 24th of November, a convention with the Austrians, which fixed the boundaries of the cantonments of the two armies, without including those to be held by the armies of the empire, nor making any provisions for the provinces invaded by Kleist. It would appear that the Austrians, who longed for peace, but who were bound by their engagements with the states of the Circles, far from opposing the king's plan, contributed by their conduct to make them desire a neutrality, that a pretext might be gained by the Austrians to extricate themselves from their promises. In no other way can we account for this convention. Finally, General Kleist having returned by Coburg and Erfurt on the 17th, all the armies entered their cantonments.

Shortly after, a congress was assembled at the chateau of Hubertsburg, near Dresden, and a definitive treaty of peace was signed on the 23d of February, 1763.

It was a singular fact connected with that treaty, that everything was restored to the condition which existed before hostilities commenced, and that not one of the belligerent powers lost thereby an inch of their former territory.

Thus terminated a singular war, the events of which have been strangely exaggerated; in it the art of combat made some progress, but the grand operations of war, strategy, and the art of making use of victory were then unknown.

CHAPTER XXXIV.

OBSERVATIONS UPON THE CAMPAIGN OF 1762, UPON THE TURNING OF THE ENEMY'S FLANKS, AND MULTIPLIED ATTACKS.

It has already been remarked that it is a difficult task to originate any new ideas upon a campaign which has occurred upon the same theatre as other preceding ones, and with combinations differing from the previous ones only in the part played by Russia.

We can also see that after the fall of Dresden, it was to the Austrian interest to conduct the war upon the Elbe, whilst that of the Prussians led them to transfer it to the Oder. Were Daun to prove successful in Saxony, it might decide affairs; but his success could not do so in Silesia; upon this fact should have been based the plan of campaign. When even the death of Elizabeth did not lead to such an important and marked change in their affairs, it was not probable that the allies would direct their efforts towards Saxony; under this view, they fell into the same error as in the preceding year; that is, they made an accessory of the principal point, and aimed their blows in a direction which could lead to nothing great.

As soon as the peace with Russia was known to the Austrian government, it had no further object in directing the mass of its forces upon the Oder; for that peace was to lead to their own, or to the war being pressed more vigorously than ever. In the latter event, Austria had only to precipitate the splendid army commanded by Daun upon the province of Brandenburg. It was at first collected in Saxony; and had always had an excellent base of operations upon the Elbe; besides which, the central position of Bohemia enabled it always to transfer rapidly the bulk of its forces to the most favorable point. The fortresses of Glatz and Olmutz, with the troops which were found in the interior of Austria, would have been more than sufficient to have opposed the operations of Frederick, who no longer possessed the means of invading Moravia, and at the same time make head against one hundred and fifty thousand well-commanded, hardy, and warlike troops.

There is little to be said upon what passed in Silesia. The king could not have foreseen that the Russians would be his allies but eleven days; and it would, therefore, be idle to criticize him for not making use of this time to attack Daun; he did whatever he could to bring an action which should result to his advantage. There is reason to think that he would have forced the matter to an action as it was, had he divined the possibility of Czernischef's corps abandoning him so speedily.

On the other hand, it is extraordinary that Daun, with ninety thousand men in hand, after the departure of the Russians, should have remained a quiet spectator of the siege of Schweidnitz. It has been said that he was there more to cover the siege than to prevent it. If we except the abandonment of Cassel by the French marshals, D'Estrées and Soubise, related in Chapter XXXI., modern history offers no such example of timidity.

The remainder of the campaign bears the impress of the spirit which directed it in its earliest stages. The king would have been wrong in attempting to deceive or mislead enemies who, so far as might be discovered, were not disposed to deprive him of a single rood of his territory.

After maturely reflecting upon the operations which had their theatre in Saxony, there is nothing more notable than the entire absence of all the principles of the art which marks them, and the marvellous part played by the army of the Empire.

Independently of the fault of forming a double line of operations in Saxony and Silesia, the members of the coalition subdivided their forces, by isolating, at more than thirty leagues apart, two armies which were to operate upon the subordinate point, and allowing the enemy, with a weak detachment, to cut them off from their communication.

What terms are suitable to designate the army of the Circles? Will posterity credit the fact that a general commanding thirty thousand men sought safety in flight, at two different times, from the presence of four thousand men, because one or two battalions were at a distance in the direction of one of his flanks? Thus it is that the abuse of systems and their technical terms misleads weak and superficial men. In those days it was regarded as a fault to have a flank turned. A general who should maintain his position after one of his flanks had been turned, would have been accused of committing a grave error; and, according to the received rules, he should have decamped without waiting to ascertain what it was which threatened his position. Consequently to operate well it was necessary to turn a flank. To attain this object an extended movement was indispensable. Hence arose multiplied attacks, weakened centres, disjointed movements, and those fine systems which have been held up as the perfection of combinations; and finally, all the absurdities with which the annals of war abounded until the end of the eighteenth century.

It may not be out of place to reiterate here a maxim already indicated, to wit: *Every army desiring to outflank, at the same time, the two wings of the enemy, should have double his force; for, independently of the acting wings, a central force will be necessary to hold the enemy in check.* If the three divisions be merely detachments, they will not produce any effect upon a central mass superior to each of them; they run the risk of being compromised so soon as it shall commence manœuvring. The battles of Rivoli and Stockach are the best proofs of this truth.

When we have an insufficient force to furnish three masses, it is dangerous to turn both wings, and of but little use to disquiet one. This manœuvre consists essentially in throwing out a simple detachment upon the wing of the enemy, whilst the principal mass shall act against his front, which is to remove the detachment from the object in view, and expose oneself to be beaten. In place of this it were better to place the accessory before the front, and move the mass against that one of the extremities, which, by its relations to the communications of the enemy, ought to give the grandest results.

It may, perhaps, be objected that this manœuvre is at bottom only the turning of a flank, but that would be a play upon words; for if a general leaves one hundred battalions upon an enemy's front, while he sends ten against one wing, he would not thereby gain one of his extremities by the mass of his forces. It is this abuse of the employment of technical phrases which colors the most stupid oversight; it was thus that it was argued that a French army, by moving from the vicinity of Sedan to Brussels, would have turned the duke of Brunswick, who was at Verdun; it was on this account that the Austrian generals thought themselves lost, in 1794, for having been turned in the course of ten marches; this was the motive which caused the prince of Stollberg to lead back the army of the Circles as far as Bareith, from a fear of being turned by some squadrons which hovered at a distance upon his flanks.

Let us return to the operations in Saxony. In glancing

over the map it will be seen that the double positions of General Hulsen and Prince Henry formed a square.

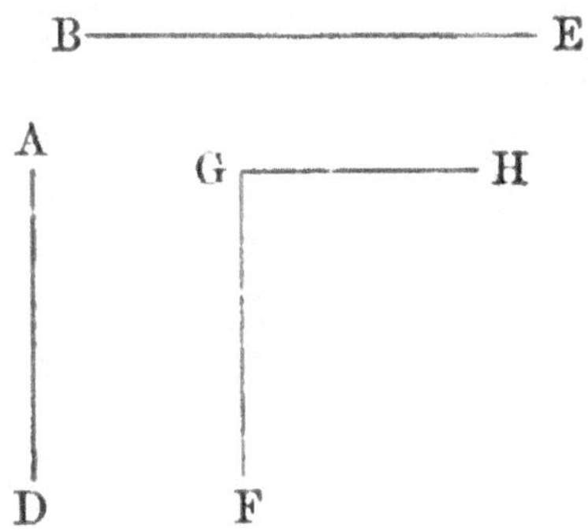

The prince's corps, A D, was separated from Hulsen's, B E, by the forest of Tharandt, a superior obstacle, behind which the enemy, F G H, could operate out of sight, and from which nothing could prevent him from taking up a position for the purpose of overwhelming one or the other of those corps, inasmuch as they had to march more than six leagues to assist each other.

The positions of Freiberg and Katzenhausen possessed even graver inconveniences, since the Mulde ran between them at such a distance that neither of the two armies could succor the other in one day. Nevertheless, since they remained three months, there was that entire time in which to combine an operation. The imperial army had a tempting game—nothing less than the putting of fifty battalions in action against a single one of these detachments. It was only necessary to attack Hulsen by Wilsdruf or Limbach, and to disquiet Prince Henry by some partisans towards Beerwalde. But the commander of this army did not know how to profit by the advantages of his positions, and confined his operations to parading along the Elbe, in order to protect the army of the Circles, which was coming from Zwickau;

truly a singular manner of employing troops and combining their movements.

If, instead of groping around in this manner, Serbelloni had, after the month of April, drawn the army of the Circles to Freiberg, and with his then superior forces attacked the army of Prince Henry, by his right, in case he had remained concentrated, and by his centre, in case he had divided his troops into two isolated corps, he might have overthrown him, precipitated his troops upon the bridges of the Elbe, and cut off his communications with Wittemberg. Then it would have been practicable to have moved seven or eight thousand men from Dresden to Meissen, by the right bank of the Elbe, for the purpose of seizing the bridges and destroying them. This division need run no risk whatever, having a secure retreat under the cannon of Dresden. The prince would also have been obliged to make a detachment of about the same strength for their protection, so that there would have remained with Serbelloni fifty-five thousand men with which to attack twenty-six or twenty-seven thousand on their extreme right, by gaining, during the action, their communications with Wittemberg. The small Prussian army, beaten in such a position, would have been annihilated even though its bridges were saved, for, compelled to recross the Elbe, in presence of a victorious enemy, twice as numerous, one half, at least, of his battalions would have been lost, either in the combat or the retreat. If the Prussians, who, up to this time, had two isolated divisions, had still maintained them, the effort should then have been made upon their centre, by Hulsen's right, in order to throw the latter upon the Elbe, and afterwards to capture the detachment of the prince, which would have had not a single communication remaining.

Serbelloni, by allowing the Prussians to take the initiative, committed no graver fault than did General Haddick. When he assumed the command, he disposed of eighty-six battalions and one hundred and sixty-seven squadrons; Prince Henry should have been destroyed by the Austrian General, for daring to maintain himself in the hazardous position he had chosen in order to prevent the junction of the forces of his enemies, which was even more rash after their junction; Hulsen ought to have been attacked by Wilsdruf or Limbach, as has been previously stated. Far from this, he sent half of his army against Prince Henry, and that half sufficed to drive him from Pretschendorf and Freiberg; from this we can judge of the effect which would have been produced by a well-combined attack of the larger mass upon the first, whose strength did not exceed twenty incomplete battalions. Haddick observed him whilst he caused the manœuvres against the prince, which was a double fault. For, if the blow which he meditated against the latter was his principal object, then he should have repaired thither in person, to superintend and carry it out with the bulk of his forces; if it was merely a secondary affair, then he ought not to have pressed it and employed in it so many troops, whilst he left Hulsen undisturbed. Haddick might have left a reliable general with thirty-seven battalions and sixty-seven squadrons near Freiberg, and have attacked with fifty battalions and one hundred squadrons the small corps of General Hulsen, which would have been destroyed. The prince, deprived of his communications with the Elbe, would have been obliged to seek his safety at Berlin, or have received a battle, in which case, his only alternative would have been to lay down his arms or cut his way through by sacrificing half his remaining troops.

The battle of Freiberg being the only one which Prince Henry had gained, became in a certain manner the foundation of his reputation; but after carefully analyzing his dispositions for the purpose of testing them by received principles, it will be seen that the only reason why he gained the victory was, that it necessarily inclined to one of the parties, and it happened to be his good fortune to receive it. The prince had before him two separated armies, and he fought them with two corps equally isolated. After he had resolved to give battle, he might easily have left some posts at the camp of Meissen, and drawing to him the greater part of Hulsen's force, he would have been able to decide with greater certainty the success of his enterprise against the army of the Circles. But far from this, he did not even content himself with preserving the isolation of his forces alone, he attacked an army of twice his own strength, in four separate columns, widely distant from each other, and the action of which was not simultaneous. That of General Forcade even remained in reserve far to the extreme left, and out of range of the field of battle. Finally, the prince, who marched himself to the principal point with the two stronger columns, parcelled them out in such a manner that there remained in hand *at the decisive moment* but five battalions of grenadiers and a few squadrons, whilst thirty-eight battalions were scattered along a line of ten leagues; half of this force engaged in secondary attacks, and the other half in a defensive camp. The attack of the Spittelwalde was executed by some battalions becoming engaged one after the other, long before the third column was in a condition to fall on. There was generally a looseness in the movements; and few battles have been more faulty; the Prussians succeeded on account of the inconceivable stupidity of their enemies and the character of their chiefs. If, far from trembling for their left and extending their defensive line towards that wing, Generals Caramelli and Stollberg had marched thirty battalions by the Spittelwalde upon the ravine and the village of Kleinschirma, and sent their cavalry upon the heights to the right, between that village and Waltersdorf, the brigade

Stutterheim would have been crushed, and the small detachments of the prince, pierced by their centre, and deprived of their communications, would have had infinite trouble to save themselves.

Tempelhof lauds Frederick for having made use of a slight movement which isolated the two wings of the Austrians at the battle of Prague, and expresses his admiration for Prince Henry for having, from a contrary principle, made four attacks without unity of action and far from the decisive point; which is most unpardonable flattery, tending to undermine every principle, and presenting to us events which are the offspring of chance as the result of profound combinations of genius. The fact is, that Frederick displayed great genius at the battle of Prague, and his brother, Prince Henry, exhibited an uncommon lack of it at Freiberg.

The conduct of Stollberg and Caramelli was the more blamable, inasmuch as they knew perfectly with what troops they were engaged; they could not be ignorant of the fact that Hulsen was encamped near Meissen with half of the Prussian troops, and that the prince had but twenty-seven very weak battalions. When seeing this little army debouching upon four scattered columns, they ought to have made use of the advantage afforded them by the woods of Spittelwalde, in order to conceal the effort which they made upon the centre against the column of Stutterheim with a certainty of complete success. But there are generals who become disconcerted when the enemy forms a multitude of columns; their embarrassment tells against them; for they ought rather to rejoice than become alarmed. A mediocre general, when he discovers a multiplicity of movements directed against his front or flanks, is afraid of being compromised; he withdraws without bringing his masses into action. Such was the conduct of Clermont at Creveldt; of Soubise and d'Estrées at Wilhemsthal; of Stollberg and Campitelli at Freiberg. Bonaparte never became frightened on similar occasions; whilst besieging Mantua, and Wurmser was advancing to relieve the place with an army twice the strength of his own, the republican advance-guard having been forced in on the Adige, he inferred, at first, that the Austrian masses were approaching by the eastern shore of the lake of Garda; but it was soon after announced to him that another column was debouching by its western shore upon Brescia. At this news he was unable to conceal his joy; for he judged, as quick as lightning, that the enemy had made a false movement by interposing between his two divisions an insurmountable obstacle. The corps issuing on Brescia, which seemed so formidable and menacing, was repelled into the gorges of the mountains and annihilated; that one which debouched upon the left bank three days afterwards experienced the same fate at Castiglione.

The peace of Hubertsberg finally brought to a close the comico-tragic scenes of the too famous seven years' war. At the commencement of the revolution, the man who had been present in the campaign of 1761 was regarded as a hero, though there were not a thousand shots fired at the Austrian army. The general who had had the honor of leading some battalions to battle, was held in little less estimation than a Luxemberg or a Turenne; they would say of him: *he was in the seven years' war!* and his patent of immortality seemed fixed as fate.

Whence originated these exaggerated ideas? Undoubtedly in the absence of talent in the age, and from the flattery and charlatanism of some of its writers. In the midst of the multitude of commonplace men who swarm around Frederick, we perceive that prince shine forth in colossal proportions. Relatively to the time, the circumstances, and his means, he accomplished much, and was always a great captain, without being a perfect one.

Whilst reflecting upon the force and unity of his organized means, we shall become convinced that he missed the decisive blow in 1756. If at that period, before the enemy was concentrated, before even the Russians were on the Dwina or the Austrian troops were in condition to oppose him in mass, and while the Empire was, as yet, as much disposed to unite with him as against him; if, at that decisive moment, he had had the breadth of view, the far-seeing glance, and the military genius that Napoleon displayed in 1805 against a similar coalition, in 1806 against the Prussians, still isolated, and above all, in 1809 against the gigantic levies of Austria, it will be seen that the war would have taken another turn; in fifteen days the king might have conducted his army to Vienna and Passau, after having pierced the centre of a line of unlimited extent, and but just garnished with a multitude of troops drawn from garrisons. This blow would have astonished Europe, and thrown his enemies into consternation, would have swelled his army with a crowd of partisans and all the princes of the empire, of which he would have become the arbiter.

At all events, that altogether military invasion was the only enterprise that conformed to circumstances; for there was no single mass in a condition to prevent it.

As we have already remarked, it was still practicable in the beginning of 1757 to have pushed his line of operations in mass through Moravia. A battle gained between Olmutz and the Danube would have procured immense results, and there existed every facility for arriving at this desirable end. In the three subsequent campaigns, the king showed himself truly great; after the bloody scenes of Prague, Kollin, and Zorndorf, which battles deprived him of the flower of his troops, there came the disasters of Hohenkirch, of Kunersdorf, and Torgau to test the firmness of his spirit. Later, when his army was composed of boys from fifteen to twenty years of age, the last refuse of an exhausted population, he was compelled to make head against armies more accustomed to war; recruited, unlike his own, from a robust and inexhaustible population, and when his fall appeared inevitable, he seemed only to aspire to make it correspond with the rest of his life; a brilliant close to a splendid career. The death of Elizabeth saved him, and Austria, guided by that evil genius which pursued her for more than a century, signed the peace at a time when the war should have been pressed with greater vigor than ever. At that period, politics, like the military art, made a retrograde step, which carried us back to near the state of ignorance of the Middle Ages. Finally, Frederick, sustaining himself against Europe, astonished the world and appeared to perform miracles, when he was only saved by the singular conduct of his adversaries. After the battle of Rosbach, which was a mere skirmish, the French armies did not operated directly against him. The Swedes made a show of entering into the campaign to obtain subsidies, and the Russians, notwithstanding their bloody success, contented themselves with the possession of a province. Nothing more was wanted to annihilate Frederick than a little unanimity of purpose and action, and a chief above mediocrity. Such a man was not then to be found in Europe, or possibly the princes did not wish to seek him; Louis XIV. or Mazarin could have found him.

However, we must not be diverted from our legitimate path by considerations foreign to the subject. Let us recapitulate the observations embraced in this work before we pass on to the history of the late wars, which are richer in events, and more fertile in lessons of war and politics.*

* See my "Critical History of the Wars of the Revolution," and the "Political and Military Life of Napoleon."

CHAPTER XXXV.

EXPOSITION OF THE GENERAL PRINCIPLES OF THE ART OF WAR.

THE fundamental principles upon which rest all good combinations of war have always existed, and to them all others should be referred, for the purpose of arriving at their true merits.

These principles are unchangeable; they are independent of the nature of the arms employed, of times and places. Genius and experience indicate the variations to be made in their application. For thirty centuries there have lived *generals* who have been more or less happy in their application. Cyrus* and Hannibal were great captains; Greece and Rome furnished many; Alexander often manœuvred with skill; Cæsar, with equal success, conducted the war of invasion and practiced grand tactics; Tamerlane even, of whom we know so little, has left us institutions stamped upon each page with the evidences of that natural genius which knows how to command men and triumph over obstacles.† While comparing the causes of the victories of ancient and modern times, we are greatly surprised to discover that the battles of Wagram, Pharsalia, and Cannæ, were gained from the same original cause.

Nevertheless, from a blindness difficult to conceive, most writers who have discoursed upon the art of war, seem to

* See the Cyropedia of Xenophon.

† Institutes of Timour, by Langles.

have given rise to researches amidst a thousand secondary details for that which can only proceed from a good direction of grand operations, or a wise employment of masses on the day of combat. From this has resulted a multitude of works, wherein the authors, arranging in their own way the insignificant details, have undoubtedly exhibited extraordinary erudition, but have endlessly confused a science which ought to be within reach of everybody. Several have gone so far as to include in works entitled the *Art of War*, long chapters on the manner in which an officer ought to carry his sword, and upon the form of the ramrod of his musket.

The result of these exhausting dissertations has been to persuade many otherwise military men that there exists no fixed principles of war, which is an absurd and untenable position.* Undoubtedly, there exists no *system* of war exclusively good, because each one is the result of hypothetical calculation; each is but a combination of the human mind, liable to error, and which, sometimes, with the aid of high-sounding phrases and technical terms arranged with art, may be made to throw a coloring of truth over the most erroneous ideas. But it is another thing with principles; they are fixed and unalterable; the human mind can neither modify nor destroy them.

To convey exact notions of war, it was essentially a condition that authors, instead of originating absurd systems, destroying one by the other, should have begun by establish-

* I once heard (it was at the chateau of Austerlitz) a general of some reputation, speaking of a charge of cavalry, say: "I should like to have some of the famous tacticians explain on what principle we came out of that charge, where the squadrons of both sides were confounded together." There can be no doubt, that in a *melée* of cavalry in which our troops are too much involved to manœuvre, the only rule is to use the sabre; but what does that prove? Was not this charge itself embraced in the grand whole of the battle? Napoleon, who ordered it, has already explained it; it was the action of a secondary mass which restrained an effort of the enemy, while the great decisive blow was dealt elsewhere.

ing the principles upon which all the combinations rest, and to which they must be referred. It was a much greater and more difficult task; but it offered sure results to compensate for the labor. There would have been no longer so much incredulity concerning the reality of the science. Mack, in 1793, would not have written that long lines are the strongest; Bulow, when treating of eccentric retreats, would not have argued that a beaten army should seek safety by dividing into as many corps as there were available roads to make use of, though these various columns, so scattered, might never again be collected, nor would there have been found any one to propose a system of cordons, which should disperse an army over all the roads of the country, at the risk of witnessing its capture, as Turenne once disposed of that of Bournonville in Alsace.

Frederick most wisely said, that the art of the great commander consisted in dividing up his enemy; but fifteen years afterwards several generals came to the opposite conclusion, that true military genius lay in dispersing our own forces. Such a subversion of ideas was the product of the confusion which then characterized individual opinions! The grossest errors would not have been advanced and defended, and the plainest and most vital truths of the art could never have been despised by military men, if, instead of vague suppositions and unreliable calculations, writers had confined themselves to the demonstration of immutable principles, and by establishing a common standard from opinions which had differed so widely.

It has been my fortune to undertake this difficult task, and possibly without the talent necessary to fulfill it properly; but it seemed important to lay down a basis, the development of which would, perhaps, be deferred a long time, had not circumstances arisen which tended to bring it about.

The only means of arriving at the desired end, was, at first, to point out the principles, and afterwards to present their application and the proofs by the history of twenty campaigns. That history was to present a clear and accurate critique upon every operation which might be found to deviate from the established rules. Were we to allow ourselves to approve of anything which should be in opposition to those rules, we should at once betray the presence of ignoble and unworthy motives, and indicate an unfitness for the labor to which we had devoted ourselves. Whatever might be the personal qualities of a general, or the reputation which he enjoyed, we should feel bound to expose all the errors which he might have committed; we should not even hesitate to repress individual affections. After such an avowal let us hope that no one will attribute our reflections either to personal friendship or envy, but solely to a desire to subserve entirely the interest of the art.

The fundamental principle upon which every military combination rests, is to operate with the greatest mass of our forces, a combined effort, upon a decisive point.

It may be easily understood how a skillful general may, with sixty thousand men, beat another with one hundred thousand, if the former succeed in bringing fifty thousand into action upon a single post of the enemy's line. A numerical superiority of troops not engaged then becomes positively a disadvantage, as it simply contributes to increase the general disorder, as was fairly instanced in the battle of Leuthen.

The methods of applying this maxim are not numerous; let us endeavor to point them out.

I. *The first measure is to take the initiative of the movements. The general who secures this advantage, is enabled to employ his own forces wherever he sees it best to direct them; that one, on the other hand, who waits for his enemy, may be incapable of originating a single combination, since he has to subordinate his movements to those of his adversary, and there may be no longer time to arrest these when they are in full course of execution. The general who takes the initiative, knows what he is to do ; he conceals his march, surprises and overwhelms one extremity or a feeble part of his adversary's lines. He who awaits the attack is beaten upon one of his points even before he may be informed of the attack.*

II. *The second measure is to direct our movements against the most advantageous feeble part. The choice of that feeble part depends upon the position of the enemy. The most important point will always be that one, the occupation of which will insure us the most favorable chances and procure us the most favorable results. For example, such will be those positions that tend to give us control of the enemy's communications with his base of operations, and to throw him back upon an insurmountable obstacle ; such as a sea ; a great river, without a bridge ; or the territory of a strong neutral power* (See Chapters XIV. and XXXI.).

In double or multiplied lines of operations, our attack should be directed against central points ; by conveying to these points the masses of our forces, we shall overwhelm the isolated divisions which guard them. The corps parceled out to the right and left will not be able to operate in concert any longer, and are, in consequence, forced to make those eccentric retreats, the terrible effects of which were exhibited upon the armies of Wurmser, Mack, and the duke of Brunswick. In single lines of operations, and continuous lines of battle, the feeble points, on the contrary, are found upon the extremities of the line. In fact, the centre is in reach of simultaneous assistance from the right and left ; in case of an extremity attacked, it would be overwhelmed before sufficient means could arrive from the other extremity to sustain it, for these means would be at a much greater distance, and could only be employed or brought up in succession.

A deep column attacked by its head is in the same situation as a line attacked at one of its extremities; both will be engaged and beaten successively, as has been demonstrated by the defeats of Rosbach and Auerstedt. However, it is much easier to make new dispositions with deep column than with a line of battle attacked upon one extremity.

*In executing strategically a general movement upon the extremity of the enemy's line of operations, not only do we put in action a mass upon a feeble part, but from that position it is easy to gain his rear and communications either with his base or secondary lines. Thus, Napoleon, in 1805, by gaining Donauwerth and the line of Lech, succeeded in establishing his mass upon Mack's communications with Vienna, which was his base with Bohemia, and rendered it impossible for him to join the Russian army, which was his most important secondary line. The same operation took place in 1806 upon the extreme left of the Prussians by Saalfeld and Gera. It was repeated in 1812 by the Russian army in its movements upon Kaluga and Krasnoï, and in 1813 by the allies, who were directed across Bohemia upon Dresden and Leipsic against the right of Napoleon.**

* It has been remarked that central lines did not save Napoleon about Dresden in 1813, nor in the Champaigne in 1814; but it can be answered, that to the system itself was due, nevertheless, his momentary success in these two campaigns. The cause of his reverses existed in the unequal nature of the struggle, in which he was engaged with only secondary means; in the difference in the nature of his troops; in the position of Bohemia and Bavaria, behind his extreme right, and, so to speak, upon his communications. Besides, it should be stated, that until then, the system of central masses had only been applied to armies of from one hundred and fifty to two hundred thousand men at most, and it would have been useless to have concentrated a larger force upon the same line, since it was already difficult to engage so many troops upon the same day, and upon the same field of battle.

We have no longer given an exclusive preference to central operations, since we have often presented those upon an extremity of the enemy's line as more

III. *The result of the preceding truths proves, that as it is preferable to attack the extremity of a line, we should be careful about attacking both at the same time, lest our forces should not prove very superior. An army of sixty thousand men, which forms two corps of thirty thousand combatants, for the purpose of attacking the two extremities of an army equal in numbers, deprives itself of the means of striking a decisive blow by multiplying uselessly the number of the means of resistance which the enemy can oppose to its two detachments. It becomes exposed even by an extended and disunited movement, so that its adversary might concentrate his mass upon a single point, and annihilate him by the terrible effects of his superiority. Multiplied attacks by means of a number of columns are still more dangerous, more opposed to the great principle of the art, above all when they cannot come into action at the same time upon the same point. As a consequence of this maxim, it is well, on the contrary, when we have masses greatly superior to those of the enemy, to make an attack upon both extremities of his line ; we thus bring into action more men than himself upon each of his wings, whereas, by keeping very superior forces massed upon a single point, our adversary may be able to deploy on it, and bring into action thereon an equal number.*

advantageous. Besides, we must not confound a central line of operations opposed to two adversaries upon the same front (for instance, that of the Archduke Charles against Moreau and Jourdan in 1796), with a line of operations entirely surrounded with enemies; the latter are far less favorable, and might become dangerous when the enemy's masses are more numerous.

Let us remark further, that a mass surrounded by all Europe roused up against it, composed of heterogeneous parties, starved by its very numbers and by swarms of light troops such as never have been seen, even though it occupied a central position, could not on that account avoid the fate which overtook Napoleon in Saxony. But one exception cannot destroy a general rule or maxim; and in all ordinary wars, a nation that fights with equal chances, that is to say, with equal means, by applying this system, will triumph inevitably, if its enemies pursue a contrary system. We can quote in support of it the most distinguished general officers of all arms, and give for proof the finest feats of arms recorded in modern history.

In such case, care should be taken to throw the weight of our forces upon that one of the enemy's wings, the attack of which promises the most decisive results; this was demonstrated in the relation before given of the battle of Hochkirch during the seven years' war (Chapter XII.).

IV. *In order to operate a combined effort with a strong mass upon a single point, it is important in the strategic movements to hold our forces concentrated upon a space nearly square, that they may be more disposable.* Large fronts are as contrary to good principles as parceled lines, great detachments, and isolated divisions, out of sustaining distance.*

V. *One of the most efficacious means of applying the general principles just laid down is to induce the enemy to commit faults contrary to this principle. By means of a few bodies of light troops we may disquiet our adversary on several important points of his communications. It is probable that, not knowing their force, he will oppose to them numerous divisions, and will scatter out his masses; these light troops, besides, will contribute perfectly to give information to the army.*

VI. *It is most important, when we take the initiative of a decisive movement, that we should be careful to perfectly inform ourselves of the positions of the enemy and of the movements which he can make. The employment of spies is a useful means, to the consideration of which too much pains can not be given; but that which is perhaps of more use is to have the country scoured in all directions by partisans. A general should send small parties in all directions, and he must multiply the number of them with the greater care,*

* It is not intended to be understood by this, a solid square column, but that the battalions may be disposed upon the field in such a way as to be capable of arriving with equal facility and promptitude at all points towards which the attack shall be directed.

*as this system is avoided in grand operations. For this purpose some divisions of light cavalry should be organized, which should not be included in the rolls of the combatants. To operate without these precautions is to march in the dark, and to expose ourselves to the chance disasters which a secret movement of the enemy might produce. These things have been too much neglected ; spy parties have not been organized far enough in advance, and the officers commanding light troops have not always had enough experience to conduct their detachments properly.**

VII. *It is not sufficient to bring about a good operation in war, to bring our masses skillfully to bear upon the most important point, it is necessary to know how to engage them there. Whenever we become established upon the desired points, and rest in inaction, the true principle is lost sight of. The enemy may then make counter-manœuvres, and in*

* The immense advantage which the Cossacks have been to the Russian army are a signal proof of the correctness of this article, which was composed in 1806. These light troops, insignificant in the shock of a great battle, are terrible in the pursuit. They are an enemy the most formidable to the combinations of a general, for he is never certain of the reception and execution of his orders, since his convoys are never safe, and his operations are uncertain. When an army has but a few regiments, their entire value can not be known, but when their number is increased to fifteen and twenty thousand, all their importance will be felt, particularly in a country where the population is not hostile to them.

On account of one convoy which they may take, it is necessary that each one should be strongly guarded by a numerous and well-conducted escort. It is never certain of making a tranquil march, for it can never know where the enemy is to be found. These cormorants compel the use of an immense force, and the regular cavalry is quickly disabled and worn out by the fatigues they are unable to endure. The Turkish militia was about as troublesome to the Russian army as the Cossacks would be to other European armies; the convoys were not more safe in Bulgaria than they were in Spain and Poland. I do not doubt, that in other armies, some thousand hussars or lancers, raised as volunteers at the breaking out of the war, well conducted, and going whither hardy chiefs should lead them, would answer about the same purpose; but they ought always to be regarded as a forlorn hope, for, if they receive orders from head-quarters, they will be no longer partisans. They will not have, it is true, the same qualities, and they would not be able to struggle long with good Cossacks; but an unavoidable evil should be opposed by every possible remedy.

order to deprive him of the power of doing this, whenever we gain his communications, or one of his extremities, we must march upon and combat him. It is then, above all, of the greatest importance that the combined attack of all our forces be simultaneous. It is not the masses present which decide the battle, but those which are brought into action. (See Chapter XXVI.) *The former decide the result in the preparatory movements of strategy, the latter determine the success of the action.*

In order to obtain this result, a skillful general ought to seize the instant when it is necessary to take the important position of the field of battle, and he should combine his attack in such a way as to cause all of his forces to become engaged at the same time, with the single exception of the reserve.

When an effort founded upon such principles fails to secure a victory, it can not be hoped nor expected from any combinations, and nothing remains but to give a last blow with this reserve, in concert with the troops already engaged.

VIII. *All the combinations of a battle may be reduced to three systems.*

The first, which is purely defensive, consists in awaiting the enemy in a strong position, without any other aim than maintaining ourselves there; such were the dispositions of Daun at Torgau, of Marsin at the lines of Turin. Those two occasions demonstrate the erroneous nature of such dispositions.

The second system, on the other hand, is entirely offensive. It consists in attacking the enemy wherever we can encounter him, as Frederick did at Leuthen and Torgau, Napoleon at Jena and Ratisbon, and the allies at Leipsic.

Finally, the third system is a mean between these two. It consists in the choice of a field of battle embracing all the strategic conditions and the proper advantages of ground, with the intention of awaiting the enemy in this position, and on the day of battle, at a convenient moment, to take the initiative and fall upon our adversary with every chance of success. The combinations of Napoleon at Rivoli and Austerlitz, those of Wellington at Mont Saint-Jean, and at the greater number of his defensive battles in Spain, should be classed under this head.

It is difficult to lay down fixed rules to determine when the last two systems should be employed when the other can not be resorted to. We must take into consideration the morale of the troops on the part of each, also the national character, more or less phlegmatic or impetuous, and lastly, the difficulties of the ground. These circumstances alone ought to guide the genius of a general, and they may be reduced to the three following:

1st. *With troops which are hardy and accustomed to war, the absolutely offensive, or initiative of the attack, will always be the best.*

2d. *That in ground of difficult access, from natural or other causes, and with disciplined and subordinate troops, it would probably be better to let the enemy arrive at some appointed position, in order to take the initiative against him when his troops shall have become exhausted by their first efforts.**

3d. *It frequently happens from the strategical position of the two parties, that an attack by main force has to be made upon the enemy in his position, without any reference whatever to local considerations. Such, for instance, would be the case when we desired to prevent the junction of two armies of the enemy, to fall upon a detachment or an isolated corps beyond a river, etc., etc.*

IX. *Orders of battle, or the most suitable dispositions for*

* The battle of Kunersdorf, which has many points of resemblance to that of Mont Saint-Jean, verifies still further this reasoning.

*conducting troops to combat, should have for their object to secure at the same time mobility and solidity. To secure this when acting on the defensive, the troops ought to be in part deployed and the rest in column, as was the Russian army at the battle of Eylau; but a corps arranged to attack some decisive point ought to be drawn up in two lines of battalions not deployed, but in columns of division closed in mass, as in the following figure:**

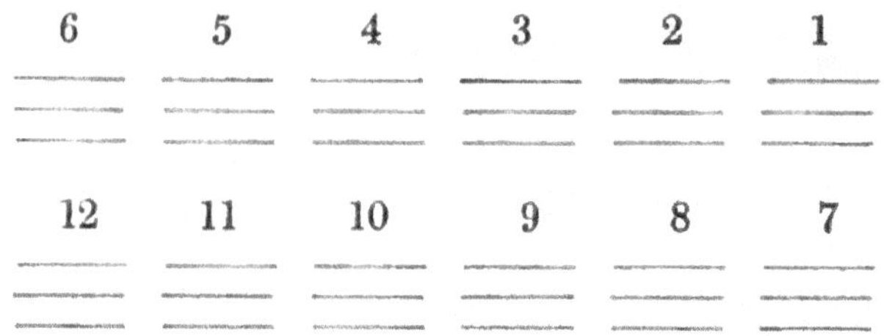

This order offers vastly more solidity than the deployed line, the wavering of which disturbs the impulsion so necessary for such an attack, and deprives the officers of the control of their troops. But for the purpose of facilitating their march, to avoid too great a depth, and farther to increase the front without diminishing the consistency of the troops, it is better to place them in two ranks. The battalions will thus be more movable, for the march of the second rank, pressed between the first and the third, is always fatiguing, vibratory, and consequently less vigorous. Furthermore, there would be all the force which it was desirable to have, since the three divisions, when ployed, will present six ranks in depth, which is more than enough. Finally, the front being increased one-third, will furnish a third more fire, in case it should be necessary to make use of it, and, at the same time, it will impose more upon the enemy, making a

* A division is two platoons or companies; thus, a battalion having six companies or platoons, will have three divisions which will really be formed upon three lines.

greater display of force with a less exposure to the ravages of artillery.

X. *In ground difficult of access, such as vineyards, enclosures, gardens, and bristling heights, the defensive order of battle should be composed of troops deployed in two ranks, and covered by numerous companies of riflemen. But troops intended for the attack, as well as the reserve, should be arranged in columns of attack on the centre, as we have indicated in the preceding article; for the reserve having to fall upon the enemy at the decisive moment, it should be done with force and rapidity, that is to say, in columns.** *A part of this reserve can be kept deployed until the moment of falling on the enemy, for the purpose of imposing upon him by an appearance of numbers.*

XI. *If the art of war consists in concerting a superior effort, with a mass against weak portions, it is most indispensably necessary to follow up closely a beaten army.*

The strength of an army consists in its organization, in the unity resulting from the connection of all the several parts with the head or the central power. After a defeat this unity or oneness no longer exists; all harmony between the head which combines, and the several corps which execute, is destroyed; their relations are suspended, and nearly always broken. The entire army becomes weak; an attack upon it

* It is said that Wellington fought nearly always with his troops deployed; this may be well for troops acting on the defensive, but for the offensive and manœuvring wings, the formation should be in columns. In the contrary case, this will be the fault of those who allow themself to be beaten with an equal force, for a general could desire nothing better than to have his adversary always make use of it.

We will recur to this subject again in connection with the generals who have been through the great European wars. In laying down an order of combat as the most advantageous, we cannot say that all victory is impossible to the party not using it; the nature of the positions, the morale of the troops and of the generals, superior numbers and general causes are considerations which must enter into the account. And in developing a general principle, it must be assumed that these chances are equal on each side.

is almost certain triumph. What abundant proofs do we find of the truth of these principles in Napoleon's march upon Roveredo and the gorges of the Brenta, to complete the ruin of Wurmser; in his march from Ulm upon Vienna; in that from Jena upon Wittemberg, Custrin, and Stettin. This maxim is often lost sight of by mediocre generals. It would appear as if every effort of their genius was exhausted on the field of battle; their ambition looks no further. Such a victory is little better than a displacement of troops without real utility.*

XII. *To render the superior shock of a mass decisive, it is equally necessary for a general to bestow the same care upon the* morale *of his army. Of what use is it to bring into action fifty thousand men against twenty thousand, if they lack the impulsion necessary to rush upon and overthrow the enemy? It is not the soldier alone who is to act, it is more particularly those who are to conduct him. All troops are brave when their leader sets the example by a noble emulation and a true, heroic devotion. It is not well that a soldier should remain under fire from fear of discipline alone, but from pride and self-esteem, not yielding to being outdone by his officers in honor and bravery; and, above all, from that confidence which should exist in his mind in the sagacity of his leaders and the courage of his companions in arms.*†

* This chapter was published in 1806. The Russian army afforded a new proof of this truth by its activity and perseverance in 1812. The emperor Alexander likewise gave a brilliant example of its application in 1814.

† The rules vary undoubtedly with different nations, and all the shades of the point of honor are not applicable to every army, as the Austrian Military Journal has remarked most reasonably upon one of my chapters. But whatever may be advanced by this journal, it is certain that severity of discipline alone did not make Suwarrow's legions so brave, for he possessed the power of electrifying them by his manner. In spite of the criticism of the author of that article, we shall persist in disbelieving that the blows of a stick furnish good motives for action. Their effect may be modified, softened, repaired; but it will never make a good soldier any more than the too general outcries and declamations against this mode of punishment. There exist other means of exciting the morale of an

A general should be able to rely upon the devotion of his lieutenants for the honor of the national arms. He ought to feel that a vigorous shock will be given wherever he orders one to be made. The first means of securing this end is to make himself loved, respected, and feared; the second is to place in the hands of this general the choice and fate of his lieutenants. If they attain that grade by seniority alone, it may be concluded in advance that they will rarely possess the qualities required to fulfil their important functions. that circumstance alone may cause the miscarriage of the best conceived enterprises.

It will be seen from this rapid exposition, that the science of war is composed of three general combinations, each one of which offers but few sub-divisions or chances of execution. The only perfect operations will be those that shall present the application of these three combinations, for this would be the permanent application of the general principle pointed out above.*

The first of these combinations *is the art of arranging the*

army, and I will cite an example of what I mean. At the affair of Culm, a sergeant of the regiment Devaux brought to the prince of Schwartzenburg a standard which he had taken, and explained to this marshal the salient and reëntrant angles formed by a stream and by the village attacked by the corps under Colloredo. An engineer officer could not have explained it more fully nor in better language, and the prince himself was struck by it. This brave man had been a non-commissioned officer for nine years; they gave him two ducats and hopes of a medal for his flag and his truly graphic narration; should he not have had a further reward, and was he not worthy of commanding a company?

* National wars, or those where we have to combat and conquer an entire people, form the only exceptions to these rules; in wars of this kind, it is difficult to subject the enemy without dividing up our forces; when we are compelled to assemble to combat, we expose ourselves to the loss of our conquered provinces.

The way to avoid these inconveniences is to have an army keep the field, and independent divisions to organize in its rear. These divisions should always be commanded by accomplished generals, good administrators who are firm and just, for their labors may contribute as much as the force of arms, to subject the provinces intrusted to their care.

lines of operations in the most advantageous manner; which is what is commonly but improperly called, *the plan of campaign.* It is difficult to understand what is really meant by a plan of campaign; because it is impossible to make a general plan of an entire campaign, the first movement of which may upset the entire scaffolding on which it rests; and in which we cannot look beyond a second movement.

The second branch *is the art of transferring our masses, with the greatest possible expedition, to the decisive point of either the primitive or accidental line of operation.* This is what is ordinarily understood by strategy. Strategy is only the means of carrying out this second combination of the art of war; the principles of which will be found in the before-mentioned chapters.

The third branch is *the art of combining the simultaneous employment of the greatest mass upon the most important point of the field of battle;* this is properly the art of combat, which many authors have denominated order of battle, and others have treated of under the name of tactics.

Such is briefly the science of war. In consequence of losing sight of these few principles, the Austrian generals were beaten from 1793 to 1800 and 1805; from the same cause, the French generals lost Belgium in 1793, Germany in 1796, and Italy and Swabia in 1799.

It is not necessary to remind our readers that we have here merely treated of those principles which relate to the employment of troops, or to the purely military part of the art of war; other combinations not less important are absolutely necessary in conducting a great war, but they pertain more to the government of empires than the commanding of armies.

To succeed in great enterprises, it is not only necessary to weigh the comparative strength of the two armies, but to take into consideration the resources of a second, which should serve as a reserve, and replace losses of every kind, both in *personnel* and *matériel.* It is also necessary to know how to judge of the inferior condition of nations from what they have had to suffer externally, and from the relative situation of their neighbors. Neither must we neglect to add to the balance the passions of the people against those with whom we have to contend, their peculiar institutions, and the strength of their attachment to them. Likewise, the situation of the provinces, and the distance of the power which we desire to attack, for the difficulties of the aggressor multiply in proportion as the depth of his line of operations increases. Finally, we must take into account the nature of the country in which the war* is to be carried on, and the solidity of the alliances which may be brought about to favor or support a distant enterprise.

In a word, it is absolutely necessary to know that science which consists of a mixture of politics, administration, and war; the basis of which has been so well laid down by Montesquieu in his work upon the Causes of the Greatness and Decline of the Romans. It would be difficult to assign to it regular rules, or even fixed principles; history is the only school in which we can find good precepts, and it is rare enough that we meet with circumstances sufficiently resembling each other to authorize us in regulating a certain epoch by one passed several centuries before. The passions of men have too much influence upon events not to have some miscarry under the same conditions in which others have succeeded.

Napoleon probably understood this science, but his contempt for men led him to neglect its application. It was not ignorance of the fate of Cambyses or of the legions of Varus which caused his reverses; neither was it forgetfulness

* This is what led me to write in 1805, Vol. V. Chap. IV., that the system of Napoleon could not be carried out in Russia or in Sweden.

of the overthrow of Crassus; of the disaster which befel the emperor Julian, nor the result of the Crusades; but it was the opinion that possessed him that his own genius insured to him incalculable means of superiority, and that his adversaries, on the contrary, were devoid of it. He fell from the height of his greatness because he forgot that the mind and strength of man have their limits, and that the more enormous the masses which are set in motion, the more subordinate does individual genius become to the inflexible laws of nature, and the less is the control which it exercises over events.

This truth, so fully demonstrated by the results of the affairs of Katzbach, Dennewitz, and even Leipsic, would make in itself a most interesting subject for study.

It does not come within the limits of our plan to give here the important maxims which Montesquieu and Machiavel have left us upon the great art of governing empires. There will be found, however, in the course of the narration of these celebrated campaigns, some reflections upon the various changes wrought by the revolution in the manner of organizing and developing national forces, together with their employment, and the probable consequences of future revolutions in the body politic. Armies are no longer composed of men voluntarily recruited from the excess of a too numerous population, but of entire nations, which the law summons to arms, and which contend not simply for a new frontier boundary, but, in a measure, for existence.

This condition of things carries us back to the third and fourth centuries, by recalling those struggles of the immense hordes which disputed with each other the possession of the continent of Europe; and if a new legislation and a new international law does not fix a limit to this levy in mass, it is impossible to foresee where these ravages will cease. War will become a more terrible scourge than ever, for the population of civilized nations will be swept away, not as in the Middle Ages, in resisting the encroachments of savage and barbarous devastators, but for the sorry maintenance of a political balance, and in order to know, at the end of a century, whether some given province shall be a prefect of Paris, of St. Petersburg, or Vienna; in either case, it being governed by nearly identical usages and laws. It is high time, nevertheless, that cabinets should return to more generous ideas, and that human blood should no longer flow but to vindicate and advance the great interests of the world.

If this truly European desire must be classed only with those bright dreams of perpetual peace indulged in by a few, let us deplore the base passions and narrow interests which lead enlightened nations to destroy each other more ruthlessly than barbarous ones; let us deplore the progress of those arts and sciences, both moral and political, which, far from leading to a perfection of the social state, seem rather to indicate a return to the ages of the Huns, the Vandals, and the Tartars.

INDEX.

CPSIA information can be obtained
at www.ICGtesting.com
Printed in the USA
LVHW101925170422
716440LV00004BA/279

9 783752 590821